Gc

MBishop

"HIS SENSES BEGAN TO DECEIVE HIM AS HIS EYES WATCHED THE ROOM MORPH, FROM THE TACKY LAVENDER, TO A FOREBODING BLACK-BLUE. THE COLOR WAS AS A BRUISED WOUND, PUSS-FILLED AND WITH THE THREATENING SENSE IT MIGHT BURST OPEN WITHOUT NOTICE. THE DRUMS INSIDE HIS EARS PEAKED LIKE A WOLF AS THEY CAUGHT A BREATHING SOUND. BUT THAT WASN'T AN AMPLE DESCRIPTION. IT WAS MORE LIKE WHEEZING, A CHOKING. IT WAS THE SOUND OF DEATH.

THE ROOM WAS NOT A ROOM. NOT ANYMORE. IT WAS ALIVE. FLESH PULSED WITH NERVES BENEATH ITS SURFACE. THE SMELL WAS BURNT HAIR AND DISEASED INFECTION. AND RAMOND COULD DESCRIBE IT IN ONLY ONE WAY: *THE BELLY OF A BEAST.*"

-from Chapter Two "The Proposition" of
Michael Bishop's "Seven Deadly Sins"

We invite you to turn to the first page and experience the next generation of horror.

SEVEN DEADLY SINS

SEVEN DEADLY SINS

BY

MICHAEL BISHOP

**Illustrated by
STEVEN McBRIDE**

CHECKMATE
PUBLISHING

http:\\www.CheckmatePublishing.com

PUBLISHERS NOTE

This book is a work of fiction. Names, characters, places, and incidents are either the product of the author's imagination or are used fictitiously, and any resemblance to any person, living or dead, events, or locales is entirely coincidental.

THIS BOOK IS AVAILABLE AT QUANTITY DISCOUNTS WHEN USED TO PROMOTE PRODUCTS OR SERVICES. FOR INFORMATION PLEASE WRITE TO CHECKMATE PUBLISHING, P.O. BOX 75312, WICHITA, KANSAS, 67275-0312, OR CONTACT THE PUBLISHER BY EMAIL AT SALES@CHECKMATEPUBLISHING.COM

Books may be ordered online from:
http://www.CheckmatePublishing.com.
Visit our website to keep up to date on special promotions and merchandise.

Copyright 1999 by Michael Bishop
http://www.MichaelBishop.com

Cover, Illustrations, Photography, and Typesetting provided by
Steven McBride of Logics Inc.
For all of your computer graphic needs, visit:
http://www.LogicsInc.com

All rights reserved.

Publishers Cataloging-in-Publication Data
Bishop, Michael, 1975-
Seven Deadly Sins/ a novel / Michael Bishop
      p. cm.
   ISBN 0-9669888-0-9
       1. Title
813'.54-dc20   99-71481
                CIP

CHECKMATE
PUBLISHING
http://www.CheckmatePublishing.com

Michael Bishop books are published in the United States by Checkmate Publishing, P.O. Box 75312, Wichita, KS. 67275-0312

First Printing March, 1999
Printed in the United States of America

CONTENTS

Child's Play	11
The Proposition	53
Night Life	89
True Love	117
Vengeance Is Mine	147
The Dark Road	193
The Perfect Place	241
The Knowing	331

To Stephen King

Though I aspire to be the Bishop of horror...
You will always be the King.

Introduction
The Birth Of Death

Everyone has been asking me the same question since I was a small child. Why death? Out of all the subjects you can write about, how come you choose horror? Well, to be honest, the answer is simple yet complicated at the same time. After much deliberation on the matter, I've finally realized I do not choose horror... it chooses me.

I've been doing what I do for a long while now. I began my first novel when I was in fifth grade, and although I am too embarrassed to tell you what that book was about, I will say it was not a happy story. Horror just came natural to me. When I sat at my desk, opened my notebook, and began to scribble down stories, another side of me took control. A side that made me want to scare my reader as well as entertain. A dark side. I never looked at the world through rose-colored glasses. Happy stories were boring and gave no rush. But being scared was fun, and still is!

The only books I ever read as a kid were horror novels. The other kids curled up at night to fairy tales and comic books, enjoying the safety that childhood brings. But not me. I stayed up all night reading Stephen King. Tucked under the bed sheets with a flashlight, reading page after page, I was transported to another universe. He led my mind's eye to places I had never before dreamed. He introduced me to characters more terrifying than any I had ever known. He told me things that scared me and fascinated me all at once.

So when it came time to dedicate this book, the person to whom that honor would go was chosen with ease. Hopefully, this novel will be a sort of "Thank You" from me to Mr. King. Thank you for all the fun. Thank you for all the fright.

And thank you for making me who I am. Without his enticing tales and incomparable imagination, I'm not sure I would have taken up writing. I owe him a debt of gratitude, and perhaps the dedication of this book will show my appreciation for his work.

But before I end this introduction, I'd first like to point something I feel is very important out to you, my friends and readers. Although I admire Stephen King immensely, our writing styles are completely opposite. I've adapted a writing style that I feel will be very well liked by the next generation of young readers. A style that is very fast paced and cuts straight to the meat of the matter. It is a style not necessarily better than others, but certainly different. I hope you enjoy it, and I look forward to scaring the daylights out of each and every one of you for years to come.

Be forewarned though. If you are expecting a slasher type novel, you've come to the wrong place. I write about what scares *me*, and the typical run of the mill stories about teenagers and axe murderers don't do a thing for me. Horror is not just about shocking people and it's certainly not about blood and gore. It is an art form that goes well beyond that. In these tales, there are lessons to be learned. Though I may have invented the characters in this book, parts of them were taken from people I have met, and others who I hope I never will meet. Evil is out there, and it is most dangerous when we pretend it does not exist.

CHILD'S PLAY

34567890

The book lay open before him as lifeless as an antique ragdoll, and for several minutes he stared blankly down at its pages. Ramond's heart was not in it tonight. Every incantation and ritual he had ever learned had been reproduced hundreds of times, and old experiences bored him. An upside-down star with a circle around it was printed on the aged cover in a dull shade of gold, with the outline raised slightly like Braille. It was a familiar symbol. All it took was a long look at the pentagram and he became convinced he must have something new.

Contact with demons was nothing novel. During the early days of worship it had been a high goal, but since then had been achieved numerous times. Likewise, conversations with the dead were getting old. At any typical seance a former living soul could be conjured and conversed with, although he was sure he had been hoaxed on more than one occasion by his simpleton friends. They did it in fun, a passing rebellion. But to Ramond it was something more... it was *power*.

  Sierra Springs, Arkansas might very well have been the buckle of the Bible Belt. To most of the townsfolk, going to church on Sundays was just as important as their children going to school. Ramond's mother had been a devout Christian as long as he had known time. On Sundays she *became* a church pew, glued to the seat, fearing she might miss a word from Brother Hemphil with his fire and brimstone sermons.

  It was the adulation of his mother, Vernadette, and other congregation members that first sparked Ramond's interest in "the faith". Sporting his light grey "monkey suit" with a lavender, silk handkerchief tucked neatly into the breast pocket, never failed to bring a compliment from a passing adult.

  "Oh, How cute!" and
  "Isn't he adorable?" were often heard.

  The clothes brought forth a change. They seemed to magically transform him from a little boy into a little man. The opportunity was never missed to dress this way. A clean cut hairstyle added to the "All American Boy" illusion. Sides trimmed just over the ears. Truly traditional.

  At the age of ten, Ramond became eligible for the duty of passing the offering plate from row to row to collect the tithes. Brother Hemphil often stated that this *honor* should be given to the children.

  "Gifts to God should be gathered by innocent children's hands," he preached.

  That reasoning, however, had little to do with the basis for which Ramond so eagerly signed up for the task. His motivation was less pure. It was the "Hot-dog" factor that made the job so appealing. Just one more way to thrust him into the spotlight and get him praise from those around him.

An added bonus was that this swelled Vernadette with pride like water bloats a dead fish. Her esteem was the most valued prize of all.

Although his mother was only a housewife, she was by no means *common*. Vernadette Lindsey Jamison's skin glowed like a perfect flesh-tone paint on porcelain. Her figure still thin enough to be called youthful, and she held a smile that could light up a dark room. Brunette hair hung shoulder length, framing her face like a portrait. It was a style much sought after.

These qualities were a source of envy by other housewives who had not the knowledge, nor the discipline, to take better care of themselves.

Physical traits alone, however, would not have made her extraordinary, but there were other attributes, and with these added to her beauty she *was* extraordinary.

Vernadette was a woman of many diverse talents. She could perform a simple task such as replacing a button with a sewing needle or arrange a sit-down dinner for ten with only a few hours' notice.

Her mind was a recipe Rolodex which gave her access to the world's finest culinary pleasures. As a born leader, she had the ability to command attention from a crowd or disappear into the background, depending on what the situation called for. There was nothing ordinary about her: including her faith.

These characteristics were the basis for which the meeker women in the Church chose her as a spiritual guide.

MICHAEL BISHOP

If you had a question, Vernadette seemed to have the right answer. There was an aura about her. A manner in which she did things that made you feel you could trust her. She could tell you what was wrong with your life without putting you down, being ever so tactful when dealing with the feelings of others. These qualities attracted others to her like a thirsty man to an oasis.

When the women made a decision to hold Friday night prayer meetings, there was little debate over whose house they would be held. Each woman promptly huddled her way into Vernadette's living room at 7 o'clock and prepared to read her Bible and pray. Making categorically sure to gossip about whoever didn't show up was always the first order of business. It was to be expected.

It didn't take long for these meetings to become tradition, and with each passing week Ramond found himself in the center of it all, playing the role of the "good son". The sessions became the central event the boy looked forward to throughout the week. He loved being a part of it. Oftentimes, being the center of attention simply because he was the only child allowed to attend.

But the "Hot-dog" factor was not his only motivation this time. When they prayed, an unmistakable energy could be felt in the air. The feeling it brought with its glorious predictability did something to the young boy. It made him peerlessly special. Part of a secret rite known only to a handful of chosen vessels. That force made him *high*.

In the back of his mind, fear arose that the group might grow impatient with him if he was unable to understand their conversations about the "Word". So he studied.

Before long, he had read the Bible from cover to

CHILD'S PLAY

cover; a feat even Vernadette had yet to perform. And remarkably, in spite of his youth, Ramond was able to remember an incredible amount of detail from the Scriptures. Often, there were times he found himself correcting his mother when she misquoted a verse of Psalms or Genesis.

This knowledge and the fact that it came from a boy only eleven years of age brought even more praise, stoking the flames and causing Ramond's biblical hunger to ignite.

Soon, as his studies flourished, the pages of the Bible began to flip through his hands like cards through the nimble fingers of a Blackjack dealer; and the more he read, the more he found himself turning back to familiar passages. Particularly ones of the fallen angel Lucifer.

There was a mystique to the Devil. An attraction of sorts. He was not bound by the will to do good or the unabridged thoughts of right and wrong. He did what he pleased, to whom he pleased, when he pleased; and somewhere deep within Ramond, in a place he feared to admit even existed, there was envy for those who walked in the dark one's steps.

The first step in his fall from grace began in the most innocent of places. A child's sleep-over party, given by Michael Billion to celebrate his twelfth birthday, began the spiraling obsession within Ramond. Under normal circumstances, he would never have been invited to such a party. Studying had left him little time for friends, and moreover he was not well liked among his classmates.

The invitation was extended to Ramond only because

MICHAEL BISHOP

Michael's mother, Janet, was an active member of Vernadette Jamison's prayer group. Michael begged and pleaded like a man being dragged down the long hall to the gas chamber, contesting that it was unfair to make him invite Ramond.

"He's weird, mamma!" the whimpering child insisted.

But his mother would hear none of it. Whether Ramond was *weird* or not had no bearing on the situation. The bottom line was that if Ramond was not invited to the party, the other women would surely put her through the "meat grinder". She could hear their insults now.

"After all Vernadette's done for us, and she didn't even have the decency to invite Ramond. She should be ashamed to show her face in Vernadette's house!"

Just the thought of rumor-mongers' chatter made Janet Billion shudder. There was no way she would let her well-kept name be dragged through the mud. Michael's cries fell on deaf ears, and in the end Ramond was begrudgingly invited.

Michael was not the only one contesting. Ramond did his share of whining also.

"They don't like me, and I don't like them. They're just gonna be mean to me!" he shrilled at Vernadette the day of the party.

But she knew as well that if her boy did not accept the invitation, she too would be subject to the jeers of the ravaging vultures in the community that lived to gossip about such things.

Ramond was forced to attend the gathering and Michael was forced to let him. The hand of fate assembled the pieces from there.

CHILD'S PLAY

†††††††††††

     The boys were not necessarily mean to Ramond that night; but then again, none of them went out of their way to make him feel welcome either. Most were surprised he showed up. Beyond that small point of interest, they ignored him.

     Just as Ramond had assumed, the night was filled with amateurish pranks and idiotic conversations of a typical "boy" nature. A large part of the chatter was tall tales and blatant lies. Stories made up only to impress. A few bragged about all the "hot" girls they had "fingered", while others tried their best not to let on they had no idea what "fingering" meant to begin with. The rest did not try to awe the crowd, and spoke of things they knew more about, like video games and football.

     On more than one occasion the mob of juveniles involved themselves in farting competitions, each one attempting to out-do the other. Overall, it was exactly what you would expect from a group of middle-class youths, until Michael brought *it* out.

     "Come're guys," he whispered in a mouse-like voice.

     "What is it, Mike?" one of the boys questioned in a way that indicated whatever it was had better be pretty damned good to interrupt the *fartfest*.

     "You'll see, just shut up and get your ass over here!" he cussed, trying to sound older than he was. His face wrinkled as he rubbed his flat nose in annoyance, while exhibiting an expression of mystery.

     The sight of even the slightest amount of passion on his normally blank face gave them all the motivation they needed. Like sheep, they filed in behind one another to see what the fuss was being raised about. Along with them Ramond followed.

"Check *this* out," Michael said, removing the square board from its hiding place underneath the bed. Instantly Ramond recognized the Ouija board, and a large frog lodged itself in his throat.

To Ramond the board was a Great Pyramid: menacing and shrouded in mystery. In it lay the keys to numerous wonders of the world. It was a line he was not sure he dared cross, but even though he knew it was wrong, he was *drawn*.

The thought of crossing that line brought with it guilt, and with that guilt came the *voice*.

"Ramond," it called in his mind as soft as a whisper.

He nervously jerked his head around to see if anyone else had heard, knowing full well they hadn't. The voice was for him alone. It wasn't the first time he had heard it. Not by a long shot. His mother's voice had haunted him for years.

When other people heard their conscience speak in their "mind's ear", it was their own voice guiding them. But not Ramond. The voice that kept him out of trouble had always been Vernadette's. Whether in reality or in his head.

"Anyone who fools with those evil things might as well be worshiping Satan outright," the voice continued to banter him. "Might as well be worshiping Satan... Worshiping Satan... WORSHIPING SATAN!"

Ramond closed his eyes tightly, hoping the darkness would allow him to escape from the clutches of his own guilt, but it served only to reverberate the words off the walls of his head.

CHILD'S PLAY

"WORSHIPING SATAN..." it continued to remind him, stirring up the greatest fears harbored in his brain like the frenzy of a disturbed hornet's nest.

It was, in his world, the biggest sin you could commit. All his research and studies had come to the same conclusion: when you play with the Devil, even to the tiniest degree, you are teetering on a thin tightrope and the only net to catch you is made up of hellfire.

I'll count to five and when I open my eyes, I won't hear it any more!, he told himself. Half as a wish... half as a prayer.

One....

"WORSHIPING SATAN!" it persisted to scream at him, paying no attention to his count.

Two....

"ANYONE WHO PLAYS WITH THOSE EVIL THINGS!" it warned.

Three....

"YOU KNOW IT'S WRONG, RAMOND!"

Four....

"MOTHER KNOWS BEST!"

Five......

Ramond's eyes thrust themselves open as he pleaded for the voice to subside. For the moment it did.

All this inner turmoil registered across Ramond's features like a ticker-tape machine, and did not go completely unnoticed. The other boys' attentions were affixed upon the board, fascinated to no end. But Michael had observed it all. Michael had seen the fear in Ramond's eyes; had felt the panic in the air; had sensed the guilt in Ramond's soul. It was the perfect opportunity to extract a small amount of vengeance. Since he was forced to let Ramond attend what he considered a very exclusive party, someone would pay. That someone was Ramond.

"Hey Ramond, get on the other side of this thing and put your fingers on it," Michael called as he pointed down at the triangular stylus. His face fought back the smile he felt inside. He was forcing Ramond to make a decision. Either do something that utterly terrified him, or be mocked and called a coward in front of everyone. Either way revenge would be sweet.

"M... M... Me?" Ramond stuttered, trying not to sound shaken.

"Yeah you! Get over here!" Michael ordered, no longer able to conceal the smile. "Hurry up, we ain't got all night."

Ramond froze. His mind racing with a million questions, all revolving around one: should he do it?

"What are you... a pussy?" Michael taunted.

"Yeah, I think he *is* a pussy," one of the flock interjected.

That was all it took to settle the question. Ramond's name already carried no respect. If he backed down now his frail spirit would not be able to handle the repercussions. The others would pick him apart if he didn't accept the challenge. There was only one thing he could do.

Unnerved, he stepped toward the board, not stopping to reconsider his decision. A plethora of emotions shot through his body: fear, anxiety, excitement. But before any of these had a chance to grab a foothold and take over, the "good son" found himself kneeling on the rough-textured carpet with his hands on the thing.

CHILD'S PLAY

Michael was not completely satisfied. Of the two choices Ramond could have made, this one would be less damaging. However, he managed for the moment to put his animosity aside and concentrate on entertaining the crowd with the board.

"Let's see what should we ask it?" he questioned his audience.

"I got it," Arnold Lifman, the class bully and undeniably the ugliest young man to ever grace the halls of Johnson Elementary piped in. "Ask it if Jenny Hoffman stuffs her bra!"

The room thundered with laughter, with some of the boys howling so hard you would have thought it was the most whimsical statement ever uttered.

"Calm down guys. If my mom comes in here she's gonna freak," Michael whispered softly. The silence of the sheep was immediate for fear the board would be taken away.

"I know," Michael began again. "Let's ask it which one of us will be the first to die." The murmur in the room halted without the slightest giggle or immature recoil. Each boy sat in a state of suspended animation, speculating if the question dared be asked.

"Oh, soldiers of darkness and spirits of the nether realms, which one of those among us will be the first to depart to the land of the dead?" Michael chanted, no doubt something he had heard on T.V. or in one of those dark horse comic books he enjoyed reading. After the plagiarized question was asked, he placed his hands lightly on the board just inches from Ramond's.

Ramond held his breath, expecting his soul to be ripped from his body at any moment and handed justly over to the Devil himself. But as they sat there, hushed and still as

MICHAEL BISHOP

a frightened possum, the board did the same.

"This sux!" Arnold proclaimed with all the intellect of a prize fighter who had taken a few too many punches to the head.

Ramond took a deep breath with certainty that the board was a farce and could not possibly work. It was a sigh of relief, but also a sigh of disappointment.

He lifted his fingers just centimeters from the lip of the stylus, with the intention to remove his hands completely, but stopped solid before completing the action. The nerve endings in his fingertips had picked up something. A *trembling*.

The primary assumption was that it had to be all in his mind. Just an overactive imagination, afflicted with guilt. But as he gazed across into Michael's eyes, it became clear he was not the only one who had noticed the sensation. Michael's face read like a glowing, neon bulletin board that flashed, "I FEEL IT TOO!"

The vibrations increased, and with their elevation, Ramond's eyes grew wider, reaching a point where they looked almost cartoonish. His lips fell misshapen as he pressed them together tight enough to cause pain. Then, without provocation, the stylus moved.

It drifted slowly at first, seemingly aimless around the board's outer limits.

"Guys, something's happening!" Michael informed. A fact that was readily apparent to all spectators. And although Michael's expression suggested he wanted nothing more than to let go of the thing and run, just as Ramond, he could not.

"No way! you're moving it Mike!" one of the boys shouted from the back, not sounding completely convinced.

"I'm not," he defended, making no effort to hide the

fright in his voice. "Are you Ramond?" he asked, not expecting an answer, and not getting one.

The triangle began to make its way to the center of the board, creating small looping movements as it passed over the letters imprinted on the surface. It flowed with smooth motions, as if it were performing an ancient ritualistic dance. With a sudden jerking motion it jutted to a nearby letter and its monocle centerpiece rested on the character for a moment.

"T," several of the boys chanted in unison as they read the magnified letter caught in the monocle's eye.

A long second passed. The tension in the air was so intense it took on an odor, similar to salt and sweat. Ramond became sure the thing was done, but as quickly as the thought came, it continued its gambol to another letter.

"H," the boys called as it stopped. This time it wasted no time in moving on.

"E," Michael said alone, voice shaking so acutely that it was barely decipherable. "THE? The... The what? Are you sure you're not sliding it, Ramo..." his words were cut short as it went back on the move.

"H," Arnold proclaimed, trying to spit out the letter before the stylus had time to choose another.

"O," the few spectators who had been silent thus far joined in with Arnold for fear they might miss out on the fun.

"S," everyone from Michael, to Arnold, to even the quietest of the lot was now in on the letter calling. Everyone *except* Ramond.

"T," the buzz of the room reported, and if the thing would have rolled over one more character, the noise level might have grown deafening. But the stylus froze on the "T" and refused to move another inch.

The mob waited, excited at the prospect of shouting

out another letter, as if they where playing some bizarre, macabre adaptation of "Wheel of Fortune." But the board was inanimate and after a few seconds, everyone understood it was done.

The instant Ramond felt the vibrations cease he jerked his limbs away as if they had been held in the stream of a blow torch. Both hands were held directly in front of his eyes as he turned them from palm, to back hand, to palm again, checking meticulously to assure they were in the same condition they had been before he had touched *it*. He stared at them for what seemed like an age as his mind tried to convince him he did not feel what his hands knew he did.

The stylus had not *just* moved beneath his hands. That would have been easy to rationalize by blaming Michael for pushing it. But the board had *lived*. As surely as if it had a pulse and breath. It had radiated energy. Pulled him to it. Spoken. Given Ramond a brief glimpse of the other side; and although he got only a small peek, it was enough to make him want to see more.

"Whaaaaat did it spell?" Michael asked dumbly after he had taken a moment to collect his scattered thoughts.

"I dunno," Arnold revealed, surprising no one.

"T-H-E-H-O-S-T, Thehost." A voice from the back offered.

"Thehost? Thehost? What is a Thehost?" Michael said, disappointment creeping into his voice at the thought that the board had not revealed an acceptable answer.

The room became a tomb of silence for a brief interlude. Ramond mulled the letters over in his head. Not really thinking about what they meant. Thinking more about the fact that the board had made them live in the first place.

"I got it!" Arnold exclaimed exuberantly as if he had just found a cure for the common cold. "It's not 'THEHOST', you retards. It's 'THE HOST'. Two different words," and after enlightening the *class* with his supreme intellect, Arnold did a clumsy victory dance. Hopping from one foot to the other.

"Well since you're not a *retard*, I guess you know what the shit 'THE HOST' means then, huh?" Michael bantered.

The boys laughed, although not heartily. It was enough, though, to stop Arnold's dance.

"I'll figure it out," Arnold stated with confidence. "The Host... let's see, ummm... maybe it's talking about some game show host or something."

"What!" Michael yelled with amusement, almost laughing the word out. "That's the best you can do, O' smart one? The question was who *here* will die first, not who on some T.V. show, dumb ass."

"Oh, yeah," Arnold conceded.

"It's *you*," a voice said. Normally that voice would not have been heard, overlooked like a rotten tomato at a fruit stand.

Ramond recognized that voice. It seemed so familiar. He gazed around the room in an attempt to discover the perpetrator. Who could it have been that dared speak up and offer their opinion in front of such a discriminating panel of judges? But his search was short lived before he realized all eyes were on him.

Had *he* spoken? Had it been his own voice he heard? Confusion began to play him like piano keys. Ramond had not meant to speak, but it seemed his mind and mouth were not in agreement on the matter. The voice *was* familiar. But it was not the voice Ramond normally heard when he spoke. It was more along the lines of the voice he heard when he recorded himself and played it back. A similar voice, but somehow different. A voice that when anyone else heard, they swore sounded just like him; but to Ramond it sounded disparate, jumbled, foolish.

"What's me?" Michael asked, for the first time interested in something Ramond had to say.

"The Host," Ramond listened to himself speak again, and was as surprised as anyone to hear the answer. It was unearthly; he had no idea what he was saying, yet somehow it was coming through him as if he were a speaker box broadcasting someone else's words.

It took a moment, but through the confusion a lightning bolt of thought struck Ramond solidly. He began to fully understand what his mouth had been saying.

"You're 'The Host'. The host of this party," Ramond continued. This time he was in control of his words, and his voice was the same he had always heard when he spoke.

"Of course I'm the host of this party. What the hell does that have to do with anything!" Michael whaled as scared as ever. His words were a denial, said in the hopes that if he pretended not to know the implication being made, somehow he would not be held responsible for it.

Ramond inwardly cursed himself for speaking up. Even when he knew the correct answer in class he never volunteered the information, so why had he chosen now to open his mouth? But deep inside, he realized without any doubt that it was not him who had spoken. The board had spoken through the letters; then the board had spoken through him.

"Holy Shit!" Arnold belched, the tumblers of his mind finally falling into place. "He's right, Mike. You're 'The Host', man. You're 'The Host' that damn thing was talking about. Jeez."

The color drained from Michael's face. Now that someone else had said it, the lines of reality painted themselves thicker. His throat turned to sand, then to glass, and his stomach did a gymnast's tumbling performance.

Ramond watched this with awe, and a part of him knew what would come next. When a volcano could no longer hold the pressure inside, it blew; and Ramond had a good idea in which direction Michael would erupt.

"DO YOU THINK THAT'S FUNNY, YOU FUCKING IDIOT!" Michael screamed as he rose to his feet. Red filled his eyes as all the fear in his soul transformed into anger. It was easier to believe he had been tricked than to accept the other grisly possibility, and he clung to his self-denial like a wino to a fifth. "IT'S NOT FUNNY AT ALL, YOU LOW CLASS PIECE OF SHIT!"

Ramond scurried to his feet in a vain attempt to make retreat. "I didn't do anything," he muttered as he lost his footing and stumbled toward the door.

Everyone was on their feet now, all silenced and glued to the surreal play being performed before them. Michael continued toward Ramond, eyes filled with hate, heart filled with terror.

"YOU MOVED IT, DIDN'T YOU?" Michael bellowed. He knew it was not true, but for his own sanity, this thought was his only comfort. "I'LL SHOW YOUR STUPID FUCKING ASS, *THE HOST*!"

Ramond instinctively headed for the door, but the

passage was blocked. Like an immovable object, Arnold stood at the exit with no intention of letting the entertainment end just yet.

"Where do you think you're going, Ramsy?" he mocked as he shoved Ramond into the awaiting arms of "The Host".

Ramond was no fighter. He hadn't the size nor the desire for the business. Even self-preservation couldn't bring the will to fight. He was defenseless.

Michael threw an unskilled roundhouse that sailed through the air choppily, but still managed to strike its mark. Ramond's lip tore open on his teeth and the taste of blood filled his mouth. He collapsed to the ground, not from the impact of the blow, but as a protective measure. Assuming the fetal position, his hands and arms were placed over his face to offer as much protection as possible.

"GET UP YOU CHICKEN!" Michael raged.

The boys became an unruly fight crowd, and Ramond heard jeers from the others.

"Get up and fight him sissy!" said one.

"I knew he was a pussy!" came another.

Their words caused a million times more pain than the punch, and would stay with him much longer. With each hateful remark they made toward him, he became more hateful toward the world.

"I SAID GET UP!" Michael contended as he placed a soccer style kick to Ramond's kidneys. It stung, but Ramond dared not uncover his face.

"God help me," he said to himself: a request. The instant the words left his mouth, Ramond felt the sensation again. The vibrations and power that had just moments before passed through his fingers were now passing through his side.

CHILD'S PLAY

"GET UP!" Michael screamed and placed another size six in Ramond's back.

Ramond felt nothing now. The vibrations commanded his full attention. He concentrated on them, trying to figure out what was happening. It didn't take long.

He knew without looking what rested beneath him. Ramond had felt its power just minutes before. It was unmistakable. The stylus jabbed into his side as if it were prodding him to take action. It was magnetic, drawing him to it as it had done before. Slowly he withdrew one arm from his face, being careful to leave the other for insurance. His palm traced a path down his chest, past his stomach, then to the triangle. The small fingers of his hand clinched it tightly as if it might jump away.

The stylus brought pleasure to the touch, like the familiar embrace of an old lover. This time there was no fear. It seemed to just be *right* somehow, and Ramond realized it wasn't just a hunk of plastic, but a source of power.

"I'M GOING TO BREAK EVERY STUPID BONE IN YOUR BODY!" Michael continued to threaten as he placed another sloppy kick, this time striking Ramond just below the back of the neck.

Enough was enough. Ramond spun onto his back and dropped his hands, a move that startled Michael into retreating a step. Their eyes met, and in that fraction of a second, Michael saw something in Ramond's pupils that he would never able to describe.

Ramond's hand slung forward with the grace of a pitcher throwing a perfect fastball. The triangle sailed through the air, spinning perilously like a Ninja's shuriken. It hit bull's-eye on its target, landing directly in the center of Michael's nose, snapping it into fragments.

MICHAEL BISHOP

Michael released a bellow of pain and fell to his knees clutching his bloody sniffer. The stylus parachuted back to the ground just inches from Ramond's thigh and he scooped it up smoothly and placed it into his pocket. It was never missed.

Arnold was shoved forward with great force out of the doorway as the door swung open. He tripped over Ramond and crashed onto the floor, spraining his wrist. In the doorway stood an irate Janet Billion. The screaming had woken her, and Michael's ear-piercing cry had panicked her.

"WHAT THE HELL IS GOING ON!" she shrieked, paying no attention to the damage she had caused Arnold. Her eyes immediately went to the blood pool in her son's lap. She rushed to his side.

"Oh'm'God! O'm'God! What happened? O'm'God, Michael are you okay? O'm'God!" she blubbered, having concerns for no one else.

His sobs were like that of a hungry infant: monotonous and continuous. Michael never lived down those sobs. They were a source of much ridicule over the next few months, as were many things concerning "the Billion sleep over incident".

† † † † † † † † † † †

Michael was rushed to the emergency room by his father, while Janet called all the parents to come get their children. Worried mothers and fathers rushed to the scene to reclaim their *helpless* young ones. Among the first to arrive was Vernadette.

That night was a mini-scandal in the town. The events of the evening were scrutinized again and again by the parents. It wasn't just the fact that there was a Ouija board

CHILD'S PLAY

involved, or that the boys were fighting. The main ridicule was that after hearing what happened, Janet Billion slapped Ramond in the face hard enough to leave a red hand print. It was bad enough to hit your own kid, but to slap someone else's was unforgivable in the eyes of the other parents.

The Billion family left town six months after that night. Janet could take the gossip and jeers no longer, and Ramond always wondered if Michael Billion was indeed the first to die.

† † † † † † † † † † † †

For weeks after that night Ramond could do little else but run the drama over and over in his head as if it was a VCR, replaying certain parts more than others.

The stylus was kept out of the ever-so-watchful eye of his mother; but at times when he knew it was safe, he pulled it out and stroked it like a lucky rabbit's foot. There was no vibration left in it. No trembling of any sort. But still, there was some twisted comfort in its touch. It had chosen him out of every other person at that party. Chosen him to receive the gift of its power. Chosen him to be *special*.

It seemed to fill a void in his life. Prayers had brought a substantial amount of power, but had never really given him that surge he lusted for. But the board was a sign that pointed him down a different road. A road that led to the glorious touch of a higher power.

There was no doubt that he wanted more. Must have more, in fact. But he was only twelve and had been brought up around people who scorned such things and would stone him with contempt if they knew of his desires.

Secrecy was a must.

MICHAEL BISHOP

† † † † † † † † † † †

Only a few weeks passed before the need to feel the power again grew too great, spurring Ramond to take action. The spokes of his red striped Huffy fluttered in the sunlight as he peddled with all the might his thin legs could muster. The store stood twelve blocks from his front door, by far the longest distance he had ever traveled on the bicycle. The rules were simply laid out for him by his father when the bike was bought.

"You are not allowed to leave the neighborhood. There are people out there who will run you over, so stay close," Brian Jamison had warned.

But the time had come to break that rule. If he got caught they would ground him, but that would be a light sentence compared to the punishment he would receive if they knew *why* he had broken it.

The risk was worth it, and even if it wasn't, it did not seem he had a choice in the matter. Ramond was far past driven.

To the left, the store sidewalk began and he expertly glided the bike under its eave near the front door and extended the kickstand.

"BOOKPLUS-YES WE'RE OPEN!" hung on the inside of the full-view door, and Ramond watched it slap against the glass as he gently pushed the door open. The store was dead, typical of a Wednesday afternoon. Ramond noticed the checker out of the corner of his eye as he passed by him quickly to begin his search.

Signs hung from the ceiling marking each section: Fiction, Non-fiction, Horror, Mystery, Religion; but none of these were of interest to Ramond. Only one category would do.

"Occult And Mystical" he spotted and headed toward the sign as he recalled how the women, championed by Vernadette, had gone as far as to threaten to picket the shop and make the owner shut his doors if he did not immediately remove the "blasphemous" literature from the store, and from their God-fearing community. But their threats went unheeded, and the section remained.

The book he had traveled so far for was found quickly. Black wrapped it from front cover to back. The gold pentagram caught his eye almost as if it was illuminated. "The Satanic Bible" was printed just below the circle in a slightly duller shade of gold.

It was beautiful. The sleek black, the shiny gold, the symbol; but best of all, the fact that it was *forbidden*. It was indeed an apple from the tree of knowledge. Ramond outstretched a shaking hand to pluck the fruit.

He traced the shape of the embossed pentagram slowly with his index finger.

"DON'T TOUCH THAT!" Vernadette's voice howled.

Ramond jerked his hand away so quickly he nearly lost his balance and fell to the floor. Regaining footing, he spun, fully expecting to find his mother standing behind him with a cocked hand ready to slap his face just as surely as Janet Billion had done. But the "Occult and Mystic" section was occupied by no one other than him.

Blood pumped through his body rapidly as his heart worked in fast-forward. The voice had haunted him constantly, but had never been that loud. That *real*.

He was standing at the fork in the road. A choice would be made here and now; and as always, the voice was there to make sure he made the *right* decision. But what the voice did not know was that the decision was already made. It had been made *for* Ramond. His desire was too great.

"Ignore it," he said out loud, not worrying that anyone would hear him. His hand reached again, clutching the book this time.

"Ramond, dear, please put the book down sweetheart. Come home to mother. Everything will be alright." The voice was syrupy. Much sweeter than Ramond had ever heard his mother speak.

He pretended not to hear as he opened the book to a random page near the center. What he read was peculiar. Some of the words were foreign to him. Some he understood. The passage was a chant of some sort. He turned the page. The next was much the same, and he realized the book was not quite what he thought it would be. He had heard of this book, as usual, from the prayer group. But to hear them tell it, this book was a simple step-by-step recipe on how to conjure demons and cast spells. There was nothing simple about what Ramond was seeing in its text. But, he thought, he was bright enough to figure it out. After all, he had figured out the real Bible, with all its riddles and odd wordings. The Satanic Bible should be a drop in the bucket.

The voice persisted.

"Ramond, don't do this. Let's pray against the Devil."

"Shut up," he said under his breath.

"Jesus, please help Ramond to overcome this evil that is trying to take hold of him. By your hand he will be spared from temptation."

"Shut Up," he said loud enough to be heard, had there been someone to hear.

"Jesus, please forgive Ramond, he is a bad boy..A bad

CHILD'S PLAY

bad BOY... A BAD BAD BAD BOY!"

"SHUT UP!" rushed from his lips as he covered his head with his hands and arms, much in the same way he had done during Michael's onslaught of kicks.

"Hey, What's goin' on back there?" the cashier's voice cracked as he called out.

Ramond snapped to attention, wanting no trouble now. Especially with so much on the line. He ducked around the corner to the "Children's" row and waited to see if any more inquires would come, ready to deny it was he who had screamed, even though he was the only customer in the place. But the cashier seemed uninterested and said no more.

"They'll never sell that book to you Ramond. You know that don't you?" the voice said matter-of-factly.

"What?" he found himself asking.

"They may sell this evil book, but there's *no way* they are going to sell it to a child. Think about it."

Ramond did think about it. Long and carefully. His mother's voice had brought something to his attention he had not considered. The owner had already taken more heat for the books than he ever dreamed. If he were to sell a book like this to a kid, the townsfolk would not only shut his store down, but be tempted to lynch him as well.

"Just put the book back on the shelf and we will pretend none of this ever happened. Come home Ramond."

"Fuck You," he whispered, more mindful of his noise level.

The words took him back for a moment. It was the first time in his twelve years of life that he had ever let a curse word escape his lips. Vernadette had always taught him that words were dangerous. The things you said could be the biggest sins of all. It only took hearing this warning once for

MICHAEL BISHOP

Ramond to keep a watch on the words he spoke. Twelve years of restraint had been removed with the speaking of a single word.

He smiled to himself. It felt good to be bad.

That defiance gave Ramond the courage he needed, and he decided to go for it. The owner wasn't here, only some cashier; and Ramond judged by the way the guy's voice had cracked that he must still be in his teens. Maybe, just maybe, he could pull this thing off after all. And if the guy gave him any static, he could just drop the book and run out the door. No one could catch him on his bike when he was pumping as hard as he could. It was a foolproof escape plan.

A stolid look was affixed to Ramond's face as he did his best to look mature. *Just stay cool and this will be over in a second*, he thought, trying to psyche himself up and subside the butterflies in his belly.

"He'll never sell it to you Ramond. Give up. GIVE UP!"

Ramond was prepared and the voice failed to stop him. He pulled the wadded dollar bills out of his pocket and flattened them against his thigh. With money in one hand and book in the other, he boldly walked up to the cashier.

For the first time, Ramond got a look at the guy at the register. His head was covered with a uniformed BOOKPLUS cap, but the sporadic strands that escaped from the brim made it apparent the employee had a long, thin mane of dark brown hair hiding underneath. His face was clear, but scars remained as a reminder of the bad acne he had suffered through. His eyes were beyond blue, almost crystal; and in them was a far away look as if he was searching for something in the distance, just beyond the range his specs could see. A

CHILD'S PLAY

signature BOOKPLUS shirt hung off his thin frame and on his chest a badge was pinned. It read "Welcome to BOOKPLUS" typed in large red letters. Underneath them "Johnny" was scribbled in black pen.

"Can I help you?" he said as Ramond neared the counter. Johnny's eyes continued to hold the far away look even though he was staring directly at Ramond. It was unnerving: sinister.

"Ahh, I wanna buy this," Ramond muttered letting the last two words drag as he set the book on the counter. His heart began to speed up again as he tried to hide his nervousness.

Johnny glared down at the book as if it were unimportant. Ramond relaxed a bit. Perhaps the whole thing wasn't as big of a deal as he was trying to make it. Perhaps he would get through this with no problems...but the celebration was premature.

Johnny's head snapped up at Ramond so quickly that his neck popped like knuckles. A smile opened up across his face like an earthquake pulling apart the earth's crust and continued to grow slowly until his teeth shown through.

"RUN RAMOND, RUN!" Vernadette ordered, and Ramond nearly followed orders like a good little soldier. But there was something in that smile. Something that was hypnotic. Something that made his knees weak and unable to move.

"So you want to learn a little about the Devil, huh kid?" Johnny said, not sounding much like a question. "Well you're not gonna learn about him in that book. You won't even understand the first page of that book. But there are ways. And they're not hard to find. Not hard at all my boy... if you know where to look."

MICHAEL BISHOP

† † † † † † † † † † †

Getting out of the clutches of his mother would indeed be a challenge, and this was a point he made perfectly clear to Johnny early on. But Ramond was not the first student Johnny had taught. Defensive mothers had been conquered before.

"It's like a play," Johnny explained. "You just say what I tell you to say and do what I tell you to do, and you'll soon have all the freedom you want."

He was right.

The charade was a simple one. Ramond told his mother he had signed up with the "Big Brother" program because he was lonely.

"I saw a commercial on T.V., momma. They said if you wanted an older buddy to hang out with you could call the number and they would find you a big brother. So I called it, and they already found me someone. His name is Johnny, and he's commin' this Friday to meet us all!" Ramond told Vernadette, trying to sound as excited as he could without sounding fake.

Vernadette cheered the idea. The program would be the perfect way, she thought, for Ramond to make a friend and have some fun. And anything that would get Ramond out of the house and around other people would benefit him. Being so reclusive was unhealthy and would stunt his social skills, she feared.

Johnny showed up every weekend and on a few "special occasions" to take Ramond out for a day of good, clean fun.

It was, of course, somewhat of a hassle for Johnny to hide his hair. But when he tied it up in a ponytail and carefully tucked it under a ball cap, it disappeared.

Vernadette and Brian Jamison trusted Johnny. They had no reason not to. He seemed like a fine boy, and Ramond was given his freedom just as Johnny had promised. It *was* truly easy.

The lessons were simple in the beginning. Johnny was careful. He did not want to scare the boy away. So the pace was slow... at first.

For the first week they did little but talk.

"What do you want?" Johnny asked.

A simple question, and Ramond's answer was simple as well: *Power*. That was all he had ever wanted. It had been the central focus of his studies. That incentive had either directly or indirectly affected every decision Ramond had made since he first felt it. If it wasn't the power that his mother's love brought, it was the power he derived from being the center of attention. It was a rush worth living for.

These answers pleased Johnny, but worried him as well. Ramond had a natural drive, and that was a good thing. *A must* even. But Johnny was not convinced Ramond understood the magnitude of his decision, so he moved slowly. After all, Ramond was still just a boy.

"I'll tell you the same thing I was told when I was in your place, Ram. Once you've seen the things I will show you, and done the things I'm going teach you how to do, you are *bound*. Bound for life. We are a very exclusive group, once in...death is the only cancellation of membership. I want you to understand that clearly. It's important. Although power will be given to you, there is a price you must pay. That price is devotion, loyalty, and honor. We are brothers. We all have the same father. Under-Stando-Kiddo?" he asked.

MICHAEL BISHOP

Ramond assured him that he did understand, and Johnny thought the boy might actually comprehend after all. But if he didn't yet, he soon would. The line was crossed and then erased. No exit.

Ramond *did* understand to a degree. He was switching teams. A life-long trade. And it was enticing. Yet some of the rules were still cloudy and terrifying.

"What about Hell? Will I go there?" Ramond inquired.

"Listen, Ram. Everything you've ever been taught, *forget*. Everything you've ever been told about Satan, Jesus Christ, and *their* God were lies. Everything you have ever seen was conspiracy. It isn't like they say. They fear us...fear what we do. They shudder what they do not understand. They believe the lies. Your mother is a *liar*. I'm sorry if that stings. I'm sure coming from me, a practical stranger, that seems like a cruel thing to say. But the truth is the truth. This world does not belong to their God. He created it, but He does not own it. He has limited power here, where as my father has boundless control. Your life could be ended with a snap of his fingers. Your life was his the day you were born. The Bible was written as a rebuke to reality. But the best lies are shrouded in truth. There are writings in that *book* that are fact, but the few truths are buried so deep within the lies that only the most astute scholars can distinguish them.

"The *truth* is that those who serve my father will inherit the Earth. We are the 'meek'. The few. We are society's outcasts. We must hide in the shadows to avoid persecution. We must lurk behind closed doors. But once my father sends his son to take what belongs to him, then, my boy, we will be the kings of the world. We'll stand in

CHILD'S PLAY

judgment upon all those who have judged us. Hell will be our refuge, but it's not something to fear. It's glorious. A kingdom. A HOME." Johnny spoke eloquently, as if he had recited the speech a thousand times and knew it by heart.

It was a powerful sermon. Ramond's fears were subsiding. The urge to push forward had never been greater.

The lessons began, to Ramond's initial delight, with a "Witchboard", which was incredibly similar to the "Ouija" board, only larger, with fancier symbols and a huge stylus that housed a crystal in its center.

"This baby cost me a week's pay," Johnny recounted. "Money well spent."

But to Ramond the entire experience was truly disappointing. They asked it a few questions. It gave a few answers. But, in all, the event was lack-lustered compared to his first experience. There was no surge in it. No *kick*.

"NEXT!" Ramond said as if he were a director auditioning a panel of young starlets. It was obvious Ramond was becoming bored, and a bored student was a bad student. So Johnny taught his disciple in half the time he had taught others.

The lessons spiraled passed Ramond: seances, ceremonies, chants, tools of the trade. He was a wonderful pupil. A sponge which absorbed all information.

He was taught the true meaning of "sorcery", using a drug-induced state of consciousness to contact the spirit world. It was a practice Ramond enjoyed immensely. He learned how not to just participate in "gatherings", but how to lead them as well. He was introduced to "The Family". Taken in. Loved.

And there were other perks. The drugs were

magnificent, and often supplied free of charge by the adults who ran the ceremonies. And sex was made available to him as early as thirteen. His age didn't matter. In his new family he was not some kid. He was Ramond "The Ram". The women, the girls, they all offered themselves to him. Taught him how to be a man. Gave him pleasure beyond his imagination.

It was amazing. There were so many who came to worship. All ages, all races, all social classes. Living like chameleons, showing their true colors only around "The Family". They flourished in the underworld. And Ramond began to understand why the membership was ended only in death.

If anyone outside the circle found out the identities of those who partook of the ceremonies, the members would be shunned as outcasts. And there were those who could not afford to let that happen. Doctors, lawyers, pillars of the community. Some of which attended a Christian church frequently to maintain their disguise. It was a tangled web. One that was woven *not* to unravel.

Many, including Johnny and Ramond, attended more than just one group's activities. They were "joiners". Jumping on the bandwagon of anything new to open itself up to them. Experiencing as much of the occult as they could in the shortest amount of time.

Ramond found the power he was looking for... and then some... for a time, at least.

Gradually, Vernadette began to notice a difference in Ramond. He had grown moody the last few months. Self-

CHILD'S PLAY

absorbed. No longer did he show interest in Friday night meeting. If he wasn't out with Johnny, he was locked in his room for hours at a time, hardly ever talking to either of his parents. Gestures of affection were becoming rare. It was drastically disheartening.

But despite all the understanding and insight Vernadette had in everyone else's life, when it came to her son, she wore blinders. In her mind, Ramond was the perfect child and she rationalized his actions, letting a bad thing get worse.

She told herself it was just part of maturing. Sure he was around little lately, but it was good that he was finally making friends. And it was only natural for a boy to reach the point where he felt he was too big to be hugging his mother. So what if he wore his hair a bit longer these days. It was just a phase. He would grow out of it. As long as he went to church with her every Sunday she assumed everything would be fine.

Each Sunday that Ramond forced himself to attend Vernadette's church, he grew more hateful of its members. To him, the entire Christian religion was based on cosmic hypocrisy. This conclusion was reached, of course, with the help of his new friends; but these thoughts had began to surface even before he met them. In those days, however, they were immediately cast out, fearing the sin of them. Now there was no such thing as sin. He had come to believe this.

Preachers, who were supposed to be the holiest of the holies, were oftentimes the worst of the lot. Each day there was a new story of one of them being brought up on charges of tax evasion, child molestation, fraud, or some other "deadly sin". Yet many in their congregations continued to defend them, even after they were sentenced and carted away. Foolishly blind.

Church goers were no better. Every word that left their mouths was so one-sided that Ramond often found himself furious just listening to them. Believing asinine things; and the sole foundation for their beliefs was a solitary book written in a time and place so out of touch with the current world that it could not possibly have any relevance for today. But Christians believed their precious Bible was the final authority in every situation, and nothing could convince them otherwise.

But the greatest hypocrisy of all was that the so-called creator would make the "Hell threat". If God was so loving, why would he let mankind go through such agony and torment? Even here on Earth were atrocities that boggled the mind. People torturing and mutilating their fellow man. Rape and child abuse runs rampant, and *their* God sits on his throne, separated from everything, letting it happen like He could give a shit less.

And if Jesus really died for our sins, how come we are still held accountable for them? How come we are judged for what we do if his blood washed away our wrong doings and granted us forgiveness? It was all a lie. And so many had bought into the lie hook, line, and sinker, including him in the past. But it was time to change all that.

Six months into his fifteenth birthday, the lie Ramond was living spread like fungus and overwhelmed him. He was a man now. Had been a man for some time whether anyone recognized it or not, and men should make their own decisions. It was decided, although not without great inner conflict, that his presence was no longer required at

CHILD'S PLAY

Vernadette's church.

She was still much loved by her son, and it bothered Ramond to hurt his mother. But it had to be done. The new life he led was blissful. He enjoyed serving his new master. It was not right to pretend allegiance to another. He did not want to be held in contempt from Satan. That might lessen his chance for power, which was a price he would not pay for anything... even his mother's heart.

She was in the kitchen, as always, when he went to give her the news.

"Mom," he whispered.

Vernadette jumped and spun, startled.

"Oh, Ramond, you nearly gave me a heart attack. Don't sneak up on me like that!" she sputtered holding her heart. It was not hard to sneak up on her when she was cooking. An artist could not possibly take more care with their paintings than Vernadette did with her edible masterpieces; and when she was *creating*, the world around her was shut out as if she were in a soundproof vacuum.

"I'm sorry, mom. Um... I... ahh, need to talk to you for a sec," Ramond attempted to recite the speech he had rehearsed.

"What is it, son?" she asked as she turned her back on him and continued her construction. It was a normal reaction. She never really listened when he spoke, and yet expected him to be all ears when she got ready to say something.

"Mom, turn around and listen to me, DAMMIT!"

Vernadette whirled around like an maniacal carousel, her emerald eyes filled with shock and anger. "RAMOND!" she squealed so loudly it made him blink. "What did you say?"

MICHAEL BISHOP

"You heard me, Mom. It's time you listened to me. Not just hear, but LISTEN!" he thundered. His eyes bulging with anger as well.

"WHAT IS THIS ALL ABOUT?" she insisted, holding back the impulse to knock the backtalk from her son's mouth.

"IT'S ABOUT A LOT OF THINGS. IT'S ABOUT RESPECT. IT'S ABOUT THE FACT THAT I DESERVE FOR SOMEONE IN THIS FAMILY TO PAY SOME DAMNED ATTENTION TO SOMETHING I GOTTA SAY!" he fired back.

"WATCH YOUR FILTHY MOUTH, RAMOND! ....Now you lower your tone and I'd better not ever hear you talk to me like that again. Is that understood?"

"O.K., Just listen to me. That's all I want," he agreed. "I have something to say that is important. If it wasn't so important I wouldn't say it at all, but I have to."

"What is it, Ramond?" Vernadette asked as a lump began forming in her throat. Something was different about her son. He had never snapped at her like this. Deep inside she knew she was about to be cut deeply with his words.

"I've given a lot of thought to this. A *lot* of thought. So don't think for a moment that this is something I'm saying out of the blue."

"Just say it, son," she whimpered, tears already drowning her pupils.

"Man, mom, don't cry." His eyes dropped to the floor. He couldn't look at her. It was wrong to hurt her like this, after all she had done. But he would...for the master. "Mom, I won't be going to church with you no more."

"WHAT?" she spewed, tears flowing freely down her soft cheeks. Of all the things she had expected to hear, this

CHILD'S PLAY

was not one of them.

"I've come to a point in my life...I mean... I... I'm a man now mom. And I gotta start making choices for myself. The choices I think are right for me. I love you mom, but I just don't believe like you do anymore,"

"What are you talking about? Where are you getting this from?" she interrogated in denial. "This didn't come from anyone. Are you even listening to me? I'm a man. I can make my own decisions. Don't think just cause I'm only fifteen I'm too immature to think for myself. You know me better than that. You know I've always been different...smarter than other kids my age... Christ is not the man I want to spend my life serving. I don't want to serve any *man*," he spoke, trying to make as little eye contact as possible.

"DON'T SAY THAT! JESUS FORGIVE HIM. HE DOESN'T KNOW WHAT HE IS SAYING. IT'S NOT HIM LORD, IT'S THIS WORLD. IT'S TRYING TO TURN HIM AGAINST YOU. BUT HE WILL OVERCOME!" Vernadette was hysterical, screaming her prayer at the ceiling as if Ramond was not there at all. Ramond's blasphemy was *too* much. A death in the family would have been better.

"MOM... MOM... I don't need you to pray for me. I can take care of my own problems without you wasting your breath. I'm sorry if you can't accept it. But this is the way it's gonna be. I don't expect you to understand and I don't expect you to support me. But I can't live a lie. The truth is the truth," he finished, stealing a line from Johnny.

She could do nothing but stare at her son. Vernadette didn't even know Ramond anymore. He had become a stranger.

She tried to find the words to change things. But the words didn't exist. Her mouth opened and only one thing

MICHAEL BISHOP

came out.

"GOD FORGIVE YOU SON... GOD FORGIVE YOU!"

✝ ✝ ✝ ✝ ✝ ✝ ✝ ✝ ✝ ✝ ✝

That day in the Jamison home was the day everything changed. It was the day the "good son" died.

She tried everything she knew to revive the little "Christian man" that once lived inside of Ramond, but it was fruitless. *Her* son was gone forever and in his place was a hollow shell.

From then on, Ramond stayed home with his father, Brian Jamison, on Sundays. Brian was what the women's group called an "armchair Christian". The term was coined from "armchair quarterback" to describe their backsliding husbands. The men lived their Christianity in very much the same way they watched their football games. Yelling at the T.V. Explaining ways they could execute the plays better than the numskulls on the field. When the time came, though, they never participated in any aspect of the *sport*.

"Abortion is murder, plain and simple," they might say.

"The government should put prayer back in our children's schools!" they would shout amongst each other.

But anytime the opportunity came to get out of the chair and actually do something, it became obvious these men were all bark.

Just about the only time you would find Brian Jamison in church was Easter or Christmas; and those times he went only out of extreme guilt for reneging on the church the other three hundred and sixty-three days out of the year.

On Friday nights, when the women came over, Brian concealed himself in his shop/garage, playing an adult version of "hide and seek", tinkering with projects he knew he would never finish. It was just an instrument to occupy his time until the women went back home where they belonged.

From the time Ramond taught himself to walk, he and Brian had never been close. He always felt his father loved *the game* more than he loved his own flesh and blood. It did not even seem to matter what *the game* was: football, baseball, even a God-forsaken sport like golf was a good enough excuse for him to flop down in front of the one-eyed-monster and ignore his family. Over the years Ramond gave up trying to establish any relationship with his father, and turned his interest toward more provocative activities.

THE PROPOSITION

ing James Version" was printed across the spine of the burgundy, leather bound book on his night stand. Several pages had been ripped out to smoke joints when he ran out of papers, but the Bible still lay mostly intact. It served as a martyr in his apartment. A thing that stayed constant through the years while everything else changed.

Seven years had gone by him in what seemed like a blink, and once again, at age 22, his mind began to turn. He had reached the point again where life was as stale as tobacco smoke. There had to be more... somewhere. Almost a decade of his practices were behind him now, and the novelty had worn off long ago. Continuing his activities only in hopes of finding something to interest him once more. The surface had not yet been scratched on the pleasures he could feel. He was sure of it, and the lust for the next step began to take its toll.

Ramond compared his craving to what Johnny had

MICHAEL BISHOP

told him about cocaine.

"The reason people get hooked on cocaine is because the first high is so good it can never be equaled again. They keep snorting and snorting, trying to find that time *rise* again. But it's never the same. Never. And those who are smart move on to a new high," Johnny admitted.

Ramond stroked the monocle that hung from his neck. The stylus had never "come alive" again, but was too treasured a keepsake to discard. Soon after he had quit his mother's church, its crystal centerpiece was popped out, a hole was drilled through it and a leather shoestring was threaded through the hole, making a shabby amulet. Over the years it had been his good luck charm, rarely leaving his neck.

But it too had grown old. Everything had grown old. The walls. The ceiling. The bed. Life.

As he looked around his room, he shuttered. Ramond's existence had become a predictable routine. The weeks ran together, each one like the last. Get up, go to work, come home, go to sleep, and occasionally make time to practice an old trick. No fireworks in his life.

It was sad and pathetic swirled together. Out of all that he had learned, all that he had worked for, and all he had wished for... he had nothing.

Every paycheck was usually owed to someone else before it was even earned. Occasionally the money was borrowed for legitimate reasons, like rent. But mostly the loans were for drugs. It seemed the only way to end the monotony. The world was a bland buffet and had lost its sumptuous flavor. His mind sought an escape from the confines of reality. Drugs were his passport. A medium that

THE PROPOSITION

carried him away to places where he could hide from society... his job... his conscience... *himself.*

The aged night stand drawer was opened carefully, creaking noisily as its rusty tracks cried in defiance at being awakened. He opened it only halfway. The thing had already been glued back together half a dozen times. It was not a chore he wished to repeat tonight.

Even with the drawer only partially cracked the sheet of acid inside could be seen as a glare from the lamp bounced off it. The acid was his favorite ride, seeming to give the biggest bang for the buck. It made him see things. Things that were more interesting than what lied in the real world.

Carefully, a small square was removed from the sheet, a ticket of sorts, and a mythical conductor could be heard in his head shouting, "ALL ABOARD".

The drop of acid was carefully placed on the tip of his tongue, a common ritual.

After twenty minutes...nothing. No pretty colors. No sound effects. No hallucinations. Zip.

Frustration set in. He had never had trouble feeling at least *something* before. Even on the weakest hit of acid. But this time the warm feeling and excitement the drug usually brought was painfully absent.

Five more seconds and he would have taken another hit, maybe even two: whatever it took to begin the process. But the voice ended all wanting.

"I have heard you," it said in tones that spoke with the low base of a tuba and the high shrill of a mandolin all at once. It came from nowhere, yet everywhere all at once.

MICHAEL BISHOP

"SHIT!" Ramond bellowed as he leaped to his feet. The Bible was knocked to the floor as he jerked the lamp off the night stand and out of the wall socket for use as a weapon. The room went black. Tightly he choked up on the lamp's neck, holding it like a baseball bat. It was a poor weapon, but it was handy and better than nothing.

"WHO IN THE FUCK IS THERE? I'LL KILL YOU, I SWEAR TO GOD!" he shouted, sure he was about to die. His skin felt like it was shrinking and tightening around his bones, as the smell in the air turned to sick decay. The panic was almost constricting, making it hard for him to breathe.

"Do not be afraid...Peace be still," it stated.

As the words entered Ramond's ears, he felt himself calm. It was magic. A feeling very much like being stoned off pot or Valium. Everything would be alright.

The lamp was released and exploded into fragments upon impact with the floor. Ramond sat back down on the bed. Then laid. A smile spread across his lips. He did not know why and did not care.

"Who are you?"

"I am he whom you seek."

"Who?... What do you want with me?" Ramond questioned as he looked around in the dark..

"Don't search with your eyes, search with your heart, I *live* there. I haven't always, but I do now."

It was God. Ramond knew without doubt. But it was not *their* God. It was *his* God. His confidant. Satan.

"I love you," were the only words he could find, as if all others were hiding in his head for fear of being chosen. It was the first time he had uttered those three words since he was fifteen. And never had they been said so sincerely.

"I know you do, son. Otherwise I would not be here.

THE PROPOSITION

Your love has drawn me. Made me take notice of you. You are special. Very special indeed."

Ramond felt something warm on his cheeks and it took hard concentration to realize it was his own tears. "I can't believe you're saying this to *me*. Thank you," he wept. It was a moment he had only dreamed of. "What can I give you? Anything, Sire. My nights. My days. My life. Anything you want."

"I do not want anything from you. Not yet anyway. I have little time, so listen close. You are searching for something. You've been searching for it your whole life. You *do* know that don't you?"

"Yes," he replied, and Ramond *did* know.

"And you don't know what it is, do you?"

"No," he agreed. His life had been spent in search. From the earliest memory he had, all the way up to present day, his life had been a scavenger hunt. Searching as a child in the pages of the Bible. Searching as a teen in the sex, drugs, and seances. Now he was a man and still searching.

It was as if he was in a vast library, looking for a book he did not know the author or title of. Ramond knew he would recognize it when he saw it, but had no idea where to begin.

"What is it I'm looking for? Please tell me!" he begged like a starving mutt.

"I'm sorry. I cannot. This is a quest you will have to fulfill for yourself. Search carefully. Answers will come to you in time. When you know what you want, seek me out. I will never be far from you. There are plans for you. There always have been."

The stench in the air lifted and the voice was gone as quickly as it had come. With it, the calm was washed away as well. Ramond's body convulsed as the overdose of adrenaline that had been suppressed was allowed to gallop about freely like wild horses in an open field. Pure energy pulsated from his fingertips. Roaches and mice scurried to their cubbyholes. They too felt the electricity.

When the adrenaline had run its course, Ramond lay motionless in exhaustion. The experience had drained him. But his mind continued to sprint.

What had just happened was unbelievable; yet he *did* believe, with everything in him. The encounter brought an answer, but also a question. What was he supposed to do? Or be?

Hours later he lay in the same spot, having not moved in all that time. Nothing else mattered but the answer. The die of his destiny had been rolled.

✝✝✝✝✝✝✝✝✝✝✝✝

For all intentional purposes Ramond had quit his job. No two week notice. No formal letter of resignation. He just never went back. There was no need to. The search plagued him like leprosy, and trying to work while his mind was occupied with something so massive would be a folly.

Just as he was told, the answers did come to him in time. Two weeks to be exact. During that period nearly every detail of his life had been sifted thoroughly in hopes something would stand out. Each grain of memory had been held under a microscope and examined for anything that might be of help. Fourteen days of this process had been toiled through with no luck. On the fifteenth day he dumbly

THE PROPOSITION

stumbled upon the answer.

Sleep hadn't come in over forty-eight hours, and his stomach yearned for something edible to fill its abyss. It was break time. Ramond grabbed some reheated burgers and greasy fries at a nearby burger joint and headed back.

As he pulled into his apartment complex, he watched as the oil stain on his designated parking space disappeared under the hood of the old green Ford his father had given him when he moved out. The car was more like a tank then a car, but was one of the few things that rarely let him down.

The view he spanned as he walked to the stairs was the same as it had always been, except for one essentially unnoticeable thing. The ancient Toyota pickup which his elderly neighbor, Mrs. Jenkins, had proudly driven for seventeen years and three hundred thousand miles, stood before him looking very much like a lame horse that had nothing left in her.

The worn out transport sat continually in the same spot, rarely found missing from its home in parking space 47G. Its sides always housed the same golf ball sized dents, with the familiar scratches and chipped paint spots. The bald tires were rotated every ten thousand miles just like her fine boy had suggested. It was yet another thing in Ramond's life that was monotonous.

But today it did change. A change that was so slight that it should not have affected anyone. A change he should not have even noticed. But Ramond did notice, and it was a change that would alter the course of his life.

As he exited the car, a breeze caught his long matted hair and blew it out of his face, over his shoulder. At that moment he noticed it. The red letters called to his eyes. A new bumper sticker had been added to Mrs. Jenkins' Toyota, with a very simple message.

"Jesus is Coming Soon!" it declared in patriotic red, white, and blue. Ramond rolled the message over the gears in his head a dozen times. It started a spark that spread like wildfire. In minutes an entire forest of thoughts were blazing in Ramond's mind. It was lustrous. It was a miracle. It was his answer.

†††††††††††

The door of his apartment came close to being ripped off its hinges as he barged through it in boyish excitement. The light switch was slapped upward harshly and he lunged for the bed, doing a belly-flop in the center of its mattress. He leaned over the bed letting his arms hang. The hair in the back of his head draped down over his face in a million mini-blinds as he secured the Bible off the floor where it had been for the past half-month. It was an old friend, and he hoped he had not ripped any useful pages out as he began ruffling through it.

Once, he had known so much about the book. Finding anything he wanted was short work and he instinctively went to the correct section. But times had changed. The Bible was now as peculiar as the Satanic Bible had once been. The writings it possessed were alien.

As if the book had known his intentions, it opened very close to the page he probed for. There, in the concordance, it would tell him exactly where in the cataclysms of the book he could find information about "The Man". As he ran his thumb down the A's, it quickly fell upon the word "Anti-Christ".

The Bible's index sent him to Daniel, Revelations,

THE PROPOSITION

Ezekiel, and Thessalonians, and in the end, proved to be moderately disappointing. If Ramond had *ever* understood the book, he certainly did not now. It spoke in riddles and rhymes, using icons that were unclear to him; and with each symbol woven into its fables and tales, Ramond's mind grew more perplexed.

Passages spoke of a scarlet dragon with seven heads and ten horns and from these ten horns grew a smaller horn that uprooted three. They recanted a story of a statue with a head of gold, torso of silver, legs of iron, and feet of clay. They laid out a tale of Kings and Armageddon and the second coming of "he that was". But all these things were too vague and entrenched with allegories for Ramond to find any useful understanding. He read for five hours before giving up.

As he lay on his back, head twinging with the first inclination of an eye-strain headache, he recalled a particular instance his mother had attempted to explain this very subject to him. This story was the catalyst that evoked the spark in his mind when he saw the red, white, and blue bumper sticker.

† † † † † † † † † † † †

"Are you warm enough sweetheart?"

"I'm okay, Momma."

"Good. I want you to get comfortable. I want to talk to you about something."

"What is it, Momma?"

"Just get comfortable. We've got plenty of time. I'm sure with this storm the lights won't be back on anytime soon," she told him as she stood up and wrapped another blanket around him. Only his head emerged from the cocoon of quilts and comforters that encased his body.

MICHAEL BISHOP

The storm was an unusual event. "Ice Storm Glenda" the weathermen were calling it. Glenda had already taken twelve victims and wiped out ninety-seven percent of the power in Sierra Springs.

Brian Jamison had turned in to his bed long before. Somewhere a few rooms from his family he lay under a mountain of cover, dreaming peacefully and oblivious to the heinous activities of the skies.

Vernadette sat across from her son and watched the fire light frolic in the glares of his candied cheeks. The storm was worth it just to have this moment with him. It seemed she was too veiled in her activities lately to spend the time and say the things to Ramond she needed to.

She seized the opportunity to have the discussion with him she had meant to have for months now. Ramond was a captive audience.

"I'm going to try to explain this to you darling, and I know you may not understand but if you have any questions just ask."

"Okay Momma." It was a common response from the boy. His mother always preempted her speeches with a long, drawn out explanation of why she was explaining something to begin with. He was used to it. Each time patiently saying "O.K. Momma," as he waited for her to fire up the pulpit and begin.

"I want you to learn this lesson because it is one of the most important you will ever hear," Vernadette paused and peered at her son with a loving gaze, studying the look on his face to see if he was paying attention. "We have in *our* beliefs what we call an 'age of accountability'. This means that when you reach a certain age you are responsible for your actions and choices. Our church teaches this age is thirteen."

THE PROPOSITION

She lapsed once again to read his face, looking for any indication that he was following her. She was warming up and knew herself. Soon she would be rolling the information out of her mouth with little thought to anything else but her own words. It was imperative he discerned so far.

Ramond's eyes gleamed back at her, bright and full of curiosity. A born pupil. His look was enough to sway her.

"So you should know all the things I am about to tell you before you reach this age; and although you're only 8 now, I think you're ready to begin learning about it now and maybe by the time you reach thirteen, you'll know enough to make the correct decision." Vernadette shifted her seat. Her buttocks were beginning to go numb from sitting in the same position too long. "Let's see, where was I... oh yes, well I told you *that* to tell you *this*. Soon, something terrible will happen. I'm not trying to scare you, but you need to know this."

"What will happen?" he interrupted.

"I'm getting to that... you see the Devil is trying to harm us. He is the deceiver and will do anything he can to destroy what God has created. That's why you and I pray against him."

"I already know that."

"I know. Just hold your horses, I'm getting to the important part...anyway, Satan will send his son to this earth. Just like God did by sending his son Jesus. Only Satan's son will come to kill instead of save. He is the Anti-Christ, because he is the opposite of Jesus."

"When is he coming?"

"Well no one knows for sure, but we do believe it's gonna be soon. And when he comes it's gonna be bad. He will try to wipe Christians out. We will be persecuted... I'm sorry, you probably don't even know what *persecuted* means. I'll try to talk more simply."

"I know what that means, Momma. Don't treat me like I'm stupid. You know I'm smart," Ramond corrected defensively.

"I'm sorry. I just don't want this to go over your head. It's soooo important that I have to explain carefully."

"Just tell me. I'll get it."

"Well, the first way he will work to destroy us is by the mark of the beast. When I say 'mark", I'm talking about the 'mark of the beast', okay?"

"Okay."

"Well, 'The Man', that's what we call the Anti-Christ... 'The Man' will try to make everyone take the mark. But anyone who does will perish in Hell. The Bible says that taking the mark of the beast is a sin there is no forgiveness for. So if you take it, it's like selling your soul to the Devil."

"What is the mark?"

"I'll tell you what *I* think it will be. I think it will be a microchip. You know like in computers? But instead, they'll put this chip in your right palm or in your forehead."

"Why?"

"Because it will enable them to keep up with everyone. They'll always know where you are and what you are doing."

"I don't understand why anyone would get that put in them. It sounds stupid!"

"Ramond, many people *will* get it. Because without it, no one will be able to buy or sell anything. Without it, no one can get food or clothes, or gas, or anything. It will work like a credit card. Only instead of the cashier scanning your card, they'll just scan your hand or forehead."

"I still don't get it. Why not just pay money for

THE PROPOSITION

things?"

"There won't be any money, Ramond!" Her voice level raised with the frustration of trying to explain something so complex. She controlled it, settled herself down. "See, Ramond, money is becoming more and more a thing of the past. Everyone has credit cards these days. It's easier to use them instead of cash. It's harder to steal cards, it's easier to keep track of what you buy, and it's safer than carrying money. Soon dollar bills will be replaced with credits. And when that happens everyone will have credit cards instead of money."

"Then why not just use the cards instead of getting a stupid chip in your head?"

"Because the cards can still be stolen, sweetie. People will have their entire life savings on these cards, and the fear of them being stolen will be too great. So they'll invent the chip to replace the card. It's not likely for someone to steal a chip from you when it's embedded under your skin. It will just make everything easier. No more writing checks. No more scrounging for exact change. Just one scan and your whole purchase is paid for and done with. The convenience of it will make millions rush to get one."

"What will happen to me if I don't want to get that thing in my head or hand?" Ramond asked wide-eyed. He was growing scared. The lesson was intense and he needed some assurance of a happy ending to this story.

"Don't worry son. Some people believe Jesus will come back and take us away before this happens. Other people believe he won't come back until after 'The Man' comes. But no matter what happens, I know he will take care of us. We are God's children and he will protect us no matter what, so don't worry about it."

MICHAEL BISHOP

"But...but what will happen to the people that say they don't want the mark?"

"I'm going to be honest with you, 'cause I think you are mature enough to handle it. There is going to be a great war. Brother will kill brother. The blood shed will be like the world has never seen. The whole Earth will be involved in a holy war. The Anti-Christ will become the ruler of all nations. He will be the most powerful man on the face of the planet. All countries will look to him as their leader, and his word will be law. I pray we are not here to see that day, but if we are, I want you to be prepared. Those who refuse the mark will be sent to concentration camps and some will be slaughtered, just like Hitler did the Jews during the Holocaust. Children, women, babies... no one will be spared from 'The Man'." She sliced her words like a guillotine, realizing what she had done. He was only eight. There was no way he could know what the Holocaust was. Or Hitler. Or concentration camps. Vernadette had gotten carried away, caught up in the message so deeply that she failed to realize its complexity. She gazed at her boy and saw the confusion.

"God forgive me... I'm sorry Ramond. I didn't mean to get carried away. I know this whole thing is scary and hard to understand. When you get a little older you'll understand better. For now I think we've talked about this enough. It's time for bed," she told him as she rose.

Ramond was intelligent for an 8 year-old, but still very confused. The main question troubling him was *"Why?"* Why would God let this happen? Wasn't He the creator? Couldn't He stop it?

THE PROPOSITION

She never spoke of it to him again. Not that she had not meant to. The right moment just never unveiled itself. It was one of the few chores she failed to complete.

The next day he went to the Bible curiously. How could she know these things? How could anyone know? It was miraculous, as if his mother could predict the future. It was a *gift* he wanted for himself.

But the Bible held few answers that he could understand, and he disregarded her speech as speculation. The book approached the subject in the same manner it approached everything else, in riddles. His mother and her friends obviously drew from it what they wanted to. Nowhere in its pages did it mention *microchips* or *credits*, although it did mention "The Man" and the mark of the beast. Saying they would come, but specifically that no man would know the time or the day. The subject quickly lost its interest.

Fourteen years later, that talk drew Ramond's attention again. Little was ever said about the Anti-Christ. Not in church. Not in the ceremonies. Not in his books. It was like the whole world dared not speak of him, as if the very mountains themselves quaked at the thought such a man might exist. And Ramond found it very odd that he had never given much thought to it again. After all, it was a subject of wondrous possibilities. The fact that a mortal man might actually be the son of Satan. And not only that, but the ruler of all. How could a phenomenon like that be kept so quiet?

But this line of thinking was not foremost in Ramond's thoughts. The real excitement came, of course, from the power "The Man" would have. As his mother had said, his word would be law. Anyone who opposed him would be dealt with severely. The "Anti-Christ" would be deity: a God in the body of a man. And this man would be second only to Satan himself. Just the idea was enough to send a freezing parade of icy waves down the path of Ramond's spinal cord.

☦ ☦ ☦ ☦ ☦ ☦ ☦ ☦ ☦ ☦ ☦

The moment of truth had almost arrived, however, certain preparations must first be made. Maybe it was preposterous. But then again maybe not. He would ask and take his chances. Just the possibility made the gamble worthwhile. The magnitude of what he intended to request was so immense his master might take his life for being brazen enough to ask. But it was what he wanted, more than anything. It was his destiny.

The black robes fell from the wire hanger as he removed them from their storage position in the closet. The cloaks were well-worn, a gift from "The Family" after Ramond's first anniversary with them. In his garbage-infested room, they were the only thing treated with care. Always packed inside a suit bag and hand washed when dirtied. He held them up in the light by the shoulders. They were a part of him, riding on his back through much of his journey down the dark path.

Somewhere deep within him, he knew this would be the last time he would wear the sacred garments. The robes would be missed, but it would soon be time to move on. Ramond wrapped himself in their warmth for their final performance.

THE PROPOSITION

The large oval mirror reflected his pale face as he sat down at the dresser. Although its drawers held books and various clothing, its top had been converted into a desk. A rusted blue folding chair had been placed in front of it and a small work lamp set on top to read by. It was a suitable workplace, and once again would serve well for his purposes.

Carefully the smoked glass bottle was opened. A nauseating fragrance released itself from captivity and was both sickening and comforting to Ramond. The upside-down funnel shaped container held a precious commodity: the blood of a black cat. The contents had been saved for an occasion of significant magnitude. Now was the time they be put to good use.

Long before, the blood had coagulated and dried to the bottle. Ramond placed an ice pick down its opening and jabbed several times. The bottled was turned upside down and its contents shaken out onto a sheet of notebook paper. The first to come out looked like a small stash of wheat-bread crumbs, then a few larger chunks fell resembling copper snowflakes. He replaced the bottle to its exact location. It was easy enough to find. In all other places of the desk dust resided, except for the small circle where the bottle had sat for some time.

The kitchen cabinets were searched for a clean glass. When one was not to be found he decided a dirty one could be used just as well. He lifted the robes and removed his tool from the jeans he wore underneath. Although few liquids had been consumed recently, Ramond still managed to fill the glass a quarter of the way with urine.

The urine was carried to the desk and set gingerly down by the paper. Both sides of the page were grasped and he tenderly lifted to the rim of the glass, resting one side on its lip. The flakes were brushed into the container with only three or four specs missing their target and falling to the carpet.

Counter-clockwise he swept his finger around the edge of the glass six times. The mixing was an important step in the ritual.

"This is my blood," his voice trembled as he spoke aloud and drank the mixture in one gulp like a shot of whisky. The swallow smoothly traveled down his throat. The taste was not as bad as he had feared.

The act may have meant nothing to Satan, but it was the only way he could think of to suck-up. Johnny had always placed great stock in small symbolic protocol, perhaps there *was* something to them. The proposition was catastrophic. Every little bit would help.

Ramond had once heard that when you drop a hit of acid on your tongue, the drug enters the bloodstream within the first second. But as he lay on the bed sideways with his feet dangling, he was sure something had happened a split second *before* the hit had actually been placed into his mouth. A jolt shuddered through his system comparable to an electrical current. Beads of sweat lined his brow like a marching band in a parade, while his chest heaved seismically in an attempt to secure air into his lungs.

His senses began to deceive him as his eyes watched the room morph, from the tacky lavender, to a foreboding black-blue. The color was as a bruised wound, puss-filled and

THE PROPOSITION

with the threatening sense it might burst open without notice. The drums inside his ears peaked like a wolf as they caught a breathing sound. But that wasn't an ample description. It was more like wheezing, a choking. It was the sound of death.

The room was not a room. Not anymore. It was alive. Flesh pulsed with nerves beneath its surface. The smell was burnt hair and diseased infection. And Ramond could describe it in only one way: *the belly of a beast.*

Serenity had not been thrust upon him this time, and he realized what a wondrous gift it had been before. He wanted to move, wanted to twist his head in all directions at once and see everything that was going on around him, but paralysis had set in. Something had taken away his strength. Muscles would not function; they betrayed him and refused to aid in his moment of need. The more he struggled, the more he lost control. Soon even his eyes would not move from side to side. They stared straight up, forcing him to witness the disgust of his surroundings. They would not close. It would have been a blessing to be blind.

It was a dream: the colors, the smell, the helplessness. Yet it was real. More real, in fact, than his perception of real.

The panic sent his mind racing with ideas: *Maybe they were wrong. Maybe the fire the Bible uses to describe Hell is just a symbol. Maybe it is used because words cannot amply describe what Hell is like. Maybe it was the only word the authors could find to describe the pit.*

And that brought forth the most terrifying questions. *Am I dead? Did I overdose?... IS THIS HELL?*

"NO, THIS IS NOT HELL, RAMOND!"

Ripples traveled through the ceiling and walls like a

stone being thrown into a lake. Vibrations from the voice caused waves to rock the room and Ramond was jostled up and down as if he was on a small raft in the ocean during a tropical hurricane. But through the bumpy ride Ramond was secure, stuck to whatever it was he was lying on like a fly caught in flypaper.

Before the voice could speak again he noticed it. A muscle had begun to work. He could feel it as surely as he had so many times before. The thing pushing up from his crotch. The resistance of his pants against it. The swelling in his testicles. For some unknown reason, he was erect.

Blood felt as if it were boiling beneath his skin as inconceivable panic pumped his heart dangerously fast. But through all the trepidation he was still aroused, and could not fathom a reason why.

The voice took notice.

"Odd, isn't it?" it spoke with a smile that was carried through its words.

The waves were lessened this time, and Ramond's attention snapped from his crotch back to his situation.

"Enjoy the feelings you have now, don't hide from them. Those who are in my presence experience the utmost emotional and physical sensations beyond what even the heavens can give. For as God loves the world and all of his creations, I love only those who serve and love me."

With each syllable he felt his body shake with an orgasmic pleasure. If life were to leave Ramond at this moment, he would die happy.

Both pleasure and pain were vastly immense, and each one complimented the other. The combination was ecstacy.

"Enough fun!"

Ramond watched mystified as the room changed

THE PROPOSITION

abruptly to a mesmerizing diamond blue. The change was sudden, not starting with one section and gradually spreading, but covering everything in one blast of transformation.

The paralysis broke, but he dared not move from his spot. His eyes rolled to his zipper. All swelling in his pants had subsided, and he knew he would have a sticky mess to clean later. The pain was gone, but so was the pleasure. A part of him wanted them both back.

"Back to my first point. When you reach Hell, you will surely know it. There will be no doubts, no questions, no wondering. The first time I came to you. This time I brought you to me. That is all the explanation you need concerning your location. Understood?"

"Yes sir," he whispered, amazed he had the control to speak again.

"You have called me, I am present. Just as promised. I assume you know what it is you desire. So make your proposition, Boy."

Ramond wanted to find a centralized point to speak to, but the voice came from all sides. It was as if every atom of the room was a speaker. The voice came from above him, below him, beside him, even through the fibers of the clothes he wore. He had no choice but speak his request into the air.

"I've been searching for so long, and have thought about this until my mind has grown numb."

"I know."

"Then you know what it is I want to ask for."

"Proposition me, Boy."

"I want only to serve you. That's all I've ever longed to do."

"Ask."

"I love you, and I..."

MICHAEL BISHOP

"ASK!"

"I want to be your son," Ramond blurted out simply.

"That's it? That's all you have to say on the matter? Well by all means then, I crown you *Son of Satan*," the voice sarcastically mocked..

"NO, Sire, don't misunderstand me. I know the magnitude of what I am asking. I have meticulously diagramed the situation. I'm not asking you to make me your son just like that. I'm asking for you to make me reborn. Take this life from me. Take my body. But let my soul have rebirth."

"And?"

"And place my soul into an unborn baby. In the body of a virgin if you choose."

"AND?"

"And you will find no better servant than I. There is not a mortal on Earth who will be as faithful. I will do as you wish. If you want me to introduce the 'Mark', it will be done. What ever you need done I will do."

"AND!"

"And...I worship you...I am yours," Ramond began to sob. Satan's response murdered the small hope he carried. He had been a fool to ask.

"You have failed to say the one thing I want to hear."

"What more do you want me to say, Lord?"

"How am I to know you are the right one for the job? How do I know you are worthy? I have billions to choose from. Why you?"

"TEST ME!" Ramond screamed. He realized it was proof Satan wanted. Not pretty words, not love, but something tangible...*proof*. "Test me. I will do anything you say. I will prove to you that I am deserving. Let me show you.

THE PROPOSITION

Please. Let me show you!" Excitement ruled his voice. If he was given the chance, Ramond knew he would succeed. And if he was tested, his dream of power would come to pass.

"Now that is the proposition I wanted to hear. I knew you would figure it out eventually. I have faith in you. I would not waste my time otherwise."

"What is it I should do?"

"Slow down. It's not that easy... I want you to accomplish a set of tasks for me," the voice demanded, this time sounding more distant.

Fear placed its hand on Ramond and squeezed. Was his father leaving him? There was comfort in the aura of the master. A comfort he did not wish to loose just yet.

"Anything you ask!" he howled, not quite sure if the distant presence would hear.

"It is known, He that rules the heavens' number is seven. He rested on the seventh day, so you shall do seven acts for me."

"I would do a hundred."

"No, not a hundred, Ramond. Just seven... and upon completion of the seventh, you shall have what you have proposed."

"You have only to ask, Lord."

"You will do the first, and upon its completion I will visit you and give you the second, and when that is done, I will give you the third and so on. Until they are all fulfilled in my name."

"Please don't hold me in suspense," he pleaded.

"The first, my boy, is a simple one. You will burn a church of any Christian faith. I'm not concerned with denomination. The mere fact that it uses the word 'Christian' to describe its members is sufficient. Burn it until it is nothing more than a pile of smoldering embers. This will begin your journey."

"It will be done expeditiously!" Ramond swore.

"One last thing, Boy. No more drugs. They will only hinder your skills. Acid did not bring you to me, *I* brought you to me. When you have completed the task I will contact you again. Remember always... The power is *mine*."

Black seized Ramond's eyes. Nothing could be seen. Nothing could be smelled. Nothing could be heard. It was the true definition of an abyss.

Moments later the sudden transformation began again. As the lights blasted back into the room, he placed his arm over his eyes to shield them from the rays. In seconds they adjusted. He was back.

† † † † † † † † † † † †

There was a new found spring in his step. A virgin smile on his lips. Life had purpose. Something that not only broke the pattern, but destroyed it. Ramond's dream lived on.

Only two Christian churches were ever attended by him, and neither was suitable for his purposes. The first, of course, belonged to his mother. Its location was ideal, lying in a section of Sierra Springs that mainly contained office buildings and parking garages. After five o'clock the lots became ghost towns as the businessmen and women disappeared to their homes and families.

But it was still Vernadette's church, and that made it unacceptable. Ramond had already taken so much from her. It was practically all she had left. There was a deep seated resentment for his mother festering in the pit of his stomach;

THE PROPOSITION

but he did still love her to some degree. At least enough not to take away her fetish.

The other church had been visited only once. A co-worker of his father had invited the three of them to attend his wedding. The Italian nuptial was held in an enormous Catholic chapel some ten years prior. The marriage didn't last, but the church still stood on the corner of Johnson and Windwood, which made it unsuitable as well. The intersection was among the most populated in town. The Italian community lived packed together in the tight vicinity, and acted as if they were an extended family. They watched each other's back, protected one another, and eagle-eyed strangers with disdain. To burn that church would not only mean getting caught, but would also be a quick way to commit suicide. Vigilante justice would be swift.

A plan was constructed minutes after the encounter with his Lord. The robes were traded for more comfortable attire, the car was warmed, and Ramond was on his way to an unfamiliar area.

"Little Ghetto" was the common nickname given to the adjacent neighborhoods, not just by outsiders, but by residents as well. The community was separated from the rest of Sierra Springs by a set of railroad tracks. Those tracks had become a recognized boundary just as surely if they had been marked with a thick red line and a sign reading "No Whites Allowed Beyond This Point!".

White townsfolk knew better than to cross the tracks. To do so would command grave penalties. It was a textbook case of reverse discrimination.

It was dangerous and Ramond knew it. But if he

pulled it off he would never be a suspect in the arson. The fear of getting caught by the police was eminently greater than the fear of being caught by the natives. If he were arrested the deal would end; but if he burned a church in "Little Ghetto", the last person anyone would suspect would be a middle class white boy. It was a gamble he took.

His dashboard clock told him it was a quarter till nine. The darkness would conceal him. He ducked down in the seat as low as he could and still see to drive. As long as he pressed on quickly, he would be safe.

Searching blindly made the experience all the more nerve wrecking. If a church did exist in this part of town, he would find it, but the exploration might be long. The area had expanded in the past few years, stretching east and west, yet still never crossing the tracks. It was a street by street hunt: third, fourth, fifth, all generic names.

A church had to be somewhere. They had their own grocery stores. They had their own gas stations, Surely they had their own church: *somewhere*.

"Fuck!" he cursed to himself after twenty minutes of driving. Ramond's knee bounced up and down nervously as he scoped the street for signs of anything looking even remotely like a church. Thirty blocks and no trace. It was as if God, Jesus, and the whole Christian faith had failed to recognize the ghetto existed.

The moment had come to pull out. A gamble was a gamble, and Ramond knew his chances of not being seen were growing thin. A large sign declared the road to the left a "dead end". It was as good a place to turn around as any.

THE PROPOSITION

Maybe he would head to a more populated street and take his chances. Time was precious and seemed to be falling down his hour glass in clumps.

The Ford turned onto the street, then halted. He looked behind him and began backing the car. Before completing the turn Ramond threw a glance through his front windshield to ensure he hadn't been spotted. The glint of his headlights reflected off something a short piece down the dead end. The heel of his cheap boot pressed firmly on the break pedal as he peered into the inky night, still not conclusively sure his eyes were not deceiving him.

Yet the harder he gazed at the path his headlights cut into the darkness, the more he was convinced of what he was seeing. The street held nothing on either side but tall oaks common to the area, but standing desolate at the *dead* part of the "dead end" stood a white wooden building with a shabbily made cross sitting atop its roof. A homemade sign supported by two rotting four by four post hammered into the ground read "Welcome to Calvary Baptist Church".

He shook his head and closed his eyes. It just could not be. But as he opened them again, the cross maintained its position. The building was real. His instincts had guided him right to it.

But inside, he knew it was more than mere instinct that brought him to this place. He was guided here. Nudged along like a lab rat in a maze, until he could not help but fall upon the correct path.

The blaring headlights were switched off in an attempt to stay inconspicuous as he jammed the car back into drive. The second the beams were severed, an eerie effect overcame the area. The church disappeared, swallowed integrally by the black night. The car slowly lurched forward, and as it moved

MICHAEL BISHOP

down the path, Ramond became convinced he had imagined the church in a deranged hallucination. Moments before the whim to switch the lights back on overcame him, he drew near enough to make out the silhouette of the cross.

The church stood half a block down the road. The street was the only entrance coming or going. The trees shrouded it on all sides except the front. It was a helpless victim.

Spinning the car on the slender road, Ramond u-turned the vehicle smoothly, pulling the tail about two yards from the church double doors. If the situation came down to making a fast getaway, it was better the car face the right direction.

The sign and the cross were the only two indications that the building was a church. Its windows did not contain the traditional stained glass decorations. No high archways or statues of Christ. Little symbolic value was given to the building.

It was the smallest temple Ramond had ever seen, covering every inch of the space at the end of the thin road, but no more. Looking around he briefly wondered where the members parked their cars. There was room for few vehicles but as he turned his head to the cheap building, he assumed there wasn't an abundance of room in the place for many people anyway.

His actions were quick as he jumped from the car. The trunk was popped and a hose and bucket were removed. Gas had been siphoned numerous times from other cars, and the tools of the trade rested comfortably in his trunk. Jamming the hose into his tank, he sucked briskly on the opposite end. The hose was true to form as the petrol began pouring into the bucket.

THE PROPOSITION

He peered at the building to get an idea of how much gas he would need. It had only four walls. The place was more a shack than a church... almost sacrilegious.

A half-filled bucket was plenty he decided as he jerked the hose out of the tank. It would be a grievous error to drain too much. Running out of gas in this neighborhood on the night its only church was burning down would be a tragedy he would pay for with his life.

Paint flaked from the building, and termites had done their work on all sides making it almost possible to punch a hole through the wall with a bare fist. The building would kindle easily. It was erected entirely of wood. Inside, the pews and alter were wood as well.

The gas flowed easily from the container as he started dousing the east wall and worked his way to the south. By the time the west wall was adequately soaked, the can was empty, leaving none for the front. It would do, he thought.

From deep within his pocket he retrieved his trusty monogrammed lighter. It had been used to light many things, but none this important. On the side of the road a dry stick was picked up and run around the inside of the bucket. He lit the tip making a makeshift torch.

The stick was thrown at the east wall, and he turned to run. Gas fumes sucked the fire in, embracing it as it neared the wall. The flames moved along the sloppy path he had poured, circling the building in a fiery hoop.

Ramond tossed the hose and bucket in the trunk and slammed it closed, then spun, just for a moment, to admire his work.

"Amen, you're dismissed," he spoke and smiled.

Stepping inside the car door, he slammed it behind him with a bang and turned the key. Slowly he pulled down the road, trying to remain inconspicuous as he made his retreat. When he reached the end of the road Ramond looked back one last time. The flames had already climbed to the bottom of the roof and their light cut through the night sky like a bullet through flesh.

More than anything he wished he could watch the cross burn. The crucifix was the one symbol recognized worldwide to signify those who despised him so. But it would still be a few minutes before the flames would engulf the emblem. He would have to be content with the image in his mind. A little piece of Heaven caught in the fires of Hell.

On the way home he did not bother to hide. He was driving much to fast now for anyone to recognize him. The getaway was clean.

† † † † † † † † † † † †

"MEMOIRS OF REVEREND JOHNSON"

All in all, "Calvary Baptist Church" only took thirty minutes to burn completely down. The last of its walls collapsed well before any sign of a fire truck had been seen. The sight drew much attention, bringing out just about every resident within a ten block radius. They all witnessed the same thing, a charred cross lying broken in the ashes of a former house of God.

Police reports stated that the fire was an accident. No investigation was even given to the matter. The building held no importance in their lives, and did not merit their time or efforts. Lengthy paperwork would be avoided if it was written

THE PROPOSITION

up as a catch-all "electrical malfunction".

  Calvary Baptist Church had no insurance and had never intended on getting any. Tithes received from its poverty-stricken members barely afforded to keep the doors open, much less pay the high price of insurance in the crime ridden area. The Church never rebuilt its walls, never reopened its doors, and never rehung its cross for all to gaze upon. The last bastion of goodness in "Little Ghetto" had been systematically destroyed.

  The Reverend was there in the beginning. Before "Little Ghetto" had taken its nickname. Before the illegitimacy rate began to soar. Before drugs were bought and sold on every street corner, and gang colors covered the clothes of every teenager that walked the street. And he had fought valiantly. The church was opened as an ointment, something to stop the rot before it was too late. It had worked for years, giving some faith, and others a reason to believe in a better tomorrow.
  Not long after its doors were opened, the Calvary Baptist Church was standing room only on Sundays. So many came to experience the joy first hand that the church was almost forced to hold services outside. And although the south side of the tracks still had problems, the congregation waged their war against crime and evil.
  Its core members were God-fearing people who could "pray down Heaven". They became the backbone of the community, with a loving aura that followed them in their lives and rubbed off on everyone they met. Their good deeds and kind hearts were the glue that kept the area from collapsing altogether.

MICHAEL BISHOP

But Johnson had been young then, and he was old now. If he was just ten years younger, perhaps then he could start over. But he wasn't. He would soon be seventy-five. Too tired to fight anymore. Too old for anyone to listen.

He watched the neighborhood as it went through its phases of demise. He had seen it before.

The first step was a disheartening of the people. Church members were no longer a congregation. Without a meeting place they were divided. And divided, their strength was gone. Many became bitter. It was frustrating to see everything they worked so hard for suddenly disappear before their eyes. That frustration caused them to give up, stop the war, surrender to whatever was to come.

The second step was the snowball effect. Honest residents began to move out of the area in fear. They knew very well what was to come. With them gone, the criminals flourished. And the more good that left, the more bad that arrived.

Reverend Johnson did not see the third step. He left well before it began. But he did not have to see it. He knew the next. It was one step down from anarchy.

Starting the day after the Calvary Baptist Church was burned, up to one year later, police statistics showed the crime rate in the area had jumped fifty-one percent. More prostitution, more theft, more violence, more death. Soon even the tracks could not hold back the crime. It spilled over them, taking victims from every walk of life.

Experts claimed that the explosion of offenses was directly related to the increase in drug distribution. Charts showed links between the crime rate and the rise in crack

THE PROPOSITION

sells. They showed how the jump in AIDS cases was due to the sharing of infected needles and increase in prostitution. They said that the sky-rocket of gang activity was a result of the increasing popularity of narcotics.

But Reverend Johnson did not need scientific data or charts. To him they proved nothing. He knew better. Knew where the real problem lay. He understood the laws of nature all too well.

Without faith, there is nothing but doom. And without love, we don't stand a chance.

Night Life

1 3 5 6 7 8 9 0

Tired and out of breath, Ramond barreled through the front door of his apartment. He closed it tightly behind him and stood with his back pressed firmly against it. The act was finalized, and his apartment offered a safe haven. Nothing this world had in it could bring him down. A delirious high consumed his emotions. Excitement like he had never experienced. In just one hour he had completed the first step. The taste of eternal power was sweet on his buds. Only six to go.

"I'M READY FOR ANOTHER!" he called to another dimension. Seconds passed. No reply.

Stopping now saddened him, but apparently it was not time. Maybe it would be better to rest. Sleep had been avoided: an interruption of the task. But it was a necessary function. Without it, he may grow too weak to pass the next test.

Ramond sprawled on the bed, legs open, clothes still

worn. In three minutes he was asleep, and the dreams came.

✝ ✝ ✝ ✝ ✝ ✝ ✝ ✝ ✝ ✝ ✝

Fifteen steps from the cliff's edge he stood as clouds floated lazily by. The view offered the most picturesque, breathtaking landscape Ramond had ever known, with layer upon layer of rich green grasses hugging the countryside. Far into the distance a forest could be seen shielding any further view of the land. The cliff's bottom met the ground about a hundred feet down, and on the land below, sheep could be seen frolicking through wild daisies. The air was fresh and untainted by man.

Soft flapping of his garments as the wind blew across them caught his attention. Looking at himself, he noticed flowing white robes hanging from his frame. They draped like sheets and were raw silk to the touch. Under his nose and beneath his chin a long silver-grey beard hung, tapering down to a pointed end.

A hickory cane lay in his grip as the length of it spiraled to the ground. He leaned on it gently, testing to see if it was as sturdy as it appeared. Confident it was, he turned his attention back to the wondrous valley before him. The rustling of the wind was the only sound heard for miles. Not even the "baaing" of sheep rose up from beneath. It was a place civilization dared not touch. As he looked around, the only word that came to mind to accurately described this place was *Heaven*.

Ramond stood in awe, trying to soak in as much of the ambience as possible. He closed his eyes and breathed deeply. The natural fragrance was pleasure. With his eyes closed his ears peeked and recognized an out of place sound. It was a

NIGHT LIFE

dripping of some sort he first thought, but as he listened closely, he was more convinced it was a hissing. His head jerked around, back and forth, quickly scanning his surroundings for anything abnormal.

A visual search found nothing. Still the sound persisted. It seemed to be all around, crawling through his ears like a mole through his underground labyrinth, but its source was unknown.

Had it not been for the flick of its tongue against his hand, it might have been some time before Ramond noticed it. The staff no longer spiraled to the ground, but rather hung from his hand with scales that glistened in the red sun. Firm hickory had been replaced with the limp body of a grotesquely large serpent with its head sticking out his fist as he held the animal's neck.

"Jesus!" he screamed as he flung the reptile in a whipping motion behind him, causing it to sail through the air several yards. He spun in its direction with no intention of turning his back to the thing.

"No, not Jesus. Not even close," the snake spoke as it slithered toward him a few feet with sudden acceleration. Had there been a place to run he might have tried, but all that lay behind Ramond was a steady drop.

The serpent ceased its motion a body length from Ramond and paused. Its head twisted upward as if it were checking out the progression of the clouds. Then, with ease, the reptile's body stretched upward until it rose above the ground and stood on the tip of its tail. The entire gesture was fascinating, and Ramond was sure it defied the laws of physics. The snake bent its head back down making a ninety degree angle, peering directly at Ramond.

"Is that any way to treat your father?" it spoke in a

MICHAEL BISHOP

voice Ramond knew unquestionably. Master, I'm sorry... I'm... I... didn't know."

"Silence!" snapped the beast, cutting him off, "I am not angry. To the contrary, I am rather pleased with you. You have done exactly what I ordered and you completed it in quick fashion. For this I applaud you," the creature finished, then turned its head back to the sky. A rippling motion fluttered through its length, brushing the scales outward as it passed through them. As the wave struck the head the serpent's body went limp, and the viper came tumbling to the earth. At the collision of the head against the ground, the animal disappeared without trace.

Ramond frantically scanned the acres for some evidence of its presence. Nothing was seen.

"Do not be alarmed," a voice called from behind.

Ramond twirled around with impressive speed. Sitting between him and the edge of the cliff was now a single, green leafed bush. It stood a foot and a half shorter than Ramond, but its type was like none he had ever seen. It was not similar to the common yard bushes lining the apartment complex. This one was stubby, with hints of pink wrapped securely in the chlorophyll green. Its leaves were smooth like a silk plant, and the foliage was enchantingly radiant.

"Surely you've heard about this one before?" the voice said in a manner that was both a question and a statement.

At the trail of the words the peculiar bush made a thin "popping" sound followed by flames rising from its center. The flames did not start on the outside, but rather burned their way inside-out, seemingly starting from the roots themselves. The glowing blaze was immense as it burned with a million times the intensity that Calvary Baptist had. Power radiated

NIGHT LIFE

off it in every direction and anything in its path could not help but feel the energy.

A cool breeze blew the flames in Ramond's direction, and he realized the blaze burned with no heat. A fire of that magnitude would surely burn with the heat of a hundred suns, but this one torched away as cool as the soft wind itself. For a brief moment, Ramond wanted more than anything to be standing directly in the middle of the burning, absorbing all the power for himself.

The bush cackled with insane glee, but the noise that escaped it sounded more like a hundred voices than just one. Mixed with every decibel of laugh was an undertone that sounded like screaming, or worse yet, suffering. The sound of the ear-bursting chuckle made Ramond cringe and stumble a step back in horror. He hoped his master did not mind his retreat.

"The burning bush. I love it... It kills me every time," it spoke letting out another short laugh that made Ramond blink his eyes hard. When he opened them, the laughter was gone and complete seriousness bubbled in the flames. "Once again, it's time to get down to business. I am aware you wish to progress to the next test, and I am eager for you to. But before I tell you what it is, I feel I should explain... Understand, it is out of character for me to explain anything, to anyone, for any reason. Normally I expect what I command to be done without question. But I will make a small exception in this case, only because I want you to be informed."

"I'm listening father," Ramond felt comfortable. The atmosphere was soothing. He could stay forever.

"Good...I gave you the first job to see if you were serious about your proposition. I am pleased to find you are.

MICHAEL BISHOP

Now you must begin to prepare yourself. Your soul is not conditioned enough to handle the rigors of being my son. But when the next six are behind you, it will be ready. Those who sit at my table must know all the earthly pleasures a human can experience. You have experienced many I know, but in all your years of worship and experimenting, there is one solemn pleasure that has escaped you."

"What pleasure has escaped me? Tell me and I will experience it immediately."

"Do not be so quick to make rash promises you may not be able to keep. The first test was *extremely* simple. This one will be a little harder for you. At least I assume it will be, knowing the kind of person you are."

"The only type of person I am is one who wants to serve you. I'll say it again, all you have to do is ask," he said reiterating what he truly felt in his heart.

"So be it. You have experienced the pleasures of a woman, even several women on occasion. Now it is time for you to enjoy a man in a physical way. Explore, have fun with it, and most of all... *enjoy*."

Ramond choked down a hard gulp. It was a request that brought him close to sobs. For the first time, he was not completely sure he could pass the test.

Open mindedness was a trait he prided himself on. He was open to women's rights and minority rights and abortion. But there was one quirk that always haunted him. Ramond was *homophobic*.

It was not something he was proud of, and definitely not something he ever told anyone. But it was a characteristic he was keenly aware of. From early childhood he could remember not wanting to use the bathroom in public places because he feared one of the other boys looking at him. In

NIGHT LIFE

high school, sports were avoided at the thought of taking showers with other males in the same stall. And if he were ever to be drafted, Ramond was quite sure he would flee to Canada. Cowardly or not, he just could not bunk and bathe with hundreds of other men.

The simple thought of homosexuality made him queasy and the idea of him performing gay acts made Ramond come close to vomiting.

The flames flickered lower and Ramond knew Satan had noticed his hesitation.

"RAMOND!" the voice exploded from the bush, releasing a wind so hard it blew the flames out. The gust caused Ramond to stumble backward and slap his hands over his ears in pain. He pressed his cupped palms on them firmly for a moment, then dropped them in front of his eyes knowing full well what he would see. His ears were bleeding. The noise had gone far to damage them and they began to ring with the monotony of church bells as the blood trickled down his jaw bones in red sideburns.

"I have spoken. This shall be done tonight. And it will be completed, won't it RAMOND?" The voice was more telling than asking.

"Yes, Sire," he managed through the ache.

"BE GONE!"

His eyes popped open with a force that was painful. Ramond laid still for a moment, staring up at the sheetrock ceiling, following the intricate web work of its cracks as his mind cleared. The steady ringing in his ears persisted and as he reached his hand up to his right ear he found it was still bleeding, although not as bad as it had been in the dream. All that remained was the nausea brought on by the thought of what he had to do.

This time he was not in as much of a hurry to perform the act, no matter how badly he wanted to pass the test. The first one was incontestably risky, but this was down right disgusting. He wondered if homosexuals felt this way at the thought of sleeping with someone of the opposite sex. It made him feel dirty, as if worms were crawling through his hair. He thought about what it would be like to kiss another man, then rolled over and spewed what little was left in his stomach on the carpet.

Ramond had it bad. It was indeed the hardest thing he could ever imagine doing. And if this was only the second, what grotesque chore might the seventh require of him? It was a thought that was forcibly removed from his mind. *One at a time*, he told himself and laid on his side for a long while... procrastinating the sex.

He, of course, had met gay men before. In a community where being queer was hated as much as worshiping someone other than God, it would have been impossible not to meet a few along the way. They were all a part of the underworld of Sierra Springs. A different class of the same brotherhood of secrecy. It was probably the same in all towns having the misfortune of being a notch in the Bible Belt. But Ramond had successfully managed to ignore the sexual preference of the few he knew.

One thing was sure, though, whoever he chose must be a stranger. Death was better to Ramond than having people think he was a *queer*. It would strip away the last shred of dignity he had.

NIGHT LIFE

Not only would it have to be a stranger, but a stranger in a different town. No chances would be taken. The stakes were too high.

Restlessly he laid in bed for hours, not bothering to clean up his regurgitated meal. He constructed yet another plan. The town, the site, the attire, everything was designed to the letter. When dusk came, Ramond was not happy.

† † † † † † † † † † † †

His attire had been chosen with extreme care. The idea was to look gay, but not like a straight guy trying to look gay. The last thing he wanted was to get gay-bashed when he wasn't even gay to begin with. So he played it conservative. At least as conservative as possible while still trying to look homosexual.

The one semi-solid fact he knew was that heterosexual men wore earrings in their left ears and gay men wore them in their right. It was little to go on, but it was a start.

When the hole in his left ear was punched, Ramond was only sixteen. The fear of the needle exceeded the actual pain, but the soreness was still enough to make him whimper. But those days were gone and Ramond had learned to tolerate pain.

Removing the silver skull and cross bones earring from his left ear, he laid it on the kitchen counter. An ice cube was extracted from the freezer and placed on his right earlobe to cold numb it. In the flame of the stove burner he held a sewing needle with his free hand. When the heat sterilized the pin to his satisfaction, he dropped the ice carelessly on the floor and tugged his earlobe, stretching it out. The needle was stuck as close to the center as possible. The pain was nonexistent. He wiggled the needle around, widening the hole a bit, then pulled it completely through.

With moderate prodding, the earring went in. He walked to the dresser and turned his head sideways to the mirror. The jewelry looked awkward hanging from the wrong side of his head. It was amazing how much difference the small accessory made.

The remainder of the costume was easily assembled. Clothes he had never worn were laid out. The first was a lavender, silk shirt given to him as a gift somewhere along the line by someone he could not remember. Its gaudiness was only topped by an enormous butterfly collar. However, it did feel good against his skin, Ramond found, as he slid one arm, then another into its sleeves. The top three buttons were left undone, leaving a spectator's view of his bony, hairless chest.

Next came a pair of black pants that stretched like Spandex. Not only did they look painted on, but hugged every nook and cranny of his frame. Even his crotch appeared to have sizable value as it extruded between his legs.

Loafers were slipped over his sockless feet, his hair was held back in a ponytail, and a wrist bracelet was double wrapped around his wrist. Dress up was over. With a final glance at the mirror he knew it was time to go. But as Ramond locked his front door behind him, he still was not happy.

Fifty-third street was a mad house at ten o'clock, making it no easy task to drive its short stretch. The town of

NIGHT LIFE

Dalton had few options as far as nightlife was concerned, and the road housed every bar in the burg.

It took two hours to reach the county, just far enough to guarantee Ramond would not see anyone he knew. Dalton was virtually identical to Sierra Springs, except its population had managed to climb out of the low twenty thousands and up to the forties. But no matter how large it had grown, the "Pew Hoppers" still had firm control of the activities.

Pubs and drinking establishments tried to sprout up occasionally on streets other than Fifty-Third, but like weeds, the Southern Baptist had them uprooted before the owners could think twice; stating time and time again there would be no "morally degrading" businesses on the same streets their children had to travel every day.

The townsfolk only left one street unchallenged, specifically because it rested in a part of town that was not only sleazy, but far enough away from their pristine lives to keep a leash on the children. Even then, it may have not been left standing by the heavily protesting women but the backsliding husbands and fathers insisted on having at least one last resort in which they could go, grab a beer with their buddies, and hide from their mundane lives and wives for a few hours of bliss.

Fifty-Third street had one stipulation placed upon it: no "Nudie Clubs". With that rule unbroken, it flourished.

"Smiley Joe's" blinked in Vegas style above the entrance. Just inches atop it, another neon masterpiece hung; one section blinked on and then off as the next section lit up. An outline of the eyes and face of a Cheshire cat glowed for three seconds, then went dark as its famous smile hung alone, brightly illuminated. It served to emphasize just how smiley

MICHAEL BISHOP

"Smiley Joe's" really was. The moment he laid eyes on it he knew it was the place. A bar that had the nerve to be that corny was bound to have one or two *sweet* men hanging around.

He parked and stepped out of the car. Three deep breaths were taken to calm his nerves. They didn't help. The shaking of his hands would be obvious to anyone who looked close. Perhaps a drink would help, he thought, as he headed for the smile.

The minute he entered the bar, Ramond felt weighed down with the eyes that were upon him. Not just casual glances, but unhidden gawks. The color turned pink in his cheeks. *Humiliation.*

A barstool closest to the door was chosen and he sat down quickly before his quivering legs gave way. Some of the customers shifted in their seats to get a better look. Ramond was a freak show attraction, just as sure as if he had been the Elephant Man.

For the first time ever he felt sincere pity for homosexuals. *Is this what they have to live with?* he asked himself. The only thing worse would be hiding it for a lifetime, pretending you are something you are not.

To a degree, he related. He too had lived his life in seclusion; saying and doing things he did not believe just for the benefit of others. Being gay was not *so* bad. It just meant you were different. *Nothing wrong with being different*, he thought. And if these people wanted to watch, then let them. At least it meant he was drawing attention to himself, and hopefully, with the help of his Father, someone *special* would take notice and approach him.

NIGHT LIFE

Three beers and forty-five minutes later, no one had solicited Ramond. His audience had stared and whispered to each other for the first beer and a half. After that, the new had worn off.

The beers began taking effect and the shaking in his limbs had stopped. An urge to be done with this one came to him. The next one was bound to be easier. It was time to end this game of cat and mouse. If a cat was not going to find him, then he would assume the role of the cat and go hunting.

Ready to pounce, he peered prudently across the room, inspecting anyone who looked ripe. Most of the men were with women or in groups. The few that were alone were alone for good reason; plainly middle aged men attempting to pick up younger women. They were sad. The kind of chaps who would die lonely.

It was hopeless. The place was a bust. There was no one who looked gay, no one who seemed even remotely interested, and no one who was worth taking a chance on. The homosexuals in Dalton had done *too* good a job of hiding themselves.

He stood to leave. The next bar down the line might serve better. If not then the next. Ramond would search the entire town if that's what it took. The disgust of the act began to subside. He was so ready to be done with it that he almost looked forward to it. If he could just find one willing accomplice, the deed would be done.

His eyes struck the man as he turned to the exit. Sitting alone in a booth under a sign that declared Budweiser the King of Beers. Had the man been there before? Ramond didn't think so. As scrupulously as he had surveyed the place for prey, it was unlikely he would have missed the fellow. But he saw him now, and not only that, but the guy was staring back as well.

Ramond smiled. The gentleman returned the gesture. Ramond smiled inwardly. The curiosity about where the guy came from disappeared like the sun behind a cloud. It was evident his lord was guiding him. And it elated him to know that he was not handling the tests alone. Satan actually *wanted* him to succeed.

Courage was found in the last drop of beer in the bottle as Ramond turned it up into his dry esophagus. He checked to make sure the man was still looking... He was.

As he walked toward the fellow, Ramond practiced the words he would say. They had been said to countless women before, and had worked on a few. This time, he hoped, they would work on a man.

As he neared, the guy's smile increased. Ramond's intentions were obvious and the stranger seemed receptive. It was a good sign.

Even sitting down it was apparent the guy was large. Not overweight. But tall and well built. Had he been a woman, Ramond might have found the fellow rather handsome. But he was a man, and the guy still looked pretty much like any other.

His clothing gave no hint of his sexual preference. The man wore the normal southern bar attire: blue jeans, boots, and a faded denim shirt. But it wasn't the way he dressed, but his body language that gave Ramond all the coaxing he needed.

"Hi," Ramond began timidly just feet from the booth.

"Hello," the guy returned with a lisp. His voice was high and irritating, and came across as more of an act than a true representation. Ramond ignored the mistrust. It was too

NIGHT LIFE

late for retreat.

"Can I buy you a drink?" Ramond spit the words out exactly as he exercised to himself.

The man rose, swallowing vision of the sign behind him. He was much taller than Ramond had imagined, standing close to six-six and weighing at least two forty. A monster.

"My name is Keith," he said with the lisp gone. His actual voice was deep and hazarding. Twangs of anger bounced from every syllable, and Ramond began to realize he had been duped. "What might your name be, Boy?"

Everyone who could see was burning Ramond with their eyes. The situation was clear. Keith had reeled him in like a large mouth bass, using a smile as bait. And Ramond swallowed the hook without a clue.

Keith and his friends had set him up. Ramond was to be the night's joke. High entertainment for low people.

"Ramond," he replied cautiously. The situation was nitro: shaky and unstable. It was imperative he handle himself carefully.

"Well, Ramond, let me ask you somethin', Boy. Are you a FAGGOT?" The southern drawl wisped through his speech making the word *boy* sound like *bouyee*. Keith's friends began circling their patsy, laughing and crooning in echo of their buddy's every word.

Ramond wanted to run for the door, but knew he'd never make it. His only weapons were his words and wits. He was smart enough to know they would not be enough.

"Look, I don't want any trouble. I'm just gonna leave and you guys can carry on."

"You ain't goin' nowhere, Queerboy. Just settle in. You gonna be here awhile," Keith informed.

MICHAEL BISHOP

"That's right!" someone to the left agreed, followed by several *UH HUH*s and *YEP*s from the others.

Ramond backed a step and turned to look over his shoulders. Every direction was blocked. The wagons were circled and Ramond was the fire in the middle.

He wanted no more of this. If he were to be beaten then let it be. But he would not stand silently and be a buffoon.

"Excuse me," he uttered and tried to gently nudge his way past the cowboy that barricaded the shortest path to the door.

"Don't you ever lay your hands on me!" the cowboy cried and placed four meaty right knuckles into Ramond's mid-section. Ramond doubled over and turned back toward Keith. He gripped his stomach tightly, trying to hold the contents in. But the beer squirted from his mouth like the falls of Niagara, soiling Keith's boots with the slop.

"HOLY FUCKING SHIT!" Keith blasted. "THE FUCKING FAGGOT PUKED ON ME!" he finished stepping backward in revolt, almost stumbling over the booth. "I'LL FUCKING KILL YOU!" were the last words he heard as the giant brought his knee cap up to meet Ramond's face. The blow came in slow motion. Ramond watched it frame by frame as it moved toward him. Just before impact he closed his eyes. Unconsciousness came immediately.

"I think you'll live. Just a big nasty bump. That's all, pal."

Ramond felt as if someone had stuck him in the washing machine and set it to spin cycle. His vision was still

NIGHT LIFE

dim, but he could hear. The voice that spoke was human; Ramond knew more by feeling then sound. It was not Master.

Recollections of what had happened began to seep back into his mind. Keith, the cowboy, the knee; all of it. But the voice was obscure. One he had never heard, and he wondered where he was.

He could feel he was lying flat, on a comfortable surface. A bed perhaps. But whose?

Slowly he lifted his upper half to a sitting position. The head rush was too much, coming close to knocking him out again. He return quickly to lying.

"Just take it easy, pal. You ain't cured just yet. Rest that pretty little head of yours for awhile. You're among friends." The words came from a male, but his accent was not southern. Northern perhaps, or maybe Midwestern.

Light came in sections, beginning with the outskirts of his peripheral vision and crawling back to the center of his eyes. He could feel where the knee had landed, on the lowest part of his forehead. An inch lower and the plastic surgeons would have been attempting to reposition his nose.

A cold rag was placed on his forehead by the stranger, and the relief it brought made Ramond feel like the man had done him the single kindest act that anyone ever had.

"Thanks," Ramond managed. The ceiling light fixture came into focus: a flowery pattern with a single dove on the ten inch rounded glass.

"No problem. That guy coulda killed ya... but nobody kills nobody in my place."

Ramond held the rag in place to ensure it did not move as he turned his head to look at the man. The stranger was short, with stubby hands and small feet. His build was normal for his height, not over or under weight anywhere except for his stomach. There, a noticeable pot belly sat up proudly looking very out of place. The wrinkles in his face made him appear to be in his late thirties, although his hair had not began to recede yet. In his eyes there was a gentleness, relaxing and peculiar. Their color matched perfectly-browned toast and hid something childlike behind them.

The man said nothing for several moments; just sat on a stool next to the bed Ramond rested on and allowed his guest to look him over. When he decided Ramond had gathered a good enough mental picture, he introduced himself.

"Horace Snide, pal," he proclaimed and stuck his stunted hand out. Ramond secured the rag with his left and reached over with his right to shake Horace's hand.

"Ramond... Ramond Jamison," he told bluntly then dropped the man's hand and went back to his rest.

"Pleasure to meet you. Boy I tell ya. I thought those guys were gonna tear ya ta pieces like jackals. Good thing I was upstairs here. Bartender ran up to get me. He ain't the kind to stop trouble ya know."

"I appreciate it. I really do," he spoke trying to sound as grateful as he could through the agony. "Where am I?"

"Why, you're smack dab in the middle of my private little hideaway. Upstairs from the bar. It ain't much, but it's a place away from the wife and kids and business. 'Bout the only place I got really. But that don't answer ya question none I don't suppose, pal...I own this place I do. Bought old Smiley Joe's here from a man named Thomas Gentry. He bought it from a guy named Frank Laurell. Hell, ain't never been nobody named Joe own this place." At this revelation he turned his head upward and let out a fat man's laugh.

NIGHT LIFE

Ramond fakely chuckled as a polite gesture.

"No, but seriously, I've owned her for 'bout five years now, I guess. Ain't a gold mine, but ain't a shit mine neither." At this Horace gave another small chuckle, but not as robust as before.

"Well, Horace, you probably saved my life. Don't think those guys liked me too much," Ramond said sarcastically, trying to keep up with the good-humored nature of the man who saved him.

"Those guys was ass holes. Plain and simple, pal. Ever since I moved here from Jersey, I've had to deal with the ignorant hillbillies, and I'm about at my wits' end with it. Don't worry none. I threw them out and told them to never come back. I would have called the cops, but..." Horace's smile changed. No longer did he beam the smile of a friend, but rather the smile of a seducer. He reached over and placed his hand on Ramond's arm. "But I kinda wanted to take care of ya myself." The signals burned throughout the room as sure as if he was unloading flares.

Ramond's Master was watching him. He could smell the aura lingering somewhere in the room. Satan had left him a trail of bread crumbs through the forest of *straight* men. The way led to Horace Snide.

Ramond dropped the rag from his head and covered Horace's hand with his own, firmly squeezing it with the intention of gentle affection. The gesture would once have made him sick. Surprisingly, it was nice.

He gave in to it, and felt a deviation inside the instant he let go. The sensation was very much like the air being removed from his lungs and bloodstream all at once and replaced with something new. He felt lighter; a burden had been removed. Ramond was mellow.

MICHAEL BISHOP

Horace bent to plant a kiss. From there it started.

"Rise and shine."

He hated being awakened; it always made him feel like his mother was getting him up for school. The light from the window illuminated the room. Horace was dressed and staring out at nothing in particular.

"What time is it?" Ramond asked groggily.

"Seven thirty-five in the A.M., pal."

It had been ages since Ramond had slept as well, as deeply. There was strange solace in what he had done; and there was a comfort in having someone close. He wasn't as sore as he imagined he would be. Horace was not a big man. It helped.

The act itself was pleasurable. If someone would have told him just hours before that he would orgasm, Ramond would have never believed it. Just the thought would have been nauseating. But he *did* orgasm. In fact, more than he ever had with a woman. It was not the masterful touch of Horace, though. It was the excitement that he was fulfilling the second test. The knowledge that what he was doing was driving him to the steps of immortality. It was a lovely evening.

But the uncomfortable part had come. It was time to go home. Ramond knew once he walked out the door he would never see Horace Snide again, and he wasn't altogether sure Horace wanted him to.

Ramond took his clothes from the floor and hastily flung them on. Horace said nothing, just stared out the window lost in thought.

NIGHT LIFE

"Well..." Ramond began not knowing how to finish the sentence. Horace snapped out of his daydream and turned toward Ramond.

"Oh, you're dressed," he said as if the world had warped ahead several minutes without his permission.

"Yeah, I gotta get back. People worry about me and stuff," he lied.

"Oh, sure, pal. I understand... Um look, pal. You don't mind going down the back stairs here, do ya. They lead to the alley. Your car's probably just right around the corner there."

"No, not at all."

"Normally I wouldn't ask, but the bartender locks the place up for me at three every night and I'd have to open the place back up to let you out."

"No, no, I understand. No need to explain. It's cool," he said stepping toward the door.

"Any time you want to come back now, the drinks are on the house," Horace invited in a way that let Ramond know he did not mean a word of it.

"Sure," Ramond turned the knob and pushed the door forward. The uneasiness of the goodbye was stifling. It felt good to be outdoors. Unrestrained by walls. Free.

"Take care, Smiley." Ramond joked hard heartedly as he stepped onto the wrought iron staircase.

"Yeah, you too... take care." Horace called after.

In the night his ponytail had come undone. The shirt was left untucked and he needed a shave. He thought he must look like quite a sight walking down those stairs, a queen who had had a long, hard night. But he didn't care. Two down; five to go. When he drove away from the parking lot of "Smiley Joe's", Ramond was happy.

MICHAEL BISHOP

† † † † † † † † † † † †

"THE EXECUTION OF HORACE SNIDE"

This was the sixth night she had staked out the room upstairs from the bar. The other five had turned up nothing, and she swore this would be her last. If nothing came of it, Annette Snide promised herself she would go to confession and pray for forgiveness for not having faith in her husband. She never made that trip to church.

Her suspicions had chipped away at her for three years now. They started the first time Horace didn't come home.

He explained that sometimes he just had to stay overnight. It couldn't be helped. The place closed in the early morning and sometimes the patrons were slobs. Clean up could take as much as an hour and a half. Not to mention counting the money and receipts and the mounds of paper work. When all was done, there would be times when he was just too tired to drive home. He needed a few hours of shut-eye first. So he crashed in the upstairs room and came home the moment he woke. It was all part of running a business, he assured her.

But Mrs. Snide did not completely trust her spouse. They had been married for nine years and she knew him. He could lie to you and you would never know. Horace was a master of deception, hiding behind the charm of his good nature. It was the kids that made her give him the benefit of the doubt. Surely he would not do anything to jeopardize the well-being of the family.

Over the three years, he had stayed overnight two

dozen times or so. Each time he finally made it home, he was tense, easily irritated... *guilty*. On his clothes there was an unusual scent. Not strange perfume; more like strange sweat.

It was happening more often lately. Three times in the last month. Still, she never questioned him. Without proof, they would only be the babblings of an overly jealous wife. She had to catch him with his hand in the cookie jar.

The first five nights he came out the front door around a quarter to three. When she saw him she raced home to get there before he did. Horace was a slow driver. She wasn't.

Kirk Snide, the oldest of the three, was the only one who ever knew she had left the house. The seventh grader was given specific instructions: "Don't answer the phone, Don't open the door, and if your brother or sister wake up and ask where I've gone, tell them I had to go to Aunt Glenda's for awhile." In exchange for his silence, he was allowed his passion, the pleasure of staying up late on a school night to watch David Letterman.

Trust in Kirk was much greater than her trust in Horace. Kirk was a good kid and very loyal to his mother. He would die before he let a word slip from his lips. Besides, he had no idea where his mother had been going the past few nights. It was better, he supposed, that he did not know.

Annette began to feel guilty herself, sitting in the car at seven-thirty in the morning, spying on her man like a deranged lover. But the sight of Ramond changed all that.

She had made it back just in time to see him, and was glad she decided to return. In the car she had waited until four before realizing that this was one of the nights he was staying. Nothing pulled her away for hours, not coffee, not food, and certainly not sleep; her mind was too intrigued to be tired.

MICHAEL BISHOP

Around six she was forced to pull herself away. The kids would be up soon for school, and it would not be good for the younger ones to know she was gone. Paul, the middle kid, would be easy enough to handle. The gullible young man believed practically any tidbit of misinformation you placed on his plate. But the youngest, Samantha Kate, was a remarkably bright six-year-old as well as inquisitive. There would be no way to guarantee her silence.

Before her alarm clock sounded at six-thirty, Annette turned it off. She had made it just in time. Even Kirk had no idea of how late she had been out. The kids were dressed and fed before being carried to their bus stop, and Annette Snide went back to Smiley Joe's.

With glazed, cold eyes she watched Ramond as he trotted down the stairs and around the corner. A hornet's sting placed itself into her heart. She had not been betrayed for some lovely, young mistress. That would have been unacceptable, but still grossly more acceptable than the truth. Instead she had been double-crossed for another man. All she wanted to know was: Why? *Why* had he done this to her? *Why* would he risk everything they had? *Why* did it have to be another man?

When he did stay at the bar all night, Horace normally did not get home until eleven the next morning, which gave her plenty of time.

Tears rolled down her cheeks as she drove home. They were not deep sobs of sadness. Instead they were light cries of anger. The kind that don't make your eyes look puffy and red; just furious and insane.

As she entered the bedroom, she noticed the

NIGHT LIFE

emptiness. It was no longer their room, it was now only her's. The item she came for was taken from his top drawer, and she headed back.

Horace sat on the bed still contemplating deeply. It was always like this after one of his "nights". He searched for an answer. His life was perfect. The perfect wife, perfect kids, he was his own boss; yet something pushed him to risk it all. The guilt was killing him, creating ulcers in his gut where there once were none. All he wanted to know was: *Why*? Why did he keep doing this to Annette? *Why* did he continue to risk everything they had? *Why* did he lust so for other men?

A knock at the door drew his attention. He figured it was Ramond returning to get something he had left or say something he had forgotten.

He pushed the door open and peered blankly at the barrel. He knew the gun. It was his. A Ruger he had bought to protect his children. He knew the lady too, although she had a look on her face he had never seen.

There was no doubt in his mind what was going on. He had been found out. The gig was up. And for his indiscretion, he would pay with his life.

No words were spoken and no attempt was made to shield his face as the bullet plowed through it. He embraced the bullet. It ended the misery his conscience gave.

Annette Snide drove to the police station amassed in her husband's blood. Outside the station's steps, a group of policeman stood chattering. She walked up to them, opened her purse, pulled out the gun, and turned herself in. She was sentenced to twenty-five to life with the possibility of parole in fifteen years.

    Kirk was sent to live with a second cousin in Oakland. Paul stayed with his only living grandparent, Grandpa Erwin. Samantha was shipped from one foster home to the next in search of someone to love her.
    Kirk and Paul saw each other only twice over the next ten years. Neither ever saw their sister again.

True Love

12 4 67890

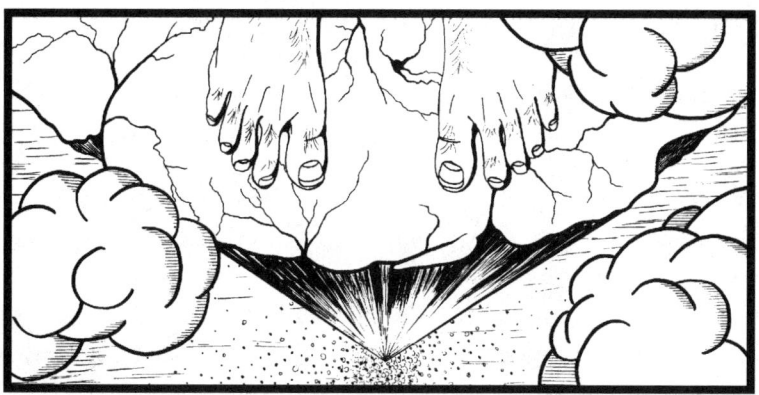

amond entered his apartment with a feeling of great accomplishment. When the going got tough, he came through. He was pleased. Not only had he proven to Satan, but to himself as well, how much he really wanted it.

A stickiness covered him, along with the stench the act of sex always brought to him. A long, steaming shower was in order. There were certain body parts he desperately wanted to wash.

Stripping quickly, he dropped his clothes to the bathroom floor and stepped into the shower. The water was the temperature of lukewarm coffee one notch too cold to be flavorful. He left the clothes on the bathroom floor as a bath mat and stepped into the stream of the nozzle. Its action was a massage, and he allowed it to flow over his back and shoulders until they became immune. He thought of "good old Horace" as he would always be remembered. The smile on Ramond's face equaled the Cheshire sign. It was a great day.

A cold chill blew through the stall and was given little thought. The only important thing was the water. He was wrapped in it and it was wrapped in him. Paradise.

The water increased in temperature three degrees. He didn't notice. Four degrees... He didn't notice... Six degrees... Didn't notice... Eight... Ten... Twelve...

Frantically he reached for the knob. *Plumbing must be acting up*, he thought, as he turned the cold on as far as it would go.

Fifteen... Twenty... Twenty-five...

"FUCK ME!" he yodeled as his skin began to blister under the heat. A handful of shower curtain was grabbed as he tried to rip it out of the way and step out to safety.

"STOP!" the voice insisted. Ramond obeyed. "Stay where you are. You must learn to control physical pain. Trust me. If you can learn to tolerate pain, it will come in very handy. Besides, you are still too weak," the Master screamed at him from all around.

The words struck Ramond as hard as Keith's knee had. They gave him determination. He would stay even if it killed him.

Fifty...Sixty...Seventy...

Red whelps bubbled on his body. The shape of the stylus monocle that hung around his neck branded into his chest, leaving a perfect outline of a circle. It was hard to breathe in the heat. It stole the oxygen, leaving steam in its place. What little air he could get was tainted by the revolting scent of his own flesh burning. The muscles of his body

TRUE LOVE

would soon give way to the pain and collapse all together. But he was going nowhere, no matter how much torment he received.

"Enough," the voice grunted as if it were growing bored with the suffering. The water no longer fell. Its absence did nothing to soothe Ramond's pain. The damage had been done. His nerves screamed their rebellion.

Not even his own body could be seen through the gummy fog that spread over him; but he was certain he must resemble a lobster. The draft blew through the shower again. This time, however, it invoked curiosity. He wondered where it was coming from. There were certainly no breeze ways in his bathroom. Perhaps he had been transported somewhere else again; but the mist of steam gave his eyes no clues.

"Where are we?" he asked, pretending his flesh did not pray him to die in order to stop its sorrow.

"That is not important. You are with me. That's all that matters. Correct?" Satan asked. "Besides, speak when spoken to."

"Yes, Lord."

"Did you enjoy yourself?" he inquired in a suddenly jovial voice.

"Enjoy myself?" Ramond questioned through the ache.

"Yes. Did you enjoy yourself? Horace Snide seemed to be rather fond of you, and you of him as well. So tell me... Did you enjoy yourself?"

It was a curious question, Ramond thought. Through the torment he answered as honestly as possible. "I will not lie, not that I could lie to you, but I had reservations in the beginning. But once again you were right, Lord. It was a very pleasurable experience. I hope I have served you well."

"Spare me. I did not give you the test to serve me well. I gave it to you to prepare you. Make no mistake. You are not doing these things for me. You are doing them for yourself. Never...NEVER forget...It was *you* who propositioned *me*." The cheerfulness was gone.

"I'm sorry. I did not mean to imply that..."

"Speak when spoken to," he reminded.

The layers of vapor began to dissipate slightly. He squinted and peered sharply. Still nothing could be seen.

"Time for number three. You're doing well. It will not be long until you have what you want. How does that make you feel?"

"Elated," Ramond pronounced.

"Good. I am starting to actually believe that you are serious about our little bargain."

"I have never been more serious about anything. There is nothing else. Only the quest," Ramond claimed.

"Happy to hear it, my boy. Happy to hear it. The next test is important because it will further prepare you for things to come. You may think you are prepared now. But you are nowhere near the man you need to be."

"I'm ready to complete the next. Right now. Just ask."

"Not so fast. Take a break. All work and no play makes Ramsy a dull boy. You don't have to do this one until tomorrow."

"Yes, Sire. What shall I do now to prepare myself?" he tentatively asked, expecting to be asked to achieve a task even more repulsive than he thought the last would be.

"You have lost your purity. You must regain it."

"How?"

"Listen carefully. The other acts were open ended. I told you to burn *any* church and have relations with *any* man.

TRUE LOVE

Granted I guided you where I wanted you, but I will no longer interfere. The remaining tests will be specific. If you forget any of the directions I give you, you will not be able to complete them and therefore the deal is off."

"I understand," he said. The fog lifted even more.

"From now on I will watch you, but I will not help you as I have been. It is up to you...With that said, here's what you are to do." Ramond listened intently. He would not let himself forget a word. "As I said, you must regain your purity. This can be done in only one way. You must take the virginity from a female."

"Is that all?" Ramond asked in disbelief. There had to be a catch.

"No that is not all, Ramond! Let me finish. Not just any virgin. A special virgin."

"Who?"

"There is a beautiful young lady who lives in Little Rock. 13 years old next Thursday. Her name is Susan Lints and her address is 1426 Plantation Drive. Take her virginity, anyway you can. But the important part is this... When you are done, you must drink the fruits of her virginity"

"I'm not sure I understand."

"It's simple, you idiot! Drink the blood of her virginity. It doesn't get any easier to understand than that."

A light clicked in his mind. He was to rape the child then drink the blood from her torn vagina. It was sick. Not just the drinking of blood, he had done that before, but the rape, the violation, the fear she would feel. It would take an animal to do such a thing. Ramond hoped he was beastly enough.

"I understand," Ramond admitted solemnly.

"Good... Cheer up my boy. It's not that bad really. She

may even enjoy it. You know how kids are these days... But it must be done. You must be pure. It is the only way."

"Why her... I mean what is so special about her?" He was becoming braver with his questions.

"There is a reason for all things. Only the reasons are not for you to know. She was chosen for a purpose and so were you. Everything serves my will. Now ask me no more, just do it." The voice had grown mild. Saying harsh things in a soft way. There was no anger, just a tone that said "this is the way things are". It was an acceptable answer to Ramond, although it was really no answer at all.

"I will do as you ask."

"I know you will."

A hard wind blew through and Ramond leaned into it to keep from being blown over. The barrier that blocked his vision was whisked away, and he saw that it was not steam at all, but a white cloud, billowing and fluffy. It flew distant from him and he watched it with vigor until he realized he was in the air. The platform he stood on was less than two square feet and if he had stepped in any direction during the confrontation he would have fallen. The entire thing was an unnatural aberration. A mountain of some sort, but instead of pyramiding down like a real mountain, it stayed the same diameter all the way to the ground.

Far below he could make out the bottom: rocky and dreadfully unreal. It looked up at him five hundred meters from his bare feet. The heat disappeared and vertigo took its place. His head began to swim with drunkenness. There had never been a fear of heights until now. So close to falling. So close to splattering. So close to the end. It was horrific terror.

"Ah, it disturbs me so to see you *this* weak. Grow a spine, Ramond. Here, let me give you a hand."

TRUE LOVE

Ramond felt it on his back, but it was invisible. The outline of its pressure was unmistakable. It was a hand, large and strong. The fingers shoved him forward like a sky diving coach pushing a frantic student from a plane. Only Ramond had no parachute.

The speed of the free fall was hard to gauge. Thirty-five, forty, a hundred miles an hour. He couldn't tell. It really wasn't like falling at all. It was more like being suspended in air while the ground moved toward you at an incredible rate of speed. The pebbles below him became stones, then rocks, then boulders. The closer he got to them, the more of his sight they consumed.

The rock directly below him was focused on the hardest. It was not the largest of the boulders, but it was the most important. It was the one he would hit. The tip was jagged, saw-like, while the rest was smooth and dull grey. His mind began to estimate the time he would smack into it. It wouldn't be long.

He wouldn't hurt me, he told himself. But there was nothing in him that believed it. It would be a painless death. His entire self would shatter like fine china. The rock was so close. So very close. So very close indeed. He could almost touch it. Reach right out and rub its grainy texture. He would hit it about... about... about... NOW!

† † † † † † † † † † † †

"A H H H H H H H H H   A H   A H AHHHHHHHHHHHHHHHHH aaaauuuuuuuu!"

His body convulsed so badly that it almost cracked his spine in two. He jerked around, twisting wildly, slamming his head and arms into the back wall of the stall. He was lying

-125-

face down in the water. His body had covered the drain hole and the liquid began to collect around him. The stream from the nozzle continued to squirt. The mist that rained down on Ramond was cold and tender and would have been paradise to the burned skin. But he noticed the skin was no longer burned. It was not even red. It was just wrinkled, the way your skin wrinkles to tell you you've been in the tub too long.

He leapt from the shower as if it were a frying pan. Once on the outside, he turned the knobs off. The water ended its downpour. He stared at the stall in disbelief for minutes. Ramond would never look at the shower the same way again.

The shirt clung to his back as the cloth absorbed the dampness. He had forgotten to dry off, wanting only to get out of the bathroom immediately. The blue jeans slid on easier, not resisting a great deal. In fact, they resisted less than usual. Had he lost weight? Perhaps. But there was no time to consider it. There was a trip to take. A trip to Little Rock. And the sooner he got out of his apartment and on the road, the better he would feel.

The speedometer read eighty the whole way. The tank was full, the day was warm, and the interstate clear. Driving always cleared his head, and his head was indeed in need of clearing.

It pissed him off. His master, the one he had chosen to dedicate every waking moment of his life to, was playing games with him. Just like everyone else, Satan was having a big laugh at Ramond's expense. It was maddening. If you couldn't even get respect from your God, then who was left to

TRUE LOVE

respect you?

He fumed for the length of the drive. The fury built, widening the scowl on his face. The anger was welcome. It could be used. If he had to be a rapist, then maybe the animosity would fuel his engine.

Just off the Little Rock exit, he pulled into a gas station and purchased a map. It was a detailed guide. Very useful. He found Plantation Drive on page B3 and made a route with his finger from it to his current location. Once a path was established, he drove to the street with ease.

1426 was not only on the mailbox, but on the front of the house as well, making it simple to find. It was an average house. Much like his parents'. Three bedrooms, red brick, fireplace, two car garage. Everything but the white picket fence.

The lot across the street was empty and the Ford was parked on its corner. Hopefully it would not raise much suspicion. But even if it did, he was in no real danger. He hadn't done anything wrong... *yet*.

Little activity was seen on the street for the next three hours. It was only two and everyone was at work or at school. Besides the occasional dog-walker or housewife out for her fitness stroll, the street was deserted.

Waiting was the worst part. He was forced to sit, nervously awaiting an opportunity to strike. Mulling over what he would do and how he would do it. He was not really a deviant. Ramond felt no need to harm the innocent. Felt no need at all to traumatize and assault a little girl. But he would and he knew it. The end justified the means. No matter how mean the *means* were.

† † † † † † † † † † †

Around three he nodded off. At four he was awakened by the girls. There were three of them. Walking slowly down the sidewalk in front of him and talking loudly. All in uniform. *Catholic school girls*, he thought. Somehow he knew. The one in the middle was Susan. The other two were plain, normal pre-teen girls. The kind you glance over but don't really notice. But the one in the middle was something completely different.

She was taller than the others, at least three inches. She had filled out much earlier than they. It was evident she would soon be a woman. Her blonde hair shined with a glow even expensive conditioners could not reproduce. In her steps there was a confidence. She held her head high and walked more like a princess than a girl.

The others felt her superiority as well. It was obvious in the way they looked up at her and listened with diligence to her words. It showed in the way they smiled at her. It showed in the gleam their eyes gave off just to be with her. But her appeal went deeper than just the fact that she flowered early. There was something else. Something about her countenance. A look that made Ramond do nothing but stare for moments on end.   Her face had no makeup, and did not need it. There was a natural glow: a pink hue to her cheeks, and her features had managed to snare something Ramond had never seen in anyone else before; yet in Susan Lints' face, it was unmistakable. Plain and simple, her face was a portrait of *purity*.

TRUE LOVE

At only thirteen years of age she was ravishing. A beauty ready for the cover of Cosmo or Vanity Fair. A heaven-touched rose among the common blades of grass. Ramond could not help but think of what she would be like at seventeen or eighteen years old. With that look, that charisma, that aura; there was no limit to what she could be.

As Ramond continued to stare, he began to feel something inside he had never felt for a girl. He was smart enough to know what it was, but not smart enough to explain why. As insane as it sounded he was falling in love. It was crazy. She was so young and he had done nothing but look at her. But that face... that face was hypnotic.

"Bye Susan!" the other girls called as she rounded the corner and walked up her driveway to the door. Susan turned to wave, giving Ramond one last look for the day. The moment froze in time. She did not notice him, but he could not notice anything but her. The image of her immaculate appearance stayed firmly in his mind's eye even after she had turned her back and walked away. It was how he would always remember her: *Perfect*.

One block was circled, then the next. He knew the bus stop would be close by. There was no way the parents of a child like that would let her walk far in the afternoon. The yellow sign with the bus painted on it was two blocks away. It would be her morning route. Hopefully, the other girls did not walk with her in the morning. They all got off the bus at the same time, so it was reasonable for them to walk together. But in the morning they would all be leaving their houses at different times. It was a feasible deduction, Ramond thought;

and if it was a correct guess, his chance would come tomorrow, sometime before eight.

For the rest of the day, she would not leave his head. Every thought was on her luscious frame. The way the red and green plaid skirt gripped her thighs. The way the white blouse hugged her firm breasts. The way her ass swayed slightly from side to side as she walked away. Even as he searched the unfamiliar town for a suitable place to defile her, she made him erect.

Tacos and burritos were his lunch and were surprisingly flavorful despite their artificial ingredients. He ate them as he drove. Ramond was in no hurry. A new thing had been dug up like a grave site in his insides: love. And it was a discovery that was well worth a good long drive and deep contemplation.

††††††††††††

Could it be? Could he really have fallen in love that fast with a mere child whom he had never actually met? It was lunacy, and he was no loon. It had to be simple lust. Just a sexual urge gone haywire. But he knew that was not the case. Lust was a common emotion. Magazines, videos, T.V., practically anything could cause lust. But Susan Lints was not just an object. She was a connection. The ideal mate he had always pictured himself with. And in a way she was an unnatural phenomenon; someone kissed by the golden lips of mother nature.

For the moment, Ramond managed to concentrate on

TRUE LOVE

the task at hand instead of the fermentation of his heart. He needed a place. Somewhere he could do what he had to do without being seen. Once again he went back to the map.

Past experiences told him the best place to go when you didn't want to be seen. Back at home when a guy and girl wanted to fool around, they went to the nearest bridge. Most of the time the workers who built it made a road under it; and there, as the cars passed above oblivious to the act below, the heated couple would rid themselves of their frustrations.

Sometimes you had to try more than one bridge. After all, great minds think alike and the first one you tried might be occupied.

The map led him to the closest creek. There were thousands of small water-ways in the heart of the South. Five miles from 1426 Plantation Drive, Shenadowa Creek slithered along a rickety path into the woods. The first bridge he came to was deep enough into the brush to keep the traffic light. A dirt road wound down the hill and under the bridge, shielding passing cars above from seeing below.

Ramond pulled off the main road and lowered his car down the hill. It was a test to see if the dirt path was dry enough to keep his car from getting stuck. It was an embarrassing problem that had happened to more than one overly excited teen; and it was not a situation he wanted to be in with a kidnaped girl in his vehicle.

The side road had a thin layer of gravel over it, providing sturdy traction for the tires. He pulled under the bridge and cut the engine. The drought of the summer dwindled the water level to a mere trickle. The creek was more a large mud puddle than an actual water-way. Graffiti lined the bottom of the bridge, announcing the youths that had visited the place before. Such poetic messages as "Crystal was here '88" and "The Tigers Suck" were scrawled across the beams in a spectrum of spray painted colors. It was a reminder of home.

The Ford stayed under the bridge for the remainder of the day. Ramond propped his feet on the seat and laid down with his head against the door. Susan Lints floated through every breath he took.

He wasn't sure how he would do it or if he could do it at all, for that matter. No part of him wanted to hurt her. Rather just the opposite. He wanted to hold her. Protect her from anyone who would do her harm. But the one person he could not protect her from was himself.

Perhaps that was why his Sire had chosen her to begin with. Perhaps Satan had known Ramond would fall for her this way. Perhaps it was just an extension of the test. But it was all speculation. He toiled over it for hours, until the sun fell and rose again. At six-thirty, he cranked his engine and headed back up the dirt hill. His mind was set. His first love would win out. His first love would be the deciding factor. It was not the love for Susan Lints, or the love for Satan. It was the love of power. As always.

† † † † † † † † † † † †

Vaseline was purchased from an all night grocery before he continued on to her house. The larger size bottle was chosen. Better to have more than enough than not enough. He drove back to Plantation Drive and parked across the street again. Every breath was deep and slow as he locked his stare to her front door. Just to see her again, just to be given the pleasure of her face, was a thrill he eagerly awaited.

TRUE LOVE

At precisely 7:13, Susan Lints strolled out the front door and down the driveway... alone.

Ramond's spirits lifted as she rounded the corner. He scanned her meticulously, carefully viewing every strand of hair, every curve, every inch, before moving on to the next.

No friends had shown up to accompany her. Ramond's theory had proven accurate. The time was now. She was walking away from him, along the newly concreted sidewalk. He let her get only a short distance before he started his motor.

In his mind he began to dehumanize her. Thinking of her as an object. An obstacle he had to overcome. It made it easier to see her as a thing than as the *gift* she was. He began to think about his Master's horseplay again. And about the smell of his own skin smoldering. It didn't bring as much anger as he hoped, but it helped.

She was in her own world, thinking about how lovely the day was and how she would finish her homework when she got to school before the first period bell rang. The sound of the car went unnoticed until it was right beside her. The door flew open and Ramond lunged from it like a starving tiger from a cage. Susan froze, unsure of what was happening and unable to do anything about it. Ramond looked around quickly. No one was near. He grabbed a handful of her hair and jerked hard toward the car.

"NO! AHHHHH!" she screamed, but made little noise otherwise. It surprised Ramond. He was sure he would have a screaming fireball on his hands. Instead she was submissive, stumbling in disbelief toward the car. They made it half way before she began to fight. First, she dug her heels into the soil beside the sidewalk. Then her hands reached up to grab

MICHAEL BISHOP

Ramond's face. She clawed at it with talon nails, drawing blood instantly.

"OWWWW SHIT!" he reeked and raised his free hand. She was tall, but he still stood a head above her. The blow crashed down, striking her in the temple. Susan's knees gave way and smeared with mud as they hit the ground. She was not completely out of consciousness, but not completely in either. Her mind was caught in limbo. Somewhere between sleep and wake. A shock state.

Ramond took advantage of her limpness and picked her up like an infant. Her head slammed against the passenger's door as he thrust her in. One more quick glance was tossed around for witnesses. There were none. He sat down and slammed the door behind him. As he drove away he made sure not to leave tire marks behind. Police were smart. The fewer clues he left the better.

† † † † † † † † † † † †

She was docile on the way to the bridge, moving only once to turn her head to Ramond. Her eyes burned through him, and he could feel her searing hate. It was a thousand times the heat of the water, and burned him much deeper.

He focused on the road ahead and did not dare to look in her direction. If he saw her, peered at her innocence, he may lose his nerve. Neither said a word: he for lack of anything to say, she because it would do no good.

Ramond steered the car back to the bridge and wound down the road to the lip of the creek underneath. The engine was cut. When the engine stopped running, stopped purring steadily, she was convinced she was going to die. Susan's mind switched off to save her from the terror.

TRUE LOVE

Ramond looked over at her for the first time. The feeling coming from her was different. Her eyes still looked in his direction. But they were no longer looking at him; they were looking nowhere: dead into the distance. He dropped his eyes to her chest. She was breathing. If he hadn't seen her lungs heave he might have guessed otherwise; but with the sight of her breath, Ramond took one of his own in relief.

Susan was in shock. Ramond understood. It was not something he had ever witnessed first hand, but in the stories he had heard about going into shock, this was what he imagined it would be like. She laid there, hunched over on the door silent and still. He pitied her deeply. But the fact that she did not move or talk or scream made it that much easier. She was no longer a *gift*, but just an object. Limp and void of life.

He stepped out of his door and walked around to her's. As he opened it, she fell out onto the ground like a sack of Idaho spuds. Ramond drug her away from the car to an open spot next to one of the bridge supports. He rolled her on her back. The uniform skirt was lifted up to her chest and her panties were removed. The Vaseline was applied liberally to himself, then to her. She did not move as he entered her. It was as if she did not know.

But as he rhythmically stroked her for several minutes, he looked into her eyes. A single tear streamed from the corner of her pupil and dripped down her cheek. The cheeks had lost their natural color and had gone as pale and plain as her friend's cheeks had been.

He did not stop as he continued to stare. With every push there was a subtle change in her. The purity began to be stripped away, like the ocean eroding away layer after layer of beach. He wasn't sure how long he should continue. The rape gave pleasure only at orgasm. It was like having sex with a blow up doll, only there was enormous guilt. Another tear burst from her eye. This time Ramond stopped. He had taken her purity. There was no doubt.

The second part of the act had lost its spectacular feel. When he was first told to drink her blood, he looked at it as a great symbolic deed. Now it was just a chore. Something he did timidly only to finish what he had done.

Her blood covered him and mixed with the petroleum jelly. He wiped two fingers worth of the defilement off of his shaft and stared at it carefully. The Vaseline gave the mixture an appearance of light red plum jelly and a similar consistency as well. He held his breath and placed the fingers in his mouth. When he could not hold his breath any longer, Ramond let out a long blow. The taste was sickening. Worse than his own urine. Worse than anything. It did not taste like purity at all, but like the horrid act of rape itself. He controlled the urge to spill his guts as he pulled up his pants.

Susan's panties were stuffed halfway in and halfway out of the belt on her skirt. Ramond did not bother to put them back on her. Her body was drug to the car and replaced inside. He drove up the hill and back to Plantation Drive hastily. The exact location where the abduction took place was revisited. Only this time with her door facing the spot. He reached past her and opened the door. Her head fell backward, but her body stayed in the car. Ramond grabbed her feet and pulled them upward while pushing forward, causing her to do a limp back flip out of the car and land face-down in the soggy earth.

Ramond took one last look. Susan laid still, face down in the mud and did not move. It was inhuman and he hated himself. Inside she was dead, but on the outside she breathed. He watched her swallow two short breaths, then slammed the passenger door closed. He wanted to see no more. He wanted to believe he was not the animal who did this.

No tire marks were left as he drove away. No neighbor bore witness to what had transpired. And Ramond had gotten away without leaving a clue.

† † † † † † † † † † † †

"THE END OF INNOCENCE"

The day Susan Lints was born was the single most miraculous and joyous day in Collin Lints' life. As he held his daughter for the first time, he could see even then something unique in her infantile face. An energy bounced off the baby, making anyone near feel a little better about themselves. At first it was dismissed. He assumed it was just the pride a father feels for his new born, and that all parents felt that way about their children. This was his first, and with no other experiences to draw from, he suspected it was just part of being a daddy.

But as Susan grew older, Collin noticed that others saw it in her as well. They treated her differently. Set her on a pedestal. Even as early as five and six he and Rita were forced to set a limit to the number of children who wanted to sleep over.

When she got old enough to walk to the bus stop, a swarm of friends would meet her at the door each morning to walk with her. So many, in fact, that the neighbors began to complain of the noise the children were making so early in the morning. Eventually Collin forbade anyone to come over during the morning time.

MICHAEL BISHOP

It seemed that everyone wanted to be in her presence and the longer, the better. It worried Collin somewhat. The boys were sure to be wolves. Flocking and stalking for the attentions of his daughter. But Susan always held herself as a lady, making friends with the boys, but no more. In a way, she was too good to be true.

When Susan was seven, the conversation could be avoided no longer. Collin and Rita had always passed small comments between each other like "That's a special girl we've got there," and "Boy we're so blessed to have her". But beyond that, Susan's *difference* was avoided.

"You know what she told me today?" he asked Rita one Saturday morning.

"No. What did she tell you?" she inquired, knowing exactly who "she" was. Whenever either of them said "she", they were always talking about Susan. It was as if she were the only "she" in the world.

"She said her teacher had to assign each kid in her class a certain seat to sit in everyday. It seems that they were fighting over who got to sit next to her. She said one boy actually punched another boy in the mouth because he wouldn't give his seat up. So the teacher gave everyone a particular desk to sit in and they aren't allowed to change it for any reason." He told the story like a boy scout leader telling ghost stories in front of a camp fire.

"Is that so? Well that Susan is something." She tried to tip-toe around his implications. She knew very well what he was getting at, knew he wanted to discuss just how and why she was so *damn* special. But the subject scared her. Rita was not at all sure she wanted to know why things were as they were. It was better to leave well enough alone, and just

TRUE LOVE

be thankful for what you had instead of questioning it.

Collin was persistent. It was time to quit acting like it was some horrible secret that must be kept at all cost. "Rita. Do you... I mean have you noticed the way everyone wants to be her friend...I mean, not all kids are that popular you know."

"Yep. We're lucky, you and I, Hon." She made one last attempt to dodge him, but she could see the look in his face. It was a stone wall: solid and unmoving. It was the look he got when he refused to let a subject go.

"Come on Rita, quit playing blind-man. You know what I'm getting at. I'm not crazy. Don't you feel it when she's around. Don't you see that she's not like her friends?"

She looked around shamefully to make sure Susan was not around, knowing very well that her daughter was out playing with the gang that came over each day. Collin had gone and said it, and oh how she wished he hadn't. Of course she had felt it, and seen it, and wondered; but to actually come out and say it... well that was almost like blasphemy.

"Why are you saying this? What does it matter? Let's just let well enough alone, Collin, please," she pleaded hopelessly.

"So what? Are we supposed to live the rest of our lives pretending she's normal? Huh? Well she's not, Rita. And I would like to discuss with you, *my* wife, what your thoughts on the matter are. I would like to have some feedback here. A little comradery. God... I've felt so alone about this, I just want someone to share this with me," he began angrily but ended with a plea of his own.

Rita shared his solitude. It was lonely keeping your words bottled up inside. She loved him so much, had since their third date. It was the kind of love that she knew would never go away. Not in crisis. Not in sickness. Not even in death. And if he needed her to share with him, she would, no matter how uncomfortable the subject was.

"I'm sorry sweetheart. It's just... Well, I almost feel guilty about talking about her. She's so wonderful. I just didn't want to... I don't know, I guess this may sound silly, but I didn't want to betray her by talking about her."

"I know. But I'm not saying her... let's call it a 'gift'... I'm not saying her 'gift' is a bad thing. On the contrary. It may be strange, but not a bad kind of strange. I just wanted to confirm that I'm not the only person on Earth who realizes that we have produced... *Angelic*."

"I don't know if I'd go that far," she said timidly, "but yes, I've noticed it too. I'm not saying I know why; but there is something about her that no one else I have ever met has. I can't put my finger on what it is. But I'll tell you this much, I thank Mary and Jesus every night for giving her to us. And I think 'gift' is a very good name to call it... She not only has a gift, but she *is* a gift."

They were both grinning like love struck teenagers. Just the evocation of her name made them feel good.

"Do you ever wonder why?" he asked.

"Collin, let's not ask why."

"No really, dear. Why do you think she is this way? There has to be a reason. It's not just a fluke."

"I told you. I don't know why, and I don't think I want to know."

"Well you know what I think?"

"What hon?"

"I think there is a supernatural purpose for her life. Something down the line that she was born to do. Don't ask me what, but that's what keeps coming to me. I refuse to

TRUE LOVE

believe that she has been endowed like this for no reason."

"Maybe so," she said smiling harder than before, "but let's not think about it any more right now," she continued as she grabbed his hand. "She won't be back for awhile. She never is when she goes to play." She gave him a seductively playful wink.

"Well then my dear, let's not waste a moment," he continued the courtship. She led him to their room where they made love for a long while.

Collin and Rita Lints watched as their daughter was voted class favorite year after year. They watched as she matured years before other kids her age. They watched as she turned rainy days into sunshine for everyone she met. And as they watched her, they never once regretted that she had been given a gift... until the day Ramond Jamison took that gift away.

Rita Lints was enjoying her third cup of coffee as the lady on T.V. bought an "E". "Wheel of Fortune" was one of her guilty little pleasures, like chocolate and romance novels. Collin hated the show and made fun whenever it came on. "Boring drivel" he called it. "Mind candy for those who have nothing better to do with their time then play a glorified version of hangman." But she liked it, no matter what he said. So when Collin left for work at eight each morning, she started the coffee, made the bed as it brewed, and was in front of Pat Sajak by eight-thirty.

"Is there a T?" the man asked just as the door bell rang.

"Be right there!" she yelled from her leather sofa chair. It rang again. "I'm coming," she called as she entered the hall. A beating rumbled from the other side of the door as someone knocked furiously. Rita got an uneasy feeling. Something was wrong. The air stunk of it. Her walk turned into a jog, then a sprint as she reached the front door and glared out the tinted glass window in its center.

At first she saw only the man wearing the light grey jogging suit. His eyes tingled with mad distress as he continued to beat on the door and ring the bell simultaneously. She recognized him. It was her neighbor, Tom Kindson. She popped the latch instantly and flung the door open.

The babbling began as soon as his eyes struck her face.

"My God Rita, I'm sorry, I don't know what happened. I just found her like this and... oh, God I'm so sorry. I...." he was bawling like a child whose parents wouldn't buy him the latest toy.

"What are you talking..." She stopped cold as Tom bent down on one knee to pick up the object at his feet. It took an extended second for her to realize he was picking up a girl, and even a longer second still to realize that girl was Susan. It was an honest pause; Susan looked so different that even her mother had trouble recognizing her.

"Dear God. I'm sorry," he bawled.

"Susan! Susan! What's wrong. Oh Jesus! SUSAN!" she screamed as if she were questioning God himself. Hysteria lined her voice as tears joined her eyes. She ripped her daughter from Tom's hands and stared down at her blank face with confusion. Susan's eyes were void of soul. Her body lacked the radiant heat of life. Her flesh was cold and clammy, like an old corpse.

Somehow, in that moment of horror and distress, Rita

TRUE LOVE

heard something she never forgot coming from the back room. The T.V. was not loud, but some part of her that she could not explain heard it with perfect clarity. "I'd like to solve the puzzle, Pat... The End of Innocence."

† † † † † † † † † † † †

The cops had zero leads and were rampaged by the media for being unable to catch the scoundrel who did the unspeakable. The town was in outrage. Each parent feared their child would be next. The event spurred the creation of dozens of new neighborhood watch groups, most lasting only a few months.

The Lints' offered a $25,000 reward for anyone who had information that would lead to the capture of the man who had done this to their daughter. No one ever collected the reward.

For eleven days after, Susan moved only when she shut her eyes to sleep. The stark white hospital sheet covered her as she lay in the hard bed day in and day out. An intravenous tube was used to nourish her. Besides the minor vaginal damage and the various bumps and bruises, the doctors found nothing wrong with her.

"It's psychological. There's absolutely nothing we can do for her. She could come out of it at any time, or she may never come out of it. Only time will tell. I'm sorry." the doctors told her parents.

Rita never left her daughter's bedside during the entire hospital stay. Not even for food. All meals were brought to her by her husband or nurses. She held Susan's hand and talked to her when she was awake. When the girl's eyes were open, which was not often, she stared straight ahead, looking at nothing. When her mother would speak she did not acknowledge. No shifting of the eyes, no nods, no signs of life at all. Until the twelfth day.

At noon on day twelve, Susan Lints awoke, looked to the left, then to the right, and sat up. It was a sudden move, unpredictable and nonsensical.

"Susan! Susan! You're back. Thank you God, she's back." Rita rejoiced as she threw her arms around her daughter. But she was mistaken. Susan was not back. Only a shell of her former self remained. "Susan? Susan?" her mother asked after getting no response from the girl. She held her daughter at arms' length with her hands on her shoulders. Susan looked at her mother with no expression. "Oh God, Susan!" Rita cried as she hugged the girl tight again. It was a step. Not as big of one as she had hoped. Still it *was* a step.

When Susan was willing to feed herself, the doctors let her go home. She made no attempt to eat unless something was placed in front of her. Even then she only picked at the food and ate little.

The young girl's room became her sole dwelling. It was seldom she left its four walls. It was the only place she felt safe. The outside world had become a nightmare to her, full of monsters and demons who would hurt her if she dared step outdoors.

Most days she stayed in bed, staring at the ceiling with empty eyes. Her mother made countless attempts to reach her daughter. Just to hold a simple conversation with her was a dream Rita prayed for every night. But each encounter was the same. Susan only bothered to answer her mothers questions with a nod for "yes" and a shake of the head for

TRUE LOVE

"no".

Rita tried for years to fulfill her fantasy of hearing her daughter speak again. But it was not to be. Her begs and pleas went unacknowledged by the girl. Eventually she grew tired...lost hope...gave up.

For all practical purposes, Susan Lints was dead. She never went back to school, or saw her friends, or left home. There was no emotion left in her. They had been stripped from her along with her virginity. She was a void. A husk of something that once lived, but now only took up space.

Her condition destroyed Collin and Rita inside. To see their little girl like this, a hollow stranger, took its toll on them. They dared not speak of it, but both knew she would be better off dead. It would be kinder. Her pain would end.

Eventually they visited their daughter's room less and less, not wanting to see what she had become any more. The feedings and bathings became a chore, like taking care of a dog or cat. Their perfect little world had collapsed around them like a house of cards.

They quit celebrating her birthday when she was sixteen. A year and a half later Susan ended her suffering.

Her parents slept soundly after another night of crying themselves to sleep. She lied awake and listened to them. When they stopped, she waited thirty minutes before she rose. Stealthily she walked down the stairs and to the kitchen. A box of matches had been kept for emergencies in the drawer by the refrigerator since she was a child. She opened the drawer and removed the matches, then turned the eye on the gas stove. The flame lit up in a sky shade of blue. It stopped her for a moment. It had been years since she had seen fire.

MICHAEL BISHOP

The flame was beautiful.

With a deep breath she blew out the fire. The hissing of the gas continued and the smell seared her nostrils. She repeated the process with the other three eyes and listened to them hiss as well.

In the center of the kitchen floor she sat Indian style, one leg crossed over the other. She did not move for an hour. When the gas fumes made her light- headed enough to nearly pass out, she opened the box of matches. Whatever it was that she was born to be was ruined. Her birthright had been stolen from her as well as her life.

No thought was given to her parents who rested above. They would die too. To Susan, it was of no consequence. Perhaps others who lived next door would perish also. It was not her problem. All Susan Lints wanted was an end.

She removed a match from the box and shut the box back. It was time to set herself free. She spoke one last time before she struck the match. Of all the things she had heard over the years, it was the one thing that stuck out most in her mind. She could not remember exactly where or when she had heard it. But for ages it had tumbled around in her head like clothes in a warm dryer.

"The End of Innocence," she whispered and struck the match on the box. The Lints family was immediately no more.

Vengeance Is Mine

Car sickness was just a part of it. The taste lingered in his mouth like old ghosts sticking around to remind him of his sins. It mutilated his stomach. Made him so queasy it was hard to keep the car on the road. Each bump and pothole brought a new challenge. His body wanted to release its contents even more so than it had at the thought of gay sex, but his mind willed him to hold on for as long as he could. At least until he made it home.

A three hour battle ensued. Mind against body. When he reached the Sierra Springs city limit sign, his raging urge to hurl pulled him to the first gas station he saw.

The "Quicky Gas" was one of many low rent mom and pop establishments the town boasted and like many of the others, the place was a haven of filth and negligence. A blue handicap symbol was faded almost out of existence near the front door. He raced the car into the spot with no concern. A bigger problem than illegal parking weighed on him. The

MICHAEL BISHOP

gastric turbulence of his insides controlled his actions.

It was not just the pain in his gut that tormented him. It was also the taste. The tang in his mouth went beyond foul. It took on fervor, holding a grudge against him. Just when it seemed he got used to the flavor, it changed, deviating itself into something new. Something even more repugnant.

The bells set above the door gonged against one another as he entered. An aging miser who looked like he should have retired years ago stood behind an ancient register. The man appeared as if he had pulled a triple shift and taken a handful of stimulants to keep him awake.

"Help you Bub?" the guy asked nervously at the notice of Ramond's hurry. His hand dropped below the counter. No doubt grabbing for a pistol of some sort.

Ramond forced himself to speak without vomiting.

"Got a restroom?" he blurted. The man nodded, but it was not a nod that said "Yes". It was a nod of relaxation. He could plainly see now that Ramond's haste was due to sickness and not criminal behavior. He pointed to a door next to the soda cooler. "Re t Ro m" was stenciled on it with cheap foil letters that are normally used to put the family name on the side of a mailbox or porch.

Ramond zoomed to it, almost ripping the door catch off as he plowed through. A muffled "Watch it, Bub!" seeped through the cracks in the door as he closed it behind him. He rested his head against the door and took a deep breath. It was a breath he regretted. The bathroom was a zoo cage. Smelling of unwashed animals and the feces of a hundred different species. The smell accelerated the climb of his stomach's remnants.

He rushed to the sink. The mirror had crusted over with some type of black soot or rust. Only sections of his face

VENGEANCE IS MINE

could be seen around the squalor. The sink was intended to be his target, but some decadent baboon had placed a fly swarmed turd directly in the center of its drain pipe. The act was so loathsome that he could not bring himself to use the basin.

The toilet was his last hope. He stepped to its side and dropped to his knees. The dried urine grasped hold of his trousers, clenching them in its pasty coating. The seat had been ripped from the toilet and set to the side, leaving a clear view of the bottom of the porcelain bowl. Incredibly, it was somewhat cleaner than the sink. The water had changed to an orange color, but no solid object could be seen in it.

Sluggishly his hand tip-toed up to flush the handle. There was extreme anxiety in touching it. There was no telling who or what had placed their unwashed digits on it in the past. But there was no other option. It had to be done. He tugged rashly on the handle and released it like it was poisonous.

The swish of the water was deafening and a few drops splashed up and struck his face. The force of the water reigned down so heavily against the bowl that its rim came close to returning to a shade of white. One more flush and it would be suitable to heave into. The handle was jerked once again and Ramond observed the mini-whirlpool revolve its way down the drain.

As the water spun, he watched his reflection in it, spinning wildly. His face twisted to odd configurations and grew smaller and smaller as the water level decreased. He did not notice that the flush was longer than the one before it had been. Time had no meaning. His eyes were chained to the water. The reflection traveled further and further away until he realized it was not just his face anymore. His body could be seen as well: whirling around like a piece of tissue paper caught in the clutches of a cyclone.

The water turned a shade darker. Then another. Then one shade darker still. Until it was black. Ramond's body began to tingle. He could feel himself slipping away.

A splash of water made him blink. When his lids reopened, he was no longer looking into the bowl, but he was *in* the bowl. Only it was no longer a toilet. It was a chasm. A black tunnel where no light entered or escaped except for a tiny pinhole of brightness miles down the shaft. His body continued to turn, spiraling toward the light. The sensation was not of falling, but like he was being pulled sideways toward that light. Exactly as he had always imagined dying would be.

"Don't you dare give up what is now inside you!" Satan ordered. Ramond knew instantly what the voice was alluding to. The blood he had swallowed was a symbol of purity; and if he were to throw it up, it would stand to reason the purity would be lost as well.

"I could not help myself, Lord. My mind and soul want to keep the blood down, but my body is rebelling against me," he attempted in apology.

"Don't give me excuses, Boy. Do you know what would have happened if you had puked out what I have allowed you to receive? If you cannot control your body, how do you expect to handle the rigors of being my son of flesh?" His tone was irritated. For the first time Ramond heard his father speak like this: rattled and shaky. Like he did not have complete control of the situation. It made Ramond uneasy.

"Sire, I swear I will not give up what lies in my belly."

"Fool, it does not lie in your belly. It now lies in your

VENGEANCE IS MINE

soul. It is a part of you. And as long as you keep it down you will remain pure," the voice said a little more calmly now. The promise that Ramond would not puke seemed to relax the mood a bit.

"I will remain pure, Father. I have no intention of giving up something so precious." It was evident the voice was coming from the light, and Ramond spoke toward it. The illumination grew brighter, allowing him to see his hand in front of his face. It neared him with increasing speed as time progressed and through it, something could be seen. Another world perhaps, but Ramond was not yet close enough to tell for sure what lived on the other side.

"Fine then... Be sure you don't."

Ramond paid only half attention to the voice. He squinted, trying to make out what was through the glowing portal. The rotation of his body made it hard to focus on one spot for long.

"Is this death?" Curiosity finally forced him to ask.

"Maybe... For some people anyway. But not for you. Not even close. But that is neither here nor there... You did good, Boy. I'm pleased. How does it feel to be pure?"

"Wonderful," Ramond assured, although besides the sickness, he felt no difference what so ever.

"Good. It is a great accomplishment. Pat yourself on the back, but do it quickly. The fourth will take you some time to complete. Possibly longer than any. And the quicker it is done, the happier it will make me."

Ramond perked up and listened more closely. "What shall it be this time?"

"There is a man who has been a shard of glass in my side for years. He has turned my own against me and swayed those who would have served me to the other side. He must be stopped; and the weapon I intend to use to stop him is you, Ramond."

"Who father?" he asked wanting to know quite badly. Surely such a man must be the Pope or a great political leader, but the true answer did not surprise Ramond much.

"His name is Jarard Collins, but his fans just refer to him simply as Jarard. I'm sure you have heard of him."

"Yes, I think maybe I have," Ramond replied, trying to make it sound as if he might have heard the man's name somewhere in passing. But the truth of the matter was that Ramond was incredibly familiar with the singer. The name Jarard was the most influential handle in all of Christian music, and had been for the last twelve years. Ramond had owned several of his records as a child. Records that were still kept today in his mother's attic along with all his other childhood remains.

When Jarard had come to Little Rock, Vernadette's entire church rented three buses and made the trip to see the man in person. Ramond was just seven then, but out of all the concerts he had gone to since, he could not remember having as much fun as he had at Jarard's. The congregation sang road songs the whole trip; and not just Christian ones either, but some of Ramond's favorites like "Rocky Top" and "California Dreaming".

Once they arrived at the concert hall, his mother bought him the sweetest cotton candy he had ever placed in his mouth and an enormous cup of soda with just enough ice to make it cold, but not too much to water it down.

But the concert itself was the best part. The singer had a voice that could only be described as "God-Given". Jarard was a born showman. Telling jokes and stories between songs. Keeping the audience entertained every step of the

VENGEANCE IS MINE

way.

His ballads were not the hum-drum hymns and outdated "Hallelujah" songs that were normally associated with Christian music. The vocalist took a different approach, adding a mixture of old and new. The music had more of a rock sound than ordinary church organ and piano. The lyrics were creative and up to date, dealing with topics fresh out of the day's headlines, such as teenage sex and drug addiction.

By the end of the night, he had made six curtain calls. Practically all of the sixteen thousand in attendance were weeping when the last note had been played. The songs struck a chord deep within the soul, turning the hardest of hearts into mushy, melted ice cream. Ramond recalled that he too wept his share of tears. The concert moved the young boy deeply. Although, apparently, it did not have a lasting affect.

He hoped his master did not know of these things. Jarard was obviously a magnificent distress to Satan, and understandably so. If his Lord knew he was actually there, weeping and woeing, mingling with the enemy, it would be like acting as an accomplice to the damage Jarard had done.

If Satan did know, he did not let on.

"Good. Then you are aware he is a singer?"

"Yes, I believe I may have heard a song at one time or another." He was laying it on thick, but better safe than sorry. He had felt Satan's wrath enough already to last a lifetime.

"Yes, I'm sure you have... Well that's well and good but I want you to make sure you never have to hear another one of his songs. At least not live anyway. I want you to silence his shrieking. It makes my ears bleed. It makes my head hurt. It makes me ill. And you, my son, will do me the honor of removing this thorn from my paw."

Ramond hoped his father was not asking him to do

what he thought his father was asking him to do. So far no great harm was being done. But to kill a man; that was a chore he would just as soon leave to the mindless maniacs that roamed the earth. Ramond *was* a lot of things, but a murderer *was not* one of them.

"You want me to kill him?" he asked, not being able to hide the hint of disgust in his voice.

"No, Ramond. I want you to do something worse. I want you to let him live."

"So how do I silence him?" A sigh of relief was breathed. He would not have to kill.

"I want you to knock the man unconscious, to insure he will not squirm. Then I want you to cut Jarard Collins' tongue from his mouth. I want that abomination severed and discarded of. Cut evenly and get as much as you can. I do not want him to utter another word as long as his soul remains in his body. Be very careful though. If you kill him, you fail. Be creative, but make sure he does not bleed to death... *Dead*, he is a martyr. But *alive*, living his days as a mute... Oh, that gives me chills just to think about it. He will be a pathetic figurehead. The perfect symbol to the world of my unequaled power, and a warning to those who are brazen enough to oppose my will... If you succeed it will truly be a great day for me, and will certainly place you ahead of all others for the honor of being my son." Satan was on a rampage. Giddiness flopped through his voice like a beached fish. His tone was almost mortal, holding normal emotion: excitement, exuberance, impatience, lunacy.

Ramond's smile widened. This was his big chance to really impress the master. To do something that would give him favor with Satan. It was a wonderful opportunity. One he intended to take with a great measure of seriousness.

VENGEANCE IS MINE

He continued to spin sideways. The light was so close now that he had to place his hands in front of his face in order to keep his eyes open. On the other side of it was a room. The walls could clearly be seen now through the hole. But they were blurry, as if they were covered in water. At the bottom of the opening there was a silhouette. At first it appeared to be a circle of some sort, but as he neared it took on a more oval shape. It was a head.

"Before you go, Ramond, I want you to know that if you get caught, your dream goes up in flames. You cannot complete the last three from a jail cell. Therefore, you lose. I never said this would be easy. I just said it would be worth it."

The light began to emit a sound very similar to a rushing waterfall. He had to scream to be heard above it.

"I won't get caught!" he assured. "Jarard will be silenced!"

The hole was just inches away and was no bigger than a body length. The head from the other side had huge eyes that stared back at him in a daze. Its pupils were green and blood shot. It was the head of a giant, covering the entire length of the hole. The face also appeared to be covered in some clear liquid; or maybe it was trapped behind the water. He could not tell for sure, but the face was eerily familiar. Close examination of it told Ramond who it belonged to. It was his own.

He shut his eyes tightly as he slammed into the wall of light and felt the water cool against his face.

Water splashed up on his brow as he stared down into

MICHAEL BISHOP

the twirling toilet water. It was as crystal clear as it had been after the first flush. He attempted to gather his bearings for a moment. The trip through the dark tunnel, with all its spinning, had given him an ambience similar to jet lag, although oddly managed to settle his stomach a bit.

A knock came from the door behind him, followed by the familiar voice of the miser at the register. "Are you all right in there, Buddy? You been in there a long freaking time. There's other people that gotta use dat thang ya know."

Ramond leapt to his feet, the gooey floor did not give up its grip on the trousers easily, but with a hard tug they pulled loose. He jammed upon the door so quickly that the clerk standing on the other side took a short step back and let out an "eep" of surprise.

"Get the fuck out of my way old man!" Ramond slandered, placing a palm on the man's chest and clearing him out of the way with a push. The old guy stepped aside in shock and turned to watch as Ramond walked out the front door.

The car was aimed towards home, and by the time he reached his front door, he knew just how he would go about silencing Jarard Collins.

†††††††††††††

"Operator assistance. What city, please?"

"Yes, I need the number for the closest Ticket Master. Preferably a number for concert information if you got it."

"One moment please." The operator put him on hold as she searched for the number. Ramond wrapped the phone cord around his fingers and tapped his pen on the cover of the

VENGEANCE IS MINE

phone book while waiting impatiently. It took less than ten seconds for the generic computerized voice to answer.

"The number is 555-9224... Once again the number is 555-92..." Click. The phone was hung up before the recording could repeat the number. He had jotted it down on the cover of the phone book and began to push the corresponding buttons on the handset.

Riiinnnggg... Riiinnngggg... Riiinggg.

"Ticket Master concert information, this is Jody speaking, may I help you?"

"Yes, I would like to know if there are any Jarard Collins concerts planned for any time soon?"

"One moment, please. I'll punch it up on my computer and see. I'm going to put you on hold for one moment."

"That's fine," he replied cooly. Fortunately, unlike some Christian singers, Jarard charged admission to his shows. It amused Ramond that the same company that handled the "Heavy Metal" concerts he enjoyed also ran the Jarard tours. It made the singer simple to find.

"Okay Sir. You're in luck, actually. It appears Mr. Collins is currently in the middle of a September concert tour. I'm showing here that he has seven more shows 'till he wraps the tour up. Where are you calling from and I'll give you the time, date, and location of the concert nearest you."

It was even better than he had hoped. With seven more shows he actually had some lead way for planning. "I'm not sure when I'll be free so if you would just give them all to me."

"Okay Sir, that won't be a problem. Got your pen and paper handy?"

"Got it," he answered flipping the phone book over to write on its back.

MICHAEL BISHOP

"Here goes then. There's a show September 13th, in Oklahoma City, Oklahoma. Then to Tucson, Arizona on the 15th. From there on the 19th he'll be in Big Spring, Texas. September 26th in Fort Smith, Arkansas, the 28th to the deep south in Glenada, Mississippi, and then he will be performing two shows back in his home state of Maine on the 30th and 31st. Would you like any further information on any of these shows?"

Ramond thought carefully. It was imperative he choose the perfect location and time. Each had their pros and cons. The Oklahoma show was tempting because it was the least number of days away, and Ramond wanted to wait no longer than he had to. But Oklahoma was too far away to be practical. The Fort Smith performance would be the closest distance by far, but he knew the Fort Smith area well. There were enough cops and Armed Forces to insure heavy protection for the singer.

He hated to wait three weeks, but the Glenada concert was the best setting for the deed. It was not large enough to merit many cops lurking about, it was not too far away from his home, and it was not too big that finding his way around would be a problem. The city was an ideal place to plan his strike.

"Yes, where is the Glenada concert being held and what time does it begin?" He prepared his pen to scribble her answer.

"It's eight o'clock sharp at the Glenada Civic and Community Center. Tickets will be on sale at all local Ticket Master outlets, at the door, or if you like you can order them by phone with a credit card."

"Ahhh, no thank you, I'll just get my tickets at the door. Thank you for your help."

VENGEANCE IS MINE

"Thank you, sir and have a good day," she said sweetly, having no idea what destructive information she had just given out. Ramond hung up the phone and sat silent for a moment. The plan was in motion. As always, the worst part would be the wait. He stretched out on his bed and shut his eyes. There was finally time for sleep. He would have plenty of chances to work out the kinks in the plan later. For now, rest was a reward he gave himself.

Rent had been paid on the first, just days before the first act was done. Had it not been paid then, it would surely have not been paid at all. Hopefully, he would finish all the acts either before the first of next month or shortly after. If not, eviction would not be far behind. There was no money left in his checking account to afford another month. He knew how it worked. The landlord would give him to the fifth before leaving a delinquency note. On the twelfth, if the bill went unpaid, eviction procedures would ensue.

If the other acts took as long as this one would, he would be homeless before he had a chance to finish. But the current test was not accomplished yet, and he set his sights on it before worrying about the next.

The three weeks leading up to the concert passed delightfully quick. A little money was removed from his dwindling bank account to buy food. He found he was not very hungry most of the time. The money saved on rations was set aside. Although he had gone beyond the realm of sensibility these past few days, there was still reality to deal with. Gas had to be bought. As well as whatever equipment he might need for future chores. Cash was a necessity. Without it he was doomed to fail. So like a squirrel hoarding nuts for the winter, Ramond put what he could aside for emergencies.

During his spare time he did little else but read and think about what was to come. Over and over he played the scene in his mind. Carefully trying to anticipate the "If's". There was so much that *could* go wrong. Regardless, he was confident. Ramond was becoming a warrior. But moreover, he was becoming an attack dog. A mindless, vicious animal that would maim anyone or anything that his master ordered him to. Only he was more dangerous than an animal. Ramond could plot and plan. He could bide his time and wait for the right moment to strike the killing blow. A perfect instrument of terror.

† † † † † † † † † † † †

The two instruments that he would need to carry out his plans were already available to him, without having to spend his precious dollars.

The first had been more a nuisance over the years than a thing of use. The T-Ball bat had stood in the closet for as long as he could recall. When he lived at home, it stayed propped against the angled corner of his wardrobe. When he moved, it went with him and occupied the same position in a new closet. He drug it around with him from place to place, never really sure why. After all, it was a symbol of failure, and not only that, but of what a disappointment he was to his

VENGEANCE IS MINE

father.

Brian had given him the bat when he was four or five. Ramond couldn't remember for sure. But what he did remember was the shame in his father's eyes as they stood on their well trimmed lawn and practiced.

"Come on, Ramond. Don't be a wimp. Hit it son. HIT IT!" he shouted at his boy. With all his heart Ramond wanted to maul the ball that stood suspended three feet in midair on the tip of the tee. He wanted to knock it to Heaven as a gift to the angels. But it was not in him. Each swing of the bat brought the same result: missing it completely or knocking the baseball only a few feet away from the base of the tee.

"Dammit Ramond. Try harder!" Brian Jamison practically begged. But Ramond was already giving everything he had. With one more swing Ramond managed to strike the ball solidly. The results were even poorer than their predecessor, and the ball rolled drunkily only three feet.

"SHIT, BOY!" his father screamed at him as he jerked the bat out of his son's hand. The tug on the bat startled Ramond, and he did not let go until the force of the pull sent him flying to the ground. His father paid him no attention as he reached down and replaced the ball on the tee. Brian's expression was overflowing with fury. His forehead folded over in wrinkle upon wrinkle as he squinted his eyes and frowned so hard his lips looked as if they might turn inside-out..

"IS THIS SO FUCKING HARD!" he bellowed as he gave a one-handed swing of the bat, slamming it into the ball with explosive power. It sailed through the air beautifully, like a perfectly folded paper plane, until it hit a neighbor's unmown grass seven houses down. Brian tossed the bat next to his son and stared down at him disgustedly. He looked only a minute before his disdain would allow him to look no longer. He shook his head and mumbled to himself as he stomped off into the house, leaving his son behind in the dirt.

The ball was gone forever, destined to become a chew toy for whatever mutt who happened to stumble upon it. But as Ramond raised himself back to his feet, he picked up the bat. A few practice swings were tried in the air. Then and there he vowed to himself that if it took him until the day he died, he was going to make his father proud of him. He was going to be the best baseball player who ever lived. And at that moment he convinced himself of that.

The bat was placed in his closet later that night. Besides the times he took it out to move it from place to place, it was never touched again. That day was the first and last time Brian Jamison took any real interest in his son. And Ramond never made good on his promise to make his father proud.

† † † † † † † † † † † †

He had no idea why he had kept it all this time, but he was glad he did. The bat was the perfect weight. Light enough to be swung easily in one hand. It had remained shiny and new even though it was well aged. On the side of the bat a huge insignia was painted. "SWINGER" it said in capital letters. The word was still in mint condition except for one small chipped piece of paint on the "E". A souvenir from the might of his father's swing. He was sure, if he could swing it half as hard as his father had, it would serve him well.

† † † † † † † † † † † †

The second object Ramond needed had ties to his father as well. A straight razor had been given to his dad by

VENGEANCE IS MINE

his grandfather. Brian Jamison had never used the thing to shave with, but he did keep it well sharpened and rust free in his garage shop. It was used as a utility knife due to the fact that it was much sharper than the store bought kind and could be used indefinitely without needing to be replaced. Ramond knew the weapon would be easy enough to get his hands on. It rested in an unlocked, plastic tool box on the top of the plywood, tool desk his father had built himself. But to retrieve it, he would have to be sneaky.

Brian watched over his garage like a hawk watches over her young. They were his prize possessions. Nothing got his juices flowing like a new building project; and it allowed him to escape from problems he did not want to deal with.

Fortunately Ramond had held on to the keys to his parent's house. They had probably forgotten he even had them, and that was a good thing. He had managed to avoid seeing either of them for some time, and had no intention of doing so now. Seeing his mother's face would only remind him of how badly he had hurt her. It was a guilt he did not need right now.

The car was parked three houses down, and much like a cat burglar he slithered up to the door and placed his ear to it. The garage was silent. He turned the key in the lock and cracked it slightly. Peeking in he saw no one. He pushed the door open just enough for him to slide his body through, but no more.

The shop had not changed much in the time Ramond had been away from home. It did not appear that his father had taken on many projects lately. As always the tool box sat on top of the counter, and Ramond hurriedly went to it and undid its latch. The razor was in its usual position on the top of all the other tools. The light reflected off of it, giving a mirror shine. It had been well cared for by Brian. Better cared for, in fact, than Ramond had.

The blade was closed and placed in his pocket. The latch was redone and Ramond exited the way he had come. His father may notice it missing, but the last person on Earth who would be suspected in its taking would be his son. Most likely Brian would just think he misplaced it. Absent mindedness was not uncommon with his father.

As Ramond walked away from the house, he did not look back. The sight brought back too many memories. Memories that were less painful if allowed to remain sleeping.

†††††††††††††

Finding the concert date was step one. The gathering of the tools was the second. On September 24th Ramond began the third.

Four days before the concert would be about right. That would give Jerard's staff enough time to reserve his hotel room and make sure everything was in place before he arrived in Glenada. If Ramond was to be successful, he would have to know where the man was staying. And with his increased prowess as of late, he thought he knew just how to find out.

Once again he picked up the phone and let his fingers do the walking. He dialed "601", the area code for Mississippi, followed by the operator assistance number.

"Operator assistance. City please?"

"Glenada. I would like the number of every hotel in the town."

VENGEANCE IS MINE

"Sir, I suggest you use the yellow pages for that information," the operator insisted rudely.

"I'm sorry. I don't have a phone book for that area," Ramond said remaining calm.

"Well, you will be charged for every number separately," she continued ill-tempered.

"That's fine," Ramond replied. Indeed it was fine. He never had any intention of paying his phone bill again, and would not have the money even if he did want to pay it. They could charge him for all the numbers they wanted. In the end, they would never see a penny.

"Okay, one moment, sir," she came back, sounding disheartened that she could not talk him out of his request. In a few minutes she came back with a list. "Are you ready, sir? I'm going to go fast so have pen and paper ready."

"I'm ready," he answered with his pen in hand and the phone book opened this time to the inside cover. She rattled off a list of eleven hotels and Ramond jotted each one down in a jumbled scrawl.

"Thank you," he told her as he hung up, actually meaning it.

He readied his dialing hand as he prepared his speech. The hotels would not give the information to just anyone, but maybe, if he asked in the correct manner, he could pry the information out of the desk clerk.

The first number on the list was dialed and he waited for an answer.

"Travelers' Lodge," the voice of an old woman answered.

"Um yes, this is Mark Johnson, manager of Easy Ride Limousine Service. We seemed to have misplaced the information on what time Mr. Jarard Collins will be arriving

MICHAEL BISHOP

at your hotel. We are supposed to have a limousine waiting for him when he checks in; so could you be kind enough to let me know what time that will be?"

"I'm sorry sir, but Mr. Collins is not staying here. You must have the wrong information," she drawled.

"That's okay, I must have been misinformed. Thank you for your help," he finished and hung up quickly. Her response was expected. There were eleven possibilities and he knew it was unlikely to find the right one on the first try. It was a matter of trial and error. He scratched the top number off the list and wasted no time before dialing number two.

Eight numbers were scratched off before he struck pay dirt. All responses from the clerks had been pretty much identical as he repeated the same tired script to each one. Finally the answer he had waited for came back from the other end on his ninth attempt.

"Golden Travel Suites," the clerk replied. This time it was a man. It was the first male voice he had reached.

"Yes, my name is Mark Johnson. I am the manager of Easy Rider Limousine Service. I'm supposed to have a car ready for Mr. Jarard Collins when he arrives, but my secretary seems to have foolishly misplaced his arrival time. Could you possibly tell me what time he will arrive so I can have the car there? You understand, I'd be in big trouble if it's not ready for him," he finished trying to add humor to his voice.

The clerk's response seemed unamused. "I'm sorry, sir, but I am not allowed to give out the time Mr. Collins will arrive. It is our policy. Perhaps if you called his people they could tell you. But I cannot."

"Yes, yes of course, I was just a little embarrassed

VENGEANCE IS MINE

about calling them back after they had already given me the information once. I just hate for them to think we run a rinky-dink operation. But thank you. I guess I will give them a call back," Ramond said excitedly as his heart sang with success. The guy had given him all the information he needed.

"Good day, sir."

"Yeah, you have a good day too," Ramond offered and slammed the phone down. A smooth circle was drawn around the phone number along with a small note, "Golden Travel Suites-Jarard Collins-Test 4."

September 28th, his alarm woke him at 6 A.M. Ramond got little sleep that night. The final rehearsal went on in his mind. The play would soon begin.

By seven he was showered and in the car. The bat was placed under the back seat and the razor was put in the glove box on top of the map of Little Rock. After a quick stop for gas and a cold soda, he was on the road.

The familiar butterflies started fluttering about halfway through the trip. They were an irritation, but they did serve to boost his adrenaline level which was a definite plus. It was the riskiness of the test that bothered him so. The rape had been risky, but this test would have to be pulled off right under everyone's nose. Luck would play a key factor, and in his life, Ramond had been unlucky far too many times to let that be a comforting thought.

It was about more than just mutilating a man. He didn't like doing it, but as long as the man was unconscious he wouldn't suffer much, and at least he would live. But the real risk lay in being caught and not being able to continue. This one would put him over the hump. It was a wonderful thought, but the thought of being incarcerated placed a layer of dread over the situation.

☦ ☦ ☦ ☦ ☦ ☦ ☦ ☦ ☦ ☦ ☦ ☦

Seven hours later, he arrived in Glenada, Mississippi. The interstate had carried him right to the middle of it all. He drove just under sixty-five the entire way and made absolutely sure to slow down at any points that designated him to do so. It was a safety precaution to avoid any run ins with the law.

Outside a shopping center a phone could clearly be seen from the road. A phone book was attached to the booth by a steel cord. He pulled over to the booth and grabbed the book. The yellow pages were flipped to the hotel section. He found "Golden Travel Suites" and read the address out loud. "9834 Lamar Avenue." The page was ripped out of the book and stuffed in his pocket just in case he forgot the address along the way.

The hotel was just off the main strip and could easily be seen towering above all the other buildings around it. Had he known anything about the town, this hotel would have been the first he would have tried. It was no doubt the biggest and most luxurious in the area, and a star the magnitude of Jarard would certainly be able to afford the best.

Ramond exited onto Lamar Avenue. There were two entrances to the hotel. The first leading off the busy, main street of Lamar. The second headed off down a side road. He

VENGEANCE IS MINE

backed his car into a parking space closest to the side road, on the left side of the building from the entrance. It would provide the easiest escape route.

Before leaving the car, he grabbed a blue jean jacket he had brought along for the occasion. It had not been worn all year, but as he slid his arms into the sleeves he found it still fit. It was looser than he remembered, but the extra room came in handy as he took the bat out from under the seat and placed it inside the empty space of the jacket's front. The jean jacket was buttoned up over the bat, concealing it under the denim. In the pocket of the jacket, he had placed a pair of black knit gloves. They were a size too small, but with work he managed to slip them over his hands. The straight razor was shoved into his back pocket before he stepped out of the car.

Looking up at the building he counted the floors. Thirty-two in all. The place looked more like an office building than an hotel, but somehow it was just as he pictured it would be: tall and majestic.

Now was one of those times he needed to be lucky. Enough for no one to take notice of him. The bat was hidden, but still provided a large enough bulge to draw attention. His arms were folded over one another in an attempt to better hide it.

Ramond walked to the front revolving door nonchalantly and entered. The lobby was lavish. Filled with huge comfortable couches and a large screen T.V. locked on a twenty-four hour news station. On one of the sofa chairs a business man sat neatly decked out in an expensive suit with a lovely striped tie. His head was buried deep in the local paper and he took no notice as Ramond entered and passed by.

MICHAEL BISHOP

The registry desk was to the right of the entrance and was currently unoccupied. A door to an adjacent room could be seen on the other side of the counter. He walked swiftly passed the desk and perked his ears. In the room, the rustling of papers could be heard. Ramond knew it was not unusual for the registry clerks to be in the back room when there was no one to check in. It was another duty of the job to take care of the mountains of paper work that accumulated throughout the day. He browsed over the sign that said "Ring Bell for Service" as he headed for the pair of elevators on the far wall.

When he reached the lifts, Ramond was kissed securely on the lips by lady luck herself. It was unnerving that he would be so implausibly favored. It went against the nature of things. He had to rub his eyes to prove to himself it was actually there, but when he looked again, the sign still hung in place. It was hand written on plain white paper, but done in a neat calligraphy style. It hung on the right elevator stating "Out of Order".

That left only one alternative. Only one way for Mr. Jarard to get to his room. He would have take the left elevator, and then he would have to go through Ramond.

Ramond pressed the up button and stood to the side of the elevator with his back turned to its doors. If there were occupants in it when it opened, he wanted to maximize his chances that they would pass by without getting a good look. After twenty seconds the doors opened to an empty lift. At 1:45 in the afternoon, the hotel was deserted.

He stepped into the elevator and pushed the button for the top floor which housed the penthouse and higher priced rooms. He estimated that would give him about thirty seconds to make his move. He surveyed the elevator with reckless

VENGEANCE IS MINE

abandon: scanning the floor, the walls, the buttons, but particularly the top. The elevator was similar to the ones he had been in before, and like the others the roof contained the escape hatch, and that was another big break that he needed.

The bat was removed from its hiding place in his jacket. He drove the tip of it into the hatch and it popped open as if it were well-oiled. He tossed the bat through it and heard it clang on the top of the elevator overhead. He had never had a great vertical leap, but Ramond did manage to jump and grab the lip of the hatch in one try. The gloves hampered his hold, making him have to grip even harder to keep from falling. He pulled himself upward with all his arm's might. Noticeably, his body had grown lighter and he disappeared into the hole in seconds. The elevator began to slow as it reached the top floor, and he shut the hatch just as the doors opened.

He held his breath, fearing any noise would be noticed. Laying on his belly, he stared downward through a crack between the hatch and the elevator top. Two men entered the elevator. Both in business attire. Ramond could see every inch of the elevator from his view point. He watched as the taller of the two reached down and hit the button for the first floor. Neither had any idea they were being watched from above. The men engaged in idle chatter on the way down. When the doors opened at the bottom floor, they left into the lobby.

Ramond felt secure. No one would know he was on top of the elevator. There was no light in the shaft, allowing him to see down into the well-lit lift, but forbidding anyone to see him. He made himself as comfortable as possible, laying where he could keep everything below him in plain view. It would be a long wait. At least nine hours. Perhaps more. But in the meantime he would rest. When the time came, he would need every bit of strength his muscles could conjure.

☦ ☦ ☦ ☦ ☦ ☦ ☦ ☦ ☦ ☦ ☦ ☦

As the day progressed the hotel slowly began to fill. Last minute arrivals checked into their rooms and prepared to go to the concert. From his position above them, Ramond heard conversations from people who had driven from as far away as four hundred miles just to watch the man belch out his tunes. Little did they know, Ramond thought, they would be watching his last performance.

It was fascinating to watch people who did not know they were being watched. It was the only time in his life he had ever seen people being completely natural. Not putting on the fake exterior they always wore when others were around.

He was able to catch two young lovers kiss and grope each other in a mad rage of lust. If time had allowed the two would have stripped down and procreated right there on the elevator floor.

One man, who resembled a seventy-year-old version of Ringo Starr, stepped into the cabin with a terrible attack of gas. Ramond had to bite his tongue to keep from rioting with laughter as the man let it rip, one right after the other, and scratched his bottom through his trousers. Eventually the doors swung open and a middle-aged lady stepped on next to him. Ramond watched her with fascination, studying her reaction.

At first she did not notice the odor, but shortly after the doors closed, her nostrils picked up the scent with full knowledge of what it was she was smelling. Ramond pressed

VENGEANCE IS MINE

his eye down on the crack hard and watched closely as the woman tried to pretend she did not smell anything. Her eyes began to water and she sucked short breaths from her mouth. Her eyes refused to look at the man next to her. Ramond did not notice Ringo's reaction. Before he had a chance to look at the man, he turned away to keep from erupting in giggles and giving away his hiding place.

Eventually the two stepped out, but he smelled the scent of the man long into the day, floating upwards through the cracks toward his awaiting nose.

He held his camouflage watch up to the crack and attempted to read it with what little light pushed through the hole. His guess was right. It was just past five. The hotel began to fill rapidly now. People crammed into the elevator like cattle into a pen. Eyes locked in front of them, fearing to make eye contact with the strangers that stood so dangerously close.

The traffic flowed through the elevator until six thirty. At around seven the place became a morgue again, as everyone filed out of their rooms and headed to the coliseum where Jarard would be arriving shortly.

In an hour, thousands of loving fans would be screaming the name of Jarard. Cheering and offering their undying love for him and their God. While here Ramond lay, on top of a dark, damp elevator shaft, with nothing to keep him company but the monotony of the elevator's *"Ding"*.

Someday though...Someday it would be different. Someday they would all know his name. None other would be on the lips of the people of the world but that of Ramond. If not out of love and admiration, then out of fear.

MICHAEL BISHOP

✝ ✝ ✝ ✝ ✝ ✝ ✝ ✝ ✝ ✝ ✝ ✝

A cleaning woman stepped onto the elevator around nine o'clock, pushing a soapy water-filled bucket with a mop in its center. The black lady had a checkered bandanna tied around her head in a do-rag. Her back was hunched over and the wrinkles in her face and hands were deep, like valleys carved out by time and weather. From her lips she sang versus of "Amazing Grace" better than anyone Ramond had ever heard, including Jarard. It was truly a joyous sound. A song so sweet it could nearly bring a tear to a dry eye.

The song came close to lulling Ramond to sleep. But just seconds after the doors closed and the hoist began moving upwards, the woman abruptly stopped the tune. Ramond bounded back to alertness and peered down, wondering why she had stopped. She seemed bewildered, like a horse spooked by something unknown in the woods. She swung her head to the left. Then to the right. Looking for something invisible, it seemed.

Ramond held his breath again. Something was awry. Not quite feeling right. Impulsively her head snapped straight upward toward the hatch as if it had been pulled by some unseen rope. She stared directly at the hatch, but it was more than that. She stared directly into Ramond's eyes.

It was impossible, he thought. There was no way she could know he was there. He was silent, and the darkness of the shaft would cloak him well enough from even the most acute eyes. But the woman *was* staring, right at the spot his eyeball rested. She stared for several seconds...seconds that seemed like an eternity.

The *"Ding"* caught her attention. Her head once again whipped back down to the doors as they opened before her.

VENGEANCE IS MINE

She made a hasty retreat from the elevator and went about her way, shaking her head like even she did not believe what she had done.

A flashback struck Ramond. Another little tidbit his mother had shared with him during his youth.

"You know, Ramond. Those of us who are pure can sometimes sense evil. It's like vibes or aura I guess. If a really bad or evil person is around me, sometimes I can just feel it. It's hard to explain, but it makes you feel dirty, or depressed. Almost like there's a weight pushing itself down on you. I've met a few people like that, and I wanted nothing more than to get the heck away from them as fast as I could," she related long ago.

At the time, like most things she said to him, it meant nothing. But sooner or later her words came back to haunt him in one particular situation or another.

It was possible, he supposed, that the woman *had* felt him. After all he certainly *did* feel her. The way she sang. The way she looked. The elderly black woman just made you feel relaxed and safe. Maybe he too had an aura about him. But was he evil? The thought rattled him. He had never thought himself an evil person; although he knew very well the things he was doing were to an extent, wicked.

But the thought that the things he had done made him a bad person never really occurred to him. At most he was ambitious, but certainly not evil.

Regardless, if the woman had known he was there, she certainly was not going to tell anybody. If she were to go to her boss and tell him "I felt an evil presence hiding in the elevator shaft," they would more likely lock her up in the insane asylum than take heed to her words. Ramond's position was still safe. But the incident did linger in his mind.

MICHAEL BISHOP

✝ ✝ ✝ ✝ ✝ ✝ ✝ ✝ ✝ ✝ ✝

At ten thirty he checked his watch again. The nervousness came back with a vengeance. It would soon be time. The concert would have ended by now, and experience told him that about this time thousands of elated spectators would be drying their eyes with Kleenex and toilet paper as they made their way back to their cars. There would be a buzz of excitement, and everyone would feel just a little bit better about themselves and about one another.

And by now, the lobby would have been roped off and cleared, allowing Jarard to make his way to his room before all the other hotel patrons got a chance to retire. They would be lined up outside the doors of the hotel, along with all the other fans who were smart enough to discover where Jarard was staying, just as Ramond had done.

It was evident by the fact no one had entered the elevator in the past fifteen minutes that the moment was near. Ramond began trying, just as he had done in the other tests, to psyche himself into a frenzy. This time he focused on the bat. What it meant. What it stood for.

He remembered how Brian Jamison had looked at him, full of disgust and shame. He recalled the promise he made to himself to make his father proud, and how over the years, no matter how hard he tried or what he did, nothing was ever quite good enough.

The memories of his father's rejection began to flow. Ramond's heart began to pump blood through his veins like a fireman's hose pumping water on a blaze. He grasped the bat tightly in his right hand and made sure the blade was secure in his back pocket with his left.

The T-ball bat was once a child's toy. But now as he

VENGEANCE IS MINE

focused his anger on it, the shaft of steel would serve as a lightning rod for the expulsion of years of frustration and hatred.

    The elevator began to drop. All the way down to the lobby floor. Two seconds before the doors slid open, he felt the man on the other side. His aura pulsed strongly. So strongly that it transcended the barriers between him and the man. Ramond thought to himself, *You really can feel people!* It was an astonishing discovery, but it did not lower the violent level he felt in his soul.

    The doors opened and a large man stepped inside first. It was not Jarard. Ramond knew by feeling as well as sight. A man stepped in directly behind the large man. Ramond recognized him. The man was older and fifteen pounds heavier than he had been when Ramond had seen him last, but he was still unmistakable. Dressed in a solid white suit with a white band collar underneath his jacket. The outfit seemed to glow in the flourescent light. Jarard had just entered the trap. Ramond was the hunter.

    The large man reached over and pressed the top floor button. Once again Ramond had gotten lucky. If there had been two body guards, he would have had a problem. But with just one, Ramond felt the odds were in his favor. Perhaps Jarard felt no one wished him any harm and he did not need an abundance of protection. He was wrong, and it was a mistake he would pay dearly for.

    The doors closed slowly and the elevator lurched upward. Ramond made his way to his knees, then to his feet. He crouched to the left of the hatch, never taking his eyes off the big man. He would be the first target. Once eliminated, the prize would be his for the taking.

MICHAEL BISHOP

The hinges of the hatch did not squeak as Ramond lifted it and pulled it all the way open. Jarard and the big man stood silently. Both tired from a long day. Neither noticed blackness opening above them. Ramond quickly eyed the spot he would land. It was clear. The big man stood just one foot back from the spot. They were both positioned like bowling pins purposely set up to be knocked down.

Ramond choked up on the bat and prepared his left hand to steady himself as he hit the ground. He had to hurry. The big man must be taken care of before the elevator reached the top. He took a deep breath, looked straight down, and leapt into action.

The bat was set in motion well before Ramond's feet touched the elevator floor. Its shaft sliced through the air in all directions like a drunken firefly attempting to hover a pattern.

"ARHHHHHHRRRR," the big man bellowed as the figure appeared before him as if it had materialized from thin air. The bodyguard lounged backward smashing his shoulder and head into the walls of the elevator. The bat struck him in the jaw a millisecond before the soles of Ramond's shoes met the bottom of the lift. Ramond's knees buckled and he fell to his back, cracking his head against the steel doors and lashing his neck forward with an awful sprang.

Jarard let out no cries of surprise or fear. He handled the situation as calmly as if it were common place to him. He placed his back in the nearest corner and covered his face, expecting his bodyguard to take care of the situation before it got out of hand.

The big man's jaw had been dislocated, and the pain stunned him just long enough for Ramond to shake off his

VENGEANCE IS MINE

own painful landing and regain his feet. The guard placed a hand inside his tailored jacket and placed all five of his huge digits around the butt of the nine millimeter held securely in his shoulder holster. Ramond began frantically swinging again, striking nothing as he had done with the ball on the tee. The guard easily dodged most of the swings and unsnapped the strap that held the gun in its holder with his thumb.

The light overhead reflected off the silvery polished barrel of the gun and caught Ramond's eyes like tinsel would a baby. It gave him a target to swing at and he gracefully brought the bat down on the barrel of the gun.

"OAAAWWWWWW SHHHITTT," the big man let out as the trigger loop snapped his index finger in two. The gun fell to the center of the elevator with a heavy thud, but with the safety still on, it refused to fire.

The man swung at Ramond with a meaty chop from his left hand. Ramond watched the blow as it slowly rumbled toward him and held the bat horizontally in front of him as a shield. The fist smashed into the rod crushing the guard's hand; but also causing enough force to reel Ramond back into the doors, roughly striking the steel with his head again.

Ramond knew the top floor had to be close. It was crunch time. If the doors were allowed to open, there was bound to be someone on the other side who could lend a hand to the singer.

The big man whined as he held his tattered fist in the grip of his other. For the moment he was vulnerable. Ramond seized the second, stepping forward and aiming his blow for the man's temple. The lug did not bother to block. His shattered hands would not let themselves take any more abuse. The bat collided with a sick "PLOMP" near his right eye. He fell instantly, head bouncing off the floor as the weight of his huge body forced it down with great velocity. Ramond had knocked a home run.

He wasted no time and spun. The digital numbers read 30. He was too close to the top for comfort. Like an expert billiard player, he grabbed the bat as if it were a pool cue. One hand on its back, one resting in the center. He pushed forward with his back hand letting the other one guide it as the tip aimed for the emergency stop button. The button was noticeably larger than the other buttons. An easy mark. The elevator grinded to a sudden halt as the bat firmly pressed it in, trapped somewhere between the 31st and 32nd floors.

Ramond let out a deep breath and relaxed for a moment. His head was throbbing and his neck would surely punish him later. Had it not been for the element of surprise, he could never have taken the monstrous bodyguard, even with the bat. So he allowed himself a short stretch.

Ramond heard a noise behind him and spun to meet it. He had forgotten, just for a second, about his victim that cowered behind him. But a second of hesitation was all it had taken. Jarard was on his knees with the handle of the nine-millimeter in his palm. The barrel of the weapon was aimed directly at Ramond's head and Jarard squeezed the trigger with a grip that had grown strong from decades of gripping a microphone.

Terror glazed Ramond's features. He saw death. But not with a proud ending as he had always imagined. But with a dreadfully sad ending; dying as a criminal, a degenerate, a failure.

But as Jarard pulled the trigger and released it, the hammer sat silent. In all his years in the ministry, Jarard had never once fired a gun. His protection was always left in the

VENGEANCE IS MINE

hands of others, leaving no need for him to take the responsibility upon himself to learn defense.

Not only did he not know how to remove the safety, but he did not even know one existed on the gun. Confusion paraded inside him. He pulled the trigger again... and again. It made only a faint click and refused to fire.

Jarard was baffled and insane with panic. It didn't make sense. Why was God letting this happen to him? Why was the weapon betraying him in the face of his attacker?

Jarard's eyes rose to meet Ramond's and in that instant they both understood. Ramond was in control. The hunter not the prey. Both men knew it as surely as they knew what would happen next.

Ramond hesitated no longer and brought the bat down on the crown of the head of Jarard Collins. The singer entered twilight. It only took one blow.

The first order of business was to check the big man. The shot to the temple was treading on dangerous boundaries. It was a blow that could definitely kill a man. Ramond kneeled and placed his ear to the man's chest. His heart beat vibrantly inside him. He was alive. When he woke he would need medical attention, and probably wouldn't remember who he was for awhile. But he was alive, and it eased Ramond's conscience greatly to know he was not a killer.

He moved rapidly to take care of the second order of business. The elevators stalling would quickly raise suspicion. He maneuvered expeditiously to the singer.

Ramond had no medical knowledge and it scared him. One wrong nick or cut here or there and the man could bleed to death. It was highly uncomfortable. Not only had Satan expressly warned him not to kill the man, but he truly did not want to kill the man. Murder was an act done by only the vilest of the vile. The taking of life was horrid to him. He could not fathom how someone could take so much from a person. It was worse than stealing, or maiming, or rape, or anything. At least with the others you left the person something. With murder, you took everything from them. Their family, their possessions, their love, hate, emotions... their breath. No, Ramond was convinced he must be very careful and he proceeded with caution.

Jarard was turned onto his back and drug to the center of the elevator where the light was the best. Ramond stared at the man, for the first time really getting a good look at him. Jarard had stayed youthful for his age. Time had been a friend to him. For a man his age the wrinkles should have dug their trenches by now; but in the performer's face, the signs of time had refused to take their damage. It sent a message to Ramond. This was what it was like to live without stress. To know you are loved and think nothing bad will ever happen to you. But it also taught Ramond that it was sometimes good to worry. The moment you stop watching your back is usually the moment someone stabs you in it.

The razor was removed from his pocket and fully extended. He grabbed the bottom of the singer's jaw and opened it as wide as it would go. Jarard's breath blew warm up in Ramond's face, full of lemon and seltzer water.

The tongue was pulled out of his mouth as far as he could stretch it. Ramond examined it closely, looking at the tip of it, then the bottom, and back to the top again. He had no idea how fast it took to bleed to death. Nor did he have any idea which part was best to cut. It would be a surgery of

VENGEANCE IS MINE

ignorance.

He noticed underneath the tongue was a string of flesh about two inches from the front of the tongue. It seemed to keep it from being pulled out any farther. Ramond decided it would be best to cut as little of that as he could. It looked important, like it may bleed excessively if he tampered with it too much. The two inches should be enough. Even if it meant he could still talk a little, it would definitely mean he would never sing again.

He ripped Jarard's pocket square from his jacket pocket and began sponging off the tongue. The organ was slimy and hard to get a good grip on. As much spittle was removed from it as possible with the silk rag, and Ramond grasped the tip of it as tightly as he could.

The blade was placed two inches up on the top at the tongue. He began sawing the razor back and forth; as if it were a hacksaw and he were doing nothing more than trimming a scrap of lumber. The blood did not spurt and he relaxed his arms somewhat, pulling himself closer to his work.

About halfway through the tongue it began to spew more, shooting blood on his chin and bottom of his shirt. Quickly, the sawing method was abandoned as he tried to hack the rest of it off with haste.

He pressed down three more times firmly making a deeper incision each time. On the third push, the member came off in Ramond's hand and the blood poured from the end as if someone had turned on a tap.

Ramond grabbed Jarard by the shoulder and rolled him onto his stomach in hopes he would not choke to death on his own blood. The former singer did not stir or move a muscle, oblivious to what was being done. Jarard's mind rested in the outer limits; a place where even the pain of having your tongue removed was not sufficient to bring you back.

The pocket square was stuffed in Jarard's mouth to slow the bleeding some. Ramond jumped back to his feet and closed the blade. He shoved it into his left front pocket and shoved the chunk of tongue into his right.

The button marked "2" was pressed. The elevator responded and began to drop. The lift fell fast. Much faster, Ramond thought, than it should. *Get a grip, Ramond*, he told himself. The pressure was mounting. He had done the deed. Now if he got caught, the consequences would be serious.

The numbers fell "7"... "6"... "5"...

On "4" he clenched the bat from the floor, then aimed toward the door in a runner's stance. If the doors opened and someone was waiting on the second floor, he would attempt to barrel past them before they had a chance to take a look inside the elevator. As an added precaution, he placed his hand in front of his face. It was better if they did not have a chance to get a look at him.

The elevator slowed its descent and the numbers slowly rolled over to "2". His heart thumped with anticipation. The *"Ding"* greeted him one last time and the doors crept open like a curtain to the finale of a Broadway play.

No one stood on the other side of the door. The hall was as empty as a beggar's cupboard. That stood to reason with all the guests being held below until Jarard had time to reach his room.

Ramond dropped his runner's stance and stood at ease. He hit the button marked "1" and stepped off the elevator

VENGEANCE IS MINE

before the doors could close him in. The sooner Jarard was discovered, the sooner he would receive medical attention and the less likely he would be to die. Ramond pushed the lobby floor button in hopes that this would speed up the process. Unfortunately, it also meant he would have to speed up his escape.

He bolted to the door marked "In case of emergency use stairs" and flung himself down a flight. At the bottom there were two doors. One with a sign "First Floor Lobby". The other marked "Emergency Exit."

As he opened the emergency exit door, he felt the cool evening air blow against his neck. Through the lobby door behind him he heard a woman's voice scream "Oh my God!", followed by other similar cries of despair. The door slammed behind him, ending his ability to hear what else was going on inside.

The escape door led to the rear of the building where garbage dumpsters and trash lined the back outside wall. A few cars had been forced to park in the back due to limited space on the sides and front. But all the vehicles were unoccupied and Ramond was the only person visible.

He rounded the corner, spotting his car before all else. It had been surrounded by other vehicles during the time he waited in the shaft; but it was easily recognized as the street light shined down on it. A few stragglers stood on the side of the building, either facing the front, or attempting to make their way toward it.

The commotion in front of the building buzzed through the night and everyone rushed to the entrance to discover what all the excitement was about.

The police cars could not be seen from Ramond's side, but their lights were flashing blue, stretching out into the road

MICHAEL BISHOP

and covering the night. Ramond unlocked his car, threw the bat over the seat, and sat inside; hoping he would not be noticed in all the confusion. No one seemed to pay him any attention as he cranked his engine and left through the deserted side road, disappearing into the back streets.

† † † † † † † † † † † †

"SOMETIMES EVEN THE ANGELS CRY"

Two ambulances arrived on the scene five minutes later. Jarard was taken in the first. The big man was taken in the second. Despite the precautions, Jarard Collins almost died anyway. By the time he had reached the hospital his blood loss was critical. It was an uphill climb, but the doctors fought to keep him alive, with the help of a few transfusions. It was a miracle he survived.

His supporters were crushed by the tragedy. When the news leaked to the media, the town of Glenada, Mississippi became a circus of news reporters and cameras. The event was seen on every news station worldwide, and the crime was hailed as the largest tragedy to ever hit the Christian music industry. Many of his fans turned away from God and the church, disillusioned with a God that would let someone so dedicated and loyal fall upon so tragic a fate. If it could happen to Jarard, it could happen to them, so why bother?

But others were more supportive, wanting to do anything they could to help. People from all over the world sent money in to Jarard's ministry. Over a million dollars came in within a few months of the incident, allowing the operation to carry on for a few months longer. But in all, the money raised was a fraction of what would have been raised

VENGEANCE IS MINE

if the singer would have been allowed to keep making records and concert appearances.

When the newness of the story had worn off, the press dropped it. With the lack of publicity, the public's interest in helping out slacked as well. Virtually no money came in after the cease of the press coverage, and within two years the Jarard ministry had collapsed, serving as just one more slap in the face to the man.

Jarard, who was unmarried, lived the rest of his life a recluse. His savings were adequate to support him for years, especially now that he never went out. He used the money to pay for regular visits by a cleaning lady and a nurse. The groceries were delivered to his door. The lawn was taken care of by a service, and all his clothing was ordered through the mail. Times were rare that he left his house for any reason. The world had become too painful for him to live in. Facing people was too hard.

The doctors were unable to restore his speech. He talked so slurred and inaudibly that if you did not listen closely, you would never understand a word he uttered.

Eventually he took to writing down everything he wanted to say. It was too heartbreaking to try to make people understand him.

Television evangelists tried to coax him out into the public eye. They begged him to appear on their shows, and said it was his duty to tell people how God gave him the strength to overcome his tragedy and be an inspiration to others.

But the truth was, Jarard never did get over the tragedy. It haunted him all his days. It was torture to hear his

MICHAEL BISHOP

voice on CD, singing a beautiful song, and know he would never sing again.

He refused the requests to be on television. It would be pathetic to hear one of his old songs being played to remind the audience what a great singer/song writer he *once* was. The last thing he wanted was to be used to solicit contributions from people who felt pity for him. He just wanted to be left alone.

Eleven years after his tongue was removed from him in that elevator in Glenada, Jarard Collins died peacefully in his bed. Upon examining the house, a massive collection of songs he had written over the last decade was discovered. The lyrics were never shown to anyone. Jarard was too ashamed that he would never be able to record them for all the world to hear. After his death, they were made public and were recorded by various artists on a special Christian album entitled "The Songs of Jarard, A Tribute."

One of the songs was number one on the religious charts for thirty-two weeks. It was sung by Terresa Colts, who inherited the title of the most popular gospel singer in the world after Jarard's fall from grace. The song told of the pain and agony Jarard felt. It told how he never gave up on God. And it told how sometimes we all hurt.

The chorus said:

It's hard to think about the misery.
But I know in my heart that He's always there for me.
When life is cruel and you don't know why.
Just remember sometimes even the angels cry.

Ten months after he was buried in his home state of

VENGEANCE IS MINE

Maine, "Sometimes Even the Angels Cry" became the most popular song of Jarard's career.

THE DARK ROAD

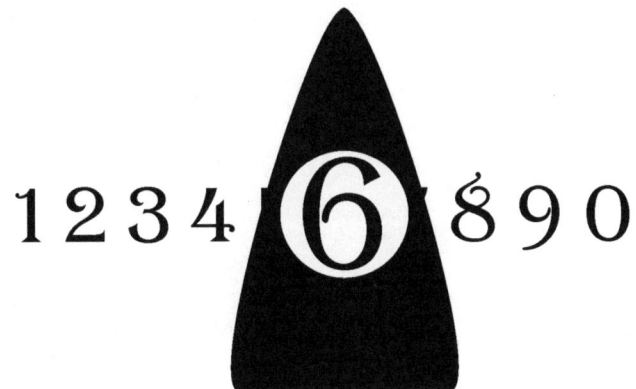

1 2 3 4 6 8 9 0

The side road Ramond had exited from led to a residential neighborhood. Every street seemed to lead to a dead end. When he turned around and attempted to retrace his steps, he never seemed to end up in the same place he started. Finally, he managed to follow behind a car that had just pulled out of its driveway. The vehicle led him out of the maze of streets that made up the subdivision. Because of the setback the trip home took him twenty minutes longer than the trip down had.

††††††††††††

About forty miles down the interstate he remembered the tip of the tongue that had been stashed in his pocket. Suddenly he could feel it, pressing down on his leg through his pants, like some loathsome sea slug caught tragically out of its natural habitat. Ramond suddenly wanted the thing away from him, and quickly.

MICHAEL BISHOP

He rolled down the window and looked in his rear view mirror for signs of spectators. There were taillights a few miles behind him and brake lights several hundred feet in front. It was safe.

Ramond straightened his leg out to make reaching in his pocket easier. The gloves had been removed and placed in the glove box, so with a bare hand he glided a path down his leg, anticipating grabbing a cold, snot-like object. Instead, the tongue had dried out and become almost scaly, like the skin of a reptile. He pulled it out with a jerk. It was still squishy, like the gummy bears kept in his pocket as a child and eaten warm and melted at the end of a hard day's play. The thought made him queasy and he chucked the thing out the window without looking at it.

A third of a mile from where he had dropped his cargo, a sign caught his attention. "Five hundred dollar fine for littering on the Interstate". Had the situation been different, Ramond may have found the irony of the sign amusing. Possibly even laughed at it. But with the thought of what he had done, and the fear of getting caught still pounding him, he was in no mood for laughter.

† † † † † † † † † † † †

The sun rose before him as he reached his parking space. It was the first sunrise he had seen in ages. Years of partying all night and sleeping all day had robbed him of the pleasure. It was gorgeous. Like the universe was giving birth to a whole new day.

Even though he was exhausted beyond belief, a smile could not be pried from his face. He was over the hump. Three to go. So far he had performed beyond his wildest

THE DARK ROAD

expectations. Things he thought he would never be able to do were accomplished with skill. Ramond had taken down a man twice his size. In a way he was like David and the huge bodyguard had been his Goliath. The taste of victory was sweet upon his lips.

As he entered his room, he removed every stitch of clothing he had on. Bare-ass to the world, he stood in the center of his room with nothing but his amulet hugging his neck as he went to work gathering his tin garbage can and placing it in the middle of the apartment. The contents of the can-garbage, rotting fruit, wrappers-were overflowing. He dumped the mess out onto the floor and replaced the trash with his pile of clothes. A match was struck and held to the others, setting the entire matchbook on fire. Moments after he had tossed the book into the can, the clothes were ablaze. All evidence of his activities was eradicated in the flames.

In the back pocket of his burning jeans, the razor turned a glowing red in the fire. It too was cleaned of all proof. Ramond was not concerned with returning it to its rightful owner.

Ramond laid his naked body on top of the filthy mattress and dozed magnificently. When he woke it was 5:30 A.M., twenty-three hours later.

Never had he slept so long. Without waking to go to the bathroom. Without waking up to change positions. Without any noise disturbing his slumber. He was a new person. Rested and ready to attack life again with zest and

MICHAEL BISHOP

energy.

It had been nearly a month since he had been in the presence of Satan and he dearly missed it. It was hard at times, but despite all the tricks that his master liked to play, and through all the pain he received, it was still a billion times better than any drug he had ever ingested.

Disappointment that his father had not tried to contact him served as the only dampening of his *life* high. But the master kept no schedule, and Ramond knew that when his sire wished to contact him, he would. Until then, there were other matters of reality to deal with.

His belly scolded him for not feeding it for such a long stretch. It had reached hunger levels that were one step from becoming malnutrition. If he did not satisfy its lust for rations soon, he would pay dearly later.

In town there was only one place open at this hour. Ramond grabbed his keys and headed for it. The joint was yet another burger chain that insisted on serving more grease than actual meat, but its saving factor was the fact that it stayed open twenty-four hours a day, seven days a week. Even on Christmas morning, some pimply-faced, prepubescent kid who had been duped into working, stood ready to take your order in his nice, neat, regulation paper hat.

Squealing tires stirred the neighbors as Ramond raced the car out of the parking lot, onto the main road. His hunger had taken on a demonic fervor of its on. It was in control as he became lead footed on the gas pedal.

The road belonged to Ramond. No one could be seen coming or going. In larger cities, traffic never left the streets, and at this time of the morning, traffic jams had already started. But in Sierra Springs, there was no such thing as a traffic jam. The coined phrase "Sleepy Little Town" fit it

THE DARK ROAD

perfectly. Not even the garbage men bothered to get up until six thirty in the morning. As long as the sun was down, so was everyone else.

☦ ☦ ☦ ☦ ☦ ☦ ☦ ☦ ☦ ☦ ☦

Three football fields in the distance, a traffic light posed the only obstacle. He watched as the quarter sized light turned from green, to yellow, to red.

"Come on change, bitch, change," he talked aloud, trying to coax the light into returning green before he reached it.

As the light drew closer, he observed it with astonishment. The red was an odd color. Unlike any shade he had ever witnessed. Orange was wrapped in the color as well, giving off a bright, glowing illumination.

At first glance, the wind seemed to be shaking the traffic light; but upon closer inspection, it were as if the lights inside that were actually moving. Twitching and swaying left and right. Dancing for spectacle in mid-air. Flickering like candle wicks.

It was clear now. Ramond realized they were burning. Inside the confines of the traffic light he was seeing the same patterns of burning as he had seen in the bush in his dream. The lights were not lights at all, but windows into another place.

Something inside him forced down on the gas pedal harder, and this time it was not the rebellion of his stomach. The car fled down the road like a convict making a jail break. He sailed toward the light, and although his mind very badly wanted to slam on the breaks and turn the car around... Ramond could not stop.

MICHAEL BISHOP

The speedometer broke ninety for the first time in nine years. Normally the car's engine was sluggish, even resistant to building speed. But new life had been breathed into the metal, and it hummed with a soft purr even a new car could not mimic.

The lights were only feet away, and he knew when he passed beneath them something would happen. Ramond didn't know what. But he did know his master was once again creating a scenario through which he could be contacted.

An eye dropped to the digital clock on the dashboard. 5:47 it reported. He took only a brief look at it before he was upon the traffic light. The road just below it was blurry and wavy, like heat rising up from a hot sidewalk. But there was no heat, only the usual cool morning temperature the fall carried with it each year.

As he passed under the light, the entire section shattered as if he had slammed directly into a gigantic mirror. The car jolted viciously like he had run over a speed bump but did not slow. The particles of the road and air around it exploded in all directions into an infinite number of pieces. Every molecule spread out on either side of the car and disappeared, leaving another world open before him.

His gape-mouthed face could only stare ahead in confusion and wonder what had happened. The road that was once there had disappeared and another, dark path had taken its place.

Ramond peered in the rear view mirror as his car continued down the shadowy road. In the distance behind him, he could see the road he had been on a moment before. A rip in time and space had been opened. Jagged portions of the opening hung like a huge pane of glass that had had its center busted in with a brick. He watched it for several

THE DARK ROAD

moments, until each piece reassembled back into its place and the hole sealed up behind him. Now all his vision beheld was the dark road stretching forever behind him.

The speedometer was spinning out of control. *Must be doing at least a hundred and twenty*, he thought. But the old Ford seemed not to notice and zipped along as if it were pushing no more than thirty-five.

For the first time he took heed to the road he was now on, looking out the side window at his new surroundings. There was something out there. Something moving. He squinted hard and peered out into the vast area on the left side of the road.

When he saw *them* for the first time, he knew exactly what they were. It was instinctive, like a salmon swimming up stream.

They were not human but they *were* humanoid. They had the same appendages as a man: two arms, two legs, one head. And they walked erect like a man, although badly hunched over. But that was where the similarities began and ended.

They had no skin as their outer covering. Instead, a mass of tissue hung from their frames in globs, like soggy clay. It seemed that the bulk of their substance would fall off and be left behind them. But somehow the slimy chunks of meat stayed on with no real shell to keep them together.

It was apparent that the things were souls. But not normal souls: *His souls.*

There was no sun in this place, but the things lit up the atmosphere as though it was always day. Each one glowed with its own distinct color. There were scores of them, but Ramond could not remember seeing two colors exactly the same. They were everywhere. A sea of walking monsters. He looked out to each side of the road and scanned as far as his eyes would allow. Like massive waves, the lights gave the illusion of flowing back and forth over the ocean of beings as they bobbed up and down to take another step.

But the frightening part was not that their numbers were inconceivable. And it wasn't that they were grossly deformed. The truly terrible fact was that each one of the hideous fiends was headed in the same direction. All in unison. Walking the same speed as if they heard a call that they must answer. And the direction they were headed was the exact same path Ramond was traveling. The road to Hell's gates.

When he finally got up enough nerve to look in front of him to see where he was going, the sight was so distinct in nature that it was unmistakable. It was Hell. Or at least the image he had always had of what Hell would look like. As a child, when he attempted to conjure up an image of a lake of fire, his brain always sent the same vision. That vision was identical to what sat before Ramond at the end of the road.

It was even brighter than what he had imagined; and even though it was still a good twenty miles away, the flames could be seen as clearly as if they were just a few feet. Normally such a light would overcome the eyes, forcing them to shut. But somehow the brightness did not disturb the pupils. It was soothing. Alluring. Beautiful.

The land all around it was too flat to have been created by accident. For as far as one could span, the fire stretched across the horizon like a tremendous forest fire burning out of control.

Ramond knew why the souls went toward it. His initial guess had been right after all. They were being called.

THE DARK ROAD

Not by some mystical voice or musical siren. But by the graceful dance of the flames. It was a choreographed number. A mixture of ballet, tap, ballroom, and all other great gambols. The flames tempted. Spoke of whatever your heart desired. They were impossible to pull away from.

The speedometer continued to spin, even though it normally pegged at ninety-five and refused to go further. The air was stale. Smelling of despair and regret. From inside the car no sound could be heard, except the low rumble of the motor. This world was in solitude.

"WELCOME, RAMOND!" the voice burst the back window as if an arrow had been shot through it. The car vibrated with each syllable. Every word brought thunder to Ramond's ears, but he tried to show no fear or pain.

"Thank you, Sire," he spoke in a low, humbled manner.

"Sorry about that. I'll try to tone it down a bit for you. After all you are still human. At least for now. It's just that my power is so great here. Of all the places in the universe that I inhabit, this is one where I have no equals. This is my domicile," Satan spoke more quietly, but still loud enough to be heard kilometers away.

"I am honored to be in your home, Lord."

"Well you're not actually in my home. Yet. Right now you are on the outskirts. Very symbolic of your life in the outside world. Wouldn't you say?"

"Yes. Sire." Ramond replied, understanding fully what the master meant.

"It's been a long while since we have spoken. But fear not. I have not forgotten our bargain, and I am happy to see you have not either."

MICHAEL BISHOP

"No, Sire. The bargain will never be forgotten. I'm close. Three more and I will have what is rightfully mine," Ramond impressed himself with how brave he had grown. The last act had strengthened him noticeably.

"Three more indeed, my boy. But you're not home free yet... Let me ask you a question."

"Anything."

"How is your conscience?"

"Conscience? I'm not sure I follow you, Lord," he replied puzzled.

"Come now. With all the things you've done, there must be some little bubbles of guilt floating around inside you, waiting for an opportune moment to burst and ruin everything."

"There's no guilt. What I do, I do for you... and in all honesty I do for myself as well. There is no guilt." But Ramond knew Satan knew he was lying. It was his nature to feel guilty. If he didn't think about it, things were fine. But when his mind did force the thought, the guilt trotted in behind it like a lost puppy looking for a home.

"Come on, Ramond. Who do you think you're kidding here. You've been a very, very naughty boy."

The words reminded him of his mother's voice that once scolded his mind. The nagging in his head had subsided years ago, and it was maddening to have the memory drudged up by the one being who should understand what he had to deal with.

"I've only done what you've ordered!" Ramond insisted. Not quite sure why Satan was treating him in this manner.

"What was going through your mind when you were raping that sweet, thirteen year old girl? Ohhh, how juicy she

THE DARK ROAD

must have been. I can only wonder what it was like beating her and then taking her purity forever. So tell me... What were you thinking?" The voice was sinister, like a detective attempting to coax a confession from a criminal.

"I wasn't thinking anything... I mean... I just did what you said... Isn't that what I was supposed to do?" He fought to justify himself. Confusion spun in him. Why was he being interrogated?

The car pounded forward even faster and Ramond could feel gravity tug his head backward. At this rate, he would reach the gates in no time. But his main concern was his master's words as the questioning continued.

"Did you enjoy it?"

"I... I don't know... Maybe to some degree. But..."

"Well *you* may not know, but *I* do. You did enjoy yourself. You enjoyed raping that girl. And it scares you. It makes you feel guilty to think that you might just be becoming... let's say... a bad boy."

"If I experienced pleasure, it is only because I am trapped inside this physical body. But what I did, I did for you. Not for foolish ecstacy. Soon, when I am not bound by this body, I will not be bothered by such mortal distractions." It was an explosive answer. Bursting from him like a balloon that could hold no more air. Ramond was pleased with himself. Under fire, he felt he handled himself well.

"Well said. But forget not, at this moment the only thing that separates you from those souls outside your window is your flesh. That is why I have caused your car to run at such a speed. They would do anything to get their hands on your flesh. To make you into what they are. Misery loves company. So heed my advice... Don't stop the car!"

Ramond took his eyes off the fire ahead and studied

the monsters once more. *Are these what souls really look like?* he wondered intently. It was terrible to think that inside his body lived an invisible thing that looked like the slugs that surrounded his car.

"Is this what a soul looks like?" He had to ask. The image would not leave him until he knew for sure.

"Some souls do, yes. But they are not born looking this way. Some blossom from wretched caterpillars to elegant butterflies. Some die inside their cocoon and are left in an in-between stage of hideousness. These failures died in a cocoon of sin before they could blossom. But while they were living, they did not serve me as you do. And as you know, I take special care in death of those who follow me in life."

Ramond took a breath of relief. Satan had reminded him of what he already knew. The reason he followed Satan to begin with, besides the power, was the promise. The promise that those who die in sin and did not serve him will be punished beyond comprehension upon death. But those who choose to serve him on Earth, will have riches beyond what Heaven can offer when they pass to the other side.

"But back to the topic at hand!" the voice erupted loudly, cracking a passenger window. "Do you feel guilty for what you have done?"

"I may feel some guilt. But once again, that is only because I'm trapped on an earthly plane with an earthly body. You have my word, guilt will not get in my way."

"Pretty words. But I know how you were raised. And I know that you have tendencies to be overwhelmed with shame. I was there that day many years ago at BookPlus, when you almost ran away because of your mother's voice. I saw the look of panic in your eyes when you thought you were doing something wrong."

THE DARK ROAD

Ramond's jaw dropped. A shock of surprise took over his system. How was it possible that anyone knew of his mother's voice? It was the one secret he had coveted his entire life more than any. A mixture of embarrassment and anger leaked in. For a moment no words could be found. But after a moment of silence he returned fire.

"I WAS ONLY TWELVE!" he screamed before he realized who he was talking to. Fear dropped the level in his voice back to calm almost immediately after the first words were released. "I'm sorry. I did not mean to raise my voice. But I have not heard those voices of guilt since I was thirteen years old. As I was taught by Johnny and learned more about you, they disappeared along with all ties to my mother. I swear to you, guilt will never get in the way of serving you. And it will never get in the way of my quest."

"Good enough. I do, actually, believe you. But none the less, the next one is a huge leap from the nickel and dime things I've had you do."

"Anything," Ramond promised.

"I wish you to take a life."

Ramond was not surprised to hear these words. After all, it was the next logical step. It was the task he hoped he would not have to do most of all. Killing was a test he would not do for his master. It was a test he would not even do for himself. But it was something he would do for the power. The lust for it was the guiding force of his existence. With that knowledge firmly at hand, he continued forth.

"Fine. Who?" he replied bluntly, not bothering to hide the fact he was not happy about it.

"When you arrive home, open your phone book to the *"P's"*. I want you to kill the second Mark Peters in the white pages."

MICHAEL BISHOP

"How would you like it done?" he asked blandly. If he was going to go through the trouble, he was going to get it right.

"I really could not care less how you kill him. As long as he is dead by tomorrow, I will be satisfied."

Ramond had grown so preoccupied with the conversation that he had forgotten that he was almost to the gates of Hell. It was a notion that took him from his angry sulking, to a thirst to reach the fire. He watched its dance with loving. Its rhythms were beyond sexual. They were all the pleasures of taste, touch, smell, feel, sight, and sound, blended into one array of bliss.

"Ah, I see you have once again become hypnotized by my brilliant creation," the voice spoke softly. Ramond hardly noticed it speaking as his foot pressed the gas even harder in an attempt to reach the gates faster. "I understand why you long so to be in it. It really is beautiful. My finest creation. Strangely enough, most people do not seek this place. In fact, most who come do so because they did not believe it exists to begin with. But they do indeed believe now."

Speed could not be calculated as the automobile blazed forward. From here the gates could be seen clearly. The bars were lined with gold, and the handle lined with silver. Two enormous pillars sat on each side and offered support. He was less than twelve seconds away.

"This place is more than fire and brimstone. It goes beyond your wildest dreams," the voice continued. Ramond did not even realize the voice had spoken. He was but seven seconds away. "But for you, my boy, it is not time yet."
Five seconds.

"You'll get there soon enough."
Three seconds.

THE DARK ROAD

"So for now."

One second.

"Go and do my will!"

†††††††††††

The car lurched in the same manner as before, but this time slowing down to practically nothing. Another hole opened up in front of him, as the molecules of the dark road were sent flying. Before him lay the road he had traveled a thousand times.

Impulsively he stomped the breaks, locking them. Ramond lost control of the car, sending it spiraling, until it stopped facing the hole. He looked back through it one last time and viewed the souls which were now walking toward him. They seemed not to notice him. Their heads pointing in the direction of something he could no longer see.

The pieces began to replace themselves, sealing the hole in front of him, leaving no trace that it had ever existed to begin with. Above it, the traffic light hung, unaffected by the night's events. The lights returned to their normal shades of red, yellow, and green, and the once shattered back window was now repaired without a single crack.

A quick review of his dash board clock revealed that it was 5:48. The entire trip seemed to have lasted at least twenty minutes, but according to the clock he had only been gone for one. It spoke volumes of what it would be like in Hell. Where twenty minutes was equal to only one of our own. For those who were forced to suffer there, the suffering would be long. But for those who would experience gratification, the pleasure would last even longer.

MICHAEL BISHOP

† † † † † † † † † † †

Ramond continued to the burger joint. Murder was not a chore taken on an empty stomach. Far more food than he could eat was ordered. There was no telling when there would be time to eat again. Ramond wanted to make the most of it.

Seven bucks were peeled from his tightly sealed wallet and handed to the cashier at the drive-thru window. After he got his food he exited a different road than he had entered. An alternate route was chosen on the way home. He did not want to pass under the lights again tonight.

† † † † † † † † † † †

For the second time in only three days, he watched the sun rise again. Its glory was not as appreciated this time, however. It was hard to enjoy the newness and wonder of life when all that loomed over your head was the thought of ending it.

Ramond scarcely gave the new sun a glance as he headed up the stairs with his sack of food. He recalled the last time he had gone through this ritual. It had been a day that changed him forever. He looked around for Mrs. Jenkins' truck, but it was not in its usual place. Perhaps she had gone out for groceries. It was not a matter he thought long on. If he was going to kill, it was better to use every second available to him to make sure everything ran smoothly. He rushed up the stairs and unlocked his door. The garbage can still cluttered the center of the room as he stepped around it and set the food on the stand next to the bed.

The phone book was lying on the bed and he noticed where he had scribbled the hotel information on the back.

THE DARK ROAD

Ramond opened it to the white pages and ate soggy fries as he flipped through it searching for the "P"s.

"C... G... K... M... N... O... ," he called out loud while flipping the pages. "P," he concluded and took time out to wipe the grease from his lips with a napkin. He dried his index finger especially well, then extended it and touched the first name in the "P"s. "Pace" he recited then skipped his finger down the page, passing the next three or four. "Page" he continued his search. "Parham... Parker... Parks... Pase... Peacock... Perry... PETERS!" he called out the last loudly. There were only five Peters in the book. One Adam. One Elaine. One Kurt. And there, at the bottom of the list, two Marks.

The long, thin index finger pressed down with increasing pressure on the second Mark. He slowly moved it to the right as he read the address aloud to himself.

"3950 Black Circle Road." Ramond knew the road well. He had passed it many times. The section of town the street was on had been satirically named "Moneydale" by people in Sierra Springs who could not afford to live in the exclusive community. Every house in town worth at least two-hundred and fifty thousand dollars was built in or around the area. It was the part of town that was furthest from the rail road tracks that marked the "Hood".

The community was set up in the northern region of town. Often when a resident told someone where they lived, they would specify that they were from *North Sierra Springs* instead of just *Sierra Springs*. The *North* added to the title seemed to have a hidden implication. One that said "I'm from the best part of town. Not from where the commoners have to live."

Some residents actually wrote *Northern Sierra*

MICHAEL BISHOP

Springs on their mail, in hopes there would be no misunderstanding.

The realization of where the house was brought a hail of stress to Ramond's temples. A house in that part of town would not only be well watched by snooty, uppity neighbors; it would also be well guarded by the finest security systems that money could buy. And he was given only one night to complete the job. His master had ordered it done before tomorrow. No time to stake out the house, or to observe the usual time the man came and went, or even to find out what the man looked like to begin with.

Sprite was sucked down through a straw before he cleared his bed and stretched out on it. The headache had already began to tear open his forehead. The jack-hammering pain beat inside his skull in unison with the pumping of his heart. His mentor had really outdone himself this time, and instantly his mind began to churn despite the pain in an attempt to devise some sort of plan to make it through this one.

†††††††††††††

The housing development on Black Circle Road was new. In fact, the road itself was new. It was the last street that had been added to "Moneydale". All the other roads in the community already had their quota of houses. The rich did not like their neighbors too close, so the lots were large, leaving enough room for only a few homes on each road. With more and more people wanting to live in Northern Sierra Springs, Black Circle Road was added to make room for those who could afford it.

THE DARK ROAD

The street dead ended with a huge circle that spun back around to the opposite direction. 3950 was the last house on the road, sitting directly in front of the circle. Ramond drove the car casually around the circle at dusk, trying to give the illusion of a motorist who had accidently turned down the wrong road. But nothing could have been further from the truth. His turn down the road was strictly intentional. To get a better look, and to see what he was up against.

It was a desperation move. Hours of lying in bed, toiling with the idea of how to go about the murder led to nothing. Ramond ran several strategies through his head, but they all fell short of being even remotely plausible.

He thought about just barreling through the front door and shooting everyone in the house dead. But that idea was more ridiculous than feasible. First of all, he did not want to kill one person, much less several innocent bystanders. Secondly, he would probably never be able to break the front door down. And lastly, in the day and age which he lived, it was highly possible that the family living on the other side of that door would shoot back.

After half a day of this line of thought, he decided to play it by ear. Maybe everything did not have to be planned out. Perhaps the stars would somehow line up correctly, and he could pull this thing off with blind luck. He had been lucky before. Ramond dearly hoped his luck had not used itself up.

The county had yet to put in the street lights, and besides the one on the corner that had been installed for the intersecting street, the road was dark. But the house itself was lit up like a Christmas tree, with lawn lights and security lights all the way around its perimeter. It stood recessed a half acre back from the road, and with the intense lighting, every detail of the house could be seen.

MICHAEL BISHOP

Ramond wheeled the car around the turn inch by inch as he studied the house. It was a remarkable piece of construction, but still paled in comparison to some of its sister houses on the surrounding blocks. Traditional white covered the outside walls of each of its three stories. The top floor consisted of only one large room, which had a small rectangular window high above the front door.

The layout in these houses was pretty much the same. The second story would house the bedrooms. The bottom would be a den, living room, and kitchen. A few bathrooms would be placed here and there, and several closets spread around.

Two huge fluted columns stood guard on each side of the door. The door had one window in its center that had too much stained glass in it to give a view of who was outside it. One would almost assuredly have to look out one of the windows to see who was on the other side of the door.

Ramond eyed the door closely. It was thick steel, grayish and fresh from the factory. It would have at least one dead bolt on it, maybe two. That, added to the lock on the knob itself and probably a chain latch, would make it impossible to penetrate. Even if he had the skill to pick the locks, the security system would give him away before he took one step across the threshold. He would have to find another entrance.

A concrete walkway led from the front door to the driveway. Straight up the driveway a three car garage was affixed on the left side of the house. The steel garage door was securely closed and held four tiny windows about six feet up. The windows were double pane and insulated. Even if he could break one open, they were no more than a foot wide. Too small to fit through.

THE DARK ROAD

Without a remote device to open it, the door would be impossible to pry open. It would be just as strong as the front door, a tough defense against would-be thieves.

The car made the loop and was facing the other direction. Ramond did not want to draw attention, but did not pull away too quickly. It was just as important to get a good look at the fortress as it was to make sure he was not seen. He noticed a cobblestone pathway leading from the right side of the concrete slab in front of the door, around to the side of the house. He pulled the car forward until he could see the right side of the house. The path traveled toward the back yard and ended at a wooden gate. The gate's hinges were attached to a pole near the house and it served as the only opening to the fence that enclosed the backyard.

He was pretty sure there was a pool in the back yard. Wealthy men rarely used their swimming pools, but they were still an important status symbol, just like their Mercedes', Rolex's, and expensive suits. The pool would have to be admired from the inside as well. So, it stood to reason, a set of patio doors would probably be at the rear of the house.

Time was up. Ramond knew if he stayed any longer someone might grow suspicious. He had already made it obvious to anyone who might be watching that he was eyeing the house and not simply turning around. But hopefully, if anyone had seen, they would assume he was a commoner out sightseeing, admiring the fancy houses and seeing how the other half lived.

Three miles away a construction crew had begun

clearing off a field in order to place yet another group of apartment complexes in the town. The workers had long since gone home for the evening, leaving the site empty. Ramond pulled the Ford next to one of the dozers and cut the motor. It would be better, he decided, if he left his car in a safe place and walked back to the house. It would rob him of a quick get away. But if he were to park the car on the road, in front of the mogul's home, too many eyebrows of curiosity would be raised.

  The gloves he had stuffed in the glove box were excavated and placed on his hands. Blood stains from Jarard had dried on the outside of the fingers, and he was both glad and angry with himself for forgetting to burn them along with all the other articles. On the one hand, they were the most damning evidence linking him to Jarard. But on the other hand they would come in exceptionally beneficial in this crime as well.

  It was still too early to go. Dinner time was not the appropriate hour for attempting a murder. He would begin the walk at eleven. By the time he got there, everyone should be fast asleep. It was better to catch them sleeping in bed than well-fed and full of fight.

  The Bible laid next to him on the passenger seat. As always, the wait was a dreaded stretch. This time he came prepared. For the duration of the wait he read the few passages the book possessed about "The Man" a hundred times each. And with each review of the words, he became more and more convinced that the "Anti-Christ" was a role he was born to play.

THE DARK ROAD

The long walk began at eleven on the dot. In all that time, he had not put the book down once. Not even to rub his eyes, even though they were strained by the poor glow of the car's map light.

The night air was crisp, breaking in two as his body glided through it with each step. As he moved further away from the center of town, closer to Northern Sierra Springs, he noticed a change in the smell of the air. The atmosphere near "Moneydale" seemed just a bit sweeter. Just a touch fresher. And just a smidgen softer. It did not shock him. The rich got the best of everything. Why not the air too?

The walk was taken grudgingly. He was in no real hurry to get where he was going. Forty-five minutes later, he arrived at Black Circle Road. Only two other houses had been completed on the road. Their inside lights were severed, while their outside lights blazed as a warning to all to stay away.

It was a good sign. A sign that everyone was, at least in their king sized sleepers, if not asleep as well. It also meant he probably would not be spotted walking down the road toward the circle at the end.

No visible sign of anyone stirring inside the Peters' house could be seen from the outside. Their lights had been turned off also, although Ramond could not remember seeing lights inside during his initial drive by at six either. A disturbing question posed itself to Ramond. *What if no one's home? What if the house is completely empty? What then?*

He did not know *what then*. If the house was indeed unoccupied, it would mean failure. There would be no way to find Mark Peters before tomorrow if he was not at home. Ramond would not even know where to begin to look.

"Calm down," he whispered to himself aloud. Speaking aloud seemed to actually make his emotions take heed. "My God would not give me a task that could not be done," he assured himself. "He wants me to succeed, just as badly as *I* want me to succeed." The first statement might be true, but the last he was not completely convinced of.

There was only one real way to find out if anyone was home. He would have to walk right up to the front door like he owned the place. If anyone did happen to spot him they would just assume he was a visitor. After all no one would expect a criminal to stroll the drive way and to the front of the house.

In seconds, he reached the front door without incident. No lights cut on inside the house. Apparently he had gone unnoticed.

Standing on his tiptoes he peered into one of the garage door windows. An oil black Lexus was parked in the left space, but the right was empty. The thought of an empty house resurfaced and doubled its efforts in bringing fear to Ramond. Surely the man owned two automobiles. Had he not, the space next to the Lexus would likely be filled with some sort of clutter: a ping pong table, a boat, something.

No comforting words came to his lips this time. Every family had at least two cars these days, and Ramond was not optimistic enough to believe a man with this kind of house would have only one vehicle.

He went to the window to the right of the front door and attempted to look in. A hand was placed above his eyes to block the glare from the lights as he pressed his nose to the glass. A lacy white curtain hung over the window, more for show than for substance. He could see right through it, into the dim living room. The shape of the couch and a few chairs could be made out in the darkness. All facing the same direction. No doubt where the T. V. had been placed. There

THE DARK ROAD

was no sign of life from the front.

An almost certainty that Mark Peters was gone swept over Ramond, and in its wake, a feeling of desperation arose. He walked around the side of the house without worry or caution, burning with the thought that he would fail, which left no room for fear of being seen.

He would check out the rest of the house, just as a formality, but he was convinced that Peters was not at home.

Rocks were trampled noisily as he neared the gate. With his head hung down, he paid little attention to what was in front of him. The latch on the gate handle was depressed with his thumb and he shoved it open without bothering to look over the top to check if anyone was around. Carelessness was not normally a trait when it came to his ambitions. But this job, he felt, had ended before it began. The quest was over.

Never in his life had one emotion changed so quickly into another. It was staggering in its transition. One moment he was on the verge of suicidal depression. In his mind there was no doubt he had failed. His life's dream, his birthright, gone because one son-of-a-bitch decided to go away for the night. He had come so close. He stood at the door of becoming the most powerful being the world had ever known and the door slammed in his face. The positiveness that it was all over plowed its brand into him.

But what he saw on the other side of the fence shoveled a blizzard of hope into him. It was such a small thing, a light in the window of the pool house; but it opened so many possibilities like a child tearing into his presents on

MICHAEL BISHOP

Christmas morning.

It meant that there might be someone in that pool house. Most likely just a servant or care taker. But they would assuredly know where Mark Peters was. And if Ramond knew where the man was, perhaps he could find him and kill him before morning. At least it left a chance. And any chance that he might still be able to achieve the power was all he needed.

The pool area was completely concreted and much darker than the front yard. The only lights shining in the back were small bug lights above the patio doors and the light from inside the pool house itself. Ramond regained his caution. He had chosen not to bring weapons with him. The plan was to work with whatever was handy. If he were to get information from the person in the pool house, he would have to sneak up on them and take advantage of the situation.

The pool house faced the patio doors and Ramond stood at the two o'clock position from it. An Olympic sized pool separated the pool house from the sliding back doors. Its water was as clear as he had ever seen. No insects or leaves floated in it. It was completely free of all impurities. Even on a cool night like this, the water was a tempting treat.

The side of the pool house closest to him had one window in the center of its side. It was this window the light poured from. Ramond ducked his head and trotted as quietly as possible to a spot just below the window.

When his feet stopped moving and their sound ceased to obstruct his ears, the noise could be heard coming from the inside. It was the sound of the radio; but not only that, it was the sound of someone singing along with it. He crawled below the window toward the front of the pool house. When

THE DARK ROAD

he passed the window he stood and began walking to the corner, hoping to peak around into the door to get a better look.

He slid his feet along the ground for fear normal steps would be too noisy. A shadow fell in front of him where the front corner of the building stood. A small rock rested comfortably in those shadows that he did not notice until his foot scraped against the ground and kicked it. It rolled across the pavement with perfect rotations, like a bowling ball headed smoothly down a lane for a strike. The rock stopped only when it reached the ledge of the pool. It tumbled over the side, landing into the water with a neat, eloquent "PLOOMP".

Ramond pressed himself against the wall tightly and froze.

"WHO'S THERE?" came a male's voice from the other side of the wall. The voice was more startled and frightened than forceful. A rumbling was made inside, as if the man in the pool house was searching for something. Ramond's inclination was to run. But to run would be to fail.

"WHO'S THERE I SAID?" The voice was closer now. Just around the corner from Ramond, in the doorway of the pool house. The beam of a flashlight lunged across the water of the swimming pool. The man took three steps toward the water and stopped, shining the flashlight back and forth across the surface of the pool.

Ramond could see the man's back. He was wearing a house-robe and fuzzy slippers. He stood a head shorter than Ramond and probably weighed about the same.

"I HAVE A GUN!" the stranger shouted, but Ramond knew the man did not have a gun. His left hand could be seen clearly, and the flashlight was held in his right. No Gun.

MICHAEL BISHOP

Ramond did an excellent job of being quiet. The man had no idea anyone was behind him. He decided to act while the guy's back was turned. It was his best chance to subdue his quarry.

The man took one step backward and turned the light toward the gate. Ramond seized the moment and rushed in. The flashlight spun around as the man turned toward the foot steps. The beam blinded Ramond momentarily but he continued to move forward. He could not see clearly for the glare in his eyes, but when he knew he was close, Ramond threw both arms forward with all his weight behind it, hitting the man in the chest and toppling him backward. The force of the blow caused Ramond to lose his balance and land on top of his victim.

As the man hit the ground his head snapped backward and cracked on the concrete. His body broke Ramond's fall, and he quickly rolled off the man and jumped back to his feet into a fighting stance.

The guy remained motionless. A pool of blood could be seen spreading from behind his head. It had gashed open upon impact.

"SHIT! SHIIITTT!" Ramond screamed. Once again set in with the thought that he had killed his only lead, he knelt down to the man's side, willing to give him mouth to mouth if that's what it took. The flashlight had rolled a few feet away. Ramond picked it up and shined it into the man's face. He was breathing. His chest heaved up and down with a wheezing sound as if he had cracked a rib or injured his lungs on the hard surface.

Ramond jumped to his feet and looked around for a container to hold water in. If he acted quickly, he could douse water in his face, wake him, and question him while he was

THE DARK ROAD

dazed and confused. When nothing to hold water was seen nearby, he wondered if a hard slap might wake the man.

Ramond shined the flashlight in the direction of the man's head and watched the pool of blood spread its way across the pavement. Something shiny on the guy's clothing caught Ramond's attention and he turned the light towards it for further inspection. A monogram stitched in purple on the guy's robe stood out. The moment Ramond read it, he knew. Suddenly everything fell into place. It all made sense.

"M.P." was sewn into the lapel of the robe. Ramond's search for Mark Peters had ended. The man he was after was not a rich tycoon after all, but a mere pool boy. He felt like slapping himself for not realizing the obvious signs in the first place. One being that very few, if any, of "Moneydale's" residents had listed numbers. No doubt the man who owned the house had an unlisted number as well. But a grounds-keeper who lived in the pool house was bound to have his own number. And there was no need for that number to be unlisted. No reason at all.

He wondered briefly why the master would want a simple servant dead. When he thought Mark Peters was a rich man, it was easier to understand. He could have been a politician or a reporter or even an evangelist. But he wasn't the owner at all. He was just a lowly employee and Ramond had no idea what good could come from his death. A big part of Ramond did not want to know. Satan's business was Satan's business. It was not his concern.

There was a decision to be made. How to kill the man. Mark Peters was helpless. Laying unconscious in a pool of his own blood, waiting to die. It was time for Ramond to play

MICHAEL BISHOP

God and decide the best way to finish him off. As he stared down at his victim, it was not a decision easily made.

✝ ✝ ✝ ✝ ✝ ✝ ✝ ✝ ✝ ✝ ✝ ✝

"Turn away Ramond. Get out of here. Don't do this."

Tears flowed from Ramond's eyes when he heard the voice.

"NO...NO... NOT AGAIN..NO MORE!" he whined. It was the voice of Vernadette. A voice he had not heard in nine years. A voice he was sure would never haunt him again.

"You've done bad things son, But there's still time to make things right. Don't take a life Ramond. Once you do, you'll never be the same person."

"GO AWAY. PLEASE GOD. GO AWAY!" he dropped the flashlight and covered his ears with his palms. He pressed his hands hard into his head. The tears were not from guilt. They came from the terrible realization that the voice was back. He had escaped it for so long, and now it had returned to torture his soul. To critique his every move. He thought he had moved beyond it. But the voice set him back nine years.

"I'm never going away, Ramond. Never! You hear me? NEVER NEVER NEVER!" it promised.

"O' GOD!" he cried one last time before dropping his hands down to his sides. The tears dried as he spoke his deny. "You're not real. You don't have any hold on me, because YOU'RE NOT REAL!" He began silently and ended in a frantic yelp.

"O' yes, I'm real. And I want to help you. You've shut me out for so long. But now I'm back to stay this time."

"You're not real. You're not real. You're not real," he

-224-

THE DARK ROAD

chanted. "I'm going to ignore you. I don't hear you. Simply because you're not real."

Suddenly, in an instant no longer than a blink, the monumental decision was made. Mark Peters would drown. It was a fitting end for a pool boy. Besides, Ramond had no hard feelings toward the man. There was no need for him to die painfully. He had heard stories of people who had nearly drowned, who claimed that once they got passed the initial fear it was a rather peaceful death. They claimed they just let themselves go and their body filled with water gently and easily. And if Mark Peters was unconscious, all the better.

"Ramond, listen to me. I love you. I only want what is best for you. You don't really want to kill this man do you? Look at him laying there with his head split open. He's never done anything to you. He's an innocent victim, Ramond, just like you. Just a pawn in Satan's hand." The voice was syrupy sweet, just like it had been many times before. And it demeaned him, telling him he was nothing more than a petty *victim*. A lowly pawn.

"I AM NOT A VICTIM. I AM NOT A PAWN. I AM A MAN AND I DO WHAT I DO FOR NO ONE BUT MYSELF... DO YOU UNDERSTAND? DO YOU FUCKING UNDERSTAND?" He surged his words at the air and stood silently for a reply. None came. The voice had left him. For now.

Bending down, he grabbed Mark Peters underneath both arms and drug him to the edge of the pool. With a hefty shove the man rolled into the water.

Mark Peters landed face down. Ramond watched as bubbles rose to the top of the pool. When the bubbles stopped

MICHAEL BISHOP

coming, Ramond made his way for the gate. The excitement of finishing the fifth step was tangled with the horror that his mother's voice had returned. The moment was bittersweet.

† † † † † † † † † † † †

"THE MOST SELFISH SONS OF BITCHES IN THE WORLD"

Dr. Jonahs Redgum was the leading plastic surgeon in the state. As his family grew, so did his need for a bigger and better house. A friend suggested he visit Northern Sierra Springs. It was only a thirty minute commute to the hospital and the area was lovely. Jonahs took a tour of the area, fell in love with it, and decided to move his family into the enchanting little community.

Mark Peters was hired the second week Dr. Redgum lived in the house. He moved into the pool house one week after that and fixed it up to his liking. It was a great opportunity. Free room and board and a place that was twice the size of his apartment. With one condition that he be given Thursdays off, he signed on as the Redgum's full time grounds-keeper.

Thursdays were the days Mark lived for. It was the day he went to see the kids. The Marsha Kite Orphanage had placed an ad in the paper a year prior for volunteers to help with the children. The main focus was on the older kids. After a child reached a certain age, the chances of them being adopted became very slim. It was these kids that Marsha Kite worried about. Out of desperation she placed an ad in the paper for someone who had the compassion to volunteer to

THE DARK ROAD

work with this group, spend time with them, be a good role model... love them.

Mark Peters called only seconds after he had read the ad. He was the only person in town to respond. Three days after placing the call he went to meet the kids for the first time.

They were tough at first. Not willing to open up easily to strangers. Most had been orphans for years, and growing up in an orphanage was like growing up in a glass bottle. They could see the outside world, see all the kids in it, having fun and enjoying life. But they were trapped inside, and could not have a family and be normal like them.

He went every week, arriving at precisely eleven A.M., taking the kids' abuse until they softened up to him.

The gesture which won the kids over happened on the third Thursday. Until then, he had found it nearly impossible to get any of them to talk to him, but then a brainstorm hit.

With him that Thursday, he brought his personal television and VCR, then stopped by the video store and rented six hours of cartoons. Surprisingly, he discovered that some of the kids did not even know what a "Smurf" was. The shelter barely afforded necessities, much less the luxuries of cable television, or VCR's. The orphanage itself was housed in a run down school building that Marsha Kite had bought with her life savings. With donations and many prayers, she gave the kids a roof over their heads.

She took in kids that other orphanages wouldn't, like runaways who happened to cross her path. No one was turned away from Marsha's home.

The kids sat in rows, glued to the screen for hours

without moving. The antics of Bugs Bunny and Elmer Fudd made them delirious with delight. As Mark left that Thursday, Marsha pulled him aside and hugged his neck. For a lady in her fifties she had the squeeze of a bear. She thanked him and said that it was the first time she had seen some of the children smile in a long time. The feeling left a glow in Mark Peters' heart that never went away.

From then, several of the kids began referring to him as Uncle Mark. The children became his life and each day spent with them was cherished.

It was a sort of game he played with himself. Trying to find something each Thursday the kids would like better than the previous one. He tried everything: cards, board games, movies, candy. A good portion of his paycheck was used each week to keep them entertained. It was hard to tell who had more fun, Mark or the kids themselves. Marsha Kites' guess would have been that both loved it equally as much.

A few months later he came up with an idea to best everything else he had done. A proposal was made to Marsha. The two of them agreed that each would pay half for an old van he had located in a trade paper. It ran roughly, had no shocks, and ate gas like there was a hole in the tank, but it was big enough for all the kids if the smaller ones sat in the bigger ones laps.

The first Thursday after the van was bought, they all piled into it and made a trip to the park. For most of them it was the first park they had ever been to. They ran and jumped and slid and swung until they were exhausted. Looking at their faces would make you think they had gone to

THE DARK ROAD

Disneyland. The day whisked by, making hours and hours seem like mere moments. When it was time to leave they protested, but not heavily. They had experienced a child's nirvana, and knew from experience it was not a good idea to rock the boat if they ever wanted to return. After that day even the hardest kids called Mark Peters *Uncle Mark.*

Next to volunteering in the first place, taking the kids to the park was the most rewarding decision Mark felt he had ever made.

The next day the threats came.

At six o'clock the next morning, Mark Peters was awakened by the telephone.

"Hello."

"KEEP THOSE FUCKING KIDS AWAY FROM OUR PARK OR YOU'LL BE SORRY, ASSHOLE!" the voice on the other end shouted.

Mark was suddenly wide awake and enraged. "WHO THE HELL IS THIS?" he fired at the receiver.

"DON'T WORRY ABOUT IT! JUST DO WHAT I SAID AND NOTHING WILL HAPPEN!" the man on the other end threatened and hung up.

Mark slammed the phone down, cracking the handle of the receiver. He put his head in his hands and breathed deeply, trying to keep himself under control. He was a passive man, but wanted so badly to put his fist through something he could hardly stand it. It boggled his mind how anyone could be so cruel. So heartless. So selfish.

He promised himself he would never forget the voice. If he ever heard that voice again, he would remember. No matter what.

MICHAEL BISHOP

The controversy should have been anticipated, but Mark Peters underestimated the self-centeredness of the people in Northern Sierra Springs. The park he had chosen had been built for the children of "Moneydale" with the taxpayers' money. The moguls of the community leaned on the mayor to foot the bill for it, and it took little prodding to get it done. The playground was constructed from the finest materials and was completed in only three weeks.

He had only chosen the park because it was the only safe playground in town. All the other public grounds had been taken over by gangs and drug dealers. It was not an element he wanted the kids to be around.

He thought little of his decision at the time. The kids were not hoodlums or criminals. They were just children who had gotten a bad break in life. If anyone deserved to be in that park it was the children of Marsha Kite Orphanage. And Mark was damned if he was going to let anyone keep them from it.

No other calls were received for that week. No doubt the perpetrator assumed the one warning would take care of the problem.

Mark had not even planned to take the kids back to the park that next Thursday, but the call had changed his mind. He loaded the excited children into the van and defiantly headed to Northern Sierra Springs.

He was on a crusade. It was a crusade for the kids, but it was also about much more. It was a social statement. A statement that said "I don't give a damn how much money you have, your kids are no better than mine." And when the kids arrived at the playground that day, plenty of people heard that statement loud and clear.

THE DARK ROAD

Once again they played until even the most energetic child was exhausted beyond belief. Mark forced himself to have fun, though it was hard to concentrate on the kids with the thought of the caller nagging his mind. He let the kids play for an extra hour just to make his point, before taking them all back to the orphanage. He had thrown the next punch and it was time to return home to see what kind of impact it had.

The caller did not even wait for morning. Mark Peters' phone had rung off the hook all day, even though he was not there to answer it. When he did arrive home to the ringing phone, he was certain of the voice he would hear on the opposite end.

"Hello."

"I WARNED YOU, YOU BASTARD. BUT YOU JUST COULDN'T LEAVE WELL ENOUGH ALONE!" the gruff voice screamed at him.

"LOOK YOU POMPOUS WINDBAG. THOSE KIDS HAVE JUST AS MUCH RIGHT IN THAT PARK AS ANYONE ELSE!" Mark had trouble keeping himself from stuttering. The anger made him want to spew all his words out at once. But he managed to scream the retort back clearly enough.

"YOU SHOULDN'T HAVE OPPOSED ME. I WILL CRUSH YOU!" the man assured, and slammed the phone down.

Mark dropped the phone and held his hands over his head again while he breathed. This time the calming exercise did not work. He picked up the phone, base and all, and hurled it across the room until the wall stopped its flight. A small hole was made in the sheet rock. Another project he would have to repair before the doctor noticed.

He was angry enough to actually strangle the man had he been close. The last thing he wanted was the kids in danger, but the situation was bigger than the children. It was an age old story of oppression. A victory might not mean an end to all the injustice in the world, but it would be a huge step in correcting the problems in Sierra Springs. It was a challenge Mark took upon himself. A battle he intended to win at any cost.

The following day he discovered who the voice on the other end of the phone belonged to. Philip Morgan, the owner of four local convenience stores called "Morgan's Fuel and Food" appointed himself as the leading opposition against the children. Morgan and a few of his golfing buddies placed a flier in every "Moneydale" resident's mailbox. They were simple in their layout.

COMMUNITY MEETING:
TUESDAY, APRIL 17. 8:00 P.M.

PRESENTED BY:
PHILIP MORGAN

PLACE:
SIERRA SPRINGS COMMUNITY CENTER

TOPIC OF DISCUSSION:
**OUR PARK AND THE WELFARE
OF OUR CHILDREN**

ALL RESIDENTS ARE URGED TO ATTEND THIS
IMPORTANT CONFERENCE.

THE DARK ROAD

Mark came across the flier while bringing the Redgums' mail inside to them. He read it in disbelief. It boggled his mind to think that someone would go through enough trouble to print up fliers and reserve a room in the community center just to stop a few innocent kids from coming to his part of town. A man that selfish was dangerous. And the fact that Morgan had a lot of powerful people behind him convinced Mark that the odds were stacked against him.

But Mark had an ace in the hole. Philip Morgan and his cronies probably did not expect him to find out about their meeting. It was a party Mark had every intention of crashing; and if he played his cards right, he knew he could end this fiasco before someone got hurt.

The days leading up to the 17th were painstaking. The more he thought about the whole situation, the more Mark became enraged. Long swims were taken to calm his nerves, sometimes even in the early hours of the morning when his anger kept him from sleeping. By the time Tuesday arrived, he had practiced the words he would say a thousand times. It was a noble speech, and even a more noble cause. He hoped he was a noble enough person to handle it all.

He arrived at the Sierra Springs Community Center at 8:10. That gave him enough time to make certain everyone who was going to come was there. The rich were punctual people, especially in matters where being late would make them lose face. They were sure to be on time for things like church and meetings.

The Center's parking lot had never been filled with so many luxury cars at one time. Every space was occupied by Cadillacs or BMW's or Mercedes. It turned Mark's stomach

MICHAEL BISHOP

to see so much money wasted on foolish status symbols when so many others could use the money for necessities. His own old model Nissan hatch-back looked oddly out of place as he pulled in next to a Corvette.

The turn out was good. The lot was full. Mark figured it would be this way. To miss a gathering like this would practically be admitting to your neighbors that you did not care about your children. Even those who did not care about the park in any way attended for this reason. Image was everything.

He passed Dr. Redgum's Lexus as he headed for the front door. The room was full. Most sat in folding chairs, while a few stood in the back. In all, the crowd topped a hundred. Mark drew little attention as he entered and stood at the back of the room. All eyes were forward, locked on a heavy-set man standing behind a podium. He was in the middle of his speech when Mark entered, but it was not his words that caught Mark's attention. It was his voice.

".......and that's just fine with me," the man in front stated, a comment that got a chuckle from the crowd. The speaker was Philip Morgan. Mark was sure of it. But more than that it was the voice of the caller. It was the voice of a coward. It was the voice of the enemy.

Mark's temper began to rise, but he kept himself steady. It was not time to speak up yet. He stood patiently in his place and bit his tongue while Morgan continued.

"But that brings me to the real reason I brought you all here tonight. Now I'm sure most of you are aware of the fact that children from the Marsha Kite Orphanage have been bussed all the way across town over to our park for two Thursdays in a row. Now if you're a concerned parent like I am, this immediately raises a red flag. I'll be honest with you at the risk of sounding cruel. It bothers me to think that my kids our playing with these kinds of kids. These kids are not regular kids. They've grown up with no adult supervision. No rules. No one to teach them right from wrong. Don't get me wrong, I feel for these kids. God knows they got a bad break from life. But that don't change the fact that they lack a quality upbringing. Just because I feel sorry for them doesn't mean I'm going to neglect my right as a parent to protect my children. Pity or no pity, my kids come first, and I truly feel something needs to be done about this before it gets out of hand." Morgan spoke more like a politician and carried himself like a preacher. The crowd was nodding at his every sentence, agreeing whole-heartily with him.

    Mark was on the verge of exploding. His fury turned him into a time bomb. But it still was not the right moment. He waited just a bit longer.

    "Well, that's my piece on the situation," Morgan continued. "Unfortunately I don't have any excellent ideas on how to deal with this problem. I'm no lawyer. I'm not sure what legal ground we have here. So at this time I would like to turn the podium over to anyone who has any suggestions," he finished and gazed around the room for any volunteers.

    "I have some suggestions!" Mark shouted from the back of the room, no longer able to keep himself quiet.

    Every head spun towards the back of the room to get a look at the volunteer. Dr. Redgum and his wife were sitting in the front row and for the first time noticed Mark. Their eyes glazed over with surprise. They knew what was to come, but no one else recognized Mark.

    "Well come on up here," Morgan called with a smile on his face. He had never actually laid eyes on Mark, and did not pick up on the voice.

MICHAEL BISHOP

Mark walked down the middle aisle to the front where the podium stood. The crowd gawked at him in curiosity trying to surmise who he was. Morgan continued to smile as he neared.

"I'm Philip Morgan," he offered and outstretched his hand. Mark took his hand and squeezed it roughly.

"Mark Peters," he spewed bluntly. "I don't think we've been properly introduced."

Philip Morgan's smile dropped like a stone. The name and the voice began to match up.

"I'd like to speak," Mark told as he nudged Morgan out from in front of the podium with a slight push.

"Now wait just a minute!" Morgan screamed at him.

"YOU STEP BACK AND KEEP YOUR MOUTH SHUT OR YOU'LL BE PICKING YOUR TEETH UP OFF THE FLOOR! DON'T TEST ME MORGAN!" Mark screamed into the microphone as he pointed a hazarding finger at the man. The threat boomed through the room. The crowd stood awe-struck. No one moved or uttered a word; including Philip Morgan.

"Now, I'm sorry for screaming like that, but I will be heard. I gave you respect and listened to you babble your little holier-than-thou sermon, so you just do the same for me. O.K.?" he asked. Morgan said nothing. His jaw hung open in a stupor. His expression held a mixture of fright and confusion. For the first time in his life, the tycoon had lost control.

"Good," Mark called without waiting for an answer. He turned his head from Morgan and gazed across the room at all the blank faces. Their complete attention was focused on him. "For those of you who don't know, I'm Mark Peters.

THE DARK ROAD

I'm the man who brought the kids to your precious little playground to begin with. These kids you are talking about like they are juvenile delinquents and street trash are my kids. I love each and every one of them just as much as you love your kids. And just like you would not let anyone talk about your kids in this manner, I'll be damned if you're going to talk about mine like this," Mark peered around the room with a dramatic pause before he began the next part.

"I didn't come here to make a long speech. I came here to tell you how it is going to be. I'm going to bring the kids to your park every other Thursday of the month. That is only two days a month, people. That is quite a small sacrifice for you to make. If you don't want your kids around them, then I suggest you keep them home on those two days. After all, this is a public park." He stopped and turned his head toward Morgan.

"If you resist or try to harm the kids, me, or Marsha in any way, I swear on my life that you will be sorry. I will bring the kids to the park every day of your stinking lives. When you come home from work, you will see my kids swinging on your swings. When you step out of your door, you will hear the sound of my kids joyfully playing in your park. Every time your child steps foot on the playground, there will be one of mine to meet them. If you resist I WILL break you. This is practically the only joy these kids have in their life, and if you try to take it away from them simply because you feel you and your kids are too good for them, then you people are the most selfish sons of bitches on Earth." He spoke his words directly to Philip Morgan. The two men stared at each other in silence for seconds. The room remained quiet. Morgan's face had turned to an unnatural shade of red. Mark knew he had made his point.

MICHAEL BISHOP

He stepped from behind the podium and made his way down the aisle towards the door. All eyes turned and watched him as he walked out, but no replies or screams came after him. Each person was shocked into silence.

Philip Morgan was humiliated. Since he was a young man he had been a leader. The crowd always seemed to follow in his momentum. But this was the first time he had ever been talked to in such a way. In a way that made him feel powerless. In a way that left nothing to come back with. He was a beaten man, and left in his Mercedes looking as such. As badly as he wanted to act, he knew it was safer to leave things alone. It was clear further action would make things worse.

It was not only Mark's victory but the orphans as well; only none of them knew it. They were never told that someone was trying to keep them from the playground. To explain that to them would mean having to explain prejudice, and it was not a lesson he wanted them taught.

For the next nine months, they were driven to the park on every other Thursday. It was a time many of them would later recall as the best days of their lives. For the first time since the shelter opened its doors, many of the children were truly happy. It was a gift that money could not buy and a privilege the world could not bring. True happiness was found only by a handful of people in everyday life, and Mark had made that possible for the kids.

He got on the swings and slides and teeter-totters with them, and played to his heart's content. He was a child all over again, and enjoyed it just as much as they did. And when the children saw Mark running and jumping and acting like he

THE DARK ROAD

was a little boy, it let each one of them know that they were loved. That love restored their faith in people. Allowed them to open up in everyday life. Gave them hope for a brighter day. The love of Mark Peters rolled the stones off the children's hearts.

† † † † † † † † † † † †

For all the good Mark Peters' life had done for the children of the Marsha Kite Orphanage, his death undid it all. The day after he was found drowned in the pool, the kids were gathered in the learning room and all sat down. Marsha was forced to explain to them that he would not be coming back. When the kids asked why, she told them the truth. She told them he was dead.

Many kids in the world do not understand death, but the orphaned kids were all too familiar with it. Each one knew what it was to die. They understood the magnitude. And in the moment they heard Mark Peters was dead, many of them wanted to die too. Their spirits were broken. Their will to live gone.

But as hard as it was to watch the light drain from their little faces, the hardship had just begun for Marsha Kite. A week after Mark's death, an envelope was found in her mailbox. It came in a plain brown envelope. There was no stamp, or mailing address on its front, suggesting that whoever wrote it had placed it in her mailbox personally.

The letter inside was typed, with no evidence of who left it. But Marsha Kite did not need any clues to tell her the identity of the writer. The letter said it all.
It read:

MICHAEL BISHOP

TO MARSHA KITE AND THE DELINQUENTS,

YOUR KIDS WILL NO LONGER COME TO THE PARK.
IF YOU RESIST, WE WILL BREAK YOU.

SIGNED,
THE MOST SELFISH SONS OF BITCHES IN THE WORLD

They had killed Mark, she was sure of it, and anyone willing to murder over something so small was too dangerous to cross. They, of course would get away with it, the rich always did. But in the end, she knew they would get what was coming to them

She was a strong woman. She had spent her entire life fighting. If she wasn't battling for the rights of blacks or women, she was battling for the rights of children. She had taken on many causes in her life, and won many more than she had lost. But time had taken toll on her and with the death of Mark crushing down, she had no more strength to fight.

The children were no longer bussed to the park. Eventually the bus was sold altogether to pay the mounting bills. Things went back to being pretty much as they had been before Mark came, except for one major difference.

The gleam in the eyes of the children had gone dull. They were once filled with dreams and hopes. But that part of them was all gone. They hardened. Placed a wall around them and promised themselves they would never let anyone break through that wall again. And the coldness they learned as children followed them into adulthood.

Mark Peters had once seen so much promise in them. He truly believed that each child had the potential to make a critical difference in the world. He never got to see that belief manifest. With his death, the potential died as well.

The Perfect Place

1 2 3 4 5 7 9 0

aunting back to his car gave Ramond time to clear his head and place everything into perspective. Oddly, the thought that he had just killed a man did not enter into his thoughts. Nor did the fact that he was walking away from a crime scene and was not far enough away to be safe. The topic that was on his mind, however, was the return of his mother's voice, and what he was going to do about it.

By the time he had made the three mile walk and reached the car, he had made a determination. The voice was not really his mother trying to ward him from evil. That was neither possible, nor rational. The voice was simply an illusion created by his mind, attempting to lay a guilt trip on him. His subconscious mind knew that his mother was the best instrument to use against him to deliver blows of contrition. It was simple psychology.

Since the condition was properly diagnosed, a cure was developed. Ramond had made the voice go away when he was young by ignoring it. That little angel that sat on his shoulder and told him right from wrong was tuned out. After a while, his conscience tired of being disregarded and disappeared altogether. Why it had chosen now to return, during such a critical time in the scheme of things, he wasn't sure. But what he was sure of was that it was a weakness. A weakness the master would surely scorn him for. And it was a weakness that must be destroyed before it was allowed to get in his way.

Somehow Satan had known the voice would return and had tried to warn him. Ramond finally understood why he had been interrogated so harshly during their last encounter. It had been to ensure that he would not fail his mission, which meant that his father really *did* want him to succeed. He cursed himself for ever doubting his master, and hated himself for being feeble. It was a problem he had every intention of remedying.

† † † † † † † † † † † †

Once again he returned to the sanctity of his apartment. The dingy den had almost become holy ground over the course of the events. It was the only place he felt safe. It offered solace. Comfort to his weary bones. And it served as his only friend.

The place reeked of rotting garbage and the stale urine from an unflushed toilet. Flushing the toilet was the last thing on his mind lately, and it was allowed to fill with urine to the point that it consumed the water that shared the bowl with it. It was a disgusting mess, but it was *his* mess; and having something he could call his own made it all right.

THE PERFECT PLACE

Soon, he thought, *soon everything will be mine. The countries, the trees, the air, the seas; every living thing on the planet will serve me and I will serve Him. Just like in the proposition.*

It was a revelation most of his thoughts hung on. The power was so close he could actually feel a part of it filling him up already. He felt strong and young and untamed, like a stallion unable to be broken. And even though his body had become as thin as it had ever been in his life, he never felt more fit.

How much weight had he lost? It was a concept he had dwelled on very little lately. Sure, his pants had become so loose that they nearly fell from his hips, but his belt was cinched tighter and tighter and he went along with his business. There was no time to worry about it. Too much work had to be done. His body was just a rotting, dying hull. A link that tied him to the earthly realm. Soon it would be of little consequence to him; but for now, he was curious to know how thin he had actually become.

He closed the bathroom door exposing the full-length, dressing mirror that hung on it facing the bedroom. The mirror was yet another item he carried with him from place to place. It once hung in his room when he still lived with his mother.

He recalled himself standing in front of it as a child as his mother tied his tie. It was a ritual done every Sunday just before they left the house. He had watched her do it hundreds of times, and was able to do it blindfolded if he pleased. But Vernadette insisted on doing it for him.

"I want you to make sure you know how to do this, because someday you're going to have a little brother and it will be your duty to make sure he is as nice and neat before church as you are. Okay sweetie?" She had told him this tale dozens of times and he always replied the same.

"Okay. Momma."

But he never got a little brother, and Vernadette's dream of having another child was crushed. She begged Brian repeatedly for years and always got the same response. "One is enough," he grunted at her before rolling over and going to sleep. Sex was a chore to Brian Jamison. Something you gave your wife as a gift on special occasions like Valentine's day or anniversaries. It was not an act of love, and was purposely avoided for fear he might father another child.

He understood perfectly why his father did not want another son. He was ashamed of Ramond as it was. Why make the same mistake twice? It was apparent, Brian Jamison wanted to make sure that he never brought another loser into the world. Ramond knew the story all too well.

The mirror had been well used over the years. Most of the time he stepped in front of it, attempting to get a piece of hair to fall into place or confirm his robes hung correctly. This time he stepped into its path for a different reason. He had to know just how shitty he looked.

Out of the corner of his eye or from quick glances, he had seen his reflection dozens of times over the last few weeks; but he had never really looked closely. Now that he did, the reflection it revealed to him was startling.

Drugs had not been taken in a month, but he had never looked more like a junky. The cheeks of his face had grown so thin and bony that they were sunken in. Huge saddle bags drooped from beneath his eyes with pink tenderness. The pink swirled above his eyes until it disappeared beneath his skinny

THE PERFECT PLACE

eyebrows. The pink even flowed into his eyes, with capillaries shooting in every direction like some morbid firework had exploded.

Across his left cheek, a cut had scabbed and clotted over. He touched it and winced as he recalled Susan Lints' claws digging into his flesh. In the center of his forehead, a purple knot had formed from the impact of Keith's knee in Smiley Joe's.

Other tiny nicks and scratches circled his face. They served as little reminders of the grueling activities that were now behind him. He wondered how many more wounds he would receive before he was done. With only two jobs left, it was hard to tell.

"Fucking A!" he cursed to himself in disgust. He really did look like shit. It was worse than he had imagined. He had to know how his body looked. Perhaps it had fared the tests somewhat better.

Tugging at the muscle shirt, he managed to pry it from his frame. It dropped to the ground as his mouth flung open.

"OH FUCK!" he yelled seeing what shone under the cloth. He had never been a big man, or considered muscular, but his body was at least normal. Now all that was left was a sack of bones tied together with a little flesh. It was a sight directly out of a commercial for starving children. In his mind, Ramond could hear the announcer saying "You could save this poor child's life for less than the price of a cup of coffee a day!"

Easily, thirty pounds had melted away. It had only been only a little over a month. How was it possible? And more so, how was he able to accomplish the feats he had done in such poor condition? He could only assume it was sheer will. That and the help of the master.

MICHAEL BISHOP

His mother would probably pass him by on the street without knowing who he was. She might even pass to the other side to avoid the odd-looking human coming in her direction. It made Ramond want to cry. Had he not been dehydrated, he just might have done that.

Rest was needed badly. When he woke, he promised himself he would go to the nearest ice cream parlor and set the world record for consuming the most calories in a twenty-four hour period. He had neglected his body to a point where it was becoming serious. The lack of food, water, and sleep was killing him. Tests or no tests, if he died of malnutrition before they were completed, all the work would have been for nothing.

He jerked his head away from the mirror in repulsion. In his peripheral vision he noticed it. His reflection had not turned when he turned. It had stood facing dead ahead. Staring at him with a deathly cold expression. He ripped his head back to the mirror. The reflection smiled back at him, while his own face held a scowl of horror.

"WHAT THE FUCK!" the left side of his brain shouted, but the right side of his brain knew exactly what was going on. More parlor tricks. A game to amuse the great one.

"Howdy, stranger," his reflection said to him. The voice coming from the mirror was not the ghastly enchanting voice his lord normally used. It was, in fact, Ramond's voice. But it was like a recording again. Similar too, but not exactly what he heard with his own ears when he spoke. "Nice to see you again. Or at least what's left of you," he continued sarcastically.

Ramond gawked at the mirror. The image of his face

THE PERFECT PLACE

looking so unequivocally evil, mixed with the sick shape of his body, pricked the hairs on the nape of his neck and sent a wave of frost from his toes to his throat.

"H-Ho-How are you, Sire?" he stuttered as he shook.

"What a stupid question to ask me. How am I? Let me explain something to you, boy. I am not mortal. I am not a talking ape like you and the billions of your kind that roam the world out there. I am a higher being. A deity. I do not have good days or bad days. I do not wake up in a bad mood or go to bed with a headache. I remain constant. I am both the immovable object and the unstoppable force. The last thing I need is a piss-ant little nothing such as yourself asking me how I am." His reflection snickered at him and in the voice there were sounds of Satan's mixed with his own. It was an odd combination. Half human-half devil.

"I meant no harm. It was just the first thing to pop into my head. You startled me just appearing all of a sudden. I did not mean..."

"Silence, enough groveling. I understand you meant nothing by it. I was just trying to illustrate a point to you. That point being that you cannot compare yourself to me. There is no comparison. I am something you cannot comprehend. Even if you are given the opportunity to sit by my side, you will still wonder what I am. And you will never find an answer. I am a mystery that cannot be unraveled. A riddle without an answer. A puzzle without a solution. It is a lesson I teach you, but it is not taught in anger. It is taught to give you wisdom. The wisdom of knowing you are ignorant."

"I understand," he quivered.

"Obviously not, because the point of my speech is that you will never understand. Not when the beginning started, and not when the end comes. Never... Now on to business," he chirped out the end. His face automatically transformed to a smile. The mood changed one hundred eighty degrees into a cheerful banter, and the voice returned completely to Ramond's.

"Mark Peters is dead. So I guess that means you were able to overcome your guilt after all. Truthfully, I was not sure you had it in you. It's good to see you develop that killer instinct. It will be important later."

"I'm happy you are pleased," Ramond smiled to himself for the first time. The conversation change gave him something to smile about. His face was locked on his reflection's. It was identical in every way, but there was something out of place. A defect that he could not quite put his finger on. He stared harder, deep into the pupils of the eyes in the mirror. There he noticed it, wrapped in the eyes so carefully it was almost impossible to see; but once you *did* see it, you could not make yourself unsee it.

Flames swayed in the eyes. It was a familiar burning. The same as he had seen first in the bush, then in the traffic light, and last in the construction of Hell itself. When you stared at it, it seemed to draw you in. Magnifying itself, letting it easily be seen. Standing boldly in the center of those flames, uncharred and unaware, was a figure.

The figure was not a man. That much was obvious. It was dark and yet colorless at the same time. It seemed impossible, but was. No emotion could be seen. It was a void. Its body was man-like in shape and stature and a head of sorts did sit upon its shoulders. But it was clear, whatever the figure was it was not of this Earth. It descended all plains and dimensions. The figure was Lucifer.

"Why are you trying to decipher what you see in my eyes? Did I not tell you that I, nor the things I do, can be

THE PERFECT PLACE

explained? To dissect me would be to place me inside a box. A box of logic and scientific rhetoric. And to place me inside a box means to cage me. I will never be caged... Perhaps, since you are so uncontrollably curious about me, I should give you a taste. A taste of just how little you can comprehend me, and a taste of just how incompetent you are to serve me." At the trail of his words, the figure that had thus far been held back safely behind the eyes leaped forward, consuming the reflection of Ramond's face. The body was still Ramond's, but the head... the head was indescribable in his limited vocabulary.

He could only look for a second before he realized it was mistake to look at all. The burning in his eyes caused them to slam shut, as searing heat melted his eyelids over his scorched retinas. Ramond was not certain that he would ever see again. The pain was devastating, as if someone had mixed acid with bleach and poured it into his sockets. He reeled backward and howled in anguish.

"AHHHHHH OOHWWWWW AAAA, OH GOD. SHIIITT. I'M BLIND! HELP ME ...I'M BLIND!...OH CHRIST!"

"Open your eyes, you pathetic fool!" The voice ordered and then paused, waiting for the order to be carried out. The voice belonged totally to Satan now.

Ramond tried to be strong, but the world spun around him and he thought he might pass out from the pain. As his hand diligently rubbed his lids he realized they were no longer melted shut. He pressed his index fingers into the top of his lids and his thumbs into the bottom. The digits were pushed in opposite directions and he forced his eyes into slits. Light flooded through them, which was a wonderful sign. At least he would regain partial vision.

MICHAEL BISHOP

"Look into the mirror, imbecile. NOW!" the Devil demanded.

Ramond turned his head in the direction he thought the mirror would be and held his eyes open. A solid block of blur was the only object he could see, but as he stared harder, the picture slowly panned into focus. The pain dissipated into the air as he gazed at his reflection. The figure had subsided back into the eyes where it belonged, and the reflection stood before him with a gaping smile painted on its lips.

"You see, boy. You have no understanding of what I am. I am so alien to you that your mind and body could not even stand the sight of me. You've still got far to go, but you have come an incredibly long way. If I had shown you in the beginning what I just showed you, your heart would have exploded in your chest. In fact, I'm impressed you were able to bear it as well as you did. You have grown strong; that is the whole point of the tests. Not just to prove your loyalty, but to prepare you for the rebirth."

"If I can't even look at you, how will I be able to sit by your side and serve you?" he asked with much concern.

"Ah, my Boy. That is an excellent question. I'm pleased you asked it. You see, Ramond, your problem is that you still have feelings. That's evident by the return of your mother's voice. They have been dulled to a point where you are able to keep them under control, but deep down inside you, they still exist. You must have no emotion. For emotion is the food upon which I feast. Emotion is the damnation of every man. It is the ultimate weakness. It brings about lust, hatred, greed, love, envy, fear, sadness. All things that can be turned against you. When you have overcome all these, and when human life is no longer dear to you, then and only then will you be able to gaze upon me."

THE PERFECT PLACE

"Show me how, Lord," Ramond begged.

"In time, dear boy. You are learning multitudes quickly. Before long, you will be right where you deserve to be... but to change the subject for a moment if I may, you look terrible Ramond. I do not say that as an insult. I relay that to you as mere observation. I understand these tests have not been easy on you. But I vow to you this... two more and I will deliver. As promised, the keys to this world and others will be handed over to you. In fact, let me whet your appetite with this. Watch closely."

Ramond opened his eyes as wide as they would go to assure he got a total glimpse of whatever it was his mentor wished to show him. The change in the reflection was slow at first, but little by little Ramond realized what was happening. The Ramond in the mirror grew a good two inches taller. The chest cavity began to inflate, not with air, but with layer upon layer of muscle. Two perfectly proportioned pecks sat outright in the center of his breast plate. The biceps in his arms balled into egg-shaped hard knots. In his stomach four pairs of muscles lined themselves side by side, creating an eight pack even the most physically fit could never attain.

Even the face changed. The jaw line became more chiseled. Distinct. His hair retracted into his head and became a pleasing shade of blond. It sported a preppie style, and looked very similar to the way the young, handsome stars on television had their mops sculptured. It was a look that suited the man in the mirror, but would not have worked on the real Ramond.

The reflection was perfect in every way. From head to toe there was not an ounce of fat. The physique was not overly muscular like a bodybuilder, but lean and sleek, like a jungle cat.

MICHAEL BISHOP

After all that he had done, Ramond still did not consider himself gay; but he had to admit to himself that the reflection was undoubtedly the most handsome man on Earth.

"This will be your body when you are reborn. It will still have some of the old Ramond flavor. But as you can see, it will be much, much better. And the kicker is that your body will stay in this condition no matter what you do to it. No exercising, no dieting, no work at all. What do you think about that?"

"It's marvelous," he managed. In his heart he wanted nothing more than to be the most handsome man in existence. It would add to his power. Giving him favor with every female alive. The thought of every woman on earth wanting to be with him aroused him instantly and the bulge pressed through his pants. He shifted his position slowly, attempting to regain a comfortable stance. He hoped, for embarrassment's sake, that the master did not notice.

"Marvelous? Is that all you've got to say about it? Well wait, because there's even more still," his flawless reflection spoke, sounding more like a salesman peddling steak knives than the *Dark One*.

He couldn't wait to see what else was in store. It was like watching a movie that revealed to you what your future would be like. The scene in the mirror did not change for several seconds. Then, on each side of the reflection, other objects began to appear. They were so transparent at first that Ramond was unable to make them out. But as they began to solidify, their luscious curves and bulging breasts gave away their identities.

By the time they fully materialized, Ramond's mouth was salivating to the point that he had to wipe the drool from his chin.

THE PERFECT PLACE

Their hourglass waists rounded upward to a bust that showed no sign that gravity affected them at all. They wore no clothing, but stood bare, wrapped around each of the reflection's arms. Their skin was a deep bronze, almost a golden shade. It was a color Ramond knew the sun could not create on normal human skin.

They each stood the same height, one head beneath the perfect Ramond. The toned muscularity of their legs showed no signs of scars or flaws. Fingernails and toenails were supernaturally well kept and each one measured the same to the exact centimeter.

Their lips a dark, disturbing red; like fresh blood. Ramond's eyes were pulled to their nipples. They were erect with excitement, like Ramond himself.

The smiles on their faces alone were enough to bring exquisite lust. Their sensual features would have made even the most devout holy-man crumble to his knees with eroticism. The total of their appearance and allure were enough to seduce a man into Hell.

The only difference between the two was the color of their hair and eyes. The one on the left had platinum hair. It reached shoulder length and hung evenly on all sides. Her eyes were more like jewels, lovingly placed into sockets. Their blue resembled topaz: untouched and uncut by man.

The other had a longer mane of hair, falling down to the center of her spine. With her head cocked to one side, her black hair left a path for her eyes to shine through. They seemed to radiate from her head, gleaming a greenness that matched the color of Ramond's iris exactly.

They were angels, Ramond first thought. After all, Satan had taken half the angels with him when he fell. And these two beings possessed ethereal features so striking that

MICHAEL BISHOP

only God himself could have created them.

But as he looked into each one's eyes, Ramond knew exactly who had formed them. Deep in the nymphs' pupils a fire blazed, and in the center of it all, the figure loomed.

"Wouldn't you like to have creatures of your own like these to do with as you please?" he inquired, looking left and right at the two vixens on his arms. They stood quietly, gripped to their master. Their face unable to make any expression other than a seductive smirk.

"Of course. No man could resist the desire, Master," Ramond admitted freely. There was no need to lie. Even though the lust he felt was an emotion, and therefore a weakness, saying anything other than the truth would be detrimental to him. His father would see through a false statement. After all, the creatures were no doubt created solely to tempt men, and performed with great success.

"Well, you will have these, soon. And much more. All you have to do are two more small things for me. And together, you and I will knock God off his throne and crush him below our feet."

"I can't wait. I will fulfill the two immediately. Just let me know what you want."

"I intend to, but enough show and tell for now," the image replied and snapped his fingers. With the snap, the nymphs faded out of existence in the same manner they came. With them the reflection began to shrink. The muscles deflated like an emptying hot water bottle. Ramond's reflection returned to normal. "That's better. Nothing to distract us while we discuss the most important part of life. DEATH!" Satan spurted.

Surely the master was not about to ask him to take another life. He had done it once already. To do it again

THE PERFECT PLACE

seemed redundant, like making a bed that has already been made.

"You don't want me to kill again do you?" Ramond pried. The repulsiveness of the act leaked through his voice, making obvious his feelings about the act of murder.

"Let's not look at it as killing or murder or whatever your trivial little mind wants to think of it as. Let's think of it in the way God himself does. As a sacrifice."

"A sacrifice?"

"Yes. You've read the Bible. You should know that God did ask for sacrifices. What's the difference you ask? Nothing at all. But if it works for God, I guess it will work for me."

"Who do you want me to sacrifice?" he questioned begrudgingly. Murder was murder. No matter whose name it was done in. Ramond felt like nothing more than a hired assassin. Fortunately, the bounty was high enough to pay for his services.

"Not so fast. This is no mere sacrifice. These last two acts are the big ones. Each one will prepare you to gaze upon me without reprisal. They will give you the giant leaps you need to take before you are ready. They must be done correctly. Due to the fact that they are a sacrifice to me, you must take great care, time, and attention to detail. These will be your ultimate gifts to me. A symbol of your undying love and devotion. You will offer these acts up to the most High One, whom you have chosen to give your life to...that would be me," he finished and smiled at Ramond with a sinister grin that looked very much like Johnny when he first laid eyes on Ramond.

"What would you like done?" he pouted. The long lecture on devotion and love did nothing to ease the disgust of killing. It was still work done by madmen and pond scum.

"God sent his son to Earth to die on a cross. That is fact. It is one of the few truths the Bible holds. Jesus Christ was killed and tortured brutally on the cross thousands of years ago at Calvary. You will never hear me refute this. I admit it without reservation. It was God's sacrifice for man. He spilled his own son's blood in an attempt to wash away the sins of all mankind. But it was an act done in vain. You see, this Earth belongs to me and every living thing that dwells on its surface belongs to me as well. That includes you humans. Which makes God's great sacrifice for naught. Sin still exists today. It always will, and no amount of the holy-man's blood will ever change that." The reflection looked down and snickered to himself before beginning again.

"But I must admit, as a sacrifice it was quite impressive. I want you to perform a similar sacrifice. Not in the name of God. But in the name of Mephistopheles."

"But I have no children to sacrifice to you?" Ramond mumbled confusedly. He was sure Satan was aware of the fact, but could think of no better way of expressing his bewilderment.

"You idiot. I am apprised of the fact that you have no offspring. If you would shut that hole in your face and listen to my instruction, maybe we could stop wasting time and you could get on with business... The point of the sacrifice is not to sacrifice any child. It's the crucifixion itself I like. It is so beautifully painful. So raw and torturous. It is one, if not the most agonizing deaths a man can suffer. You really have no idea of all the little things that go into it. You suffer in so many different ways. It's not just the nailing of the hands and feet. It is so much more.

"You will soon get to witness its complexity first

THE PERFECT PLACE

hand. And if the truth be known, it is a death that I invented personally. I had my minions practice on scores of mortals until I perfected the technique. I had the act ready when God sent his son. It was my men who carried it out. I was a willing accomplice to the sacrifice. I knew, even then, that it was in vain, but the opportunity to hurt him by torturing his son was too sweet to pass up. I love the brutality of it so much, I want you to recreate it for me. The first act of two that will finalize our pact." Satan's voice beamed through the words on the trail of each syllable. There was lust in his tone when he spoke of the brutality and the death of Christ. He talked about pain and torment in such a way that it came across as romantic. Suffering turned into an art.

"Who would you liked sacrificed, Lord?" The conveyance of his master's desire for the act made the crucifixion less repulsive to Ramond. He knew it was an incredibly sadistic way to put an end to a man's life, but the knowledge that it would be such an important move in the process of attaining power made the thought of it easier for Ramond to deal with.

"The sacrificial lamb lives by the name John McCalister, and shall die by the name *Traitor*. He is a man your age, Ramond, and just like you, he is full of life and zest. Of course these things you will take from him, but I did think it would be wise to let you know that Mr. McCalister will not lie down while you kill him. He is a fighter. A man of curious resources. And he could easily surprise you if you let him."

Ramond wasn't sure what Satan meant when he spoke of the man as a traitor. But he was clear on the other point being relayed to him. John McCalister would be a tough target, and Ramond would have to be on his guard if he wanted to succeed.

MICHAEL BISHOP

"Where can I find John McCalister?"

"He lives in Olive Branch, Mississippi, a suburb of Memphis. He is a commuter and works in Memphis at a local supermarket. The man has worked hard in the past month, and has already assumed the position of Assistant Night Manager. There are three 'Pig in the Basket' stores in Memphis. His lies on Winchester Road. That should give you sufficient information to find this man."

"Yes sir. It does. I will find him and when I do..."

"When you do, you will hang him from a cross in honor of me."

"Yes sir," Ramond mulled quietly.

"What's the matter Ramond? You don't seem excited about being so close," Satan spewed.

"No, Sire. Don't get me wrong. I love serving you and I love the fact that I am so close. It's just... It's just that torture is such an awful thing."

"IT'S NOT TORTURE, YOU COWARD! IT'S A SACRIFICE!" The voice exploded and as it did, the figure in the eyes leapt forward once more and became the head. Ramond did not even try to look this time, but the small glimpse he accidentally caught was enough. His eyes seared shut again, and the unequaled burning rose in his face. "IT'S A SACRIFICE AND YOU WILL DO IT AND LIKE IT!"

"YES... OH GOD...YES. I'M SORRY...PLEASE!!! OH PLEASE!" Ramond moaned as he groped at his eyes. He ripped at them and rubbed them for what seemed like ages. He ground his palms into his sockets trying to relieve the burn, until he realized they did not hurt anymore. The pain had left seconds ago, but Ramond was so busy with his whimpering that it took time for his brain to catch up and realize it.

THE PERFECT PLACE

One eye slowly opened and then the other. They were back to normal and his vision was twenty-twenty. All that stood before him was a mirror. The reflection in it was his own. When he raised his hand in front of his face, the reflection did the same. When he stepped back, the reflection stepped with him. Leaning forward he stuck his nose directly to the glass and left a smudge mark in the shape of his nostrils. He looked into his own eyes for any sign of the flames. None remained. All he saw were bloodshot pupils and sandbags that could secure a levee. No sign of Satan. His reflection was no longer possessed. The mirror had been exorcized.

He stepped away. Ramond had seen enough of himself for one day. But he had also been given a peek into the future. A future where he was a perfect specimen. It brought a coy smile to his lips. A smile that was soon nullified by the thought of torture.

† † † † † † † † † † † †

The rest he had promised himself was long overdue. He cleared his mind and refused to think about the chores ahead. The odorous covers were pulled over his head to block out the world. Pure, undisturbed rest laid before him as he settled in for a night of sweet slumber.

It took just minutes for him to fall asleep, and just a bit longer for the dreams to begin. They were not the hell-induced dreams brought on by the Devil. They were self-induced nightmares brought on by his own sick mind. Which was worse, he was not sure.

MICHAEL BISHOP

† † † † † † † † † † †

They touched him and caressed his naked body. It was heaven. The one with the green eyes slowly licked his lips, as the blonde went down. The tip of his tongue flicked across her nipple, and her moans were more like the soothing strums of a harp. They were the essence of sex. The perfect female objects. They did what was commanded without question or hesitation, and Ramond began to see a little of himself in them.

He pushed green eyes's hair back as she frenched the inside of his ear. Shivers flooded his body at her touch. Ramond was in utter ecstasy. And the best part about the nymphs was that the fire no longer marked their eyes with the brand that said they belonged to Satan. Now they belonged to Ramond. Slaves to his desire.

He could not control himself, he had to watch blue eyes while she was doing her thing. Her lips on it was the best part of the experience, and the thought of watching her work only aroused him more. Looking past the dark haired vixen, he had a perfect view of blue eyes. Only it was no longer blue eyes.

The child's familiar face met his own as she continued to bob up and down. The Catholic uniform still clung to her frame. Her own blood could be seen dried to her upper lip where Ramond had punished her. And although he could not see it, somehow he knew her panties were still tucked half way in and halfway out of her skirt.

He wanted to scream at the sight of her, but no noise or motion scampered from his lips. She smiled in recognition of his horror and continued to perform.

THE PERFECT PLACE

"I WANT MY BLOOD BACK!" Susan Lints said, although her lips never strayed from what they were doing. The words came from her, somewhere, but was more telepathic than physical.

Ramond was frozen in time. Unable to move, or shriek, or hide from the little girl who was no longer so helpless.

The innocence was gone from her face, just like it had after he had raped her. Her face wrinkled witch-like as she did her job. There was an evil in her, as if all the purity she had once possessed had been replaced with an equal amount of wickedness.

The piercing feel of ripping flesh and the gushing of blood filled Ramond as she bit into his member. Jarard's tongue passed through his mind as he assumed the cutting of it might have felt similar to this atrocious pain.

It took her several hard chomps to completely separate his penis from him. Her smile broadened as she leaned up, sitting on her knees. Half hung from her mouth as the blood dripped from the severed end. Her tiny mouth kept on chomping away. She took inhuman bites. Her jaws separated like a serpent swallowing a rodent, and she took as much as she wanted down her throat.

More and more of it disappeared into her mouth as she swallowed it bit by bit. A shrill laugh escaped from her, although once again her lips never showed a sign of it. It was just understood. There was no mistaking that the sound came from inside her, in the pit of her soul.

Blood spurted high from the hole between his legs. Some of it struck Susan directly in the face. The rest just disappeared off the bed.

He managed to glance to his side. The bed was no

longer in a room, but in a massless void. Besides himself, the bed, and those who shared the bed with him, the rest of existence was a black abyss. Nothing was above, below, or beside Ramond. They were floating in emptiness.

The licking in his ear was calming, and almost made the pain of being dismembered tolerable. The chills shot through his body like snow dogs pulling an unmanned sled. The licker stopped kissing his ear and drew Ramond's attention away from Susan and the darkness.

The green eyed goddess no longer serviced him. She had been replaced with good-natured Horace Snide. Horace said nothing as Ramond looked him over. The pot-bellied man just stared back with an expression that resembled love.

Horace's mouth opened as if he might speak. Instead, the tip of his tongue oozed from his mouth. It slithered from his lips slowly. Six inches. Then eight. Then a foot. It continued to stretch until it reached a yard. The organ had a mind of its own and moved around like an eel in the ocean.

The tongue came toward Ramond's face and stopped in front of his lips. It flicked its tip back and forth, lapping Ramond from below his nose to his chin. It continued licking while saliva flowed freely from Horace's wide mouth.

The spit traveled the path down the tongue until it hit Ramond's lips. It began to drench his face, then trickled down his chin, to his chest, and finally down to the place where his testicles laid without a shaft to keep them company.

The blood and spit ran together creating a foul scented concoction, much like the farts of the old man in the elevator. The soaking mouth water continued to pour with increasing rapidness. It was warm. Almost soothing. It seemed to make the pain in his crotch subside a little as it ran over the bloody stump.

THE PERFECT PLACE

He heard the giggle again in his mind and his head blasted back to the girl. Susan chewed on the last bites of it, but no more could be seen coming from her mouth. She had cleaned her plate, and Ramond just hoped she would not come back for dessert.

The saliva did not run off the bed. Instead it collected on it. Making a rectangular pool all around him. The flow increased from the mouth, and Ramond had to press his lips tightly shut to keep the spittle from running into his own mouth and into his lungs. The liquid river stacked up around him, covering his legs first and rising fast.

Even though he was propped up on pillows, it did not take long for the puddle to cover his mouth and begin flowing into his nostrils.

Air was blown out of his nose to keep the substance out. It reached his eyes. The spittle was so irritating that he closed them securely. A steady flow of bubbles poured from his nose, but the air was running out quickly. He had failed to take a deep breath while there was still time; and the higher the tide rose, the more eminent a mistake it became.

His oxygen was running out. There were few moments left. The thick liquid bogged him down and as it increased it pressed harder down upon him. Through his clogged ears he was able to make out a muffled noise. At first it was nearly inaudible, but the closer he listened the louder it got. It was a gurgling, he thought, and listened closer. As his last supply of air dwindled, he realized exactly what the noise was.

Even though Susan Lints was covered just as he was, she was still laughing at him. It was a gurgling, phantom laugh. It mocked him and played a sour tune of revenge. It was a laugh that said, "I got you fucker! I got you!"

MICHAEL BISHOP

It may have been the sick, twistedness of his mind, but something within him had to see her one more time before he went. Just one last look into her face before it was all over. He eased his eyes open, expecting to glare through a sticky mire. But as irrational as dreams are, the scene had changed again, and he found himself in new surroundings.

He was no longer laying in his bed, but his back was still laying against something. It was hard and rough. A quick feel of his hand behind him and he realized it was concrete. His eyes had not yet adjusted. A new liquid now surrounded him. It was harsh on the eyes. Stinging. He used moderate force to keep them open.
The liquid was crystal blue. A color he had seen somewhere before. When his eyes finally adjusted themselves, Ramond immediately recognized where he was.
The pale face stared down at him with stolidness. It was not condescending or judgmental. It was impassive and unaware of his presence. The man's arms floated limp at an angle just below his chest. As he stared into the dead eyes of Mark Peters, Ramond knew exactly where he was.
 The hard concrete bottom scraped his back and he grasped that he was lying at the bottom of an immaculately clean pool. Mark himself had probably kept the pool looking this good, Ramond thought to himself as the light began to fade from his eyes. He had gone without air a bit longer than humans were allowed and his life was almost spent.

In that moment the stronger side of him took control. It was the side that had pushed him from the beginning, even though his body was growing more frail by the hour. It slapped him and screamed, *DON'T GIVE UP NOW, YOU*

-266-

THE PERFECT PLACE

PUSSY! REMEMBER THE DEAL. REMEMBER THE PROMISE! REMEMBER THE POWER!

The voice stirred something in him. Made him feel invincible. His foot hit the bottom of the pool with great force as he pushed himself upward. His eyes locked on the surface above as the glow slowly faded from his brain. He was not sure he was going to make it. But he was sure if he failed that it would not be without giving it his all.

It would only take a few more seconds, but he was already on borrowed time. Ramond barely managed to make out the body of Uncle Mark as he floated up past him. The surface and all of its magnificent air was just within reach, and he thought he just might make it.

Just as the tip of his skull broke the surface, Ramond bolted upright in bed. Oxygen couldn't enter his lungs fast enough as he sucked it in. He breathed through his nose, then his mouth, then his nose again. The rapid air flow burned his nostrils. He choked on the wind current. When he was sure his body had regained all the air it had lost and more, he regulated his breathing back to normal.

This dream was not merely a joke taunted by Satan. He was sure. This time his mind had created the scenario. It punished him for his crimes. It made sure he did not forget the horridness of what he had done. He knew he must hurry and finish the acts. If he did not, he was sure to break. His own mind had already begun turning against him. And with your own head as your enemy, it's just a matter of time before it breaks you open like a chick who no longer wishes to be cooped up in its egg.

MICHAEL BISHOP

Six hours of sleep was gained before the dream came. The bags under his eyes had subsided a bit, and he felt recharged and ready to put an end to his quest. His body had gotten used to getting little sleep. Once, a night where he got under eight hours would have resulted in irritability and laziness for the entire length of the day. But now, what little sleep he was able to get was like time spent charging a battery. It rejuvenated him. Enabled him to last a few hours longer.

He resurrected from his bed and changed clothes. The garments he wore had grown gamey. Fresh attire made him feel almost as good as the sleep had.

†††††††††††††

The bottom drawer of his dresser was opened and a book was removed. "The Complete Illustrated Child's Bible" the spine read. It was the first Bible he had ever owned, and had been traded in at an early age. It, of course, was not a real Bible, but a simplified version with fables and tales of Christ and the many other heroes of the Bible. Every few pages there was a drawing, illustrating whatever story the book was telling at that point. The pictures always seemed to have a bit too much blue in them, as if the artist had an abundance of that color and wanted to make sure he made use of it.

Because the child's Bible was not genuine, Ramond had put it aside and insisted his mother buy him one that was real. Vernadette went to the local bookstore soon after and purchased a leather bound edition with his initials engraved on the cover. The Holy Bible was presented to him with pride, and in time was used more than her personal Bible that

THE PERFECT PLACE

she had owned for years.

The child's Bible was the Bible Ramond carried to church. After all, in church you really never read anyway. You listened to the preacher read, which made having a Bible yourself useless. So he took the illustrated book along with him. If it were to get lost or damaged, it would be no big loss. But if his leather bound prize were to become misplaced, that would be a most unpleasant occurrence.

He opened the "Illustrated Child's Bible" for the first time in years. It had been kept only because of the memories locked away in its pages. When he was bored in church, which happened to be most of the time, he would sneak a pen from his mother's purse and draw his own illustrations on the back side of the pictured pages.

He stared at the first thing he had drawn. It was done on the back of a picture of David swinging a sling over his head. Ramond's picture had less of a clear meaning. It was a collage of circles and triangles. In each one he had drawn eyes and a smiley face. Stick arms and legs had been added to the creations during later tiresome sermons. The figures resembled cave drawings, and he smiled at himself for ever being so young.

The pages were flipped in search of another picture. Not a picture he had drawn himself, but rather one that belonged in the book. It was the reason he had taken the Bible out to begin with.

Illustrations of Noah and Samson and Moses were passed by until he came to the one he sought. This picture too was barraged with an overuse of blue. The majority of the art was a sky background. Its blueness stretched for miles with no clouds or sun to add spice or variety. But the main focus of the drawing had been sketched with incredible detail.

He held the book close to his face admiring the grueling time that must have been spent adding every drop of blood and sweat in the character. In the center of the page, Jesus hung crucified on two wooden stakes that had been intersected into a cross. A thorny crown had been smashed into his skull, and the blood ran into his eyes as he gazed down at his accusers.

The crowd below him could not be seen. The picture cut off just below his feet. But the rendering showed pity in Jesus's eyes. It was a look that said even though he was suffering beyond comprehension, he still felt more sorrow for those who had done this to him than he did for himself. It was a powerful piece, and Ramond studied it for a long while in silence.

The work had never before been this closely scrutinized, but he was still surprised he had never noticed Jesus' hands before. Over the years spent in church, he must have spent hours on that picture alone; but in all that time, never once had he noticed that the nails were not driven through Jesus' hands like he had always been told. Instead, they were in his wrists. Between the two bones that extended from the hand.

It was a marvelous revelation, and it made perfect sense. The more he thought about it, the more he understood that you could not crucify a man by nailing his hands. He examined his own hands front and back. With all his weight hanging from the flesh in his palms, they would surely rip through and he would fall from the cross. But if the nails were placed through the wrist bones, they would be secure enough to keep from ripping completely through.

THE PERFECT PLACE

This must have been what the master meant when he said he had his minions practice the act to perfection before he tried it on Jesus. It was a process that, no doubt, would be trial and error, until you figured out exactly how to hang your victim.

Had Ramond not seen the picture, he would have ignorantly nailed the man through the hands. It would have been a mistake that would have ruined the sacrifice. He felt very fortunate he decided to dig up the old book.
It was returned to the drawer and he closed it shut, never to reflect upon it again. It was another chapter in his life that had been ripped out and thrown into the wind, like they all eventually would be.

On a tablet he jotted down a list of supplies. It would take many tools and much work to bring the crucifixion to life. Every detail was probed in his mind, and with each idea he wrote down the object he would need. When he was done, the list fully covered the page.

The location was the second hurdle to overcome. Ramond couldn't exactly plant a cross and crucify a man in his front yard. Privacy was of the utmost importance. He, nor his family, owned any private land, which narrowed his options considerably.
A decision had to be made. He could either travel to Olive Branch and hunt for a suitable location there, or bring

MICHAEL BISHOP

John McCalister back to Sierra Springs, to an area of his choosing. Each side had its advantages, and the ruling was not to be made hastily.

Olive Branch was bound to be well-wooded, as the majority of Mississippi was. It should not be too hard to find a secret place, deep in the heart of some secluded woods, where no one could hear screaming or see what he was up to. And the fact that he would not have to drag McCalister far was the sweetest part of the dish.

But there were a few kinks in the chain. He was not familiar with the area. In truth, it would probably take a map just to find the town to begin with. To find a suitable site and erect a cross before the landowner discovered him was unlikely. It would be hard enough to build the cross in the first place, and looking over his shoulder every five minutes for an old man with a shotgun determined to protect his land from trespassers would make it impossible.

The option of sacrificing the man in his hometown had about as many strikes against it. The idea of kidnaping John McCalister and carting him hundreds of miles away left Ramond with a bad feeling. He had been warned that McCalister was a fighter. There was no telling what could happen in the time it took him to take the man from point A to point B.

Another catch was that if he carried out the job in Sierra Springs there would be a much greater risk of being linked to the crime. If the body ever was found, the police would begin by searching locally for the murderer. A guy who looked the way Ramond did would be the first person the cops would try to finger.

It was not an easy decision, but the hometown team

THE PERFECT PLACE

won out in the end. The fact of the matter was it would be easier to work on his own turf. The materials for the job were easier to get in town, due to the fact that he knew exactly where to go to pick the items up.

The clincher was that Ramond already had a spot in mind for the sacrifice. The more he pictured the place in his mind's eye, the more he became convinced it would suit his purposes well. Hopefully by the time the body was found, the seventh test would be completed and he would no longer have to worry about the repercussions. It was a chance he would have to take, as was the kidnaping and transporting of John McCalister.

† † † † † † † † † † †

At seventeen, Ramond was invited to a unique wedding. The bride was a hefty young colt named Wendy Demton. Her lover and husband-to-be, Tony Janner, was given the title "Apprentice Master" in a bland cult that had taken the name "Clan of the Five Stars".

The clan was another sect that quickly came and went in Ramond's life. A putrid array of people who joined together in an attempt to begin a different kind of church. In the end, it became identical to all the other groups that were formed in hopes of creating a distinct style of worship.

The ceremony took place on a stretch of land in the center of an overgrown cotton field. The cult members worked diligently to clear the area for the special day when Wendy and Tony were to become *one* forever. The land was deep behind a curtain of woods, hidden from the prying eyes of outsiders, and unknown to all but a chosen few invited guests.

MICHAEL BISHOP

A card table was set up near an enormous oak tree. Chips and dip were set on the table instead of an actual banquet. Ten feet from the tree, a large circle was scraped into the dirt. Inside that circle a pentagram was drawn, and between all five points of the larger pentagram, smaller pentagrams were drawn. The five pentagrams within the circle sparked the idea for the handle "Clan of the Five Stars".

Inside the carving, the bride and groom stood holding hands and gawking foolishly at one another. Carrollton Irish, the sect's founder, stood before the couple in the bottom tip of the large triangle. The significance of the symbols and the position of each person inside the symbols, Ramond did not know. Most likely, the participants did not know either. As with so many groups, they made up the rules as they went along, like a secret club that young boys might start in a treehouse.

A crystal glass filled to the rim with fresh goat's blood was passed through the group of spectators. Each guest was expected to take a drink from the cup to signify unity among the order. It was a common protocol among Satanists. The bride and groom were then supposed to guzzle the last remains of the blood from the glass.

THE PERFECT PLACE

Ramond was not at all pleased at the thought of drinking after so many strangers. When the glass was passed to him, he dampened his lips in the brew and performed his best impression of a gulp, before handing the blood to the man at his right.

The groom was cloaked in a white sheet that had been slit at the top to allow passage for his head. The bride was dressed in similar garb, except the color of her sheet was black. Supposedly the garments were a symbol of marriage between the light and the dark: the good and the bad.

According to the Five Stars' belief system, there was no difference between the two. All things were neither holy nor evil, but neutral. All actions were simply meant to be. Therefore, there were no bad deeds and no good deeds.

After this rhetoric was explained by Carrollton, the two were declared wedded in the name of the Spirit of the Earth. The chubby blonde kissed her awkward, bowlegged spouse deeply, and the spectators cheered and clapped with great enthusiasm.

Ramond pounded his hands together out of politeness only. The entire festivity had taken under thirty minutes, and was the most boring he had ever had the displeasure of attending. The marriage would not be honored or recognized by any court in the land, and Ramond knew it. It was all for show, an act in order to draw and impress unsuspecting members.

The scenario was common. A member would invite someone to a *secret* ceremony, and stress to them just how secret it was and that they must not tell a soul. That was the bait. An attempt to perk curiosity. Once there, the ceremony was projected as being so meaningful and moving that no one could resist joining. For some it might have worked, but

MICHAEL BISHOP

Ramond had seen this charade a dozen times before, and could spot it as soon as the invitation was given.

The invitation was accepted only because Larry Husk, the one who gave it, was a co-worker, and Ramond did not want to disappoint him; but when the wedding was done, he wished he would have politely declined and saved himself the pain of boredom and loss of time.

The first chance that availed itself, he gave the bride and groom his insincere best wishes and vowed he would come to the next meeting. He pulled the Ford onto the dirt road that led to the clearing and never went back.

Through the underworld grapevine, he had heard a little more about the Clan of the Five Stars. It had been constructed by Carrollton Irish two months before the wedding. The thirty-seven year old had inherited a few cotton fields upon the death of his last living relative. Most of the land, excluding the section on which the ceremony had been held, was sold off to finance various groups which he attempted to form. Each cult he founded was primarily the same, set up exclusively so that he might declare himself supreme leader. It was his own little way of voting himself *class president*.

Naturally, there was always a crop of rebellious teenagers who were willing to join any club that made them feel important, but the ending resulted the same each time. The groups bickered and argued until they fell apart at the seams.

The same was true with the Clan of the Five Stars and the sect broke apart three months after Wendy and Tony were married. Wendy and Tony broke up one month after that.

Carrollton Irish attempted to start a few other groups

THE PERFECT PLACE

after the clan's demise, such as "The Lords of the Inner God", "The Bride of the Earth", and "The Ethereal Searchers", to name a few. All were even bigger failures than the "Clan of the Five Stars", and eventually Carrollton's financial resources ran out. With it, so did his chance at leadership.

Just six month earlier, Ramond had heard that Carrollton Irish was missing. No signs of his body were found. No clues to his whereabouts located. To the world he was a ghost. Mystically disappearing without leaving a vapor trail.

† † † † † † † † † † † †

Carrollton Irish may have vanished, but it was a sure bet that his little stretch of land, deep in the wood of Sierra Springs had not. Ramond headed toward it with great anticipation. He had to see if it was as perfect as he remembered. An area created for sacrifice.

Typically, Ramond would never have been able to remember the route to an out-of-the-way spot far in the heart of the forest, but once again fate swung the pendulum of good fortune his way. At the time, it was meaningless to him. Larry Husk, who had so desperately insisted he attend the nuptial, had drawn him a wonderfully detailed map of the spot. Ramond eyed the map and assured Larry that with such a specific map, he would find it easily.

He didn't.

The dirt road was no straight shot by any means. The main road had dozens of smaller side roads that branched in every direction. They led to farmhouses, barns, other fields,

MICHAEL BISHOP

and some simply led to nothing at all. It was blatant arrogance that made Ramond decide he did not need the map in the first place. He looked at it only for a moment before he began trekking down endless gravel-covered roads.

After an hour of searching fruitlessly, he began to curse himself for not studying the map to begin with. It was useless now with no point to start from. He could be anywhere on its pencil-drawn roads, and with no landmarks to judge his location, he was driving blindly through the wilderness.

Somehow, the roads twisted and merged until he ended up back where he had started, at the intersection of the main road and the gravel road. He grabbed Larry Husk's map and ran his finger a dozen times over the path he would take. It was like the kids' puzzles he had as a child, beginning at the start of a maze and finding the only path that was not blocked until you reached the exit.

At every new road he came to, Ramond stopped the car and reached for the map to confirm it was the correct turn to make. Not a single wrong turn was made as he followed the paper. Sure enough, as it was signified by a big X in the center of the paper, X marked the spot.

He swore to himself as he stepped out of the car and into the presence of the awaiting bride and groom, that if he ever had to come back to the sight, God forbid, he would remember the way. Map or no map.

Five years had passed, and the directions were still engraved in Ramond's memory like an epitaph on a tombstone. He made no wrong turns as he skillfully guided the Ford through the series of twists and turns. In under fifteen minutes, he had arrived at the site.

THE PERFECT PLACE

It looked nothing like he remembered, thanks to the many weeds and thick brush that had accumulated on the area. The spot, though, was unmistakable. It laid at the end of a narrow path that was not wide enough to command the word *road*.

It was not covered with gravel like the others. This passage was financed by Carrollton himself, to ensure even the road workers did not know it existed. It was flattened with a rented dozer and topped with loose, red clay dirt to keep the weeds from growing back over it. The dirt had done the job well. The brush had managed to overtake everything else, but the pathway was free of the foliage.

The oak tree was the marker that convinced Ramond it was indeed the right spot. It towered proudly above all else. The leaves just beginning to transform into a breath taking pumpkin orange. Soon they would lie amongst the growth below and rot away, feeding the hunger of the weeds.

He stepped out of the car and stared ahead at the land. The place was not perfect yet, but it would be. Once the brush and weeds and briars were cleared out, and the grass was chopped down. Once the cross stood in its center as proudly as the oak tree stood on its side. Then, it would indeed be *perfect*.

The acres were as private as any he could imagine, and with Carrollton Irish out of the picture, no one should stumble by. Most likely, the body of his sacrifice would never be found. Sure it was possible that years down the road some construction crew might excavate the bones from the earth; but by that time, Ramond would be long gone from this world.

His only regret was the backbreaking work it would

take to prepare the area. Much was to be done and he took one last deep breath of air before stepping back into his car. The air was even sweeter than it was in "Moneydale". Perhaps, in the end, it was the animals who had it best of all.

†††††††††††

Upon entry to his room, Ramond grabbed the supply list he had made and revised it. There were many tools not on the list that he would need. Seeing the piece of land and the ominous job it would take to ready it, brought all the tools he would need to mind.

After each item was purchased, he would be broke. The money in his account would just cover things if he shopped wisely. He dearly hoped the seventh act would not cost a dime. After this one he was not sure he would have one to spare. If it did, he would be forced to rob a liquor store or gas station. It was not a pleasant thought. For now, he focused on number six.

†††††††††††

Sierra Home Hardware had no competition in the town. The store was the only one in Sierra Springs that dealt in hardware supplies and building materials. Ramond pulled into a parking space close to the front entrance. At nine in the morning, the store had just opened its doors and was free of customers. He pulled the list from his back pocket and grabbed a pen from the glove box. He would check each item off as he bought it to make certain he forgot nothing. It was imperative that he got every tool he needed for the job. Each one was a necessity.

THE PERFECT PLACE

The most expensive item was purchased first so that he could budget his money for the rest. He stepped beneath the aisle marker number 20 and went to the gas-powered trimmers. Most used weak line, suitable for slicing grass and small weeds. But this job would take more power than they produced.

At the end of the row, he spotted a trimmer with a brush-cutter attachment on clearance. The weed-eating season was coming to an end and the store had placed all the trimmers on sale in order to make room for Christmas supplies. It had been marked down fifty percent to $75.00. It was a bargain. With the time it would save him, it was more than just a tool; it was an investment. The bushwhacker was scratched from the list.

He set the trimmer in his basket and pushed it to the tool aisle in the hardware department. This time his choice was made a bit more carefully. At least fifty different kinds of hammers hung on the rack. One by one, Ramond picked them up and held them in his palm. He inspected the different weights between them, the head size, the length of their shaft, their material, and their price.

After fifteen minutes of deliberation, he decided to go with a large fiberglass hammer. Its construction would almost guarantee it not to break under heavy strain, and it was on sale too. But the point that sold it was the grid on the tip of it. Its head was formed with notches on it. Every strike on the nail would cause the hammer to grip it and not slip. It was a man's hammer.

Ten other odds and ends were placed into the buggy and he headed to the checkout counter. He told the cashier that in addition to the items in the basket, he would be needing some boards. She filled out a pickup slip, handed it to him and directed him to the back, where the lumber would be located and loaded for him.

Before heading to the rear of Sierra Home Hardware to obtain the most important purchase of all, he filled the back seat with the tools he had bought. The grand total had come to $152.37, leaving him just enough for gas money to get to Memphis.

The store's personnel wore bright green t-shirts with the Sierra Home Hardware logo on the front and back. As Ramond pulled around the back of the store and through the gates leading to the lumber yard, he spotted a uniformed employee and pulled the vehicle next to him. He rolled down the window and nodded.

"Howdy," the worker greeted.

"Hello, I need to pick this up," he said not bothering with small talk as he handed the slip over.

"Let's see," the red-skinned guy started as he stared down at the paper as though he were attempting to teach himself to read. "One six by eight by twelve and one two by ten by ten. Both treated, number two pine."

"Yep," Ramond agreed.

"Where you plannin' on puttin' 'em? Them some big boards ya know," the hillbilly articulated.

Ramond kept his cool. The dark side of him wanted to snap at the man just for having such poor grammar, but he knew the process would go more smoothly if he were polite.

"I was thinking we could just strap it to the hood of the old car here," he replied with a smile.

The man scratched his head and looked at the roof of the car with fascination. "It's gonna get scratched up if we do

THE PERFECT PLACE

that. Besides, you'll have an awful lot hangin' off the front and back if you do that. Ain't very safe. You better go get a truck er somethin and come back later." It was obvious the man did not want to be bothered with doing his job right at the moment. Ramond took a deep breath and begged himself not to explode.

"Well, I don't think I'm going to be able to get a truck. So, if you would, I'd like to try to tie it down if we could. I don't mind if it gets scratched. It's old anyway. Couldn't hurt it much more than it already is," he spoke patiently and politely, and did a professional job of holding his true thoughts and feelings in.

"Well, alright then. Let me go get some help. Them things is heavy. Be right back," he said as he walked out of sight around the side of the lumber bin.

Ramond sat still for several minutes with no sight of the hillbilly. He began to think the man had abandoned him altogether, but just before the urge to lay on the horn won over, the man rounded the corner with an even bigger, more stupid looking man. The two carried the six by eight by twelve on their shoulders. One in the front. One in the back.

They placed it on top of the car as gently as possible, but it still made a loud bang. The roof sunk in a bit, but held its ground. Ramond exited the car to get a better look at the situation. The man had been right about one thing, the board hung off a good four feet in the front and back and looked rather dangerous. The entire car resembled a metallic knight about to engage in a joust.

"Maybe if we tie it down real good it'll be alright. Ya think?" the hillbilly asked the newcomer. Both ignored Ramond completely.

"Should be. I'll fetch some line," he reported before

disappearing around the corner. Ramond assumed *line* was another term for rope, and hoped the second man would be swifter than the first.

"I'll go get the other board while he's getting cord. The other board ain't near as heavy as that 'un there was. I can lift it by myself," he boasted as he walked away.

Both returned simultaneously moments later. Once again each one had an end of the board. Ramond guessed the board was a little heavier than the man had thought. Either that or the hillbilly was not as strong as he thought he was.

They set the second board on top less carefully, paying no mind to damaging the car. "Brought a red flag to pin to the front of the boards too. Just in case," the other man told Ramond with a smile and expression on his face like he had done some incredible feat by bringing the plastic red flag.

"Thanks," Ramond managed fakely.

The two men began wrapping the board to the car as if they were entombing a mummy. They were not stingy with the roll of twine they had brought to tie up the lumber. They tied it in two dozen places, including in the center, running it through the windows of the car. The job was done well. The knots were secure and tight: Boy Scout knots.

"You oughta make it. Just don't slam your brakes too fast, hear?" the hillbilly joked and the two men burst into giggles. Ramond laughed along with them in relief that he would soon be out of the company of these dullards.

"I won't," he assured as he slipped into the car. The advice was actually not bad, had it come from someone just slightly more intelligent.

He drove from the gates slowly and inched his way from the parking lot. Back roads were taken when available.

THE PERFECT PLACE

If a police car saw him, he might get stopped. The wood jutting so far from the car was definitely illegal. But he knew his hometown well, and the roads it possessed. The gravel turnoff was reached without incident, and by lunchtime Ramond was on his way back to the spot where the tedious work would begin.

† † † † † † † † † † †

The grass was thigh high and he hoped he would not disturb a sleepy asp nestled deep in the brush, away from the rays of the sun. Snakes seemed to be everywhere in the forests of the South, and Ramond had dealt with enough serpents lately to last him a lifetime.

The brush cutter's rope pulled with little resistance and the motor roared to life. There was not a house within seven miles, and Ramond doubted the sound of the motor would carry that distance. The woods belonged to him. He shared them with no one but the animals that surrounded him; and even they came nowhere near the sound of his labor.

Even the heavy duty brush cutter was obviously meant for smaller jobs. It became evident as he placed its spinning, three-pointed blade on top of the first section of growth. It whined and cried, indicating it was not at all pleased with the thickness of the area it was being asked to topple. But as Ramond persisted to push the blade forward, it slowly grinded through the quagmire of foliage.

The work was slow. *Extremely slow.* The area was not only weeds, but saplings, and honeysuckle, and kudzu. It took what seemed like an eternity to make a dent in the stuff; and just when Ramond thought he was getting a foothold, the gas-guzzling machine would choke and die, demanding more fuel be placed into its engine. By the time the light of the sun began to fade on the horizon, the car had already been siphoned down to a quarter of a tank to feed the weed wacker.

The taste of gasoline lined the bottom of his mouth and gave a sick smell with his sweat. He stepped back and stretched out his aching muscles. The bags beneath his eyes had returned with a fury, and his belly rioted internally for something to fill it. The palms of his hands had grown numb where the vibrations of the weedeater had worked them all day. And Ramond's back felt as if it would break if he tried to straighten up entirely.

The oak had been a helpful friend. The sun whipped his face with hatred and left it red and scorched. But the tree had blocked out a great portion of the rays, and kept his skin from being seriously damaged.

Even after he had pulled off the Jarard caper, he was not this tired. In fact, there was no other time in his existence that he had reached this level of fatigue. The day had been a battle of wills. His against the forces of nature. With the help of his chosen weapon, the brush cutter, he had won the battle.

The aches and exhaustion were well worth it. Ramond rotated his body slowly three hundred and sixty degrees, scanning the land he had carved into. A half circle had been cut into the grass, and the scene looked something like it had the day of the wedding. In his mind he pictured the guests standing around. Most of them dressed in black or some other dreary color, symbolizing their outrage at society.

His eyes darted to the oak as he recalled the table that once stood underneath it. The tree would come in very handy, he thought. It seemed to add the final touch on the fact that

THE PERFECT PLACE

the place was so overwhelmingly *perfect*. Almost as if it were created solely for the purpose he intended to use it for.

✝ ✝ ✝ ✝ ✝ ✝ ✝ ✝ ✝ ✝ ✝

Hillbilly may have been mind-blowingly stupid, but he was irrefutably correct on one point. "Them things is heavy," he had said in reference to the boards, and Ramond discovered dismally that the things *were* indeed heavy.

The ropes were cut easily enough with a utility knife he had picked up. He cut them leaving long strips. They would be useful later. The two by ten by ten was removed first. Its weight was massive, but it was still in a range that he could handle. Ramond dragged it to the center of the clearing, where it would be used.

It was the six by eight by twelve that was the stopper. The solid slab of wood was considerably larger than a railroad tie. It was thicker than a telephone pole but rectangular in shape. The green tint of the wood was an indication that it had been weather-treated. The mill that had formed it had soaked it with a liquid that prevented the board from rotting in the outdoors. The treatment made the board at least twenty percent heavier than it would normally have been.

He climbed on top of the car and pushed the thing to the side of the hood. His muscles allowed him one more boost and he managed to tumble it off the car and onto the ground. It ripped the paint from the hood as he scooted it across the surface, but the damage was of little concern to him.

The task of moving the thing to the middle of the clearing was going to be a real bitch. If the ground had not been so rutty, he could have driven the car right to the center.

MICHAEL BISHOP

But Ramond feared he would get the car stuck; and if that happened, it would be very difficult to explain to anyone what he was doing out there in the first place.

Side over side, he rolled the board toward the center. The six inch side faced up, then the eight inch, then the six inch again. He worked it like this for twenty minutes. The cool night air spurred him on. The temperature began dropping considerably since the sun went down, but he still sweated pools as he toiled with the lumber.

For every minute he pushed, he rested for a minute. When the board finally reached its destination, Ramond collapsed next to it.

His body flailed against the ground. The sweat propelled down his cheeks as he sucked air in by the mouthful. Crickets shrilled all around him. Until now, he had not noticed their song coming from the woods. His work had commanded all his attention before. But now that he had a moment to rest, he listened to nature with awe.

In the background, almost out voiced by the crickets, the muffled croak of a toad could be heard in the darkness. A dog howled in the distance, searching for a friend to comfort him. An owl hooted from somewhere to his right, perhaps perched in the oak. It was amazing how things that were so well hidden could make so much noise. Ramond saw nothing in the night, but as he laid in exhaustion, the orchestra of animals played a symphony for him, until the world was gone altogether.

A friendly sunbeam attracted his eyes through closed lids and Ramond awoke. Dawn had broken, and he had slept

THE PERFECT PLACE

without incident through the night. It wasn't often that sleep overcame him with a ferociousness like this. Especially when he had not planned to sleep in the first place. He did not beat himself up for resting early. He deserved it. A good day's work deserved a few hours of shut eye but not too much. There were no urges to go back to sleep and his body accepted the fact that it had received all the rest it was going to get for a while.

He rose from the ground and walked to his car. It was time to unload all the tools he had bought earlier. Diligently, he carried them to the center of the clearing and prayed that he had not forgotten anything. A row was made as each one was laid next to the other for easy access. When he was done, the clearing looked like a carpenter's workshop. Each tool serving a specific purpose.

The infamous gloves were placed back on his hands. He had come to appreciate his failure in ridding himself of them. The hole was chosen to be dug first. It was as good a place to start as any.

The post hole diggers were taken from their place. The wooden handles were spread apart as he thrust the mouth into the earth. The digging was strenuous, especially for someone who had never had any experience in hard labor. But Ramond managed, on sheer willpower.

The ground was not hard nor soft. It was of ideal consistency for his purpose. The metal tips of the diggers went into the ground only inches with each strike. He was not sure how long the task would take to complete, but he was determined to work as long as it took.

He jerked his head around, looking at the six by eight.

MICHAEL BISHOP

The hole would have to be the right depth and width or it would not work. It would have to be wide enough for the post to fit in, but not too wide or it would slant, causing its weight to free it from the earth.

The depth of the hole was exceedingly important. Too shallow, and the cross would lack stability. Too deep, and there would be no room to place McCalister on the thing. Ramond did quick calculations in his head. The post was twelve feet, give or take an inch. John McCalister would hopefully not be over six feet or so. If he were to dig the hole about four feet deep, that would give him eight feet of pole above the ground.

Would that be enough? Ramond worried. McCalister would only be two feet off the ground if he did it that way. It did not exactly bring the spectral wonder of Jesus hanging high on the cross; but it just might work.

John McCalister was not going anywhere once he was nailed down. No matter how high or low he was. And as long as his feet did not touch the ground, gravity would create the exact same effect as if he were hanging fifty feet in the air.

The width of the hole was a simpler matter. The shaft was six by eight. If he dug the hole about eight inches at it widest place, and six at it most narrow, the cross should fit into the slot like a baby into a diaper.

When he was through calculating the size of the hole, he continued to dig. The earth was ripped, plug by plug, until tiny rips were worn into the fingers of the gloves. When the hole was finished, Ramond's leg could not reach the bottom. It was bound to suffice.

With the gloves still offering protection from splinters, Ramond grasped hold of the end of the timber closest to the

THE PERFECT PLACE

hole. With great effort, he pulled and rolled it right up to the lip of the opening. The back of it was positioned to lay directly in front of the oak's largest limb. Ramond stood and eyed the board to confirm it was in the right place. When he had determined its position was at the correct angle, he turned his attention back to the mammoth tree.

The oak rose in dominance of all else. No other tree in the area came close to matching its mass. Its branches sprawled out in all directions, covering a large circumference with its shadow. Twigs shot off from every branch like a thousand tiny fingers.

Every few feet, the tree had sprouted knotholes and bumps. Ramond felt sure he could shimmy up the trunk, using them for footholds. The bark was rough, providing excellent traction for scaling.

He grabbed one of the leftover plastic bags and began filling it with everything he would need after he reached the limb. The bag was shoved into the front of his pants, and Ramond gave the climb a try.

The high tops he wore slipped off the knot's rounded edge as he placed his weight on it. The fall had not been far. His foot was placed back on the knot and he tried it again. This time with success.

Every stepping point was chosen carefully as he timidly placed a foot on each new knot. The bag crammed in his trousers offered protection from the bark against his belly, but his arms were being shredded each time he pulled himself up.

After a painful climb, Ramond reached the lowest branch. He lifted himself up and straddled it, letting his legs hang limply below. The hardwood was uncomfortable on his tailbone, but the chance to rest more than made up for the minor inconvenience.

The view of the countryside was breathtaking from this height. It looked very similar to the heavenly place his master had shown him in the dream. Ramond found himself staring silently in wonder. He took only a short time to smell the roses and enjoy the landscape before he forced himself back to work.

Shelf after shelf of the hardware store had been searched for a pulley that explicitly stated it was for "Heavy Duty Construction". When he located one which specified this, he placed it in his cart. He pulled the pulley from the plastic bag and admired its construction. It was small, but well made. The strap was thick and braided of stress resistant nylon. The box had offered a money back guarantee, and claimed the pulley would hold a baby elephant. Ramond was not exactly sure how much a baby elephant weighed, but he was sure it was less than John McCalister and his cross would be. It was a theory he would soon test.

He wrapped the strap around the sturdiest part. The teeth on the strap buckle bit into the braid as he pulled it tight. The six inches of excess strap was then tied underneath as an added precaution.

Reaching his hand under the pulley, he tugged hard on it. It gave no sign of pulling loose. The metal glistened in the light as it hung from the limb, swaying in the breath of the wind.

The second item, a one hundred foot length of yellow rope, was removed from the bag. It was thin nylon, but was as strong as chains. He held the tree limb with one steadying hand and made an attempt to thread the pulley with the other.

THE PERFECT PLACE

After two tries of not coming close, he managed to push the rope through the pulley's eye on the third.

He pulled the rope through until an equal amount hung on each side. When the slack he required was attained, he dropped the other end and watched as it rapidly raced for the ground. His tree top mission was completed.

The climb down was easier than the climb up. With gravity working for him instead of against him, he sailed down the oak in seconds. Being back on solid ground did his heart good. He thought of kneeling to kiss the earth, but then thought better of it. The dirt was better left to the insects.

†††††††††††††

The eight inch side of the timber lay up as he placed the two by ten on top of it. The dented tooth hammer stood out from the pile of tools as he secured its handle in his right hand. With his left hand he removed a one pound box of nails from one of the remaining bags. The first nail was placed in the center of the two by ten and nailed down. The next was placed just below it. He wildly beat the nails one after the other into the wood with no particular order. When he was done, they zig-zagged up and down the timber. But it was sturdy no matter how it looked, and Ramond's aching hands were glad when the box of nails ran empty.

He grabbed each edge of the board and attempted to jiggle it from side to side. There was no give. The Cheshire smile came out in him again. He was cruising down the hill now. The worst part of the work was over. At least until the crucifixion began.

The end of the rope was wrapped and tied, making a

loop in its center. With great struggling, he lifted on the tip of the cross with one hand, raising it the tiniest bit. With the other he wiggled the rope underneath, and stopped it about four inches down the top of the shaft. When the rope was in a satisfactory place, he stood above the cross and pulled it upward, cinching the slip knot. It would hold.

This job was almost money in the bank. But he knew the most important part of the sacrifice was yet to be secured: John McCalister.

The trip was timed to assure that when he got to Memphis, he did not have to wait. He had been told McCalister worked the night shift. If he arrived at the grocery store around 5 A.M., the man would still be at work, but would be headed for home before long.

His work in the clearing was completed around noon. The trip to Memphis would take just over four hours, which meant he had a dozen free hours to kill before it would be time to head for Tennessee.

The *perfect* place was left just as it was. No tools were picked up. Nothing was hidden. Ramond was sure no one would stumble upon it. The spot was his secret alone. A secret he intended to share with just one person.

The fried chicken was not half bad, and along with the taste of buttermilk biscuits, the meal was the best he remembered having in a long while. He ate inside the

THE PERFECT PLACE

restaurant and finished his Sprite on the way home. Now was the time to sleep. Everything that could be done was done.

He would wait for 1 A.M. to visit. Until it did, he planned to conserve his strength for the fight of his life.

At 1 o'clock in the morning, the Ford's tank was filled. Four hours later, as he reached the city limits of Memphis, the fuel gauge was sliding ever so close to the "E". If he'd had the money he would have filled it then. But paying for tools had left him with just enough cash to make it to the city and no more. He would have to gas up later, after he had McCalister. It was risky, but there was no other choice.

Olive Branch was somewhat of a mystery to Ramond, but he knew Memphis well. The town was a hotbed of underground meetings and "Family" activity. He had traveled here many times over the years to participate in various rites. Interstate 240 was taken to the "Local Traffic" exit, and he followed it to Winchester Road.

A "Pig-N-The-Basket" supermarket was immediately spotted, lying directly in his path as he entered Winchester. Ramond pulled the Ford into the parking lot at a quarter to five. If McCalister happened to be off on this night, he was in trouble, and would have to wait for another opportunity.

But he did not want to wait. He had worked hard to set things up, and he was anxious to test it out. Most of all, he was ready to get this thing over with. The guy would suffer. There was no way around that, but the sooner it was over and out of mind, the better. Whether it could ever be completely forgotten, Ramond doubted.

MICHAEL BISHOP

Before he got himself lathered up over the "What Ifs", he entered the store to see for himself if the man was there.

He grabbed a cart and pretended to shop. As he went down the cereal aisle, he grabbed a box of Captain Crunch and set it in his basket. Whenever an employee walked by he gave a casual glance at their name tag, searching for one that read *McCalister*.

The store colors were red and white. All employees were forced to suit up in an awful smock which bore the store colors along with a logo of a pudgy pig driving a cart as if it were a race car. The smocks made the employees easy to pick out; but as he observed one after another, he saw no *John McCalister* among them.

Perhaps, he thought, since McCalister was a manager, he would be dressed in a shirt and tie instead. He honed the area looking for any managerial types who fit the description. Still no sign of McCalister.

"Mr. McCalister, code 99 to the fruit section, please. Mr. McCalister 99 to the fruit section," a female voiced crackled over the intercom system. Ramond had struck oil, and tried to be as subtle as possible as he rapidly made his way to the section set aside for fruits and vegetables.

John McCalister had somehow managed to beat him to the fruit section, and was standing over an elderly lady with a grimace on his face when he arrived. Ramond strolled nonchalantly as close to the two as he could without raising suspicion, and eavesdropped on their conversation.

"I'm sorry, Ma'am, but you can't stand here and sample the grapes. If customers eat the produce we lose money," McCalister informed her as politely as possible. His voice was average. Not deep and not feminine. He stood an

THE PERFECT PLACE

inch or so taller than Ramond, but had a frame that made him look shorter from a distance.

Just below his tie, the beginning of a pot belly could be seen poking out. His face was clean shaven and resembled a little boy's more than a man's. His cheeks were pudgy and his hair was cow-licked and childlike. But in McCalister's eyes was a curiousness. The kind of curiousness that gets a man killed.

The woman was the exact opposite of what a sweet old lady should be. Her face was wrinkled so badly that a permanent frown was etched in it. Her expression was one of insult and disdain.

"How am I 'spose to know if they're any good if I don't try them?" she sassed at him.

"Well Ma'am, it's okay to try one or two, but you can't stand here and eat a whole bunch," he informed her, still keeping his polite demeanor.

"Well that's the stupidest thing I ever heard. Them grapes ain't no good nohow. You charge $1.99 for a pound a grapes, you think you'd have somethin' worth a durn," she mumbled, more to herself than to him, as she walked away and headed for the door.

Ramond watched the scene with grave amusement. Apparently, a code 99 had something to do with people eating the fruit, and the thought that it happened frequently enough to merit its own code amused him even more.

John McCalister shook his head in bewilderment as the woman left. Then he turned around and started back to wherever he'd come from. He noticed Ramond standing close by and stared at him strangely for a moment. Then he remembered his polite manners and quickly threw a smile on his face.

MICHAEL BISHOP

"How you doing, sir?" he rhetorically asked Ramond as he walked past.

"Fine, thanks," Ramond replied cheerily. He watched as McCalister walked through a plastic divider into the stock room in the back. McCalister seemed like a nice enough guy, Ramond thought. It was a shame to kill a nice guy. There were so few around these days.

Ramond left the market and returned to his car. Now that he knew what McCalister looked like, he could sit and wait for him to leave the store, then follow him back into Mississippi on his way home. The timing of the trip was figured well, and he did not have long to wait.

† † † † † † † † † † † †

At 5:35, McCalister stepped out of the store and walked to his car. The tie that had been around his neck was now in his hand, and his top button was undone to allow his throat some relief. McCalister drove a car that was not new, but was probably a *new*, used car. Its floor room shine and fresh paint gave this fact away. It was a shine that was impossible to reproduce after you got it home and drove it a few weeks.

The sun had not began to peek its head out from beneath the other side of the earth, but the parking lot was so well lit that daylight would not have made much a difference. Ramond could clearly see McCalister, buckling his seat belt like a good little boy. When John McCalister cranked his engine, so did Ramond.

He had seen plenty of movies showing a vehicle being

THE PERFECT PLACE

tailed, and he was pretty sure he knew how to do it. He would stay close enough to see McCalister's every turn, but not too close to let him know he was being tailed.

Being that there were few cars on the road at that hour of the morning, it was difficult to hide the fact that he was obviously following the man. But the thought never entered John McCalister's head, and he never once looked back at the car behind him.

Ramond followed the man just under ten miles into Olive Branch, Mississippi, to a small low-income housing community set up there. Olive Branch was so close to Memphis that it was practically a part of Memphis, and Ramond was surprised that he had never heard of the town before.

McCalister pulled into his driveway and cut his lights. Ramond pulled his car into a lot four houses down. A red sign could be made out in the center of the yard that marked the house "FOR SALE". It was a safe place to roost.

Through the darkness, Ramond could see only the silhouette of McCalister as he stepped out of the car and disappeared behind his front door. Ramond cut his own lights and engine. He gave McCalister ten minutes to settle in, then opened his car door and tiptoed across the neighbor's lawn to the man's house.

Unlike the houses on Black Circle Road, the houses on this block were dark and gloomy. He did not have to worry about staying in the shadows, because the shadows were everywhere. He made it to McCalister's home without making a sound, and ducked his head underneath the man's bedroom window.

The houses were miniature and cheaply built. They

were constructed like single bedroom apartments with a small band of grass wrapped around their outside to give the illusion of having your own home. Each one was built from a single set of blueprints and had the same layout. One cramped living room, one bathroom, one bedroom, and a kitchen barely able to house cockroaches.

He peeked in the window to get a look at what he was up against. John McCalister had the T.V. set on in the bedroom, directly in front of the bed. Its light provided the only illumination in the room.

McCalister had already undressed and crawled into bed. "Good Morning America" was on the T.V. and he laid watching it, moments from dozing off.

It was obvious McCalister had no wife. And the one bedroom abode left no room to accommodate a roommate. He occupied the house very much the same way Ramond occupied his apartment ...alone.

Dawn would be breaking soon. It was imperative he act before the light had a chance to pierce the darkness. Ramond scooted away from the window stealthily. McCalister heard nothing as his heavy lids began to close. When he was far enough away from the window to assure he would not be heard, he began a full trot to his car.

He opened the car door, stepped inside, and started the engine. The car was backed out of the drive with the lights off. He drove just past McCalister's driveway, then eased the car into reverse and backed into the drive quietly.

McCalister's vehicle occupied the first position in the drive, and Ramond parked his directly behind it. The parking brake was pulled and he reached under the seat groping for the bat. The metal rod found his hand easily, and felt

THE PERFECT PLACE

comfortable in his palm.

From the glove box, the filthy knit gloves were removed and placed on his hands. He intended to leave no fingerprints for the *pigs* to find.

The driver's door was left cracked. He had not been discovered thus far, and did not want the noise of the door closing to stir McCalister. He snuck to the trunk of the car and placed the key into the lock. The mechanism gave way and the hatch opened revealing an empty trunk. It was just the right size. Big enough for a man, but not too big to give McCalister room to move around and create mischief.

He left it open as he stepped to the front door. No sound came from inside. McCalister had not yet realized he had a visitor. Ramond examined the door closely. It was cheaply made. Exterior doors were supposed to be solid; but despite the fact that the door was metal, its center was as hollow as a rotten stump.

A corroded knocker hung from its center, rusted immovable. The front door had no window around it or in it. Not even a peephole was placed into it to provide the resident visual assurance of who lurked on the other side. The lack of a peephole threw Ramond for a loop, and all his plans were changed in an instant by the small detail.

The original strategy was to kick the door in. Then rampage into McCalister's room while he was still half asleep and before he could gain his bearings. Once he had McCalister in his sights, he would bludgeon him into submission, drag the body to the trunk, and be gone long before anyone bothered to check and see what the loud noise next door had been.

But now, thanks to the absence of a peephole, there

was another option. An option Ramond decided to try.

The bat made a light metal to metal rapping noise as he tapped it on the steel door. The rustling inside occurred almost immediately. John McCalister was apparently a light sleeper, for one reason or another.

Light scampered underneath the door as McCalister turned the living room lamp on. Ramond listened to the foot steps increased in intensity as they neared the door.

"Who in God's name is it?" McCalister questioned sleepily.

Ramond stood paralyzed. The question should have been anticipated. But somehow, in the midst of changing plans, it took him by surprise. His mouth opened slightly and let out the first words that came to his lips.

"Mr. McCalister, this is Officer Jamison, city police. I'm afraid I have some disturbing news for you," Ramond expelled in his deepest voice. The words sounded entirely phony to his own ears, but perhaps McCalister would not be so observant.

A long second passed, and the cold wind blew through the clean night air. The sound of latches being unbolted followed the pause, and Ramond stood at the ready.

What he must do next was perfectly clear to him, and he slanted the tip of the bat upward as he tried to recall how tall McCalister had been and where his face would be. The man was not an idiot, and would not just open the door without knowing who was there. McCalister would, no doubt, open the door just inches and peek out, leaving the chain lock securely in place. When he saw that no uniform stood on the other side, he would slam the door closed, relock it, and call

THE PERFECT PLACE

the police. Ramond saw this vision unblurred in his mind, and his job was to stop McCalister before he could do this.

He watched as the doorknob slowly turned clockwise. As expected, it was opened only a few inches, and Ramond could see the brass chain hanging from one side of the crack to the other. Just beyond that chain, McCalister's curious eye peered out into the darkness.

The second it took for John McCalister's eye to focus in the darkness was longer than Ramond needed to strike. By the time he realized the man on the other side of the door was not a cop, the tip of the bat had already been jammed through the crack. It smashed McCalister hard in the nose and sent him flailing backward. He tripped over the throw rug in the center of his living room and crashed to the floor.

Ramond grabbed the doorknob and shoved his shoulder into the door with his feather weight behind him. The chain gave way with virtually no resistance, and Ramond came close to falling himself from the excess force he had put behind the blow.

McCalister held his bleeding nose and attempted to crawl backwards on his bottom. The blue pajamas he wore clung to the rug and hindered his movement. The shattering of his nose sent enough tears to his eyes to destroy his vision. He could not make out his attacker, but he could see a form growing nearer. With panic, he attempted to make his way back to his room for refuge.

Before McCalister even got close, Ramond had already assumed a dominant position above him. McCalister heard his assailant's breathing so close to him, and stopped his struggle to escape. It was too late to run. His hand was dropped from his bloody nose as he peered upward.

McCalister wanted desperately to see the face of the intruder before it was all over. All he saw through the water in his eyes and the dazed horror of his mind was the outline of a skeleton hovering above him, holding a large shaft. He could not tell what the shaft was, but he felt certain it was a sword. The pale rider of death had come for him, and McCalister shut his eyes as the shaft was thrust down upon him.

Ramond brought the bat down hard on the right side of his victim's skull. He had never seen fear in a human's eyes like he had seen in McCalister's. Susan Lints, Jarard, Mark Peters... none came close to expressing the degree of horror that McCalister had. It made Ramond shiver with disbelief. He swung the bat seeking to end that look. It only took one blow to knock McCalister out.

† † † † † † † † † † † †

It was peculiar how the thought of stealing disturbed him. Especially after what he had just done. It almost seemed worse to steal from the man than it did to pound him senseless with a bat. Unfortunately, there was no alternative but to take the man's money. The car was empty, and Ramond's pockets were barren as well. If he did not *borrow* a bit of money from McCalister now, he would never make it home.

McCalister's wallet was in the first place Ramond looked. Crumpled up in the corner of his room was the pair of pants he had worn during his night shift. In the back pocket of the slacks, his wallet was neatly folded. Ramond often treated his billfold in the same manner. The next morning it

THE PERFECT PLACE

was difficult to remember which pants he had worn the day before, but once he did he always knew where his billfold was.

The wallet was cheap leather. The kind bought in drugstores. Ramond found two new twenties and three fives tucked away in its side compartment. It would be enough.

He placed the cash in his own billfold and dropped McCalister's on the bedroom floor as he hurried back into the living room. It was best to get while the getting was good.

The body plopped into the trunk as Ramond dropped the man into the compartment. He was not as heavy as Ramond had thought he might be, and with reasonable pulling, jerking and maneuvering, he was able to move McCalister into the car easily. Ramond grabbed the man's arm and leg that still hung out of the trunk and brashly crammed them inside. When all appendages were clear, he slammed the top and jumped behind the wheel. The ferrying would now begin. It was the most nerve-wrecking journey of Ramond's life.

The sobbing began about an hour after he got out of Memphis. He had not bothered to gas the car in the city. It was best to put distance between himself and Olive Branch before someone realized McCalister was missing, and he thought McCalister would stay knocked out until he reached a good place to fill up further down the road.

The fuel peg was on empty when the whining began,

and Ramond drove the car thirty more minutes without pulling into a station.

It was a two-sided fear. If he stopped, someone might hear the man's cries and cause trouble. But if he continued to drive on fumes, the car would eventually run out of gas. When he was sure the car would go no further without a drink of fuel, he exited and pulled into the nearest gas station.

As he walked around the car and removed the fuel cap, he was delighted to hear the man had silenced his cries altogether. It boggled Ramond's mind. Why would McCalister not cry out? It was as if he did not want anyone to help him.

Ramond filled the car, paid the cashier and was twenty miles down the road before the answer came to him.

McCalister knew as long as the car was in motion he could not be harmed. He was safe in the trunk while the car barreled down the road, and free to cry and moan and raise as much hell as he wanted. But once the car stopped, his life might very well stop too.

Ramond could picture the man, laying there, curled into the fetal position, silently waiting for the trunk to fly open with some maniac standing over him with an axe or gun.

The gas stop must have taken years off McCalister's life... not that he had years to live anyway.

The Ford did not stop as it passed through Sierra Springs. Ramond's nerves were on pins and needles. McCalister had cried for three hours straight. He cried so

THE PERFECT PLACE

loud, in fact, that the shrillness of his voice had turned Ramond's forehead into a mine field. Each howl set off another mine between his eyes.

On the last hour of the trip, McCalister made no noise at all. Surely he had cried himself out, Ramond thought. But as bad as the cries had been, the silence was worse. John McCalister knew he was going to die, and that fact scared Ramond. A man who knows he's going to die has nothing to lose. His only thought is survival, and he will do anything to defeat the reaper of death. When Ramond was finally forced open the trunk, he knew he would have a grizzly on his hands.

† † † † † † † † † † † †

The *perfect* spot lay straight ahead and he crawled the car forward and backward on the narrow path, until he was able to back the car into the clearing. He pulled as close to the cross as he could without getting the car stuck. The sun had been up a few hours now and the dampness created by the dew had just began to dry.

As he gazed into the rear view mirror, Ramond checked to make sure everything was in place. The tools laid in the same position he had left them, the cross was intact; the area was untouched.

His keys were clenched tightly as he stepped to the trunk. No sound came from it. Not a moan. Not a rattle or bump. No sign of life at all.

He lowered his head to the trunk timidly as if it might bite his face for spite. His ear was pressed directly to the cold metal. He held his breath and listened closely for any sign of his *friend*. Still no clamor came from inside. It was as if John McCalister had somehow escaped somewhere along the highway at fifty-five miles per hour.

Was the man alive? Ramond juggled this question for moments. Escape was impossible, and Ramond did not think anyone was capable of laying in a trunk *that* still and *that* quiet. The only logical conclusion was that somehow, during the past hour, McCalister had passed on.

Was there enough air in the trunk? This question came next. He had never really thought about it. Ramond had assumed the trunk was aerated enough to support life; but it was an untested theory.

Then the most frightening realization entered his thoughts. What about exhaust?

The car smoked so bad at times, that he could smell the toxic exhaust from way up front. An unventilated area such as the trunk, so close to the tail pipe, might just be enough to kill a man.

If McCalister was dead, so was he. He knew very well Satan would never accept a sacrifice with the sacrificial lamb already dead. It lost its meaning. Its symbolism. But most of all it lost all the pain and suffering his Lord seemed to relish so much. The thought made Ramond quaver.

He carefully placed the key in the trunk's lock. The bat was clenched tight in his left fist. The lines of tenseness spread through his face. One way or the other, it was time to unwrap the surprise.

The mechanism in the trunk clicked signifying the lock had opened. Ramond placed his hand off the key and onto the underseal. He took a deep breath and closed his eyes

THE PERFECT PLACE

tightly. He would count to three. When he hit three, he would open his eyes, raise the top, and find out for sure if a live or dead man lay in the trunk.

"One," he made no effort to remain quiet as he counted. The number was audible for anyone who could hear.

"Two," he continued, eyes still squeezed close.

"THR...." he started the number, but the trunk flew open before he could conclude the word. The top came up with a force that could have only come from a pair of legs. It bashed Ramond's hand and splintered into his chest, sending him flying backward into the dirt.

The surprise of the jolt nearly stopped Ramond's heart, and he stared up from his position on the ground, expecting to see a dead man rise from the trunk and come to finish him off.

Instead, McCalister leaped from the back and landed feet first on the soil and bolted for the clearing, trying to escape.

John McCalister's feet were running before his mind knew where. He only looked at Ramond briefly, to locate his captor and avoid his direction at all cost. Escape was the only thought going through his mind, as he darted away from the car and in the direction of the woods. There, he would have a better chance of alluding his kidnapper.

McCalister ran with the speed of a rattler's strike, even in his bare feet. By the time Ramond made it to a standing position, the man had an insurmountable head start on him.

It was due only to the fact that John McCalister was running out of fear and paying no attention that he did not notice the hole in front of him.

MICHAEL BISHOP

His left foot disappeared into the hole Ramond had made for the cross, and he tumbled forward, doing a complete monkey flip. The fall dazed, but did not injure McCalister. His kidnapper was still a few steps behind, and if he hurried to his feet and made it to the woods, he would be home free.

Ramond did not slow when he saw McCalister stumble. The opportunity spurred his steps faster. Running with the bat in his hand kept him from going full speed, but he was determined to catch the guy if it killed him.

McCalister placed his palms on the ground and began to push himself back up. But as his eyes struck the cross he hesitated. At first it did not register what the thing was; but it didn't take long to realize what laid before him. The expression on his face went from simple fright, back to the unequaled terror. That moment of hesitation was all it took for Ramond to close the gap in the foot race.

McCalister snapped out of it when he saw Ramond was upon him, but it was too late. He made it back to his feet, but did not have time to run before the bat was slammed into the side of his jaw. The blast sent him flying back to the ground, and the bones in his face contorted sideways as they broke.

McCalister was still conscious, but highly dazed. Ramond grabbed the bat like a golf club as he swung it. The rod sliced through the earth, and rushed to meet the back of McCalister's head. McCalister passed out from the pain more than the force. Ramond had scored a hole in one.

THE PERFECT PLACE

McCalister's face looked as if it had been through a sacrifice of its own. The blood from his nose had dried leaving a red mustache, and there were bumps and scratches on every part of his head.

He had fallen beside the crucifix, and by gripping his pajama top and pulling, Ramond was able to position him on the cross.

The twine that had been left over was taken from the pile. The first pieces was wrapped around McCalister's wrist tight enough to cut off the circulation, and the rest of it was carefully wrapped again and again around the post and over the wrist.

He repeated this on the other side. When he was satisfied neither of the arms could be budged, he moved on.

Thick, fibrous duct tape was wrapped just below McCalister's knees. Ramond could not work the twine under the cross that far up; therefore, the tape was used to lock the legs in place. He cut close to thirty pieces from the roll and careful laid them from the right side of the cross, over McCalister's legs, and stuck the gummy underside to the opposite side of the lumber, hindering the movement of the man's lower half.

He stood above McCalister, straddling him with a foot on each side of his body. He gazed down into the lifeless face. John McCalister was a pathetic sight. A victim.

It would suit Ramond fine if the man stayed unconscious through the whole ordeal; but he knew it was unlikely. Once the spikes were driven, the pain would snap him back to reality, and to the agony that awaited him.

When Ramond had pitied the man all he cared to, he

reached once again for the hammer. The nine inch nails were sold loose in a barrel in the center aisle of Sierra Home Hardware. He had purchased four, although he was pretty sure he would only need three for the job. The fourth was "just in case", bought in the unlikely event he would screw one up.

Spike number one was placed in the center of the left wrist. The image in the illustrated Bible came to his mind and he placed the nail exactly where the artist had placed it in the picture. An effort was made not to break the twine in two as he nailed. The first blow of the hammer was the worst.

Ramond slowly lowered the head of the hammer to the head of the nail and aimed. The hammer was then raised way above his head and his eyes bulged out at the target. With all the strength in him, he drove the teeth of the hammer down upon the spike. It shot only halfway through McCalister's wrist and stopped somewhere between the two sides of his skin.

John McCalister went from slumber, to wake the moment the nail entered him. The wail that left his vocal chords was inhuman. It was the sound of all the pain in the world brought down upon one man. It was a sound a mother made at the loss of a child. It was a sound the angels made when they cried.

Ramond dropped the hammer and clasped his ears. The shriek was so horrible, his ears almost went deaf to protect themselves. The terrible moans continued, but Ramond forced himself to continue.

The spike stuck straight into the air as the blood drained around the rope. McCalister wrist's pulled forward,

THE PERFECT PLACE

digging the braided twine into his skin. He struggled to free his left arm, then his right. Both were glued down.

Ramond picked the hammer back up and aimed again before he lost his nerve. His aim was poor this time. The second blow missed the nail head completely and pounded the lower part of McCalister's wrist, leaving a perfect imprint of the hammer's teeth. The pain of the blow was nonexistent compared to the pain of the spike, and McCalister barely acknowledged the strike.

The hammer came down again, and Ramond kept his eye on the head this time. The nail was shoved through the wrist and a quarter inch entered the wood. McCalister's back arched to the point of almost breaking as another shrill yodel left his lips. The pressure he place against the ropes subsided somewhat, and Ramond understood that it was because the nail had finally struck wood. The added resistance from the nail made it harder for McCalister to work the ropes. One more strike and it would be deep enough. He raised the hammer and pounded the nail one last time with fury.

McCalister's screams were no longer waiting for him to hit the nail. They came one after another. Without repetition. Never making quite the same sound twice. One scream was a guttural groan. The next like a little girl's cry. And still another like a man who has caught his wife in adultery.

Ramond could take no more. The screams were unbearable. He swiped the tape from the ground nearby and cut off a large piece. McCalister's mouth was fully covered with the strip. His screams were muffled, and Ramond felt relieved.

McCalister's eyes rolled back in his skull as the tears flooded down his cheeks. Apparently, he had placed some on reserve and had not spent them all while he was in the trunk. Ramond tried not to look, and did his best not to listen as he moved to the other side.

The right side's ropes had been worked with less effort by McCalister. His wrist had yet to gain the tiny cuts and rope burns. He turned his head away from Ramond and stared at the nail already in place. He did not want to know when the next blow would come. His mind could not handle that knowledge. It was better to let it be a surprise. It was better not to anticipate the suffering.

Ramond was glad the man did not look at him. It made the work easier. He placed the next spike in the other wrist and prepared to drive it.

Flustered and wanting to be done with it, he smashed the next nail without skill. The hammer ricocheted of the nail head and it drove into McCalister's wrist at an awkward angle. The blood spurted from the wound, splashing Ramond's chin. The flow tapered off and drizzled after the initial downpour.

McCalister's head spun so quickly toward Ramond it seemed like magic, as he lioned out a stifled roar. His eyes cut Ramond. There was hatred in his stare. A scolding of sorts. They seemed to say "If you are going to do it, at least have the decency to do it right!"

Ramond forced himself to ignore the man's deadly gaze. He concentrated on nothing but the nail. The hammer's head was brought down three quick times, plunging the nail deeper with each blow. It was a good thing he had the twine around McCalister's wrist. The tear in his arm had grown larger than the nail head. Had the twine not been there, John

THE PERFECT PLACE

McCalister's wrist could possibly have come through the nail.

The crucified man's teeth ground together with a nauseating churning. With nothing else to bite down on, his body involuntarily forced him to grit his own incisors, chiseling and chipping them like a sculptor carving into marble.

Ramond did not bother to admire his work, but moved directly to the feet. McCalister wiggled his toes and shifted his feet in defiance. It was obvious he was not going to make the nailing of his feet an easy chore. Ramond dropped the spike on the ground and attempted to still the man's feet.

He struggled with them for a moment, trying to place one on top of the other, but McCalister would have none of it and slid them off just as quickly as Ramond could put them on. Frustration took hold of Ramond. He decided to take the only course of action left.

The spike was placed directly in the center of the right foot, halfway between the heel and the toes. The first blow of the hammer skidded the spike an inch through the foot, crushing bones as it went through. That sound mixed with the man's anguished sobs brought tears to Ramond's eyes. He was suffering so badly that Ramond could almost feel the pain radiating off of him. It was cruelty beyond what he had ever known, and a small twinge of guilt inside him made him wondered if the power was worth all this.

He struck the nail head again. He wanted to hurry up and raise the man. Not to add to the pain, but rather to hurry up and end it. He wanted very badly for McCalister's life to end soon. The sooner he died, the sooner his suffering would be over.

With the nail lodged through the foot, the toes had

stopped moving altogether. McCalister made little noise compared to before. He was obviously grasping for breath. The screaming and weeping had taken the wind out of him, and the tape over his mouth was making it almost impossible to breathe. Ramond did not want the man to suffocate. He ripped the strip off his mouth with a hard yank.

McCalister coughed and spat, sending a tooth fragment flying through the air. Then drew in a deep breath.

Ramond wasted no time getting back to the feet, but before he could begin again, he heard the man speak.

"No. Wait," the victim choked out so weakly that at first Ramond thought he was hearing things. He brought his eyes over to McCalister's face. The look in the man's eyes told Ramond he had heard right.

As he opened his mouth to speak again, Ramond decided to seize the moment. While McCalister's attention was diverted, he quickly grabbed the loose foot, placed it under the other, and began to pound the third spike into it.

The sounds of crunching bones could be heard once again as the spike barreled through both feet and into the wood. McCalister's words were lost as he cried out in agony. His feet were motionless. Even the toes were immobile and began to turn blue. The bones and nerves were destroyed, rendering them useless. They were as dead as McCalister himself would soon be.

It was done. Everything was attached. McCalister went through successive periods of catching his breath, then screaming, then breathing again. As Ramond stood, he dared not look down at the man. He wanted nothing more than to make his Lord proud, but if he was going to finish this test, he

THE PERFECT PLACE

would need all his courage. Looking at the misery that *was* McCalister, wiggling on the cross like a worm dangling on the end of a hook, would do little to surge him forth.

He walked toward the pulley, gazing up at it with fascination. Grabbing the loose end of the rope hanging from the tree limb, he turned and headed to the Ford. The trunk still stood open and the keys hung out of the lock. He lowered to his knees, turned onto his back, and pushed himself under the car's rear axle. With a hard tug, all the slack was pulled out of the rope and it was wrapped around the axle until just enough was left to tie off.

As he laid there on his back, he could hear McCalister's sobs; but even worse was that even from this distance, Ramond could hear his teeth grinding. It was amazing how hard the man's jaws were crushing down. If he continued the gritting for long, he would be certain to snap all his teeth out one after the other.

The rope was fastened and he crawled from beneath the car. Grabbing the rim of the open trunk, he pulled himself up. When he had reached his feet, he jerked the keys from the lock and closed the trunk.

The rope was strung from the car to the pulley, then from the pulley to the cross. Ramond followed it with his eyes before sitting down in the front seat. He cranked the engine and let it warm as he gave a short prayer to his God that everything would fall into place and work correctly.

Releasing the parking break and shifting to drive, he touched the gas pedal with the gentleness of silk on skin. The Ford rolled forward slowly and the little remaining slack in the rope tightened as the pulley wheel turned. His eyes watched through the rear view mirror as his great invention came to life. The squeak of the pulley and hum of the engine drowned out McCalister, which made it easier to concentrate on raising the cross.

The rope, which was tied to the stump behind McCalister's head, caused the man to lean his head far to the side as the cross began to slide forward in the dirt. It tore through the earth until its bottom struck the far side of the hole.
The sacrificial lamb could not get his head completely out of the rope's way and it ripped at his neck, bringing up blood whelps on the left side.
Ramond moved the car slowly, not wanting to ascend too fast and cause the cross to over shoot the hole altogether.

As the cross left the ground and headed toward a vertical position, McCalister's screams could be heard again, even over the car's motor and with the windows up. The higher the cross lifted, the more weight was placed on the nails. The holes ripped wider and wider, and the bones and rope became the only things keeping the man attached.
The pain had been bad enough when he was lying. Even with no weight at all being placed on his wrists. But that pain was a dream compared to the agony McCalister now endured. With each yelp, the true measure of torment was expressed.

As the cross reached seventy-five degrees, McCalister's teeth began shattering in his mouth. Ramond gave the car a bit more gas and it moved forward the last few feet. As the cross straightened, the earth just in front of the

THE PERFECT PLACE

hole began to tear away.

At ninety degrees, it had torn away enough of the soil to allow it to slide into the hole. The entire creation, McCalister and all, fell in a blink into the awaiting opening. The fit was perfect, like a sword in a sheath. And when the cross hit the bottom of the hole, a jolt shot through the boards causing the greatest damage of all to the man's tattered skin.

From his sheltered position inside the car, with the windows tightly rolled up and the doors closed, Ramond heard the sound that came from McCalister. It was a noise that no man should have made, and yet one did. It was not a scream, or a howl, or a cry, but more a release. A release of every shred of pain. A release of each wrong deed the man had ever done. A release of all the hatred in his heart. All concentrated into one tragically dark song.

The bellow had an energy that could be felt even from inside the car. It radiated through the glass. And as Ramond peered wide-eyed in his rearview mirror at the man hanging from his cross, he could not begin to ponder the affliction his body was going through.

The car was backed up five feet and Ramond cut the engine. He backed up only to give the rope slack and allow McCalister to hold his head upright instead of pinned to the side. He waited in the confines of the vehicle to make sure no more of the sounds would come.

The moans had returned to that which a normal man could create, and he decided it was safe to leave the car. Even from across the clearing, blood could be seen oozing from the nail holes. Tears made their way back to Ramond's eyes as he looked at what he had done. No attempt was made to be strong. If he was weak it was for good reason. McCalister was a sight that would bring remorse to anyone.

He stepped toward the man and stopped a few yards from his shattered feet. He made himself look... made himself remember what he had done. It was a sight he would have to force himself to get used to. As horrible as it was, it was surely to be the first of many. When Satan reclaimed the Earth, Ramond felt sure multitudes would suffer such a fate, and he wondered what McCalister had done to deserve such a deplorable end.

Physics played a large part in crucifixion, and Ramond began to understand just how complex the process was. As Satan had already told him, it was not simply just the nailing of the hands and feet. It went far beyond that. There were levels to the pain, and the nailing was just the first of many.

Gravity pulled down on McCalister's body and tortured him in two ways. The first was obvious. The weight of his body ripped and tore at his flesh and bones with no respite. The second was more subtle.

As his body weight reached for the earth, McCalister's chest fell below his outstretched arms. This position made breathing an impossibility. When the body could go no longer go without air, he was forced to place all his weight on the nail in his feet and push himself upward.

Every breath was marred by a scream or a moan, and the woes of anguish competed for the air his body so badly needed. McCalister could only stay extended for a short time before the pain in his feet would be too great and he would have to lower himself, shifting the pain back to his wrists.

A man could live hours like that before smothering to

THE PERFECT PLACE

death. Suffocating until the need to breathe forced you to administer your own body more pain. It was mental trauma, as well as physical torture. A truly peculiar and perverted death.

Ramond watched the man rise and descend three times with curiosity. After he fully realized why McCalister kept pushing up and falling, the repulse forced his gaze to the ground. He could see no more. If he did, he might lose his passion for the power altogether.

He turned to leave, but from behind him he heard an audible and irrefutable "Wait!"

Ramond spun in astonishment. McCalister had extended himself upward and forced his body to enable him to talk through the pain. When he saw that Ramond had heard him, he lowered himself back down again until he could find the courage to place the weight on his feet once more.

He wanted very badly to leave. But out of all he had done to McCalister, he felt he at least owed him the decency of listening to his words. McCalister obviously had something to say, and like it or not, Ramond would make himself listen.

McCalister extended again five seconds later. It was clear in his eyes that he had something important to relay.

"Listen," he grunted. The single word almost made his knees collapse, but he locked them into place determined to say his piece. "You don't understand. I..."

"RAMOND!" the voice shrieked, cutting off McCalister's words from Ramond's ears. Although McCalister did not hear the name spoken, the way in which Ramond scowled and shut his eyes caused him to stop speaking. The voice belonged to Ramond's own private Hell... his mother.

"NO!" he screamed into the wind. "YOU DON'T EXIST!"

For a moment of loving bliss, McCalister's mind replaced the pain with confusion. He had no idea who or what his assailant was talking to, and in the midst of the insane situation his mind reeled with bewilderment. He allowed himself to descend again, while Ramond talked to the air.

"I do exist, sweetheart. Don't you understand that? Listen to me Ramond, there is still time. Take the man down and rush him to the hospital. The power is in your hands. You can save his life if you hurry," the voice of Vernadette pleaded.

Ramond dropped to his knees at McCalister's feet, with his arms wrapped around his head and his eyes closed. He shouted at the ground as the tears pulled away from his eyes and sprinted down his face. "GO AWAY! PLEASE, JUST GO AWAY."

"Sweetheart. I am here to help you. The man above you has done you no wrong. He is suffering mercilessly. You must put and end to this. RIGHT NOW!"

"I CAN'T. IT'S TOO LATE!" he bawled.

"IT ISN'T TOO LATE. YOU CAN DO IT. GET THE MAN DOWN, NOW!"

"Listen to me!" McCalister called down to him, interrupting his inner conversation. McCalister had had enough. No matter what was going on with this man, he had to tell him something, and he was determined to say it.

Ramond dropped his arms from his head and looked up at McCalister. For a moment he had forgotten all about the

THE PERFECT PLACE

man and the sacrifice. McCalister hung directly over him and stared down at him with bulging, blood shot eyes. The strain was evident in his face, as he stood upright to speak.

"I have to explain something to you. It's important. You have to listen," McCalister grunted. Ramond gazed up in fascination. The man *was* a fighter. Anyone who could speak through that much torment was a true warrior.

Ramond had every intention of hearing the man out. McCalister's words were sure to be better than his mother's. He sat in silence, on his knees, gazing up at the man, waiting for him to speak.

But before the first word left McCalister's lips, Ramond blacked out.

†††††††††††††

One knee blocked his view as his eyes burst open. He was laying on his side in almost a complete fetal position. The feeling of disorientation he usually felt when he woke up was not present. From the moment Ramond's eyes opened, he knew exactly where he was and understood fully that he had blacked out for an undetermined period of time. He rolled on his back, gazing at the sun which still lay high in the sky. Couldn't have been more than twenty minutes, he thought.

The lack of sound from the cross drew his attention. The cries had stopped. McCalister was dead. The blood had stopped trickling from his wounds, signifying the circulation in his body had ended. His head hung down. His eyes stared at his feet. All weight hung from his wrists as his fingers drooped limp from his hands.

MICHAEL BISHOP

A strong stench fouled the air. It was a familiar odor, and Ramond eyed McCalister's crotch. At some point during Ramond's blackout, his victim had relieved himself; although, most likely, it did not bring much relief.

The sight of the dead man's limp body nailed to the cross, bloody and covered in urine was catastrophically pitiful, but somehow there was solace in it. McCalister no longer churned his teeth. He no longer had to force himself upward to receive air. The waves of agony no longer pulsed through him. It was over. He was gone.

Ramond got to his feet, totally clear headed. Fainting spells were not commonplace to him. In fact, he had never passed out before in his life. Not even when he was drunk.

Still the *nap* was, in a way, a blessing. It kept him from having to listen to whatever it was McCalister wanted to tell him. And it kept him from having to see any more of the horrible script being played out before him. As awful as the thought might be, he was glad the man was dead. For his own sake, more than John McCalister's.

Unsure about what he was supposed to do with the body, he decided to leave it. Satan had never mentioned how long the body should hang, and Ramond never thought to ask. But after completing number six, he was not about to screw it up by removing the body too soon. It was possible the sacrifice was supposed to stay up a few days. There was no way to know. At any rate, the body would be fine for a while right where it was. No one would find it out here. Only the overlooking trees and Ramond knew the clearing existed.

The tools were picked up and placed in the trunk, along with the bags and whatever other clutter lined the

THE PERFECT PLACE

ground. He crawled under the car and untied the rope, then pulled on the end that was attached to the cross until it unthreaded itself from the pulley above him and fell to the ground. He left the rope in the dirt, simply because he did not want to get close enough to the body to cut the other end down.

He was ready to leave. The atmosphere had changed somewhat since he had awakened. His head was just a bit *too* clear. Too keen. That, and an extinct John McCalister, tainted the clearing. It was no longer his *perfect* place. It was now a site owned by the dead.

He did not look in the rear view mirror as he cranked the Ford. He had seen enough for one day. The tires spun and threw up dust as he wheeled away. The moment was melancholy. A part of him wanted to rejoice. One more test and the power of the universe would be his. But when thoughts of celebration arose, darker thoughts of the sacrifice smothered them.

And on top of the guilt murder brought, was the vexation of Vernadette's voice. It was uncontrollable. A hindrance. Somehow, whatever it took, he would have to find a cure for the voice in his head.

††††††††††††

"DYING ALONE"

It did not take long for Joan McCalister to become hysterical. Her only son was missing. A struggle had been found at his house. Blood on the carpet. Money missing from his wallet. And the chain on the door snapped like a rotted rubber band. Any loving mother would have been just as distressed, and she did not sleep a wink for four days.

Every waking moment was spent by the phone. When it rang, she snatched it up on the first ring with a frantic "Hello?" Each time, her hopes were dashed when it would just be a concerned friend or another family member offering their sympathy and support.

"He'll turn up, have faith Joany," everyone told her, and for awhile she truly believed he would.

In all the time she sat by the phone, the police never once called. They didn't have to. She contacted them every few hours, leaving no reason for them to get in touch with her. And with no clues to go on, they had nothing to tell her when she *did* call except "We are doing the best we can, Mrs. McCalister. If we hear anything you'll be the first one we call. Promise."

But that was not good enough for Joan. She refused to just sit by and let her son's disappearance go unsolved. She refused to be a victim. There was too much fight in her. After a week with no leads, she decided to take the matter into her own hands.

Joan McCalister did not always see eye to eye with her son, but in the past few months their relationship was on the mend. Her husband Bob had been killed two months earlier. The brakes of his pickup truck had failed rounding one of the many dead man's curves old southern roads were famous for. The truck collided with a tree and like most old dogs who had trouble learning new tricks, Bob was not wearing a seat belt. His body was thrust through the windshield and snapped like a twig as it slammed into a tree.

THE PERFECT PLACE

Upon his father's death, John rushed to his mother's side to comfort her. It had been ages since he had wrapped his arms around her, but she needed him and he was determined to be there for her. John's strength gave Joan strength as well; and because of him, she was able to wade through her grief. Learning to live without the love of her husband was not easy. But with a caring son to lean on, the days grew easier as they passed.

She had begged John to move back in. There was plenty of room in the old house and the money he saved on rent he could pocket and save for his future. But John was not ready to give up his space. He was just beginning to get his life together. It was something he would have to do on his own.

She couldn't forgive herself for not insisting her son move home. Each night she just kept thinking if she had only asked him a few more times, if she had just been more insistent, if she had just pleaded, he would be at home with her right now safe and sound. She blamed herself, and promised no matter how long it took, someday she would see her son again. She had lost one loved one already. Determined to bust Hell wide open to find him, she made plans.

The crusade started immediately. Joan drove into Memphis with a few recent photos of John and had a copy shop print up several hundred "MISSING" fliers. Her days were spent pinning the fliers to every telephone pole, bulletin board, and store window she could find. Two weeks later, she had tacked up over three thousand of the papers, leaving her name and number as the contact.

MICHAEL BISHOP

Not a word came from anybody.

An incredible fear began to grip Joan McCalister. Why hadn't she heard from anyone? Surely someone, somewhere, must know something about what happened to her son. How could he just vanish into thin air, without a trace? Why would anyone want to harm him? These questions haunted her every waking moment.

He had to be alive. After all, they hadn't found a body yet, and that had to mean *something*, she told herself.

Maybe she wasn't doing enough; maybe if she just tried harder, she could bring her boy home. Perhaps she wasn't getting her message to the right people, she reasoned. It was upon these revelations that she stepped up her efforts.

The next morning Joan woke early, dressed, and hit the streets with a renewed energy. If she could just make the right people hear her, someone would have a piece to the puzzle. It would be a start; and a start is all she needed.

Money from Bob's insurance policy was used to buy radio air time and newspaper space. A description of John was read over the radio and a picture was placed in the paper. She ran the ads in every paper in a 200 mile radius of Olive Branch. A large reward was offered to anyone with legitimate information leading to his whereabouts. All of this in vain.

Day after day she read her ads in the paper and listened to the requests on the radio. Each time she came across them she ran to the phone convinced it would ring at any moment with the answer to her prayer. But the phone never rang, and nothing panned out.

THE PERFECT PLACE

Days became weeks. No concrete leads were found. The campaign was sucking her bank account dry. But there was still fight in her. She refused to give up, even though the police had done so long ago. She knew she could do more. She was convinced that with enough willpower and determination she would see John again.

The next logical step was taken. A reputable private detective was hired to find her son. It was a last ditch effort. Hiring the man would cost her every last dime she had, but if he found even the smallest of clues it would be the best investment she ever made.

He was told to work night and day, whatever it took. He was to find John McCalister, or die trying.

It only took the man a week to conclude that John McCalister had fallen off the face of the earth. He had run himself ragged for seven days, exhausting every avenue and possibility before moving on to the next. With no clues, no witnesses, and nothing to go on, he informed her that it was hopeless. The man told her to give up, cut her losses, and move on with her life. It was over.

The search had become more than just a need to know. It had been a sort of companion to her; and without it, she was alone.

It gave her a reason to get up in the morning. It brought with it a new day and new possibilities; and when the realization that it was indeed over struck her, she died inside. Living alone was worse than physical torture. It was mentally irreparable. Knowing when she went to bed, she would go to bed alone. Knowing when she woke up, there would be no one laying next to her. Knowing when she made dinner she

MICHAEL BISHOP

would be the only one to enjoy her cooking.

    Everything Joan McCalister did, she did by herself. When she passed away four years later, sitting in her husband Bob's favorite easy chair, she did that alone as well.

The Knowing

1 2 3 4 5 6 8 0

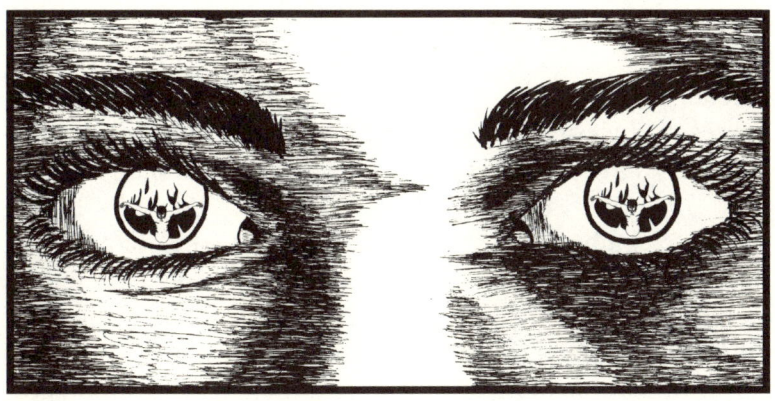

The stagnant air of his apartment smelled like the fresh baked bread of paradise to him. There truly was no place like home. Ramond wanted nothing more than a cold bath to soothe his tired skin and a victory nap as a reward to himself for the sacrifice.

Thoughts of McCalister pushed out the door of his mind while the cool water filled the basin and chilled his skin. A thousand kinds of grime clung to his crevices. There were granules of dirt, grass stains from weeds, bark from the oak, shavings from the twine, blood, sweat, and umpteens more hiding about the parts of his frame.

All the germs were annihilated by the soap, and their particles sailed down the drain as he pulled the plug. There was nothing like the feeling of being clean, except for maybe the feeling the power brought.

As he dried his back, he fantasized about what it would be like. Having a perfect body. Having respect from the world. Having gifts more amazing than magic and witchery. It was all at his fingertips, just beyond the grasp of his reach. Just one step more and he could grab it. The road had been hard; but where it led was well worth the journey.

A bathrobe that once belonged to his father was wrapped around him. It was one of the many articles of clothing he inherited over the years as Brian Jamison's midsection expanded out of control. The robe was warm and comfortable, not at all like ceremonial cloaks. He embraced it as he entered his room and peered lustfully at his bunk.

The bed was not distasteful to him. It brought no memories of a saliva pool, or Susan Lints eating away at his penis. Instead it called to him. Summoned him to rest his weary bones. He hated to put his spotless body against the unsanitary linen, but the floor offered less cleanliness.

He leapt onto the mattress with the enthusiasm of a child leaping into a sandbox. The bed sheets were thrown on the floor in a wad. The air in the apartment was tepid enough, and their filth was not something he wanted on him.

His eyelids slammed down like prison gates. Ramond could tell it would not take long to pass into sleep. His mind had already begun to fade like the reception on an outdated television. But moments before he floated completely into slumber, a bang on the door brought him back. Rest was halted. Disturbed by an unexpected guest.

Looking out the peephole he saw nothing. On the other side of the door only air and sunlight presided. *Must have been some kids playing a prank,* he thought annoyed. As he turned to walk back to the bed, the knock came from

THE KNOWING

behind him again.

"What the hell?" he spoke aloud and stuck his face back to the peephole. Once again, it reported that nothing was on the other side of the door but and empty walkway.

He could not understand it. Without thinking he turned the knob and pulled the door wide open. What he saw on the other side nearly caused him to rip the knob from the door. He placed so much pressure on the handle, in fact, that the top screw holding the knob in place popped out.

The man at the door was normal looking enough. All appendages were in correct proportion to their counterparts. Even his clothing was nothing Ramond had never seen before. An expensive looking suit hung perfectly from his body. Solid black, lacking pinstripes or any signs of a seam or taper. Underneath the black jacket, he wore a collarless button down silk shirt that matched the color of the coat. His trousers were creaseless and cut with a stylish three pleat. The outfit was definitely tailor made.

The nails on his fingers were well manicured, and his face was shaven so well it seemed that nothing grew there to begin with. His jaw line was chiseled, squared off. Adding to his good looks.

But the eye catcher was his head. The entire thing was as smooth as a cue ball. No hair at all could be seen on his skull. It almost seemed to be polished.

His age was hard to guess. He could have been fifty, but from a different angle he looked not a day over thirty. Still in the dark, he could have been mistaken for a teenager. There was no way of telling.

None of this, however, had caused Ramond to nearly break his hand with his death grip on the knob. It was the

MICHAEL BISHOP

knowing that did it. The man did not need to say a word. The aura that blasted from him said it all. It was Satan incarnate.

"Gonna invite me in?" the familiar voice asked nonchalantly. With the question, he invited himself in, stepping past Ramond with long, silky strides. "Housekeeper's day off?" he inquired as he glanced around the room. A long finger was raked over one corner of the dresser and held in front of his face as he studied the dirt on his fingertip.

Ramond stood awestruck. Seeing the master in the form of a man was overwhelming. And not only that, but he was standing right in front of him, critiquing his cleanliness. It was enough to dumbfound any rational man.

"Shut the door, Ramond," he commanded matter-of-factly. Once again without waiting for a response from his host, the man pointed at the door, and with a flick of his finger, the knob broke loose from Ramond's hand and the door slammed shut by itself. Ramond jerked his hand back from the knob as it moved from his grip. He stared at it long with wonder. The situation was just too much. His mind was not yet able to make sense of everything. It was happening too fast.

"Ramond, what is wrong with you? You are truly a poor host," Satan teased with a coy smile that let Ramond know he understood his behavior.

"I'm sorry, just surprised to see you... like this," he attempted in explanation.

"I understand, my boy. It's not every day that the God of this world stands in the center of your room and attempts to make idle chatter with you. No need to explain your idiotic reaction. Take as long as you want to get used to the idea. I

THE KNOWING

want you paying attention and alert as we discuss the future."

"I'm ready... really. It's just... peculiar," he felt ignorant when he spoke. It was different when you had to speak to a person instead of an omniscient voice. The form his master had chosen to take was intriguing, yet threatening as well.

"Yes. It is peculiar. And to tell the truth, I hate wearing these suits. They are so gaudy and uncomfortable."

"It looks like a very nice suit to me. Expensive and tailor made," Ramond complimented, trying to relax.

"Not the suit on my back, simpleton. I'm speaking of this *skin* suit around me. It's absolutely disgusting to have to force myself into this ridiculous looking flesh. Not to mention degrading looking as lowly as you... you *mortals*." When he spoke of humans, his face puckered and wrinkled with repulse as if he were talking about eating bugs. Ramond listened to him speak in silence. He felt doltish for the misplaced compliment and dared not speak again.

Satan waited a moment for a reply from Ramond. When none came he started again.

"I did not come here to talk about such things, though. This visit is for business, as it seems they all are... I just want you to know, Ramond, I was there. I watched every single move. From the start to the end."

He did not have to wonder what the Master was talking about. He knew without doubt Satan was referring to the crucifixion; and the fact that he was there did not astonish Ramond at all. After all, what good is a sacrifice given in your name if you are not there to experience and enjoy it first hand.

"I'm impressed," his Sire continued. "You showed fascinating ingenuity. The way you put the whole thing together, using the rope and pulley... pure genius. With a wonderful performance like that, I will be proud to have you as my right arm."

To have Satan say such a thing to him, face to face, brought such pride from within him that his emotions could barely be controlled. All the pain and agony he had put himself and others through seemed worthwhile. So worth while, in fact, that he felt he could do six more if that's what it took. Anything to reach the ultimate goal.

"Go ahead and gloat, Ramond," Satan said looking straight through him. "You deserve it." A smile attached itself to Satan's face, like a leech on an open sore. He took steps toward Ramond before he spoke again.

The sight of his Master coming toward him took him by surprise. His arrogant smile disappeared as the complicatedly gorgeous face of his Lord stood nose to nose with him.

In the eyes there was no fire. No figure standing in the flames. There was no need for them. The Master was not inhabiting another person or object. Instead, it was actually him, in the human form he had chosen to take. This was not a possession, but an incarnation. The difference was monumental.

The hand of Satan reached out and placed itself on Ramond's shoulder. With it, every emotion he had ever felt ran through his body in unity. It was the highest and lowest he had ever been; and though it only lasted for a brief moment, his body tingled from it for hours to come.

"You have done so well for me, Ramond," the Devil said with an ere of respect floating in his voice. The grip increased on Ramond's shoulder. His eyes were so deep. Almost transparent. Ramond felt as if he could see forever in

THE KNOWING

those eyes. See ages past. See times to come. See all the knowledge the world held. And if the Master had allowed it, he might have gazed forever.

"You have been a better troop for me than you'll ever know. The things I have had you do have excelled far better than even I had foreseen... But, my boy..." Satan paused, relinquished his grip, and turned his back to Ramond.

".....but there is one more..." He paused again and stood in his place for a second as if he were deeply contemplating the situation. Then Satan spun toward him. A move so sudden, Ramond took a step back in startle and balled his fist. Satan's eyes were wild and wide, and a dastardly gape came across his face as he screamed.

"THE SEVENTH!" It rolled off his tongue like a ringleader standing center stage announcing his last side show freak. And it was spoken in a manner that Ramond thought it might be the most important thing anyone had ever been asked to do.

"You have only to ask!" he assured, fired up by his mentor's performance. Ramond was sure that whatever it was he could do it, and do it better than anyone else.

"If you are truly strong and have overcome all your weaknesses, it should be a piece of cake. I'm aware of your financial status, but this one won't cost you a red cent. And the second it is completed, I will swoop down from my ever watching perch and take you home with me," He charged the words with hypnotic power. He exuded pure energy. The way he spoke would motivate even those who possessed no ambition, and to Ramond it was the ultimate driving force.

"Name it," Ramond sputtered.

"One more sacrifice. And the most important of the seven," he announced, as he took a step toward Ramond again, making eye contact that was impossible to look away from. "You see Ramond, you may have only one Lord, and that must be me."

"But you are my only Lord!"

"Let me finish," he whispered gently. "If you want to join me, you must sever all ties. Every single, solitary one. There shall be no link between you and this world. Is that understood?" The question was not asked angrily, but it was clear to Ramond there was only one acceptable answer.

"Yes... But I have no ties here. I'm ready to go with you now. Nothing holds me to this world," he insisted.

"There is still one hindrance that keeps you from seeing my true form. A tie that binds you here. A sacrifice you must make before you can take your rightful place."

"What?" he asked clueless.

"You must have only one father and you must have only one mother. And that's me. I am to be your all. I am the one who will transform you and mold you into a man-god. Therefore, the other two who hold claims to you must be blotted out."

The motivation and energy disappeared from Ramond as he began to get the message. His head told him it could not be true, begged him to make it not true. But he could not let self-denial take control. He knew what was being asked of him.

"What are you saying? I don't understand," he lied. He understood totally and they both knew it.

"I think you understand just fine, Ramond. Brian and Vernadette Jamison will be given to me as the last test. Their death will be your ultimate sacrifice to me. God gave his son for you. You will do the opposite and give your parents for me. When it is accomplished, all ties you have to this world

THE KNOWING

will be eradicated and you will be ready." The words were spoken as casually as someone reading a grocery list.

Ramond's head spun with pressure. The whole thing was lunacy. What had his parents done wrong? This had nothing at all to do with them. Why should they be punished for what he wanted? All the doubts and questions started a civil war in his mind, and the guns of battle caused an explosion.

"WHY?" he screamed back at the man not caring who he was. For the first time, he made a stand and questioned what he was being told to do.

The answer he got in return was spoken quietly and was the simplest answer he had ever been given.

"Because I said so," he whispered at Ramond with breath as thick and cold as frost. It was arrogance at its peak. The words of a parent to a child.

Ramond's eyes bulged at the response. It gave him no answer, but also left him with no retort. It was so final there was no room to argue. He could only stand and gawk at the man in disbelief.

He stepped toward Ramond and met him eye to eye. Satan's stare was filled with hate and fury. The look spoke for itself and said "Don't you ever question me, boy!" He peered at Ramond like this for moments, until Ramond neared tears. Then the man's voice deepened and became louder, sounding less like a man, and more like the king of Hell.

"You *will* do this," the voice grunted. "You *will* do it immediately. You *will* do it in my name. And you *will* do it without any more questioning. Isn't that right, BOY!" At the end of the orders, the incarnated body began to grow. It increased in height a foot and thickened to equal proportion.

The face changed too, although not in a way Ramond

could describe. Its age sailed past decades of time. It was a eternal, not bound by the aging process. It was free of impurities or flaws. And although it was angelic in nature, it was ghastly combined with the voice.

He could not speak as the creature stood a head above him and stared down with contempt.

"Don't pussy out on me now, Ramond. You're close. Right at the door to me. All I have to do is open it for you. And all you have to do is the teensy, tiny little task of killing your parents. Is that so much to ask? But there is something I failed to mention, and maybe this will make it easier. You see, that voice in your head, the voice that you hate so much, the voice that causes you so much pain and distress as it nags you into submission; the voice of your mother... that voice can only be silenced in one way," Satan paused to take in Ramond's changing expression. His face perked up as his curiosity came into play.

"Tell me how!" he pleaded like a man dying of cancer would beg a doctor who had the cure.

"It's simple. In fact, I'm surprised you have not figured it out by now. If you kill Vernadette, who is the real root of the problem, the voice will stop. No more being scourged by her mocking. No more worrying when it will pop up and what you will do when it does. It will be gone forever. And you have the power. All you have to do is what I said. And you will do it. Right?"

The idea that he could actually stop the voice was the only thing on his mind. To be free. To end the insanity for good. The idea was a definite temptation for murder.

"I said, RIGHT?" Satan demanded.

Ramond's attention returned to the large body above him. Fear chose the reply. "Yes...Yes Lord. Whatever you

THE KNOWING

say."

"Good," Satan replied, his voice oddly returning back to casual. He took a few steps back and returned to normal size. Ramond did not notice the shrinking until it was complete. More parlor tricks.

"I will come for you when it is final." The man threw a glance at the door. When his eyes struck it, it seemed to read his thoughts and opened for him. Light flooded in from outside and lit up the man's face. For a twinkling, he looked almost normal: Unmenacing.

"I'm off," Satan reported. With three steps he was out the door. It closed behind him without a touch and made no noise as it shut securely.

Ramond rushed to stare out the peephole. He knew what he would find before he even looked, but a part of him had to look anyway. The peephole reported to his eye just as he expected. An empty walkway. He had gone just as he had come. Magically.

Sitting on the edge of the bed, Ramond fumbled with his hands, working them against each other in nervousness as he mulled over his predicament. Could he do it? And what if he couldn't? What then?

Murder was one thing when it came to strangers. There were no emotional ties. There was no knowledge of who would mourn them or how the world would be without them. He didn't have to dwell on it. He could alienate himself. Shut them out of his mind. Even pretend they were as insignificant as animals if he wanted.

But with someone he knew it would be a different

story. The knowing would be unbearable. The knowing of the loss the world would suffer from their death. The knowing of how many loved ones would stand over their casket, weeping and wishing to God that he had not let them die. The knowing of all the hopes and dreams they had, only to lose their life before they had the chance to fulfill any of them. The knowing was pain.

But this went well beyond the fact that they were not strangers. These were his parents. The two people who had brought him into the world. The ones who had bought him his first bike at six, the kind with the training wheels. They were the ones who had thrown him a surprise birthday party and had hired a real clown to entice some of the other kids into actually showing up.

Most of all, Brian and Vernadette Jamison were the only two people on Earth who Ramond could actually say he loved. And although, up until now, he had thought he wanted nothing more than to serve the Master and gain the power, maybe there was something he wanted just a little bit more: the long life of his parents.

On the other side of the coin lay his dreams and lust for the most dominant position a man has ever held. All the work, all the pain, all the frustration would be wasted effort if his folks were allowed to live.

And what would Satan's response be if he failed to kill them? That question frightened him most of all. The Devil was erratic. There was no predicting what he might do. Perhaps he would kill them himself just for spite. Ramond did not want to experience his wrath.

He knew if he could summon the courage to get rid of them everything would be fine. Satan had promised to come

THE KNOWING

for him when the act was done. And surely after he was taken away with the Master, he would not be allowed to feel grief over the killing of his parents. If he could just endure until it was over, his Lord would take care of the rest. The pendulum began to swing toward murder's side.

But the main factor that determined the pendulum's swing was the riddance of Vernadette's voice. As a child, he could not do anything without it tormenting him. Every move he made, it haunted him and scolded him for his actions. It was hell to live with, and the possibility of ending it was too good to turn down. The affliction would finally end.

Brian Jamison would be the easier of the two. After all, if Ramond allowed, he could bring himself to hate the man. All the neglect, all the shame, all degrading remarks could boil up feelings that might just let him carry out the act. The two of them never clicked like a father and son should. It was a tragic relationship. One that could have been so much, but in reality was nothing. An underlying factor did remain, however; Brian Jamison *was* still his father and he *did* love him.

Vernadette Jamison, on the other hand, could have easily been mother of the year. She had an uncanny knack for being there when you needed her. The advice she gave rivaled that of the well written dialogues T.V. moms were paid to rattle off. Time was always made for her only son, no matter what was on the agenda. Only when Ramond changed did they separate, making their relationship tragic as well. It was so much, turned to nothing.

MICHAEL BISHOP

It was due to the fact that Vernadette would be much harder to kill that made Ramond decide to get her first. If he killed his father first, there was a chance he would chicken out and not be able to go through with killing his mother. And with his father dead and his mother still alive, he would fail the last test. Instead of being taken away by his Lord, he would be left to suffer the consequences.

With Vernadette the first to go, the hard part would be over, and the rest would be smooth sailing. The decision was well thought out.

† † † † † † † † † † †

Ramond knew their routine well and accordingly decided to wait until 6:30 before he left his apartment. About this time, his mother would be starting dinner. Timing it perfectly so it would be fully prepared and ready to serve by seven thirty, the same time they ate every night.

Brian, no doubt, would be flipping the television from channel to channel to catch the latest sports news. In his easy chair he would be laid back, beer in hand, rooting for one team or the other. Occasionally checking the T.V. Guide to make sure he was not missing a better sporting event on a different channel.

The two of them were predictable. With or without Ramond in their lives, their patterns remained the same.

His old neighborhood regurgitated thousands of dormant memories as he coasted through it. The beam of his lights bounced off the reflectors of a bicycle as he neared his old homestead. It reminded him of the Huffy he championed with pride as a kid, and how he pretended it was his horse and

THE KNOWING

he was a gun-slinging cowboy.

Every tree on the street had been climbed by him. He had played in every yard at one time or another. The neighborhood had once been his whole world. And in that world, he could be anyone he wanted to be. His idols were superheros, like Superman and The Incredible Hulk. All he ever wanted was to be a powerful being who had millions of adoring fans. After all these years, things had not changed that much.

He pulled the car to the right side of the driveway and parked near the curb. From the seat next to him he scooped up the butcher knife he had taken from his own kitchen. The handle was cold in his hand. Its blade about the same length as the nails he had driven through McCalister; only it would be driven through Vernadette instead.

No one, as expected, noticed his arrival. Little could rip them from their positions in the house. And, most likely, neither one would hear the car anyway, each too engrossed in what they were doing to notice a small detail like a car motor outside.

Exiting the car, he did a fast walk to the garage door. He entered his father's tool room in the same manner he had done when the razor was stolen. The door leading from the garage into the house was at the north end of the room and he ventured toward it. As he passed the shop table he scraped the knife across its surface, leaving a trench behind on its top. When he reached the door, he stopped to survey the situation and plot his attack.

The door had the only lock in the house which he did not have a key for, but it was an obstacle easily overcome. Ever since the garage had been added on, a key had been kept on the ledge above the door. Ramond had used it countless times through the years to let himself in when he came home from school and no one else was there.

In those days, the ledge was too high and he had to stand on an overturned bucket to reach the key. But now, as he slid his hand from one side of the ledge to the other, he ran across the key about halfway, reaching it easily with no help from a bucket.

The key was slipped into the lock, but before he turned it, he gazed through the paneled window in the door to make sure the coast was clear. A curtain covered most of the window, but a crack was left at its bottom just wide enough to see through. He peered into the house and listened. As his eyes struck the washer and dryer, his ears picked up the sound of them running simultaneously. *Must be laundry day*, he thought, as he twisted the key in the lock.

The knife was placed between his teeth to free up both hands. Then his left palm was placed on the door beside the glass and he turned the knob with his right. With a fast shove, the door flew open without a squeak. This technique had been learned through many years of sneaking out of the house to attend various parties and gatherings after his parents went to bed. He entered the room and closed the door behind him quietly.

As he removed the blade from his mouth, Ramond scanned the laundry room. The running washer and dryer were an added bonus. The pair of appliances were ancient and made an awful racket. They would go far to cover up his footsteps and any other noise that might give him away.

In his head he pictured where each of his parents would probably be. Around the corner from the laundry room a small hall led to the kitchen. The kitchen was the largest

THE KNOWING

room in the house, and to Vernadette, the most important. It was the room she did most of her thinking and secured the majority of her quiet time.

To the left of the kitchen, a swinging door led to another hall. The long carpeted hallway gave access to every other room in the house, and down it the dining room, bathroom and bedrooms could be found.

At its very end lay an open doorway, leading to the room Brian Jamison held dear. The living room contained the two things he loved most: the thirty-eight inch Magnavox television and his Lazy Boy recliner with the optional cup holder on the left side. The chair had served as his bed on more occasions than his actual bed did, and Ramond could imagine him sitting in the chair now with the remote in hand.

From the living room, with a sports announcer blaring in his ear, Brian would hear nothing from the rest of the house. What little noise Vernadette made would be heard by only the pots, pans, and clean white floor.

Ramond peeked around the corner of the hallway. Unsurprisingly, Vernadette could be seen standing over the stove stirring various pots and pans with her back to him. Above her shoulders steam could be seen rising in puffs, dissipating as they hit the air ventilator that hung above the stove.

The aroma rushed to meet his nose as he watched her. The scent was instantly recognized. It was her "Spaghetti Italiano". His nose remembered the fragrance even now, and his stomach sang out in cramped pains for just one taste of the mouth watering sauce. That ache showed him just how much he had missed her perfect cooking.

He stepped out into the open, knife in left hand, and

MICHAEL BISHOP

walked toward her in the quietest way he could muster. His foot rolled from ball to front, in a rocking chair motion as to not make any stepping noises. The sound of the washer and dryer, and hum of the stove ventilator covered all traces of his steps as he slowly walked across the tile past the counter in the center of the room, to within stabbing distance of his mother.

In killing her, he wanted to be as quick and merciful as possible. The faster she died and the less she suffered, the better. But ensuring that she remained silent throughout was also a major consideration. If she were to scream out, there was still a chance Brian would hear her even over all the other noise. And since Ramond wanted to have the advantage of surprise over his father as well, keeping his mother silent would be a must.

Slitting her throat would be the best way, he thought. The knife was sharp by no means, but he felt that with enough pressure placed on it, it would do a good enough job of slicing. With a cut throat, she would not only bleed to death quickly, but would also have no way to shriek. It gave the best of both worlds.

Her back remained turned to him. It would be so easy just to reach around her and end it all before she even knew what was happening. She had no clue he was there. Her mind was impaled into her work, musing over the heavenly scent her sauce gave off. Ramond increased his grip on the knife and raised it to the level of her head.

The handle shook in his hand. The guilt was starting before he even struck. A deep breath was sucked in to calm him; but it only forced another magnificent whiff of the sauce

THE KNOWING

to sail down his nostrils.

He stood still behind her as she worked. He was hesitating. It only took a slight moment of pause to give the voice time to attack, and it took the opportunity with fierceness.

"DON'T KILL ME RAMOND, PLEASE!" the voice of his mother begged in his head.

It did not startle him this time. He knew it would come. It would have been foolish to think it would stay away during a time when it could be put to an end. Self-preservation would force the voice to fight him, attacking him during his moment of weakness and doubt.

He did his best to ignore it and gripped the knife a bit tighter. *Just kill her. Get it over with!* he told himself. But with that thought the voice rattled him again.

"I love you, son. I love you with all my heart and soul. Do you really want me dead?" it asked him with tenderness and sadness mixed in its voice. It was insane hearing the voice in his head, and seeing his mother in front of him at the same time. The voice had never before come when Vernadette was present. It made it all the more appalling.

You can stop the voice. Just cut her! DO IT! his own mind screamed for him to take action before it was too late.

"By the way, Ramond, do I look thin to you?" Vernadette's voice questioned him. The words boggled his mind. Such a statement was so oddly out of place in the situation, it reeled him with confusion. Why would it ask him a question like that?

But as he looked at his mother, he realized the voice was right. She did look thin. Had she not been eating? He pondered the question briefly.

MICHAEL BISHOP

What does it matter if she has been eating? She'll be dead in a minute, so just do it! he told himself. But somehow it *did* matter if she had been eating or not. It brought a reality to Ramond. The reality that he still cared about her well being. She had grown thin and he wanted to know why and what he could do to help.

"*END IT!*" his head screamed at him one last time. But it was hopeless. Ramond lowered the knife. He could not kill his mother. He knew it now. She meant too much to him. He had forgotten for such a long time, but as he stood behind her thin frame he began to remember.

He remembered her incredible devotion to him. The way she used to sit at his bedside each night and tell him a new story from the Bible. The hundreds of Sundays she got up and dressed him for Sunday school. All the skinned knees she kissed and all the times she nursed him when he was sick.

How could he have ever thought of killing her? This was his mother for God's sake. What kind of monster had he become? The thought of how close he had come to slitting her throat made him ill. It was inhuman. He had transformed into a beast in the last few months. A walking tragedy.

But deep inside him, Ramond's heart held a spark of hope. As he stared at the back of Vernadette, he felt something he had not felt in ages: compassion. He still had a conscience and a heart. He was not totally reprobate after all. Tears rolled down his cheeks and he ached inside to be in the arms of his mother, for her to tell him everything would be alright like she did when he was a boy. He had not been close to her for years and longed to feel her soothing touch.

Until that moment, Ramond had never realized how

THE KNOWING

lonely his life had grown without his mother. All the things he had done, all the groups he had joined, all the power he had searched for seemed so minute compare to his mother's love.

"Mom," he spoke softly through the tears. Vernadette jumped forward, slamming into the stove and slinging the stirring spoon that was in her hand into the back splash, then turned towards him. A scream of surprise left her, although it was not loud enough to attract attention.

"Ramond?" she questioned with a confused stare. After a moment, recognition began to show on her expression. "Ramond! What have you done to yourself? You look... well... you look..." she could not bring herself to be cruel. She looked at him like he was a ghost for a moment before she began again. "What are you doing here? You scared me to death." Her eyes dropped to the knife. Her expression changed to concern. "What are you doing with that knife, Ramond?"

He stared down at the knife like he wasn't sure why he had it either, then tossed it in the sink to his right. Her motherly gaze was all it took. He couldn't control his emotions any longer. He flung his arms around her and held her tight. It was a gesture that surprised her as much as seeing him there in the first place. This was the first sign of affection he had shown in almost a decade. And although she was not at all sure of what was going on, after a moment, she returned the embrace to her son.

"I love you, Mom. I really love you!" was all he could say as he rocked her from side to side.

Sobs rushed to Vernadette and she began to cry unlike she had cried since the day he told her he did not believe as she did. She had heard him say the one thing he had not said since he was fifteen. And to hear her son say "I Love You" washed away all her fears, confusion, and uncertainty.

All that mattered was the love between them. It was the single happiest moment in Vernadette Jamison's life, and would never be replaced by another.

†††††††††††

It was time for a fresh start. If that was possible. The nightmares of his sins would keep him awake at night, but Ramond felt that with his mother's help, he could turn his life around.

He wanted to tell Vernadette all the things he had done. It would have helped to get it off his chest. To tell someone would mean it was not a secret anymore. Not something you kept bottled up inside.

But telling his mother of his deeds was out of the question. Having Vernadette look at him as a rapist and murderer would be much worse than living alone with the guilt. It was a cross he would have to bear alone.

Would the Devil forget his failure? Most likely not, but that was a worry for another day. Like it or not, it was over with. There was nothing more to be done about it. He would live with the ghosts of his past, but pushing forth had to be attempted. Ramond had not given up on life just yet.

A part of him still considered itself a Satanist; but other parts of his soul began to raise doubts. In any case, fear kept him from worshiping the Devil any longer. Satan's reprisal for treachery would still have to be taken into consideration. For the time being, he felt it would be best to

THE KNOWING

stay neutral in the war of the spirit. He was not a Christian, and not a Satanist. He was an Atheist, the easiest road of any to take.

† † † † † † † † † † † †

There were measures that had to be taken before he could move on. Skeletons that had to be locked in the closet.

The body of John McCalister must be disposed of. There would be no magic tricks from Satan to protect him if the police found the body. And, he thought, John McCalister deserved to be buried. The man had never done anything to him personally. He deserved the right to be laid to rest respectfully.

But with all the good intentions, it was still drastically taxing to go back to the *perfect* place one last time.

Only five days had passed, but the weeds had already began waging their battle on the clearing. The brush Ramond had not completely demolished was flourishing, growing with incomparable speed in the sunlight. The foliage he had gotten rid of was spawning new life from its remains, leaving various weeds, briars, and bush peeking up from the earth's soil, striving for new life.

The body had not been discovered. This was a fact he could clearly see as he pulled into the circle. It still hung lifeless from the assembled lumber, and it was still unsettlingly gruesome. In fact, it was now even more gruesome. Ramond was forced see a part of the death he had not considered before: the scavengers.

MICHAEL BISHOP

The size of the buzzards was astounding. Some of them bore wingspans that neared the length of the Ford. At least twenty flew overhead. If anything should have been a signal flare to passerbys, the birds should have. Even a large buck nestled in the forest, laying lame and waiting to die would not have attracted this much attention.

But no one had noticed, and it was almost a shame, Ramond thought. Had someone seen, they could have stopped the systematic picking apart of John McCalister's corpse. They could have cut him down and taken him away, protecting his earthly hull from the attack of the flying beasts.

As he exited the car and moved closer, he realized why most of the birds were circling above instead of eating. The truth of the matter was, there was not much left to eat. McCalister's dead eyes were no longer staring at his feet, simply for the fact that they were no longer there. The scavengers had picked the eyelids off, then removed their gooey contents.

The clothing he wore lay in tatters just below the cross. The pajamas had been torn to shreds in an attempt to get to the tasty flesh underneath. By now, there was practically no flesh left. Just an outline of a man. Only enough stringy ligaments to keep the body from falling to the ground below.

The buzzards were not the only scavengers to have a go at McCalister. Both legs were completely missing past the knee. They appeared to have been ripped off in a ravaged fashion, leaving strings of meat hanging. Apparently, a pack of coyotes or some other four-legged creature that could reach no higher than the knees had converged upon the gamey legs in a fight to secure the most tasty parts. They dragged the limbs off, bones and all, leaving no trace of their

THE KNOWING

whereabouts.

One bird still sat upon the skull of McCalister picking away at the remains of hair that lined the top of his cranium. The shrill "Caw" it made gave Ramond shivers as he approached. At his presence, it flew to the heavens to join its sadistic brethren in their circle flight. They would soon move on to repeat the process on whatever dead thing caught their sight next.

The scavengers had inflicted their own kind of punishment on McCalister. It would be just another nightmare Ramond would be forced to live with.

No longer did a body hang from the cross. Only a sad reminder of what once was a human being with a heart, feelings, a family, and a life.

He reached out and touched what was left of the man's right thigh. Quickly, he jerked away in disgust as the section he touched crumbled to the earth. The skin flaked and bubbled in the sun. Another day or so of intense rays beating down upon it and the outer layers would be cracking and falling off like dandruff.

The decaying process was not readily seen. The birds had picked the parts away before the rot could take hold on any one section. But the smell of the rot was not taken by the birds, and its stench added to the revulsion.

The smell would have easily made Ramond vomit had he not anticipated it and began breathing from his mouth. It did not smell like death. This smell was different. It was more like five day old garbage. At this stage, it didn't seem to matter that what hung from the cross was once a thriving living creature. Now, it was just another chunk of trash, meant to be decomposed and taken back to the earth from

MICHAEL BISHOP

which it came.

All this, combined with Ramond's newfound compassion, made him feel much more guilty than he did when he had given the sacrifice. The main difference was that this time the voice did not come to torment him. The voice had stopped from the moment he decided he could not kill his mother, and had not returned since.

Perhaps it was because he was trying to make things right, but Ramond thought it was more than that. It was the fact that his mother was on his side now, and had she known about the situation, would have given her blessing on the burial of John McCalister. It was much better to have Vernadette as a friend than a foe. Life was more tolerable.

He had wondered about the best way to take his lamb from the cross. Now, with the work of the buzzards, it was a moot point. With a slight tug around the waist area of McCalister, the bones and remaining flesh easily came free. The twine had been gnarled into bits, giving no resistance as the wrist bones pulled from it. The remains collapsed on Ramond in a heap. They were light and stiff, not bending over his shoulder but sitting like a board flung over it. He laid the remains on the ground as gently as he could for fear it might crumble like a moist sugar cube. The time had come to erase all signs of McCalister's existence.

Ramond wrapped his digits around the orange plastic handle of the shovel. The tool, which his mother used in the backyard for light gardening, was lightweight and ideal for grave digging. His hands were just beginning to heal from their blisters and sores, and they screamed in annoyance as he

THE KNOWING

overturned the first weed-ridden chunk of earth. He turned another, then another, making no attempt to make the hole six feet deep. When it was just deep enough to cover the bones so that no animals could dig them back up, he rolled the remains into the shallow grave.

Pieces of the man's clothing were gathered from the area and thrown into the hole with him. When Ramond had filled the hole with everything he wanted to bury, he scooped up the first shovel full of loose dirt, intending to fill the grave.

A thought came to him before he tossed the dirt into the hole. There was one more thing he needed to bury. The shovel was dropped and the soil in its end scattered about the ground. From beneath his shirt, the glass eye of the stylus was removed. It sparkled like a diamond in the sun and cast a reflected circle of light over the grave.

The amulet had been with him from day one. It had given him his first taste of power, and had been a key instrument in the course of Ramond's life. Since the dream of possessing the power had begun with the stylus, it seemed only fitting that it be buried along with the dream itself.

He took the necklace and held it away from himself in a clenched fist over the grave. It swung hypnotizingly back and forth. There was no power left in it. Now it was nothing more than a piece of glass. He released his grip and watched it fall on top of McCalister's corpse. Two dead objects sharing the same grave.

He grabbed the shovel again and hastily filled the hole. It took far less time to cover the area than it had to dig it. When it was full, Ramond patted the raised soil down with the end of the shovel, leveling the pile. It was done. A ghost had been laid to rest. Perhaps it was just more useless symbolism. But if it helped him to sleep better, it was well worth it.

Soon the weeds would begin seeding the dirt above the plot. In a few weeks, there would be no sign that the earth had ever been disturbed. McCalister would rest forever in an unmarked grave.

✝ ✝ ✝ ✝ ✝ ✝ ✝ ✝ ✝ ✝ ✝ ✝

Brian Jamison had never cut a tree or log of firewood in his life; nevertheless, in his shop a large chainsaw had hung for years. It was more a status symbol than anything else. A piece of equipment to be shown off to the other men when they dropped by for visits.

Ramond thought he could make use of it. He dragged it out of the back seat and brought it to the foot of the crucifix. The cross now looked more like a tombstone than a sacrificial element. It rose high above the grave and its blood stains served as a reminder of the suffering experience on it.

The old gas inside the chainsaw's tank was stale and did not want to burn; but with four tugs on the starter rope, the gas finally blazed and set the motor into action.

He had never used a chainsaw either, but he quickly taught himself the ropes as the saw hungrily bit into the bottom of the timber. It took just seconds to rip through the board. The cross tumbled to the right, landing one of its arms first, then toppling flat on its back.

The pulley was left in the tree. There was no way he was reclimbing the oak. Enough had been done to cover his tracks and it was time to move on. The weeds he once dreaded would cover up anything he had forgotten. In all likelihood, no one would ever know what took place here

THE KNOWING

except he and the late John McCalister.

As he drove away from his *perfect* place, he tried to erase it all from his mind. He kept telling himself that the act was done by a different person, in a different time. If he could only convince himself of that, he might be able to sleep at night.

An eviction notice was discovered on his door when he returned to his apartment to gather his things. It was not a problem. He had no intention of staying in the apartment any longer. With all that had happened to him there, and with the fact that Satan had stood in his very living room, Ramond did not want to live there another minute.

Vernadette offered her house to him. As long as he got another job, he could stay as long as he needed. She did not ask how he lost his last one. Like most things in her son's past, she knew it was better that she did not know.

The usual stench greeted him as he entered the place. Brian would come later in the day and help him move the heavier pieces, but Ramond knew he had to clean the place before his father arrived.

Small things were taken care of quickly, like removing the straight razor from the ashes in the garbage pail. He placed it into his pocket with every intention of returning it to its proper place in his father's toolbox. Every item he had ever collected that dealt with the occult, from books, to posters, to goblets and robes, was then placed into the can.

MICHAEL BISHOP

His parents never had a clue about his cult activities. It would stay that way.

The bed sheets were also discarded. Their crusted surface had hardened to an almost breakable level and the odor collected in the fabric would never come out.

One thing after another was disposed of; and with each one that was thrown away, so was a piece of Ramond's past. It was a change he briskly accepted.

†††††††††††††

"I'm not so sure about this, Vern. I mean we don't know what the kid's been doing, or what he's into, or anything."

"Brian! I'm surprised at you. This is our boy. If he needs our help, then we're gonna help him."

"I'm not saying we shouldn't help him. I'm just saying maybe we should be askin' a few questions here. That's all I'm saying. If the kid's on the up and up, then that's fine; but if he ain't, then I wanna know about it. For all I know, he could be pushin' drugs. Now, I don't want that sort of thing in my house." He knew it was a touchy subject. Vernadette had always been quick to take offense when you talked about her boy. It didn't seem to matter that it was his boy too.

"Look, Bri, I normally don't put my foot down...I mean I think I go your way most of the time...But this time, we're gonna do it my way. Have you taken a good look at your son? He looks like death warmed over. Now, he didn't say how or why. But what he did say is that he's gonna need a place to stay for awhile until he gets another job and gets back on his feet; and that to me sounds like he's trying to do the right thing. So why don't you give him the benefit of the

THE KNOWING

doubt for once in his life?" Her words were so fast that they were barely coherent, and although her tone was not a scream, it was definitely louder than a normal conversation voice.

"Calm down, Sweetie," He tried to soothe her.

"Well, it's hard to calm down when you're sitting there talking about our son like some stranger. And I'll tell you the truth, I don't care where he's been and what he's done. The important thing to me is that he's here now. And that should be important to you too!"

"It is important to me!" he defended.

"You know all I ever asked is that you be a father to your son," Vernadette's words were becoming quieter as tears began slowly running down her cheeks. "And now you have a second chance. Why won't you just take it?"

He rose out of his chair and walked over to her.

"Don't cry, honey," he pleaded as he wrapped his arms around her and cradled her. "I'm sorry. I'm just cynical. You know that. 'Tis the nature of the beast." He looked at her and smiled. She managed to make herself smile back.

"I just wish..."

"I know what you wish," he cut her off. "And I'll try harder. I mean it. If you say he's getting it together, then I'll take your word for it... and his."

Her smile widened and the tears disappeared. "You mean it?" she asked.

"I do. I'll tell you what, when he gets back from cleaning up his place, and after we get all the moving over and done with, I'll make a few phone calls to some of my buddies and see if I can land him a job somewhere. How's that sound?"

Her face beamed back at him. It was a face anyone

would fall in love with. "It sounds like a father." She leaned forward and gave him a short kiss. "Thank you Brian...It means a lot to me," she said as she gazed into his eyes.

"I know it does... I love you."

"I love you too."

In a twist of irony, one of the managers at Sierra Home Hardware owed Brian Jamison a favor. He cashed in the favor by getting his son a job interview for a full-time position.

The position paid little more than minimum wage, and although Ramond hated to take such a low paying job, he knew it was a paramount step in regaining his parent's trust.

For the first time in his life, he had a sensible plan for his life. In six months he could save enough money to get another place of his own. From there, he would put a percentage of his check into a savings account and save for a better car. Maybe even find a steady girlfriend and think about settling down. His plans were not extraordinary, but they were *new* dreams; and with the *new* dreams came optimism and possibilities.

With the passing weeks, his hair was trimmed shorter and shorter. Brian adored the short hair style, saying it made him look more like a man. A part of Ramond, surprisingly, agreed with his father.

Meat began to form on his bones again, as Ramond's

THE KNOWING

frame packed on fifteen pounds. Vernadette stated time and time again "It does my heart good to see my son eat well." And as Ramond shoveled each fork-full of food into his awaiting mouth, he thought that it did his heart good as well.

Her cooking was so rich and flavorful, even better than he remembered it being as a child. Each dish was spiced and seasoned perfectly and had an unmatched freshness.

It was nice to eat meals at the table. It gave them a chance to sit together and talk. They were actually becoming a family.

Sunday, two months and four days to the day of John McCalister's burial, Ramond awoke to the smell of fresh baked, buttermilk biscuits. On top of the aroma, a hint of bacon hung in the air. The perfume of the food called to his stomach. He stretched heartily before rising to follow his nostrils to the dining room.

A hard week of work was behind him and it was a wonderful feeling to know he could enjoy his day off, kick back, and relax. Maybe even watch a game on the tube with his dad while they sipped on ice cold Coors. The activity was indeed simplistic, but even simple things have their charm and appeal.

He climbed out of bed and exited his bedroom.

"Mornin' Dad," he said as he passed his father in the hall, then did a double take. "Whoaa you're dressed up. What's up?"

"Well, your mother convinced me to go to church with her this morning. The pastor is beginning his three part sermon on how to keep your house like God's house

MICHAEL BISHOP

...anyhow I thought I'd go, seeing how there are no good games on today," he said jokingly and gave Ramond a smirking smile as he fumbled with his tie. "Come on, let's go get some breakfast."

"O.K." Ramond agreed wholeheartedly.

He followed Brian down the hall, into the dining room where Vernadette was just placing the scrambled eggs on the table. Her hands were covered in striped oven mitts and around her waist an apron hung that read "Kissin Don't Last, Good Cooking Do". Underneath the apron she wore a sunny yellow dress. The outfit made her look like she was twenty-five again, and Ramond wondered how she managed to do all she did and still stay looking so young and pretty.

"Well, don't you look handsome, Bri," she said planting a kiss on his cheek. "Here, let me help you," she told him grabbing at his tie. In seconds, she achieved what he could not do in the ten minutes he stood in front of the bathroom mirror trying. It struck Ramond funny how once this "Ward and June Cleaver" scene would have made him wretch, but now how he was delighted to be a part of it.

"Smells good," Ramond commented sincerely. Her smile shone down on him like the rays of Heaven. "Let's eat," he suggested.

"Does my heart good..." she began.

"I know, I know... does your heart good to see your son eat well," Ramond interrupted.

She gave him a sheepish leer. "What? Have you heard that before?" she kidded in her most innocent voice.

"Maybe once or twice," he offered back, playing along. "I hate to repeat myself, but, let's eat."

"Alright, alright," she said as she took her place at the table. "Brian, you wanna say grace, please?"

THE KNOWING

"Dear Heavenly Father, thank you for this food we are about to receive and please help those who have none, in Christ's name we ask, Amen," he prayed with a bowed head. It was the same stale blessing he repeated once or twice a year when he was asked to give the blessing. The words to it had not deviated even once in all the years Ramond could remember.

"Thank you, honey," she said as she handed Ramond the eggs. The dishes were passed around the table clockwise until all plates were full. Ramond wasted no time in stuffing his mouth with a slice of bacon and a piece of biscuit.

"How's work going?" she asked him, making small talk.

"It's not bad," he said with his mouth full. The food in his mouth was choked down out of courtesy before he continued. "There's talk I might get promoted from the back, up to hardware." He said exuberantly, more anxious than he realized to reveal the good news.

"Well, that's great, Ray!" Brian burst into the conversation with obvious pride in his voice. "I knew you could do anything you set your mind to."

If you only knew what I have already done when I put my mind to it, Ramond thought to himself. With effort, he forced the thought and all thoughts that came with it, out of his mind. It was something he was doing more and more these days. Blanking everything out until nothing was there. The nothingness was leaps and bounds better than the memories feeding upon his mind, and he found himself traveling inside the blankness increasingly these days.

"Thanks Dad," he managed after a long moment of unblemished silence. The meal helped ease his mind. The bacon was lean with little fat to ruin its taste, and the biscuits were perfectly buttered. With the bread melting on his palate, there was little room for any other thoughts.

When the meal was finished, Brian and Vernadette prepared to leave for church. Ramond watched as his father added the last minute touch to his suit by slipping into his blue pinstriped sport coat. She handed him the car keys and grabbed her Bible as they headed out the door. Ramond walked them to the front and stood in the doorway as they walked to the car.

"Enjoy the service," he shouted after them as he waved goodbye. Brian Jamison gave him a mock grin as he ducked his head and sat behind the steering wheel.

"We will, sweetie," she assured him, then paused. Her lips parted slightly as if she had something to add. Ramond could read her face like a book. She wanted to tell Ramond that she wished he would come, but more than anything he hoped she wouldn't.

Vernadette gazed at her son for a moment silently, then closed her mouth without speaking again. She knew it would not help things if she pushed. If he wanted to come back to church, he would on his own. She scowled and nodded her head to him, then ducked into the car herself.

A sigh of relief swept through Ramond, and he continued waving as they drove away and disappeared around the corner. A smile touched his lips. His mother had been smart enough to keep her mouth shut. The air was cool, but the inside of the house offered warmth and relaxation. He had nothing to do and plenty of time to do it. It was undoubtedly going to be a fine day.

THE KNOWING

The chair his dad loved so much was indeed comfortable, he discovered as he sat down in it. The remote control was never far from the chair, and Ramond found it at once. Lifting it from the table his dad rested the beer cans on, he pushed the large red "On" button and the television sprang to life.

Flipping past channel after channel of televised church services, he stumbled on an old rerun of "Hogan's Heroes". It wasn't much in the way of entertainment, but it was better than watching loud men in expensive suits tell him how to live his life.

As Hogan was sent to the cooler for the millionth time that season, Ramond's eyes grew heavy. It wasn't often he got up so early on his days off, and coupled with a full belly, he grew sleepy. In minutes, the well-cushioned chair took his mind away, as he dozed off in much the same way his father had done so many times before him.

A knocking on the front door jolted him back to reality. He had not slept long, but grogginess still dulled his senses like a shot of novocaine from a dentist. Without hesitating he muddled to the door and flung it open.

The blow came fast. *So fast* he never saw it. The moment the object struck his head, he returned to dreamland. This time it was an involuntary trip.

The sound had escaped his lungs before he was fully

aware of what was happening. As his eyes bolted open, his only thought was pain. He knew the sound came from him, but it did not come from his vocal chords. It came from somewhere deep down. Some place he never knew existed until that moment.

He pulled his arms forward. The thick cord dug into his wrists making rope burns on them. Helplessness was the first emotion to spring out of the pain. It took only a second of struggling for him to realize he could not move. Ramond was pinned. Held down like a mouse in a trap.

The second strike on the spike sent it sailing through his left wrist into the board. The howl came again. This time with a higher shrill to it. The tears drenched his cheeks as he felt blood gushing and falling off the edges of his wrist bones. He forced himself to look.

The young man kneeling next to him looked nervous as he held the large ball-peen hammer in his hand. The sweat on his brow glistened in the sun and a drop fell and mixed with the blood flowing down Ramond's arm.

The rope the man used to tie down his wrists was thick, and even though Ramond was fifteen pounds heavier, he knew he would not be able to budge it. Still, instinctively, he pushed and forced against it, hoping for a miracle... expecting nothing.

The man had nailed the spike directly into the rope, not worrying that it might break. It made no difference if it did split in two. The spikes were different than the nine inch nails Ramond had used. These were similar to railroad spikes. They were pointed at the bottom and grew progressively as they went up. The head was huge, and rope or no rope, once the spikes were driven into the wood, it would be impossible

THE KNOWING

to pull it through the wrist. Once nailed, there was no escape.

The only thing worse than the pain was the knowing. Ramond's first-hand knowledge of crucifixion taught him one thing for sure: as bad as the pain was now, it was going to get worse. *Much worse.*

The man shakily hammered on the spike until it passed all the way through the wood and exited the other side. With each strike, the vibrations sent a fresh wave of torture through Ramond's body. The pain was not just isolated in the wrist. It was carried to every inch of his flesh like a river with hundreds of tributaries. Accompanying each wave was a cry that sounded different to Ramond each time. It was a cry he had no control over.

The man was done with the left and stood to move. Ramond's eyes immediately shifted to his other wrist. Twisting and straining under the rope, he exhausted every supply of energy left in him trying to stop the pain from being repeated on this side. His hands clenched into a fist, and then released, and then clenched again.

As the man entered his range of view, Ramond took the first real look at his captor. The man was much larger than Ramond, explaining why he did not wake up after the blow. The guy stood what looked to be about six foot three, and easily weighed two hundred and sixty pounds. His golden blonde hair hung limp, stringing down his shoulders, and his face was round and pudgy like a baby's.

The fellow was line-backer size, but did not look to be over nineteen or twenty. And although he was nervous, it did not appear that he was nervous for conscience's sake. It looked more like he was jittery for fear of messing things up.

MICHAEL BISHOP

It was distinct, the man was much colder than Ramond had been during his sacrifice.

One large boot was placed on the palm of Ramond's hand as the man knelt down. He tried to wiggle his fingers under the weight, but all efforts were to no avail. His hand was locked motionless.

Ramond tried to speak, but each attempt was interrupted by a moan or a cry. His voice made sounds without his consent. The pain allowed him to do nothing but cry and bellow.

Another spike was placed on top of his right wrist and he closed his eyes tightly in anticipation. The *"ting"* of the hammer hitting the spike was heard a fraction of a second before that place within him released another shriek. He found the sound hurt even his own ears, but as the pain drifted through every nerve in his body, he was defenseless to stop it.

His jaws clamped down on his teeth, grinding them together spontaneously. They pressed so hard against each other that fragments began to crack off and collect in his mouth. Several slid down his throat like shards of broken glass, and he choked and coughed as he tried to swallow.

His eyes sprung open like a jack in the box as the man struck the spike for the second time. Somehow, he had to speak. Had to warn the man. Maybe if he could explain things, the man would not kill him. But each time Ramond tried to say a word, another blow would be delivered and all speech would be swallowed by his howls.

He followed the man's eyes as he gazed over at the left wrist. When the blonde was satisfied that both spikes were

THE KNOWING

nailed into the wood equally, he rose and walked toward Ramond's feet.

This was his chance. In the time it took the man to walk to his feet he could stop himself from screaming long enough to speak. Ramond grabbed a breath and uttered a last whimper of pain before mumbling the first thing that came to his mind.

"Wait," he blubbered and relinquished another bellow of pain at the realization of how painful speaking was going to be.

The man took no notice of the fact that he spoke. He was quickly on his knees at Ramond's feet with another spike in hand. Grabbing his ankles with a huge hand, the blonde bent Ramond's knees slightly and placed the spike on his feet. Ramond quickly shuffled them, removing one from the top of the other in an attempt to buy himself time.

"Wait, you don't understand," he gasped as he kept his feet moving.

The man frowned in agitation. Then the look of annoyance turned to anger.

"OH GOD, PLEASE DON'T!" Ramond begged, knowing he had pushed the blonde too far, and knowing what he intended to do about it.

The hammer smashed down on Ramond's feet, shattering the bones that led to his toes.

"STOP MOVING YOUR FUCKING FEET!" the blonde shrieked in a voice full of hatred and lunacy. The pain of breaking bones was searing as it flowed into the endless sea of other pains he was experiencing. His feet stopped their shuffle as the man bent his knees again and placed one on top of the other.

MICHAEL BISHOP

The fight was going out of Ramond. The only advantage he had left was the knowledge of what was going on. If he could just tell the man that he was being used. Let him know that if he did not stop now, someday the same thing would happen to him, maybe he could make the blonde see the light.

But the pain did not subside and the blonde sent the spike hurling through Ramond's foot. The place inside him was now sobbing instead of screaming. The cries were ethereal and he knew he could not speak above them. Three more hard blows on the nail and it was through his shattered feet and into the wood.

The tears were unstoppable as they burned Ramond's eyes and blurred his vision. Breathing was becoming harder through the crying and screaming. It took conscious effort to make the "crying place" inside him subside for a moment while he sucked in oxygen.

The man stood and walked behind him. As Ramond looked around and saw no pulleys or ropes, he understood perfectly what the blonde was doing.

The guy was towering and strong. He would be able to lift someone Ramond's size without any help from ropes or pulleys. The lumber he used to construct his cross was lighter than what Ramond had chosen. It would take little effort for the monster to raise him into position.

Ramond gazed past his shredded feet and saw the hole dug in the ground for the cross to fit in. He also noticed the cross he was nailed to was considerably larger than the one he had constructed. It was easy to see that he would be hanging no less than six feet in the air.

This was a sick joke. He wondered how many had

THE KNOWING

taken this path before him, and how many were still to come.

What was coming next was well known to him. In his mind a prayer repeated itself with the consistencies of his moans. *Please God. Stop my heart!* it begged. But his heart continued to pound as the cross began to rise.

The pull on his wrists was immediate as his body rose. Gravity jerked down on him with cruelty. The ascent was quick and with each degree the cross gained, the pain increased. There was a pause every couple of seconds where the cross remained still. Undoubtedly, the blonde was stopping to get a better grip further down the shaft. The extra time did nothing but elongate the torture.

As a vertical ninety degrees approached, Ramond watched below him as the tip of the cross ate away at the soil on the lip of the hole. A second later, the cross began its bullet descent into the opening. He remembered how McCalister had reacted when the cross crashed into the hole. He remembered the unequaled pain the man must have felt. And he remembered the howl McCalister let out. He knew it would be even worse for him. The knowing was almost as bad as the pain.

The scream radiated from every pore in Ramond's body. Every atom that made up his structure cried out to the world when the jolt ripped the flesh from his wrist and his feet.

"JESUS!" the man screamed as he cupped his ears tightly with his hands and collapsed to his knees. The shrieks continued. Short and repetitious, until Ramond was sure his own ears were bleeding.

Had he any idea the depths of suffering caused by this

MICHAEL BISHOP

kind of death, he would have never been able to kill McCalister this way. Death was a gift compared. The agony of crucifixion was beyond comprehension, and yet, he knew there was suffering still to come.

The blonde had bent his knees, which made it easier to raise up and gather air. But it also placed more weight on the feet, increasing the torture of the act. In addition, it allowed the victim the ability to get more air thus increasing the time spent on the cross. The bending of the knees was just one more step to further the punishment.

Ramond began extending upward to seize air. His feet begged him to go ahead and suffocate. Their anguish was too severe. But the natural urge to breathe was too strong. If he could just get enough air to speak, it would be worth hanging on.

After all, McCalister had done it. Somehow, he had managed to over come the pain long enough to speak, and would have enlightened Ramond, had he not passed out. He had to try to warn the blonde. It was the only hope.

Through his tears and fluttering eyelid, Ramond caught sight of his murderer standing in front of him, inspecting his work. The one advantage of the *bent knee* crucifixion was speech. You could extend higher, allowing more air to be obtained. The last opportunity was at hand as he crushed the weight of his body on the foot nail and prepared himself to speak.

"Don't do this," he grunted between breaths. The pain in his feet would soon make his legs involuntarily fold. Teeth were being snapped off in chunks as his jaws clamped down like a vice. Little time was left. "I know what's going on. This is a mistake," he managed in a voice that came close to hiding

THE KNOWING

the pain. The last of these words peaked the man's attention, and for the first time Ramond's heart leapt with hope.

"Let me explain," he quickly added, holding himself up a moment longer. "It's a trick..."

His words were quickly terminated by the blonde's nodding head. It fell forward, as if it had fallen asleep on his shoulders and left the rest of his body unaware of it.

Ramond's feet could take the pain no longer. He collapsed down placing the weight and tearing back on his wrists. His eyes never left his captor. The pain took a back seat for one moment of ecstacy as his mind fully concentrated on what the blonde was doing.

"Hello Ramond," the man said as his head jerked upright again, making direct eye contact with him. The blonde smiled with a satanic arrogance that Ramond immediately recognized. But the voice was the clincher. For the first time, he did not perceive it as the voice of the Master. It was now the voice of death.

"You broke our bargain. You welshed on our proposition. I guess you thought I would forgive and forget. Well, as you can see, I didn't forget...And I'll never forgive. 'Tis not the nature of this beast," the possessed blonde stated as he approached Ramond's feet. The face, controlled by Satan, looked up at him with satisfaction. From this distance, even in his condition, he could see the fire and the figure in the man's eyes.

"I have so much to tell you and so little time. Before you die I want you to know exactly what a fool you've been. I want you to see all the things you have done and how easily you have been manipulated. When you cross to the other side, I want you to cross with the knowledge of what a pathetic, wretched human you were.

"See the fire in this human's eyes? See *me* standing in the center of it all? I was in your eyes too, Ramond. I controlled you just like I control this dolt. You did not pass out before McCalister had a chance to talk. I merely took over. I could not let him spill his guts to you. Just like I cannot have you spill your guts to blondey here. That wouldn't do... no that would not do at all."

There was no saving him now. Ramond understood this much. He tried to shut the words out by concentrating on the pain. It almost seemed a fair trade. But the words were penetrating and everything rung clear in his head.

"I spoke to McCalister through you, and basically told him what I am going to tell you now... There is no one to blame for this but yourself. You chose to be here. You chose to come to Hell with me. Certainly, I have drawn you, and guided you, and placed circumstances and people in your path to help bring you here; but ultimately, the choice was all yours.

"See, Ramsy, you all have a choice. From the beginning that is just the way *he* chose to set things up. You are not mindless drones with a single destiny that you cannot change. It is not like that at all. You were created as free thinkers. Created to make your own choices. It just so happens that your choices brought you here," he spoke as fast as an auctioneer, taking great joy in his words.

"There was never really a chance of becoming my son. My son has already been chosen. He was not born from your world. I created him and placed him where I wanted him. But it was your fantasy and fantasies are the best bait to lure prey to me. McCalister had the same fantasy, but just as you, he betrayed me. Although he did make it a bit farther

THE KNOWING

than you.

"He managed to complete half of the seventh. While his father was resting comfortably in bed one night, John McCalister sabotaged his brakes. The next day the man drove right into a tree. But, like you, McCalister was a momma's boy and could not bring himself to off the old lady. So he had to be punished for his treachery. I used you as the tool. Just like I'm using this guy to take care of you," he said looking down for a moment at his host's body.

"And I know what you're thinking... What would have happened if you had killed your parents? What then? Well, I'll tell you. If you had butchered your parents, you would have been on your own. I would have left you to the justice system, and they would have probably given you the chair. Which is a death no where near as lusciously devastating as crucifixion." The face smiled at the mention of crucifixion.

"Enjoy what you are feeling now. It is heaven compared to what you will experience once you die. Then, you will really be mine. Eternal torture. You'll look back on your crucifixion and wish for it again, just to give you a break from the real suffering. But it won't ever be this good again. Believe that much."

Ramond did believe, and that belief made him extend for another breath, prolonging life as long as possible.

Satan's words were worse than the pain. They showed him what a fool he had been. Made him realize his entire life had been controlled. Told him he was spineless and feeble. The words did their job of adding to the misery.

"I'm not done yet, boy. You have yet to realize just what a puppet you have been. Listen to this..." The blonde paused and looked up at him to make sure he was paying attention. Ramond had no choice but to listen as he spoke again, this time using a different voice.

"RAMOND, PLEASE DON'T KILL ME!" It was the voice of Vernadette. Even that had been a trick. It was the most horrifying realization Ramond had ever had.

The blonde threw his head back and laughed sadistically. The point had been well made, and Satan paused to gloat over his deceit.

"Since you were a child, I have used that voice to bring you to me," he bragged. "I watched and rejoiced to myself at the pain that voice caused you. And I used it again and again over the years to suck you in.

"I have always been aware of you. I chose you at an early age, and you lived up to my expectations. You did wonderfully on the acts you managed to complete. The people I wanted you to hurt will never again interfere with my plans. It's all a game, Ramond. A perpetual cycle. I used McCalister to get people out of my way, and when he was used up, I sent you to get rid of him. Then I used you the same way, and when you were used up, I sent big boy here to finish you. And most likely, I'll be forced to send someone to get rid of him when he's of no more use. Although he is more sadistic than you or McCalister were. He may just pull the seventh off. But that's of no concern to you now. What is of concern is what I will do to you when you arrive at my home. Hell is not just fire and brimstone. It is much, much more than that. I can't wait to show you."

The blonde reached up and placed a hand on Ramond's left foot, grabbed the heel, and pulled downward, deliberately causing more pain. Ramond's face grimaced and he let out another unearthly moan.

"Hear that sound? That's not just your body writhing in pain. No, indeed not. That sound comes from your soul.

THE KNOWING

Crucifixion is a death so torturous that it is felt down in your very spirit. And *your* spirit is mine. Let the animals have your body. I only want what is inside. And I believe it's almost time to take it. As much as I would like to leave you hanging here, suffering for the duration, I cannot. I don't have the time to stay here for hours; and if I leave, this guy will come to. I can't risk having you tell him the whole gory story. Therefore, I'm afraid I'm going to have to kill you before I go.

"But I'm a sporting soul. You've got one chance to live. If you're strong enough to look at my real presence and survive, I'll grant you the rest of your life... on the cross, of course... Fair enough?"

Ramond understood either way he would end up in Hell. If he *was* strong enough to withstand a final test of Satan, it would only mean the crucifixion would last longer. It was a no win situation, and he really did not care anymore what the outcome was.

The man brought his face as close to Ramond as he could. His eyes peered upward as he prepared himself to come out.

"Look closely now. Are you ready?... Oh yes, one last, little thing... Michael Billion *was* indeed the first one at that slumber party to die!" he revealed as the figure leapt from the eyes. Ramond stared intently at it and grasped his first true look at Satan. It would be the first of many. In less than a second his heart burst in his chest. Ramond went home.

The blonde woke up with no cloudiness in his head. It was not like him to pass out. He gazed up at his sacrifice and saw that Jamison was dead. He was glad. It would save

MICHAEL BISHOP

him from hearing any more screams.
      He rose to his feet and spoke.
      "This sacrifice I give in your name," he chanted to the air.
      The cycle continued on.